Brian Gallagher was born in Dublin. He is a full-time writer and has had five stage plays produced, *Paid in Full* (1987), *Fitting In* (1988), *Brothers and Sisters* (1989), *A Job for Life* (1990) and *Duet* (1992). His radio plays broadcast by RTE include *The Last Summer, I'll See What I Can Do, A Change of Mind* and *Funny 'Ol Game*. He has had short stories published in Ireland and Britain. Outside of writing, his interests include tennis, music and inland waterways. He lives with his family in Dublin.

D0452862

BRIAN GALLAGHER

TOWN HOUSE

Published in 1993 by
Town House and Country House
42 Morehampton Road
Donnybrook
Dublin 4
Ireland

Copyright (c) Brian Gallagher, 1993

The author of this book received financial assistance
through the Author's Royalty scheme of
The Arts Council / An Chomhairle Ealaíon, Ireland.

All rights reserved. No part of this publication may be
reproduced, stored in a retrieval system, or transmitted in any
form or by any means, electronic, mechanical, photocopying,
recording or otherwise, without the prior permission of the
publishers.

A CIP catalogue record for this book is available from the
British Library.

ISBN: 0-948524-58-8

Cover design by Bill Murphy
Typeset by Typeform Ltd.
Printed in Guernsey by The Guernsey Press Company Ltd.

For Miriam, with love

Author's note

During the early 1880s British rule in Ireland was being challenged on two fronts. In Westminster Charles Stewart Parnell's Irish Party sought Home Rule for Ireland by parliamentary means, while in Ireland the National Land League agitated at local level to seek agrarian reform on behalf of the tenant farmers.

The land-owning aristocracy had been able to demand high rents, evict tenants by the thousand, and generally suppress dissension, but with the formation of the Land League the small farmers began to unite in seeking basic rights of tenancy.

The refusal of all locals to work for or have any dealings with the Mayo landlord, Captain Boycott, gave a new word to the English language, and a new and potent weapon to the Land League in pursuing its demands.

In placing my fictitious characters in the midst of historical events I occasionally have had to take the liberty of putting my words into the mouths of actual people, but while stressing that what follows is a work of fiction, the historical detail nonetheless reflects the actual course of events in 1881/2.

Prologue

Second Lieutenant William Scott knew he would soon be dead if he didn't control his fear. The blistering summer sun was making him sweat heavily, and he could feel the rivulets of perspiration creeping down his back, but he knew that the perspiration running into his eyes wasn't caused just by the sun, but by fear — heart-pounding, stomach-tightening fear.

Taking a deep breath, he tried to put from his mind the awful consequences of capture, and instead concentrated on listening. A cacophony of cries came from the bazaar, but straining his ears he could hear the harsh tones of the guards shouting to one another. His command of Pashto was limited, but he didn't need fluency to understand. They were spreading out to comb the bazaar for him.

He shifted cautiously behind the bales of foul-smelling wool which hid him, and risked a glance up the alley. Just as he did so one of the guards appeared at the alley-mouth. The man hesitated a moment, glancing down at the over-hanging rows of dyed wool. Suddenly he stepped forward, forcing the wool aside with a swing of his rifle.

Scott froze. He could hear the man moving bales at the entrance. The alley was a dead end, and if the Afghan continued bale by bale, Scott knew he'd be as good as dead. He cursed the guard for his thoroughness, and, thinking of his death, he cursed himself too. Cursed himself for studying Pashto during his cadetship in Sandhurst. Cursed his bravado in accepting a mission to spy on Sher Ali's military strength in Kabul. Why couldn't he have stayed in Peshawar with his regiment? Why couldn't he have been like the other young cavalry officers, playing polo, gambling on tent-pegging competitions, complaining about the

1

absence of eligible women? Instead he had to be the one, Pashto-speaking Scott, who'd volunteered to dress like a native and ride one hundred miles behind enemy lines.

At the time he had convinced himself that it was his duty. If the British didn't intervene in Afghanistan the Russians would. And if the British were to intervene, they had to know the military capabilities of Sher Ali. In his more honest moments, however, he knew that duty was only part of the reason. Adventure and bravado came into it too, and though he wouldn't have admitted it to himself, there was also a desire to prove to his family that he, William, was as good as any of the others in the long line of military Scotts.

The guard was getting closer now, still checking behind every bale. Stifling his panic, Scott realised he might have one chance. It was a slim one but it was better than being shot dead in a foul-smelling alley, or worse, taken alive, a hated *ferangi*, caught spying on Sher Ali.

The Afghan was now only feet away. Scott knew what he had to do. If he could kill the guard quietly and don his outer garments, he just might escape in the confusion of the bazaar. Careful not to make any rustling sound, he slipped his hand inside the loose-fitting Afghan coat he was wearing and withdrew his dagger.

The guard was so close now that Scott could clearly hear the man breathing as he moved the bales of wool. Clasping the knife, Scott prayed that the man would give up. He didn't want to have to kill him. He didn't know if he *could*.

The Afghan was now one sack away. Scott grasped the knife, his palms moist with sweat. His mouth was dry, and he could feel his heart pounding madly. Suddenly the Afghan pulled the sack away. Scott saw the man's startled expression as they came face to face. He willed himself to action, but looking into the Afghan's cataract-infected eyes he felt rooted to the ground. Recovering, the man raised his rifle and opened his mouth to call out.

Scott sprang forward. He clasped his left hand over the man's mouth, strangling the cry, and swinging around, he drove his knee into the Afghan's back. Dropping the rifle,

2

the man arched backwards in pain, and in one swift movement Scott slit the exposed throat with his knife. Avoiding the gush of blood, he held the man firmly, then, feeling the body go limp, he laid it on the ground. Immediately he took off the man's loose coat. It was bloodstained near the collar but it didn't show against the dark colour of the material.

Scott quickly removed his own dirty coat and pulled off his stained white turban. He crouched beside the dead Afghan and reached for the man's turban. Seeing the bloodied throat, he was suddenly struck by the horror of what he had done. He wanted to be sick, but steeling himself, he swiftly undid the turban, wound it around his own head, and quickly pulled on the dark brown coat.

Hauling back two large sacks of wool, he created a small enclave, into which he threw his own discarded coat and turban. He dragged the Afghan's body into the enclave, then pushed back the two sacks. Picking up the rifle, he glanced around. To anyone casually looking down the alley nothing would seem amiss.

He took a deep breath, then walked to the mouth of the alley and looked out through the draped wool at the crowded bazaar. Sher Ali's men would be combing every corner of it, so the sooner he made his move the better. If he could just brazen his way out of the bazaar, he knew where he could go to ground in Kabul. In his money belt he had forty gold pieces – more than enough to buy sanctuary until things quietened down. Then he would get a fresh horse and make for the Kyber Pass and safety.

Pushing the overhanging wool aside, he stepped out of the alley. The important thing was to get to one of the exits quickly, but not so quickly as to draw attention. He must behave like one of the searchers.

He moved forward and as he passed cautiously through the bazaar numerous people glanced his way, but all seemed to accept him as one of the searching guards.

His apparent search was gradually bringing him closer to an exit gate, which he recognised from an earlier exploration of the bazaar. As he approached he looked carefully at its environs. It hadn't been sealed off yet. He forced himself not to rush, then, stepping unchallenged through the gate, he felt a wave of exhilaration sweep through him.

Moving faster now, he disappeared into the back streets of Kabul.

One

The day of the eviction was a beautiful autumn day, sunny, but with an invigorating crispness in the air. Kate waited at the bottom field, nervous yet excited at the same time. Normally she would have been in Nursing School in Enniscorthy at this hour, but this morning she had left her starched white uniform aside and dressed instead for the kind of action she knew was at hand.

Her father hadn't wanted to resist, but since getting Lord Masefield's eviction order the family had been visited in the night by Whiteboys, one of the many illegal groups opposed to the landlords. Shouting through the windows, the masked Whiteboys had made it clear that if the Lannigans meekly surrendered their farm, their lives would be in danger.

And so they now waited expectantly in the November sunshine, a mixed group of neighbouring farmers, barefoot children, black-shawled old women and aggressive-looking Land League activists – all ready to defy the forces of the Crown.

Kate looked back across the neatly tended fields towards the cottage. From its thatched roof fluttered a Land League banner, boldly proclaiming NO EVICTIONS! HOLD ONTO YOUR LAND! The windows were sealed with planks of wood, and the barricaded half-door was surrounded by the waiting crowd. The sight sent a shiver up her spine, and she knew that irrespective of the Whiteboys, this was a stand she wanted to make.

Suddenly she heard the sound of horses' hooves. Rising immediately, she crossed the wooden footbridge and ran to the corner of the lane. She looked round the corner and saw an advancing column about one hundred yards away. At its head rode Lord Masefield, mounted on his large grey hunter. He was followed by the sheriff and several wagons carrying an eviction party of ill-clad labourers, and marching along the road on both flanks was a large party of Royal Irish Constabulary.

Kate felt her pulse quicken. She stared ahead boldly for a moment, then turned on her heel. She walked calmly round the bend, then sprinted down the lane and across the wooden footbridge, her auburn hair catching the sunlight as she ran towards the house.

At her approach there was a stirring of all those who had been lounging about the cottage.

'They're coming!' Kate cried. 'They're coming up the lane!'

Tim O'Connor came forward to meet her. He was a tall, broad-shouldered man with a mop of curly hair. O'Connor was president of the local branch of the Land League, and, it was whispered, secretly a leading Whiteboy.

'How many, Kate?' he asked.

'Masefield, the sheriff with about twenty of his men in wagons . . .'

'How many police?'

'I'd say about twenty-five, thirty.'

'Right,' he answered, 'we know where we stand.' He turned to address the crowd. 'OK, we know why we're here. Those manning the house, inside now.'

Kate saw her father and her brother Michael step forward, each clasping a roughly hewn wooden stave. Though Michael was only three years her junior she had always regarded him as a child, but now, at seventeen, he had started to fill out, and she noticed how he carried himself with a quiet determination.

Kate crossed and joined her family. Now that the moment was here her young sister Deirdre was having difficulty holding back the tears, and little Denis stared ahead grimly, his young face taut with anxiety.

'Mind yourselves,' her mother said softly. 'And, Michael, go easy, don't do more than you have to.'

'Tis alright, Mam,' he answered, 'we'll be fine.'

O'Connor approached. 'Come on, lads, inside.'

Kate felt a lump in her throat. 'Good luck,' she said.

The two men nodded, her father nervously, Michael less so,

then they quickly crossed to the cottage door, followed by O'Connor and three others. O'Connor turned at the door and faced the crowd. He waited for a second or two until there was silence, then he spoke. 'What do you do if threatened with eviction?'

'Hold onto your land!' roared the crowd.

O'Connor gave a quick grin, raised his clenched fist in the air, then entered the cottage. Immediately the men could be heard shifting furniture within, to block the door on the inside.

One of the Land Leaguers approached Kate's group. 'Women and children over to the side please. Women and children over here,' he called importantly. Kate moved reluctantly, following her family and the other women to the left of the path leading to the cottage door. She hated the passivity of simply standing by, but no amount of persuasion had been able to convince her father to let her take part in the occupation of the cottage.

Suddenly a cry went up from the crowd as Lord Masefield came into view, followed by the sheriff's wagons and the two columns of police.

Masefield rode slowly forward. Imperious in the saddle and looking straight ahead as though the assembled crowd did not exist, he stopped before the cottage door, his angular face set in an expression of studied indifference as the sheriff's workers and the Royal Irish Constabulary deployed.

After a moment Masefield reached into an inside pocket and withdrew an envelope. When he spoke his voice had a nasal drawl. 'Denis Lannigan, I call upon you to cease this illegal occupation of my property. I have compensation for you, generously offered. You have no hope of success, so stop this foolishness at once, accept your compensation and vacate the property peacefully!'

Tim O'Connor's voice was heard immediately. 'Lord Masefield?'

'Yes?'

'The Lannigans have worked this farm for twenty-one years – have they ever not paid you your rent?'

'That isn't the point.'

'We've always paid,' Kate found herself calling out, 'every

7

time the rent went up! We don't owe a penny!'

'Hush, Katie,' her mother whispered.

'No, let him hear, Mam,' answered Kate, but the landlord disdained to turn towards her, and instead addressed the men within the cottage.

'You know as well as I do that this is not about rent,' said Masefield.

'No,' cried O'Connor, 'it's about more profit for you leasing one big farm than several smaller ones, and you don't care if the tenants broke their backs cultivating the land and improving their farms!'

'I'm offering compensation,' answered Masefield evenly, 'you'd be wise to take it.'

'Your greed would deprive this man and his family of their livelihood, so why don't you shove your compensation up your arse!'

A gasp of shocked delight ran through the crowd. Masefield's pale cheeks turned pink in anger, and his mouth tightened. Turning in the saddle, he faced the waiting sheriff. 'Reclaim this property!' he cried.

Jumping down from his cart, the sheriff called out: 'Right men, get your tools.'

An angry murmur ran through the waiting crowd as the eviction party prepared for action.

'Lapdogs!'

'Lickspittles!'

As the sheriff moved towards the front door a contingent of the local men moved forward, their bodies shielding the door. The sheriff stopped and looked enquiringly at the inspector commanding the RIC. The policeman stepped forward, stopping before the blocked doorway. 'Clear a passage,' he said. The men stood immobile. The inspector turned to his detachment. 'Draw batons!'

Turning again, the inspector addressed the defiant men. 'I'm giving you one final warning – clear that doorway.'

Nobody moved. Then an old woman standing behind Kate cried out: 'Hold onto your land!' As the chant was taken up by the crowd the inspector turned and walked away, quickly followed by the sheriff.

At a nod from the inspector the police charged. Within seconds there was chaos, with women screaming, men being batoned, and children crying. Seeing the police attacking the men at the door enraged the crowd, and suddenly a cache of heavy wooden staves was produced.

Wielding the staves ferociously, the local men charged the police and the sheriff's men. The surge of battle swept towards where Lord Masefield was protected by the inspector and six constables. 'Draw you guns, man,' he shouted at the inspector, as his horse started to rear, 'draw your guns for Christ's sake!'

The policeman hesitated a moment, then called to the constables. 'Draw arms!' Quickly withdrawing his own revolver, he fired four shots above the crowd. The sound of the shots brought the fighting to a halt.

'The next ones won't be in the air!' cried the inspector. 'Now back off.'

The crowd regarded him sullenly, unwilling to retreat.

The inspector indicated the six policemen with rifles trained on the protesters. 'Don't make this more bloody than it has to be,' he said. 'Back off, now.'

For a moment nobody moved, then the crowd slowly and resentfully shifted backwards. Without waiting for the injured of either side to be dealt with, the sheriff and six men ran towards the door with a battering-ram. The door splintered but held. Again they rammed. There were more splinters, and watching the inexorable progress, Kate felt sickened. How could they ever have thought they'd win? Stick-wielding farmers against armed policemen?

The sheriff's men were moving with a swift efficiency now, and a well-delivered blow from the battering-ram shattered the door. The inspector sent a sergeant and ten constables to the smashed entrance, batons at the ready. They stood aside as the sheriff's party rammed again, breaking and forcing back the furniture barricading the inside of the doorway.

Once an entrance had been cleared the policemen stormed inside. Kate felt her throat go dry as screams and blows were heard from the cottage. One of the policemen staggered back out the doorway, blood flowing from his face, and a cry of satisfaction ran through the crowd.

The shouts and blows inside the cottage reached a crescendo, then died down. The sullen crowd murmured angrily as the police emerged, manhandling the defenders towards the waiting wagons.

Pushing forward anxiously, Kate noticed with satisfaction that a number of the constables were bloodied and bruised, then she caught sight of her father and Michael. An ugly gash ran the length of her father's face, and Michael was carrying his arm as though it might be broken. Her brother's homespun grey shirt was splashed with crimson from his heavily bleeding nose, but at least both men were walking upright.

'Kate, Kate, how are they?' her mother cried.

'They're not too bad, Mam. They're not too bad.'

Just then Tim O'Connor and one of the other Land League activists were carried out unconscious and battered, and laid in the wagon where basic medical attention was being given by two of the sheriff's party. Three RIC men were finally helped from the house to the First Aid wagon; then the sergeant called to the inspector. 'All clear now, Sir!'

Lord Masefield spurred his mount forward. 'Sheriff?'

'Sir?'

'Torch the roof!'

'Right away, Sir.'

At a nod from the sheriff, three of his men quickly lit torches.

'No!' screamed Kate. 'No!'

Her mother took her arm. 'Easy, child, easy. 'Tis no use . . .'

The three men ran forward and tossed the burning torches onto the thatched roof. Instantly the flames took hold, the dry thatch cackling and spurting into flame.

Lord Masefield wheeled about on his horse, addressing the crowd. 'Let that be a lesson to you all. The forces of law and order are not to be defied. I shall reclaim any of my land as I choose!'

The flames were racing now, the whole roof ablaze, and Kate felt an awful sadness as her house, focal point of a lifetime's memories, burned fiercely. She knew that when the roof was gone they would tumble the walls. There would be no question of reoccupying the house – the sheriff's men would leave nothing standing. She looked over towards the wagons and caught sight of her father. His bloodstained face had a haunted, lost look as he watched the inferno. Her heart went out to him. Poor, weak, good-natured Dad.

A whinny from Masefield's horse caught her attention and looking round she saw the landlord sitting masterfully in the saddle, his lips drawn in satisfaction as the cottage blazed. Kate felt her temper rising and before she knew what she was doing she had broken from her mother's grip and run forward, grabbing one of the discarded staves from the ground. Masefield saw her coming and swung around, bringing his riding crop down in a swinging arc as Kate reached him. On reflex she parried the blow with the stave, then quickly swung again, striking Masefield soundly on the leg. He cried out, and in the next instant Kate felt a searing pain run from her shoulder down through her arm, as a policeman struck her with his baton. The stave fell from her numbed right hand and the RIC man pinioned her left arm behind her back. Masefield, recovering from the blow to his thigh, leaned forward in the saddle, then powerfully swung his riding crop down, catching Kate on the temple. She screamed in pain as she fell backwards, the roof of the blazing cottage the last distorted image she glimpsed before slumping unconsciously to the ground.

Two

The January snow swirled through the air, covering Dublin in a heavy blanket of white, and the city, normally resounding to the clatter of horses' hooves and the rattle of cartwheels on cobblestones, was strangely quiet. James Carey sat by the fire in the small upstairs bar, watching through the window as the snowflakes eddied before the street lamp in the road below. He was a big, bearded man in his mid-forties, and his fashionable clothes and well-fed look proclaimed to the world that here was a successful man of business. Sitting beneath a softly hissing gas lamp, he leaned back in his chair and drew contentedly on his cigar.

'Jim?'

'Yes?' answered Carey.

Mullett was standing behind the counter of the small bar, and Carey noted with satisfaction the look of anxiety on the publican's face.

'What time do you make it?' asked Mullett.

'Four minutes to eight. Why don't you relax?' continued Carey languidly, 'we can't start the proceedings till our friend arrives, and he's not due till eight.'

'Right,' answered Mullett brusquely.

Carey drew on his cigar again, then turned to the other two men seated about the fire.

'Isn't there something . . . something magical about snow, all the same?' he mused.

'Not so magical if you're out on a building site, trying to do a day's work,' laughed Dan Curley.

'Oh don't I know, Dan, don't I know. I served my time too remember. But when you're in out of it – nice and warm and snug – then ye can't beat a bit of snow.'

'You're not in out of it much if you're drivin' a horse and cart all day though, are ye?'

Carey looked at the speaker, Ned McCaffrey, then back at

Curley in mock dismay. 'Begod you're a right pair of killjoys,' he cried. 'There's only one thing will cheer you lads up. Landlord!' he called across the room, 'these prophets of doom need liquid sustenance.'

'But you got the last one, Jim,' protested Dan Curley.

'Sure what if I did?' answered Carey magnanimously, 'wouldn't it be a poor lookout if a man couldn't treat his pals? Jimmy!' he called across to Mullett, who was arranging bottles behind the counter. 'The same again for all of us.'

'Maybe we should ease off till after the meeting,' answered Mullett.

'Are ye listening to this, lads?' Carey turned to McCaffrey and Curley. 'A publican turning his nose up at business!'

'I was speakin' more as the chairman than as a publican,' answered Mullett.

'When our friend arrives, and we start the proceedings, sure won't that be time enough to be chairman?' retorted Carey. 'Right now, one more drink won't hurt us, will it, lads?'

McCaffrey and Curley smiled non-committedly, not wishing to offend Mullett, yet neither wishing to refuse Carey's offer. 'So three more pints and a small one,' Carey continued in a half-bantering, half-hectoring tone. Mullett paused a moment, then shrugged and went to get the drinks.

Typical, thought Carey, makes a point and then doesn't defend it. How had Mullett ever been chosen as chairman ahead of him? If the London Directory of the Land League wanted to set up a 'society that would make history', as it had been described, they should have chosen him, James Carey, to lead it. Sure wasn't it obvious that if you were setting up an assassination society then you needed a real leader of men at the helm? A self-made man who had the common touch, but could command loyalty and respect? Hadn't he, Carey, got those credentials? Hadn't he started as a bricklayer and risen to having his own building firm and being a property owner?

Instead they had opted for Mullett as chairman, with Curley, McCaffrey and himself as the guiding committee. Well, he'd bide his time. They would soon see that if the new Society – the Invincibles – were to succeed against the targets selected, then they would need someone like James Carey running the show. For the assassination targets were, even Carey had to admit, ambitious. When it came to tackling the kind of foes they had chosen, it would soon become evident that the organisational skills of a James Carey were needed, not just on the committee, but heading it. Yes, he'd simply bide his time.

From behind the mahogany counter Mullett approached with the drinks on a tray. He placed a small whiskey before Carey and a pint of stout each before Ned McCaffrey and Dan Curley. He hadn't pulled another pint for himself. Alright, Carey thought, if you want to play the martyr, you can watch us drink. He turned to the others. 'Right, lads, down the hatch!'

'Sláinte,' said Curley, raising his pint.

McCaffrey lifted his drink and nodded. 'Thanks, Jim.'

'Not at all, lads, a bird never flew on one wing, what?'

As Carey spoke a knock was heard on the door. They placed the drinks on the table.

'There's none of our papers or anything out, is there?' said Mullett quietly.

'Not a thing,' answered Carey, patting his coat pocket to indicate their whereabouts.

'Right.' Satisfied, Mullett crossed to the door and opened it.

Standing on the landing, his long overcoat, hair and moustache flecked with snow, was a man in his early twenties. Even beneath the loose-fitting overcoat, Mullett could discern a burly, muscular frame.

'The barman sent me up – I'm Joe Brady', the man said somewhat brusquely.

'Come in, come in,' said Mullett, drawing him into the warm room. Curley rose and approached them, hand outstretched.

'You're very welcome, Joe,' he said.

'Thanks, Dan.'

'Let me introduce you,' said Curley. 'This is James Mullett, our chairman.'

'Glad to have you with us, Joe,' said Mullett, shaking hands. 'This is Ned McCaffrey . . .'

'Pleased to meet ye.'

'And, Joe, this is Mr James Carey, the builder. I'm sure you've heard of him.'

14

'I have of course. Nice to meet you, Mr Carey.'

'The pleasure is mine, Joe, the pleasure is mine. Here, take off your coat and warm yourself at the fire.'

'I will, it's perishin' out.' Brady slipped off his coat, dropped it on a stool, then rubbed his hands before the fire.

'You've a fine physique, Joe,' said Carey, 'what trade are you in?'

'I'm a stone mason.'

'That's where you get the muscles, eh?' said Carey, resting a hand on the younger man's shoulder. 'Well, we're going to need a few strong lads like yourself, Joe. There'll be work aplenty for you.'

'That's why I'm here,' answered Brady.

'Let's get to business so,' said Mullett. He approached the young man and looked him in the eye. 'Dan has explained to you our objectives?'

Brady met his gaze. 'I know what's needed,' he answered.

'You're ready to take the oath then?'

'Yes.'

Mullett reached into his jacket pocket and withdrew a long, narrow dagger which he slowly unsheathed and raised in the air with his left hand. 'You grip it with your right hand,' he said.

Watched by the three seated men, Brady closed his large right hand around the handle.

'Now repeat the oath after me,' continued Mullett. 'I of my own free will, and without any mental reservation whatsoever . . .'

'I of my own free will, and without any mental reservation whatsoever . . .'

'will obey all orders transmitted to me by the Irish Invincibles . . .'

'will obey all orders transmitted to me by the Irish Invincibles . . .'

'nor to seek nor to ask more than is necessary . . .'

'nor to seek nor to ask more than is necessary . . .'

'in carrying out such orders, violation of which will be death.'

15

'in carrying out such orders, violation of which will be death.'

Mullett lowered the knife and spoke solemnly. 'Now you're a member of the Irish Invincibles.'

'And a thirsty one, I'll be bound,' said Carey heartily. 'You'll join us in a drink, Joe, what'll it be?

'Pint of Guinness, Mr Carey.'

'A pint of Guinness, Mr Mullett Sir, for our new recruit,' said Carey jovially. He was amused by the look of annoyance on Mullett's face, for it was obvious that the publican resented the sudden switch from chairman to purveyor of drinks.

'Take a seat at the fire, Joe,' Mullett instructed, attempting to retain some authority. 'Warm your bones, and I'll bring you a pint.'

Brady joined the others around the fire as Mullett went behind the counter of the small bar.

'Where do you come from, Joe?' asked Ned McCaffrey conversationally.

'North Anne Street.'

'Ah well, that wasn't too far of a walk . . .'

'No.' He turned abruptly from McCaffrey to Curley. 'When do we go into action, Dan?' asked Brady.

'When we get our orders.'

'The point is, Joe,' Carey interjected, 'this has to be planned carefully. We want to make Mr Gladstone sit up and take notice. You see he thought he was being very clever, bringing in his Land Reform Bill – and locking Parnell and the leaders of the Land League in prison for opposing him. The old carrot and stick. But what did Parnell say in the House of Commons in 1877?'

'I don't know,' said Brady.

'I'll tell you, Joe,' said Carey, enjoying his role of speechmaker. 'He said "When we are pleasing the English, we are not winning". And Mr Gladstone would be very pleased to look nice and liberal, and reasonable, with his land reform – and have Forster over here using brute force to smash the Land League resistance while its leaders are in jail. But we're going to displease him, Joe. It'll take time, and planning, and patience. But when we strike, it won't be to frighten a bullying

16

bailiff or to burn the crops of some parasite of an absentee landlord. When the Invincibles strike, our targets will be sent back to Mr Gladstone – in six-foot pine boxes!'

Mullett approached, handed Brady his drink, then took a chair himself. Brady nodded thanks as he took the pint, lowered half the glass in one swallow, then wiped the froth from his moustache. 'How will they be killed?' he asked Carey.

'With knives,' interjected Mullett.

'No guns?' Brady sounded mildly surprised.

'We could get guns,' answered Mullett, 'but remember "Garfield"?'

'Garfield?'

'The American president, Joe,' said Carey.

'Oh . . . right . . .'

'He was shot in July – and didn't die till September,' continued Carey.

'Also knives are quieter, makes it easier to escape afterwards,' added McCaffrey.

Carey leaned forward. 'We've arranged to get twelve-inch surgical knives, Joe – believe me, they'll do the job as well as any gun.'

'Where will you get them?'

'In London. You see we have . . .' started Carey, but Mullett quickly interrupted him.

'You don't have to know that, Joe, the committee will provide the weapons.'

Brady turned and looked Mullett straight in the face. 'Who'll use them?' he asked.

'Whichever Invincibles the committee thinks most suitable.'

'I'd like to be considered,' said Brady, 'I'd gut those bastards any day!'

'We'll certainly bear in mind your feelings for the English,' said Mullett drily.

'Not just the English – anyone who's against Irish freedom. Informers, collaborators – they're all enemies of Ireland.'

'That's the spirit, Joe,' said Carey warmly, 'that's the spirit!' He turned to Curley. 'Begod, Dan, I think you've brought us a good recruit in Joe here.' Carey stood, stretching himself to his

17

full height. 'Gentlemen, I'd like to propose a toast.' He raised his glass. 'Death to tyrants and freedom to Ireland!'

They raised their drinks and toasted, and Carey looked over the rim of his glass at Brady, the newest Invincible. The young stone mason was blunt, strong and ready for physical action. Yes, thought Carey approvingly, he might be just the man they needed.

Three

Captain William Scott walked happily along the fog-enshrouded length of the Mall. There was nothing quite like a night at the theatre to lift the spirits, and he had just come from a fine performance of Gilbert and Sullivan's latest operetta, *Patience*, at the newly built Savoy Theatre. Being the first public building in London to be entirely lit by electricity, the Savoy was the talk of the city, but Scott had been more impressed by the high production standards of the D'Oly Carte company than by the new lighting. He was a frequent theatre-goer, reasoning that as long as his regiment was stationed in London he would be foolish not to indulge his love of the stage – even if some of his fellow officers regarded going to the theatre alone as slightly odd.

Softly humming a tune from the show, he reached the end of the Mall, and turned left. In the thick January fog he could just make out the yellow glow of gas lamps at Buckingham Palace. Scott enjoyed the sensation of walking in the fog, it seemed to give the familiar surroundings an attractive air of mystery. He came to Birdcage Walk, carefully crossed the road, then entered Wellington Barracks, casually returning the salute of the sentry. Still humming softly to himself, he sauntered towards his quarters.

'Captain Scott,' a voice called.

Turning in the fog, he had difficulty in identifying its source, then a figure materialised from an archway to his right. On approaching, Scott saw a big-featured, heavy man in a colonel's uniform.

'Captain Scott?'

'Sir?'

'I'm Colonel Penrose. I'd like a word if it's convenient.'

Though politely phrased, Scott realised it wasn't a request. 'Of course, Sir.'

'Your adjutant has provided a room where we may talk in private. It's this way . . .'

'Very good, Sir.' Scott followed the colonel up a flight of stairs, his mind racing with curiosity. Why would a colonel want to meet him in a darkened doorway?

Penrose stopped at the head of the stairs, unlocked a door and ushered Scott inside. 'Take a seat, Captain.'

Bemused by the sequence of events, Scott sat. The office they had entered was one used by the adjutant, and it would normally have been long since deserted at this hour, but now a fire blazed cheerfully in the grate.

Colonel Penrose locked the door, crossed behind the large oaken desk which dominated the room, and lowered his bulk into a chair. He was an impressive-looking man in his late fifties, the heavy fleshiness of his cheeks only partially disguised by broad grey sideboards. Leaning back, he looked at Scott, a fleeting smile of amusement playing about his lips.

'I expect you find this rather curious, Captain?'

'Somewhat, Sir.'

'Simple enough really. I wanted to meet you away from any prying eyes. Hence the late hour and empty office.' Penrose leaned forward and opened a folder on the desk. 'I've been studying your file, Captain. India, Afghanistan, Zululand, and the Transvaal . . . Quite a lot of active service for an officer' – he glanced at the file – 'just gone twenty-six?'

'Yes, Sir.'

'You rather distinguished yourself in Afghanistan, Scott.'

'Thank you, Sir.'

'We felt you might like to undertake another . . . unorthodox assignment . . .'

Scott looked quizzically at the older man. 'We, Sir?'

'I've spoken to your colonel, of course,' said Penrose easily. 'If it should be decided that you'd be suitable for this job – and assuming you agree – you may be seconded to us for a term.'

'Seconded to whom, Sir?'

'A section of Military Intelligence. You are, I take it, a career officer?'

'Yes, Sir.'

'I can assure you, Captain, that your bravery and ingenuity

20

in Afghanistan did not go unnoticed. Another such performance could go a long way in advancing your career. A very long way . . .'

'What sort of mission have you in mind, Sir?'

'An undercover assignment again.' Penrose smiled suddenly. 'Your Mr Quentin was very convincing . . .'

Scott looked at him in amazement. In a Christmas entertainment for the regiment, he had played the part of Mr Quentin, an American gambler, in a melodrama staged in the barracks. But how did Penrose know?

'You kept up the accent very well,' said the colonel.

'You saw it?'

'Yes indeed. I always try to do my homework, Captain.'

'I see . . .'

'Could you maintain such an accent – impersonate an American offstage?'

'Well . . . yes. Yes, I'm certain I could, Sir.'

'Certain?'

'We had a groom at home when I was a boy. He'd been born and raised in Pennsylvania before his family returned to Devon, and he never lost the Yankee accent. I seemed to spend half my childhood mimicking him.'

'No wonder your Mr Quentin was so convincing. Tell me, Captain, apart from the accent, do you think you could maintain an entire persona?'

'Act out the part . . . continuously?'

'Yes.'

Scott leaned back a moment, thinking. 'If it were the right sort of part, I believe so, Sir. With sufficient preparation, I think I could act it out.'

'Indeed . . . presumably your Uncle Philip's influence . . . ?' Penrose allowed himself a small smile, seeing Scott's astonishment.

'How on earth . . .'

'I told you, Captain, I do my homework for an operation like this. Your uncle must have been rather the black sheep of the family. Something of a military clan, the Scotts – I rather fancy your grandfather didn't care to have an actor for a son.'

'My Uncle Philip was an excellent man, Sir. I had the

highest regard for him.' Scott allowed a note of coolness into his voice, notwithstanding Penrose's superior rank.

'Your dutiful loyalty does you credit, Captain.'

'With respect, Sir, my fondness and regard for my uncle are not dutiful, but genuinely felt.'

Colonel Penrose calmly raised a hand, dismissing the topic. 'We shan't argue over it, Captain. The point is that your background – both military and . . . theatrical – would appear to equip you rather well for this particular mission.'

'Might I ask what the mission is, Sir?' asked Scott, a touch of reserve still in his voice.

'We'd like you to spend some time in Ireland.'

'Ireland, Sir?' Scott's surprise showed clearly.

'You thought it would be America?'

'Well yes . . . the accent and so on . . .'

'I'll explain that presently,' said Penrose. 'What do you know of the political situation in Ireland?'

'Only what I've read in the papers, Sir. I've never been there.'

'You're aware, presumably, of Mr Parnell's Irish Party – and their aims?'

'Yes, Sir, they seek Home Rule for Ireland.'

Penrose laughed mirthlessly. 'In any sensible society it would be treason – here we give them the run of the House of Commons.'

'Well . . .' Scott started hesitantly.

'Yes, Captain?'

'Well . . . without sympathising with their views, Sir, but they have been elected to Parliament.'

'Quite. And if they restricted their shameful behaviour to Parliament, I dare say we could tolerate it. The reality, of course, is that they're working hand in glove with the thugs of the Land League, to get Home Rule by violence and intimidation.'

'I thought, Sir, that the Land League was for agrarian reform – controlled rents, rights of tenants, and so forth.'

Penrose shook his head. 'My dear Scott, the need, the *alleged* need for agrarian reform in Ireland, is simply the first step on the road to ultimate disloyalty to the Crown. You don't really think those ruffians will be happy with lower rents? That's simply the thin end of the wedge. Once we allow them to think that Jack is as good as his master, everything breaks down. They'll want the whole bloody country. That's Gladstone's mistake as a Prime Minister, he's too soft with the Irish.'

'I'm not awfully conversant, Sir, but isn't his Chief Secretary in Ireland . . . Mr . . .'

'Forster?'

'Yes. Isn't Mr Forster taking rather a firm stand? I mean, Parnell and the League leaders have been jailed?'

'Oh yes, they're in Kilmainham Jail, Captain – and for all the difference it makes they could be in a suite in Claridges. Every day brings fresh outrages. Cattle maimed, rent withheld, landlords threatened, crops burnt . . . Your people have land, Scott. Can you imagine what it must be like for the landowners?'

'Sounds unbearable, Sir.'

'It is. And the Land League is able to continue – even with its leaders in jail – because Forster's hand is stayed. With the backing of the military, Forster could smash the thugs and traitors, but Gladstone, with his liberal bloody conscience, shies away from it.'

Scott kept discreetly silent, not thinking it good form to criticise the Prime Minister.

'I'm telling you all this, Captain, so you'll know the background . . .'

'Yes, Sir.'

'What we've discussed so far is public knowledge, what I'm about to tell you is not. This is to be treated with absolute secrecy, you understand?'

Scott felt a frisson of excitement, but kept his voice calm. 'Perfectly, Sir.'

Penrose leaned forward and spoke more softly. 'Our intelligence has become aware of a new threat in Ireland. It appears that an offshoot of the Land League has been formed, called, rather fancifully, "The Invincibles". The members of this group are extreme nationalists. Their objective is said to

23

be political assassination.' He paused and looked at Scott. 'They plan to start by murdering the two most important men in Ireland – the Chief Secretary and the Viceroy.'

'Christ Almighty! They . . . they really plan to kill Forster and the Viceroy?'

'So it would appear.'

'My God . . . it's outrageous.'

'Indeed, Captain, indeed. Not the way we settle our political differences here, but then these gentlemen don't play by civilised rules.'

Scott's initial shock was now giving way to curiosity, and he longed to know his place in this dramatic scheme but sensed that impatience would be poorly received while Penrose was briefing him. He decided, however, to probe a little.

'Your knowledge of their activities, Sir . . . it seems fairly detailed . . .' He let the statement hang.

Penrose looked at him evenly. 'If you're asking where it comes from, Captain, I don't mind telling you. Its chief source is Superintendent Mallon of the Dublin Metropolitan Police – he has a long-established network of informers. However, the situation in Ireland may well call for a military, rather than a civil, response. Which is why we'd like our own man on the spot.'

'You'd wish me to investigate these . . . Invincibles?'

'No, Captain,' Penrose smiled fleetingly, 'we'd wish you to join them.'

'Join them?'

'In your American guise.'

'Why would an American wish to join them – assuming he could?'

'Because the Irish-American community is a hotbed of anti-British feeling. Fenians, Irish Republican Brotherhood, Clan na nGael . . . God only knows how many half-baked societies they have plotting against the British Empire.'

'If I were to present myself to them, Sir,' Scott asked carefully, 'wouldn't they surely check me out with their people in America?'

'They'd probably try. But since the potato famine of the

24

forties, perhaps two million Irish have emigrated to America. Mix them with fifty-one million Americans scattered throughout a vast continent, and tracing one individual becomes rather difficult.'

Scott looked thoughtful. 'I'd have to create an entire history for myself, Sir. If I could effect entry to their group – and that may be a very big if – wouldn't they surely question me very thoroughly?'

'Yes, we have thought of that,' replied Penrose. 'Fortunately the nature of such groups tends to be . . . unstable, to put it mildly. Their security in particular is somewhat slap-dash. Nevertheless, there would be no question of your going to Dublin without completely absorbing the culture and history to back your role. That means everything from Roman Catholic dogma to Fenian songs.'

'Would I be expected to sing, Sir?' Scott's voice contained just a hint of humour.

Penrose softened slightly. 'I can appreciate a touch of the cavalier in a young officer, Scott, but please, don't underestimate these people.'

'No, Sir.'

'It would be a mistake to confuse their fanaticism with stupidity. Although they're naïve in ways, and might well bungle things, they're also single-minded in the extreme, and that makes them dangerous. They could succeed – have no illusions about that.'

'I take your point, Sir.'

'You're under no obligation to accept this mission, Captain. It is dangerous, and all the preparation in the world cannot cover every eventuality. Having said that, the chaos and rebelliousness which assassinations could unleash don't bear thinking about.'

'I can see that, Sir.'

'The reason you're being asked to take such a risk is because of the significance of pacifying Ireland. The reality is that we cannot countenance rebellion on our doorstep. If we were seen to be defeated this year by the Irish in Ireland, then why not next year the Indians in India, the Chinese in Hong Kong, and so on.'

25

'I do see the implications of it, Sir,' said Scott.

'Will you undertake the assignment then?'

'Yes, Sir, I'd be honoured . . . provided . . .'

Penrose immediately raised an eyebrow quizzically, his expression suggesting that he wasn't used to junior officers issuing provisos.

Scott continued undaunted, 'provided that I'm allowed a fair degree of flexibility . . .'

'Flexibility?'

'Yes, Sir. I know from experience, that once in the field one must be free to make one's own decisions. It may be normal military practice to take orders from superior officers, but undercover operations are unpredictable − decisions must often be made instantly and without consultation.'

'Yes, I do see that,' said Penrose, with a trace of reluctance. 'Very well, Captain, once in the field, you will be given a suitable degree of freedom.'

'Fine, Sir.'

Penrose got up from the chair and came around the desk. Scott immediately rose, seeing Penrose reaching out to shake hands.

'It's good to have you along, Scott.'

'Thank you, Sir.'

'You'll have a month to immerse yourself in the new role − we sail for Dublin in mid-February.'

'Both of us, Sir?'

'Oh we shan't travel together, naturally, but I'll be taking up a post in Marlborough Barracks in Dublin. It will allow me to act as your liaison officer.'

'Very good, Sir.'

Penrose withdrew an envelope from his pocket and handed it to the younger man. 'There's a ticket here for tomorrow morning's seven-thirty train to Norwich. You alight at Thetford, where you will be met and transported to Valbeth House.'

'Valbeth House, Sir?'

'It's a secluded country manor where you won't be disturbed. You'll be spending the next month there with your tutors in matters Irish/American.'

'I see . . .'

'I need hardly stress that no one – *absolutely no one* – must know of this mission. Simply leave here quietly in the morning and catch the train – civilian clothes. It's all been cleared with your colonel.'

Scott looked at Penrose. 'Everything seems to have been arranged in advance, Sir.'

'Yes.'

'You must have been pretty certain I'd undertake this mission?'

Penrose smiled. 'Mystery, adventure and career advancement in the name of the Crown – what young officer could resist?' He took the file from the desk and nodded curtly. 'Goodnight, Captain.'

'Goodnight, Sir.'

Penrose crossed to the door, unlocked it, and left. Scott found himself staring after the older man, somewhat perplexed by the abrupt end to the discussion. Hearing the colonel's footsteps fading as he descended the staircase, Scott crossed to the window. After a moment he saw the figure of Penrose emerge from the archway and walk briskly across the courtyard, gradually disappearing into the fog. What was it about the man that was unsettling? Scott sensed an inate air of superiority about him, but a degree of arrogance – it had to be admitted – was common enough in officers of all ranks. Perhaps it was a smugness, as though he would always know more than he would be prepared to reveal. But damn it all, one didn't have to like the man to like the mission he had offered! And what a mission . . .

Scott knew enough of the army to realise that success in an assignment of this importance could be richly rewarded. His excited thoughts were interrupted by a loud chime from the clock as it reached the hour. He glanced up. Eleven o'clock. In just eight and a half hours he would be on his way to Norfolk. He looked out again into the fog-covered night, and wished, impatiently, that it were morning.

Four

Dr Hamilton Williams realised that it was imperative to control his mounting excitement. He had hurriedly crossed Oxford Street and turned down Bond Street, and now, seeing the sign for Weiss's, the instrument-makers, he slowed down. If he were to succeed in his mission he knew he would have to behave with a cool self-assurance. He paused a moment outside the shop door, then took a deep breath and strode in purposefully.

It had been several years since Williams had last been in Weiss's, but he remembered the layout and crossed without hesitation to the surgical counter. An assistant looked up, took in Williams's well-dressed appearance, and nodded deferentially.

'Good morning, Sir, may I be of assistance?'

'Yes, I'd like some large surgical knives, twelve-inch blades . . .'

'Do you have an account, Sir?'

'Yes. Williams, Dr Hamilton Williams.'

'Very good, Sir. And how many did you require?'

'Oh – say a dozen,' replied Williams casually.

'A dozen, Sir?' Though perfectly polite, there was no doubting the note of query in the assistant's voice.

'Yes, I'm off to serve in the Colonies – can't be popping back for replacements. You haven't opened a branch in Demerara, I presume?' he smilingly asked the assistant.

'Eh, no, Sir, not in Demerara,' the man answered with a respectful smile.

'Best make it a dozen so. Always lots of amputations out there I'm afraid . . .'

'Indeed, Sir. Shall I have them delivered to your residence?'

'No, no I'll collect them now. Speed things up . . .'

'Very good, Sir. If you wouldn't mind waiting a couple of moments, Sir?'

'Certainly.'

With a pleasant nod the assistant turned and went out one of the doors behind the counter. Williams realised with a start that it wasn't the door leading to the store-room where surgical supplies were kept.

Despite a growing sense of unease he forced himself to glance about the shelves with the casual air of one awaiting delivery of a perfectly mundane item. The time passed with agonising slowness, then after several moments, and to his great relief, the assistant suddenly re-entered from the store-room door.

Placing two cardboard boxes on the counter, the man produced a pen. 'Now, Sir, if you wouldn't mind signing for these. Just here and here please . . .'

Williams signed. He was pleased to notice that his hand was perfectly steady. The assistant carefully dried both signatures with blotting paper. 'Thank you very much, Sir. Now, this one's your receipt.'

'Thank you.' Williams took up the boxes.

'Well, *bon voyage*, Sir.' The man nodded at the box of knives. 'Hope you don't have to use them too often . . .'

'Oh, I fear they will be needed,' answered Williams, 'I assure you though, they will be put to good use. Good day.'

'Good day, Sir.'

Turning, Williams walked to the door, allowing himself a small smile as he stepped outside.

Five

All the arguments were over now, the pleading, the cajoling, the threatening. It was fixed. Kate's family was taking the boat train to link with the ship for New York. After that they would travel on to Stanley, Ohio, where, as her father never tired of putting it, 'they'd make a fresh start'. All except Kate, who, in spite of all argument to the contrary, was staying behind.

She was uncomfortable now as she watched the smoke from the waiting train rise in the freezing January air, to hang in a cloud beneath the blackened roof of Kingsbridge station. Her mother was re-checking their tickets, and Aunt Julia fussed about the packed lunches, as they too tried to put off the moment of departure.

Kate knew it was breaking her mother's heart to have the family split up, and she genuinely felt sorry for her father, dressed in his best clothes and standing uneasily on the platform, uncertain where to look or what to do next; but she also knew it had to be this way. Kate could not leave Ireland; not yet anyhow.

Attempting to bolster her convictions, she cast her mind back to the previous November when the family was homeless, and her father and Michael were jailed for unlawful occupation and resisting arrest. Kate and Denis and Deirdre had stayed with neighbours for about a week, while her mother went up to Dublin to visit Michael and her father in prison. People said that their sentences of two months each in Kilmainham Jail were light when compared to O'Connor and the Land League activists, who had all received two-year sentences.

While in Dublin her mother had stayed with Aunt Julia, her widowed sister-in-law, and Julia, with typical generosity, had insisted that the whole family move in with her, to facilitate visiting Kilmainham Jail.

Kate remembered with perfect clarity how on that awful day, as they left Knockcarney forever, all her bitterness seemed to crystalise. The loss of their farm, the disfiguring scar on her temple from Masefield's riding crop, the men in prison, the family having to leave the country – she realised she just couldn't accept it. Before she could continue her normal life, a blow had to be struck against the evil that had blighted them. She would simply have to stay in Ireland and channel her anger somehow. She knew instinctively that immersing herself in a violent, protracted struggle wasn't in her nature, but neither her pride nor her innate sense of justice would allow her simply to be driven away. And so, tearfully leaving the friends and neighbours of a lifetime in Knockcarney, she solemnly vowed that she wouldn't leave the country until she had made some gesture against the injustice of the British-run regime.

The shrill sound of the train's engine releasing steam brought Kate out of her reverie. She looked round as her mother, struggling to control her voice, started to speak.

'Well . . . well we'd better . . . we'll be late if . . .' Her voice trailed off as the tears formed in her eyes. Aunt Julia reached out her arms and embraced her sister-in-law silently.

With a lump in her throat, Kate reached out to Deirdre. 'Goodbye . . .'

'Bye, Katie . . .'

As they hugged, Dennis and Michael approached.

'Bye, Kate . . .'

'Bye, Dennis . . .' Her heart aching, she kissed his upturned forehead.

Aunt Julia and her father shook hands solemnly as Kate and Michael said their farewells.

'Look after them, Michael,' said Kate.

'I will, I promise . . . and mind yourself, Kate,' he said softly, then awkwardly he embraced her. Kate hugged him, then patted his shoulder as she saw her mother waiting to say goodbye. Kate had hoped not to worsen the departure with emotional farewells, but seeing her now, with the tears flowing down her cheeks, Kate gave in to her own tears. She reached

31

out and held her mother. 'It'll be alright, Mam . . . it'll be alright . . .'

'Oh, Katie . . .'

'Come on now, Mam, or you'll have us all in floods.'

Her mother sobbed. 'Katie darlin' . . . mind yourself . . .'

'I will, Mam . . . I will . . .'

Her father approached them. 'God bless you, Kate.' He held out his hand. Kate took the large gnarled hand in both of her own.

'You too, Dad . . . you too.' She hesitated a moment, knowing he felt awkward about public displays of affection, but in spite of his weaknesses, she felt a sudden rush of love for him. Reaching forward she hugged him and kissed his cheek. 'Goodbye, Dad . . . We'll be together again . . . we'll be together again in better times.'

As though it were the cue he needed, he latched onto the note of hope. 'That we will, that we will indeed . . . Now away with us or we'll miss the train. Have you the tickets there, Bridget?'

'Aye.' Drying her eyes with a handkerchief, her mother composed herself, then turned and handed their tickets to the conductor at the gate behind them.

'Right so,' her father said, his voice shaky, 'Well . . . God bless . . .'

There was a chorus of tearful 'God blesses' and 'don't forget to writes' as, gathering their belongings, they moved through the gate. Kate crushed up to the barrier separating passengers from well-wishers. Then, with a last wave from her mother, the family moved on and was swept up in the crowds going forward to board the train. Kate remained looking after them, tears slowly trickling down her cheeks, until they were finally lost to sight.

After a moment Aunt Julia touched her arm. 'Come on, child, there's no more to be seen of them.'

'Yes.'

'Come on,' she said gently, 'we'll get a cab home before we catch our death of cold.' Tenderly she placed her hand on Kate's arm, then guided her away.

*　　*　　*

32

A row of cabs was lined up outside Kingsbridge Station, their drivers chatting and stamping their feet in the cold. Kate and Julia emerged from the main door and approached the first of the cabs, Julia wrinkling her nose in distaste at the pungent smell of fresh horse manure.

'Good morning, ladies,' the driver greeted them heartily in a strong Dublin accent. 'Where will it be?'

'Drumcondra please,' answered Julia.

'Right ye be.' The cabman opened the door for them, helping Julia and Kate up the step. 'Drumcondra it is. Visitin' the archbishop in his palace, what?' he enquired jovially.

'Binns Bridge will suffice,' Julia answered coolly.

Kate recognised the tone as the one adopted when Julia felt a social inferior was being over-familiar.

'Fair enough,' said the cabman, subdued by the disapproval in Julia's voice, as he mounted the cab and clipped the horse into motion with the reins. They moved off, crossing Kingsbridge and the slow-moving waters of the river Liffey.

Glancing across at her aunt, Kate saw the lines of fatigue about her eyes. Julia looked back, smiled briefly as though in apology for her tiredness, then leaned back against the padded seat and closed her eyes. Though a vigorous and healthy woman, Kate realised that in the harsh morning light her aunt suddenly looked her sixty years.

Kate observed her affectionately, remembering how the family, and in particular her mother, had been relieved by Julia's tact in never making them feel like the recipients of charity. Her aunt had gently but firmly refused all offer of payment for housing and feeding them, insisting that they keep their savings intact for when they would reach America. Instead it had been agreed that Kate and her mother would work in the shop, and for the past two months they had helped in running the grocery store. In fact, Kate had agreed to continue working full-time in the shop until the hospitals took on the annual quota of nurses the following July. It was an agreement that made her feel a little guilty, for she had no intention of working in Dublin that summer – not if her plans worked out. She had decided to wait until her family was safely out of the country before acting on her vow, and now the time had come. Of course it would be essential not to implicate Aunt Julia, who, despite her family devotion to the evicted Lannigans, considered herself a loyal subject of the Crown.

Kate glanced out the window of the cab, recognising the junction of Church Street and King Street as they swung right to begin the long straight run up Bolton Street to Drumcondra. Since coming to Dublin she had got to know the city quite well, and although initially a little daunted by its size and the pace of city life, she had soon adapted to the point where she now knew her way about sufficiently well to travel with the same easy confidence as the native Dubliners. She calculated now that they were about half way home and she looked closely at Julia's face to ensure that her aunt was still dozing.

Satisfied that this was the case, Kate reached into her pocket, unable to resist a final reading of her letter. It would finally be safe to send it now. How many times had she written and re-written that letter? It had been so difficult to express her feelings, yet the first impression to be made by the letter could be all-important. Opening the envelope, she looked at the sheets of her neat, rounded handwriting, reading it under her breath one last time.

> Kate Lannigan
> c/o P.O. Box 124
> GPO, Dublin
> 30th January 1882

Mr James Carey
19a Denzille Street
Dublin

Dear Mr Carey,

I have read in the papers about your standing as a nationalist candidate for the Dublin Town Council. I am very sorry you did not get elected, but the article described you as a man with a long-established background in nationalism.

It is this last matter that I am writing about and I hope you can help me. If you cannot, I hope you might be able to introduce me to someone who could.

I decided I must take action after my family was evicted, and forced to emigrate. Our house was burnt down by Lord Masefield, my father and brother were put in jail for two months, and I myself am physically scarred for life.

I hope this does not sound like the ravings of a woman who is unhinged. Really I am quite sane, but I need to do something about the injustices that the English and their landlords are doing here.

You are probably wondering why I do not get involved in the struggles of the Land League, but what I want is not a campaign that would last for years, even though I admire the progress the Land League has made, but I want to strike one powerful blow and then rejoin my family abroad.

I am sure there must be patriotic people who could use a willing recruit, and I am not afraid to take risks. If you want to check the truth of my story, the eviction was on the 11th of November last in the townland of Knockcarney, County Wexford, and the landlord responsible was Lord Masefield. The Freeman's Journal had an article on it at the time.

I have not contacted you until now as I wanted to wait until my family was safely abroad. I am staying with a relative and I do not want her to be associated with this in any way, so I am using a P.O. box.

As we both appear to be against the same injustices, Mr Carey, I really hope you can help me and I look forward to your reply.

Yours faithfully,
Kate Lannigan

Kate folded the letter, reasonably pleased that it stated her case fairly accurately. But would Carey respond? She'd simply have to wait and see, though now that the time had come she was suddenly impatient to post it and set events moving. Sealing the envelope, she heard the flat accent of the cabman calling out a greeting.

'Skin-the-Goat, the hard man!'

'Ah the bould Mick!' came the answer.

'Whooa there,' cried the cabman.

Feeling the cab slowing down, Kate looked out the window. They were at the junction of King Street and Bolton Street, and she saw that her driver's greeting had been addressed to another cabman of middle-aged, but robust appearance.

'Are ye goin' to the do tonight in O'Rourke's? Should be plenty of free gargle?' shouted the driver.

'Do ducks swim?' answered the man hailed as Skin-the-Goat.

'See you then,' called the first cabman.

'Right . . .'

Looking out the window during this exchange, Kate saw a red pillarbox on the pavement. A quick glance established that Aunt Julia was still asleep, then, just as the cabman was about to move off, Kate stuck her head out the window. 'Excuse me,' she called, 'can you hold on a minute? I'd like to post a letter in the box there . . .'

'No problem, Miss.'

Kate quickly descended from the cab and crossed the road. She looked for a moment at the letter on which so much depended, then slipped it into the pillarbox. Crossing back to the cab she smiled at the driver. 'Thanks.'

'Not at all, Miss, not at all.'

Kate climbed back into the cab and they moved off. It was done now, she'd set her plan in motion. Leaning back in her seat, she wondered where it might lead . . .

Six

Dr Hamilton Williams felt his pulse begin to race as he approached Westminster Palace Chambers. Since delivering his lethal cargo of surgical knives to Frank Byrne, secretary of the Land League of Great Britain, Williams had been waiting impatiently for the call to further action. It had finally come this morning, and he was to present himself at the League offices at eleven o'clock.

Williams entered the building and climbed the stairs to the first floor, then turned left along the corridor. He paused a moment outside the door marked F Byrne, Secretary, and gathered himself. It wouldn't do to rush in looking too eager. He adjusted the angle of his hat, straightened the lie of his overcoat, and, satisfied with his composure, knocked confidently on the door.

'Come in,' called a voice from inside.

Entering he saw Frank Byrne approach smilingly, but to Williams's surprise the other occupant of the room was an obviously pregnant woman, seated beside the desk.

'Good morning, Hamilton, glad you could make it.' Byrne shook Williams's hand, then indicated his hat and coat. 'Here, let me take these . . .'

'Thank you,' answered Williams, glancing at the woman as he took off the coat. She was about seven months pregnant, he guessed.

Byrne placed the hat and coat on a stand, then turned. 'Hamilton, I'd like you to meet my wife. This is Dr Hamilton Williams, Dear.'

Suppressing his surprise at Byrne having his wife present, Williams crossed to shake hands.

'How do you do, Mrs Byrne?'

'How do you do, Dr Williams?'

Her handshake was firm and confident, and she smiled pleasantly.

'Take a seat, Hamilton, take a seat,' said Byrne easily.

'Thank you.' Williams drew up a deep, comfortable-looking leather chair as Byrne crossed behind the desk and seated himself. Byrne smiled.

'Well, I'm sure you're wondering what's happening about the knives,' he said.

'Yes,' answered Williams.

'They came back from Bethnal Green yesterday. Collins had the sheaths made, so transporting them will be much safer now.'

'That's good.'

'We've given a lot of thought to your offer,' continued Byrne, 'it was very good of you to volunteer . . .'

'Someone has to bring them to our men in Dublin,' said Williams.

'Yes. The point is though, that having procured them successfully – thanks to your good self – it would be foolish to risk losing them at this stage.'

'I don't think I quite follow you.'

Byrne leaned forward. 'The problem, Hamilton, is that if we use any of our usual messengers or anyone known for their Land League affiliations – like yourself or myself – they'd be liable to questioning and searching by the police on leaving the country.'

'Are you telling me I'm not being given the Dublin mission?' The disappointment was clear in Williams's voice.

'It's too risky, Hamilton. I'm sorry. Truly I am. But we cannot put the Invincible programme at risk by using a known nationalist as the courier.'

'Then who will you use?'

'I'm doing it,' said Mrs Byrne.

'You are?'

'Yes. Unlike the chief League members, I'm not known to the police.'

'Yes but you're . . . you're obviously with child.'

'Precisely. And what policeman is going to suspect a woman, seven months pregnant, of carrying assassination weapons?'

'But . . . the rigours of a sea-trip, the stress of concealing weapons . . .'

'Come come, Doctor,' Mrs Byrne chided smilingly, 'thousands upon thousands of Irish women have had to cross the Atlantic to America, and they've delivered healthy babies – I'm only going to Dublin. And as for the stress . . . well, living with Frank here while he fussed and worried over the safe delivery of the knives would be far worse than delivering them myself.'

Byrne smiled sympathetically at Williams. 'You won't change her mind, believe me, I know! You're a man of action, Hamilton, and I know you're disappointed, but the committee are all agreed that this is the safest way of moving the weapons.'

'I see,' answered Williams.

'And we would be eager to use your skills again,' continued Byrne, 'it's likely to be a long struggle against the British. There'll be future missions for a man of your bravery and daring . . . believe me.'

'Thank you . . . thank you, Frank,' answered Williams, flattered and considerably consoled by the secretary's words, and, despite his initial disappointment, aware of the tactical sense of using Mrs Byrne. He rose and crossed to her, extending his hand. 'May I wish you *bon voyage*, and the best of luck in delivering such a vital cargo?'

Mrs Byrne shook hands. 'Thank you, Dr Williams,' she replied, looking him mischievously in the eye. 'And for Ireland's sake let's hope my delivery is without complications!'

Frank Byrne laughed heartily at his wife's joke and Williams smiled pleasantly as the other man poured three glasses of whiskey.

Byrne raised his glass in a toast. 'I give you a "safe delivery".'

Williams and Mrs Byrne smiled and raised their glasses. 'A safe delivery . . .'

Gusts of wind blew down Sackville Street, scattering the lightly falling snow in all directions, and the afternoon streets were crowded as the citizens of Dublin went about their business.

Barely conscious of the snow, Kate alighted eagerly from her tram at the base of Nelson's Pillar, a one hundred and twenty feet tall column from the top of which a statue of the one-eyed sailor overlooked the main street of the capital. Briskly crossing the wide thoroughfare, she entered the main door of the General Post Office, and went to the counter marked Poste Restante. It was eight days since she had written to Carey, and she knew that a response one way or another must be awaiting her.

Sensing Kate's presence, the clerk behind the counter looked up from a ledger, raising his eyebrows quizzically.

'Can you tell me if there's anything for Box 124 please?' she asked, a note of excitement creeping into her voice, in spite of herself.

The clerk, an overweight, grey-haired man in his fifties, lowered his pen wearily. 'One moment please.' He rose slowly, his demeanour suggesting that Kate had disturbed him from far more important work.

Watching him reluctantly round the counter to where the letters were kept, Kate felt a surge of irritation against the man. It was a golden rule in Aunt Julia's shop never to make a customer feel that their purchases, however small, were ever an interruption. Just as she was thinking of how a few days working for Aunt Julia could work wonders for the overweight clerk, the man returned carrying a single letter, and in her excitement Kate immediately forgot all thoughts of his shortcomings. It could only be Carey's reply.

'Sign here, please,' said the clerk, laboriously lowering himself into his chair while Kate impatiently wrote her name on a form. The clerk took the form, blotted her signature dry, then handed her the letter.

'Thank you,' she said, taking it eagerly as the man returned wordlessly to his ledger.

Moving through the crowded main hall of the Post Office, Kate crossed to one of the tables at which people addressed letters and applied stamps. She found a vacant space and quickly opened the envelope. It contained a single sheet covered in large, somewhat uneven handwriting. Her heart pounding, she swiftly read the letter.

19a Denzille Street
Dublin
5th February 1882

Dear Miss Lannigan,
I have received your letter of the 30th inst., for which many thanks. I may be in a position to assist you in the matter referred to. If you could meet me at the above address on Monday next, February 12th, at 8.00 pm, we can discuss the matter in more detail.
I await meeting you with pleasure.

Assuring you of my best attention,
I remain,
Yours faithfully,
James Carey

Elated, Kate stared at the letter. She was past the first hurdle at least. Reading through the letter again, a little more analytically this time, she noticed that it was the composition of a man used to writing business, rather than personal letters. But the tone was encouraging, and on whatever pretext was necessary with Aunt Julia, she would meet Mr Carey.

Pocketing the letter, she left the Post Office and re-entered Sackville Street, a spring in her step despite the February snow.

Seven

Captain William Scott found himself unwinding, as usual, as he took his after-lunch walk through the grounds of Valbeth House. The cold February rain had stopped, to be replaced by a weak hazy sun, and even in its barren, winter starkness, the Norfolk countryside looked appealing. Scott had come to relish these daily walks along the banks of the Valbeth stream during the three gruelling weeks of preparation which he had undergone here.

Could it really be only three weeks since Penrose had briefed him on the Invincibles, he wondered. Having to absorb so much information on Irish-American affairs, he had lost all sense of time, immersing himself each day in the seemingly endless round of tutorials, library study and written exercises.

Whenever he had felt his enthusiasm lagging, he'd reminded himself that on a mission like this a small detail could mean the difference between life and death. And so he had studied American politics, Irish history, the Roman Catholic religion – the Irish version of which seemed amazingly colourful compared to the Church of England – rebel songs, and a host of assorted topics which would back up his identity.

Choosing that identity had been the most important exercise – and one which he had insisted on doing alone – for he had to devise a credible character whom he could portray and maintain upon his arrival in Ireland. And thus Captain William Scott had created Bill Ryan – the logic behind the name being that if he responded automatically to a call of William, it wouldn't expose his cover.

Scott knew that it was important to keep the deceptions as near to the truth as possible, and so with his family background of horse-breeding and his own love of the animals, he'd made Bill Ryan a horse breeder from Pennsylvania who would be visiting Ireland to consider starting a stud farm.

Reaching the end of the path by the stream, Scott climbed a

small rise, then rested a moment. The hazy sunshine glinted on the stream's waters, and looking back up the valley he could make out the chimneys of Valbeth House over the treetops. Everything looked so pastoral and serene that it was hard to believe he was training here to infiltrate a terrorist group.

He checked his watch. Five minutes to two. His final interrogation was scheduled for half-past three today, and his two tutors – Cox, from Military Intelligence, who specialised in American politics and Irish-American subversion, and Fowler, a retired Foreign Office official whose brief was Roman Catholicism and Irish-American culture – would be questioning him with Colonel Penrose.

Better head back and have a last look through his notes, he thought; a good performance today would practically guarantee that the mission went ahead. He pocketed his watch, then started back down the hill towards Valbeth House, eager, now that the time had come, to pass this final test and then to take on – and beat – the so-called Irish Invincibles.

'Ready, Cox?' asked Colonel Penrose.

'Yes, Sir,' answered Cox, the gaunt-faced intelligence officer.

'Fowler?'

'Yes, Colonel, quite ready.' With a weak smile, the plump Fowler indicated the neat rows of paper on the table before him.

'Very well, I'll call him in.' Penrose crossed to the door and opened it, his heels echoing on the panelled floor of the Valbeth House Library. He beckoned to the dark-haired young man who was waiting outside in the corridor. 'Very good, Scott, we're ready now . . .'

Entering the room, Scott laid his hand on the colonel's arm.

'The name's Ryan,' he said in a perfect American accent, 'Bill Ryan . . .'

'Oh . . . yes. Quite.' The faintest hint of a smile crossed Penrose's face as they walked to the long table, behind which sat Cox and Fowler. Rounding the table to take the vacant seat between them, Penrose indicated a single chair on the other side of the table. 'Take a seat, Mr . . . Ryan,' he said.

'Thank you,' answered Scott, seating himself comfortably.

'What brings you to Ireland?' asked Penrose.

'I'm a horse breeder. I'm thinking of starting a stud farm here.'

'Really – and from what part of the United States have you come?' asked Fowler.

'Philadelphia.'

'Ah, a fine old city, quite historic . . .'

'Yes, Sir,' said Scott.

'A long established city – your Birth Certificate would be registered there . . .'

'No,' answered Scott. 'I was actually born in Kentucky.'

'Where exactly in Kentucky?' asked Fowler.

'Somewhere on the road from Bowling Green to Horse Cave – I'm afraid there were no Birth Certificates issued there.'

Penrose leaned forward. 'That's rather a long way from Philadelphia, isn't it?'

'My father was a travelling horse dealer; we moved around a lot in the early years.'

'And later on you settled in Pennsylvania?' continued Penrose.

'That's right.'

'In the capital – Philadelphia?'

Scott looked at Penrose evenly. 'We settled in Philadelphia, but Harrisburg is the capital of Pennsylvania.'

'So you know a lot about Pennsylvania?' Cox cut in.

'As much as most residents, I guess.'

'Then you'd know where the world's first oil strike occurred?' said Cox.

'Yeah, over in Titusville . . . 1859 . . .'

'What place outside Philadelphia is called after a small town in Wales?' continued Cox.

'Oh, you must be talkin' about Bryn Mawr.'

'Yes,' answered Cox, 'and the canal linking Pittsburg and Philadelphia has to cross what mountain range?'

'The Alleghenys,' said Scott. 'Had to winch the canal boats over on flatcars . . .'

'Yes indeed,' said Cox. 'Oh, just before we leave

Philadelphia – what river joins the Delaware near Province Island?'

Scott paused a moment. 'Province Island . . . eh, that'd be the Schuylkill River . . .'

'You say you were born in Kentucky, Mr Ryan?' asked Fowler.

'That's right.'

'Then no doubt you'll know who wrote the popular song 'My old Kentucky Home?'

'Eh . . . no, can't say I do . . .'

Fowler looked taken aback. 'How surprising, Mr Ryan. Not familiar with Stephen Foster, and you a native Kentuckian . . .'

Scott shrugged depreciatingly. 'I guess I was never what you'd call a musical man. Besides, we moved from Kentucky when my Momma died. I was only two at the time.'

'Ah yes,' said Fowler pleasantly, his plump frame filling the chair as he leaned back. 'Yes. Tell me this, your family were Catholic, were they not?'

'That's right,' said Scott.

'And your father a horse breeder?'

'Yes.'

'Perhaps you'll tell us then, who is the patron saint of animals?'

'Saint Francis of Assisi,' said Scott.

'Who is more senior in the Catholic Church, an archbishop or a cardinal?'

'A cardinal.'

'How many days are there in Lent?'

'Forty days.'

Fowler leaned forward slightly. 'What conditions make for a mortal sin?'

Scott paused briefly. 'Clear knowledge, full consent, and it must be a serious matter.'

'Indeed,' replied Fowler, 'a serious matter such as missing Mass on a Holiday of Obligation – say like Ash Wednesday?'

'Ash Wednesday isn't a Holiday of Obligation.'

'No, of course not – but the Feast of the Assumption is?'

'Yes '

'On what date does the Assumption fall?'

'Eh . . .' Scott looked uncertain. 'Off the top of my head . . . I'm not sure.'

Fowler raised an eyebrow. 'A Catholic who doesn't know the date of Our Lady's Assumption into Heaven?'

'Well, to tell you the truth, I guess I'm kinda lapsed as a Catholic,' said Scott, contriving to look just a trifle sheepish about it.

'Lapsed?' echoed Fowler. 'Since when, may we ask?'

Scott barely hesitated. 'Well, you see my father had been ill for years before his death. He suffered . . . he suffered a lot. I guess it sorta undermined my faith a bit . . .'

'Your father moved to the United States in 1848,' said Penrose, 'was he a nationalist then?'

'I guess so . . .' said Scott.

'Then how come *your* interest in Irish nationalism is only developing *now*?'

'Well, the fact is, most of his life my father kept his politics to himself. He'd lost his wife and was struggling to raise a son and build a business in a new country. It was only at the end – when he knew he was dying – that he told me all about Ireland's history and the potato famine and so on . . .'

'And it intrigued you?'

'Sure did.'

Cox cut in. 'With your new-found interest in Ireland, did you join Clan na nGael – or any of the other republican groups?'

'No, Sir, I didn't.'

'Why not?'

'I wanted to see the things at first hand, to come to where the real struggle is goin' on,' answered Scott. 'My father had a big insurance policy on his life, so I used some of it to travel to Ireland.'

'Nevertheless as an Irish-American with an interest in Irish politics, you must have heard of the New Departure?'

'That's right.'

'What is it?' insisted Cox.

'In 1878,' answered Scott, 'John Devoy of Clan na nGael offered Parnell and the Home Rulers the conditional support of the American movement.'

46

'Mr Ryan,' called Fowler suddenly.

Scott immediately turned in answer to the name.

'Mr Ryan, you say you developed a strong interest in the history of Ireland?'

'Yes.'

'Can you tell me which patriot was known as "The Darlin' of Erin"?'

Scott hesitated, then replied: 'Wolfe Tone.'

'Wolfe Tone,' repeated Fowler, 'and tell me, who said: "when my country takes her place amongst the nations of the earth, then, and only then, let my epitaph be written"?'

'Robert Emmet, in his Speech from the Dock.'

'Why was he in the Dock?' asked Fowler briskly.

'He was captured and tried when his rebellion failed.'

'In what year was that?' persisted Fowler.

Scott paused briefly, then said: '1803.'

'Very good,' said Penrose nodding, 'very good indeed.' He turned to his two colleagues. 'I think that will be all for now, Gentlemen. Thank you very much for your efforts.'

'Not at all, Sir,' answered Cox.

Taking their dismissal cue, Fowler and Cox rose. Fowler nodded pleasantly to Penrose and Scott, then moved towards the door.

'Good afternoon, Colonel, Captain Scott,' said Cox.

Watching from the corner of his eye, Penrose noted with satisfaction that Scott had not responded at all to his real name.

'Good afternoon, Cox,' Penrose called after the departing tutor.

Penrose waited until the door had closed after the two men, then turned. 'Very well, Scott, you may revert to being Captain Scott again.'

'Thank you, Sir,' he answered with a smile.

'You think well on your toes, Captain – the lapsed Catholic business was quite convincing when you didn't know the Feast of the Assumption. Having said that,' continued Penrose with a slight change of tone, 'if you'd *known* the date, the inventiveness wouldn't have been necessary.'

'Yes, Sir.'

'Which brings me to your one serious error.' Penrose leaned forward, looking Scott in the eye. 'If you don't know something, *don't guess*. Wolfe Tone was *not* called the Darlin' of Erin; that was Robert Emmet.'

Scott grimaced.

'Far better if you're unsure of something to do as you did with the religion business – say you're not sure and invent a plausible reason for your uncertainty.'

'Yes, Sir. Point taken.'

Penrose relaxed slightly. 'Well, Scott, you'll be pleased to learn that we depart for Dublin next week.'

'Excellent, Sir,' he replied enthusiastically.

'You're not quite ready yet. A bit more work is called for on the Irish history end of things. However, you've a full week to brush up on that and any other shaky areas.'

'Don't worry, Sir, I'll certainly apply myself.'

'Do that, Scott – you don't need me to tell you what a sticky wicket you'd be on with these Invincibles people if you make any mistakes.'

'No, Sir.'

'Right, that'll by all, Scott.'

'Yes, Sir . . . and thank you, Sir. When we get there . . . I won't let you down.'

Penrose looked at him thoughtfully. 'No . . .' he said. 'No I don't believe you will.'

Eight

'Joe?' Tim Kelly's voice was a soft whisper.

'What?'

'Are you nervous?'

Joe Brady turned his bulky frame and faced his companion directly. In the moonlight Kelly's clean-shaven face looked even more youthful and innocent than usual. 'No,' he answered gruffly, 'I'm not nervous.'

'Neither am I, Joe. I thought I might be, but I'm . . . I'm excited – but I'm not afraid.'

'Good.'

Softly stamping his feet, Brady looked over towards the gas-lit main road of the Phoenix Park. It was a crisp February evening and a hard frost had already formed on the grass. Good, he thought, feeling the cold, the fewer strollers the better.

'I've never done anything like this before,' added Kelly, 'have . . . have you ever . . . have you ever killed a man before, Joe?'

'This isn't a man – it's a rat! An informer! I haven't killed anyone but I'll kill this squealin' bastard alright.'

'Yeah, we will together, Joe! Mr Mullett will be proud of us.'

Brady grunted. 'Mullett isn't God Almighty.'

'Still and all . . . he gave us these,' said Kelly defensively, indicating the long surgical knife in his hand.

'Keep that in your pocket,' snapped Brady.

'OK, Joe, OK. They're some weapon, aren't they?'

'Yeah.'

'I wonder where they got them.'

'From London,' answered Brady. 'Someone must have smuggled them in.'

'Fair play to him, whoever he was.'

'Yeah. What time is it now?'

Kelly took out his watch and tilted it to catch the moonlight.

'A quarter to seven, Joe.'

'Slip over to the park wall and look up Conyngham Road. He's due any minute.'

'Right,' answered Kelly, and quickly moved off into the shadow of the nearby trees.

Brady stamped his frozen feet again. They had been in place nearly fifteen minutes now, awaiting the arrival of the traitor Matt Flynn, who was due to enter the park from the Conyngham Road steps. A sympathiser working in the British HQ in Dublin Castle had passed word on to the Invincibles that Flynn was definitely an informer, and that he would be meeting Superintendent Mallon tonight, for a pay-off.

The rendezvous was the main road of the Phoenix Park, directly opposite the Wellington obelisk. The Duke of Wellington – another traitorous bastard, thought Brady, looking at the two hundred feet tall monument to the soldier who had defeated Napoleon; for this was the man who, on being reminded of his birth in Ireland, replied that being born in a stable didn't make one a donkey. A real smart alec, thought Brady. A toady and a smart alec – two things Joe Brady hated.

'Joe.' Kelly materialised from the shadows. 'There's no sign of him yet.'

'Damn it, he should be comin' by now. We want to get him before the Peelers arrive.'

'It's only ten to, Joe. He's not meeting Mallon till seven.'

'What did Carey say?' answered Brady harshly. 'This fella's always early for appointments, always there first. The whole plan is based on that.'

'I know,' answered Kelly.

'OK, you wait here, Tim, stand in the shadows. I'm going down to the wall for a look.'

'Right.'

Turning quickly, Brady moved into the darkness of the evergreens and crossed the uneven slope leading down to the boundary wall of the park. Reaching the wall, he carefully leaned over and looked up Conyngham Road. No one was about, the only sound on the deserted thoroughfare being the contented munching of a horse, its owner's carriage parked in front of the house across the road. What the hell was keeping Flynn?

Brady leaned over the wall again and looked down along the road. Still nobody to be seen. Glancing behind the horse and carriage, he could see down into a cutting where two lines of railway track shone in the moonlight before disappearing into the tunnel leading under Conyngham Road and the Phoenix Park. The cold steel of the tracks made him think of the steel blade in his pocket, and unconsciously he closed his fist around the knife's handle.

Out of the corner of his eye he caught a sudden movement, and swiftly turning, he glimpsed a heavy-set man hurrying across the road about one hundred yards away. The man moved quickly to the steps leading into the park and then vanished into the shadows. Immediately Brady turned and speedily but carefully ascended back towards the road. Reaching the edge of the belt of trees, he made out the shape of the waiting Kelly.

'Tim,' he cried softly, 'he's comin' up the steps.'

'We might have a problem, Joe,' said Kelly urgently.

'What?'

'I've been watchin' the main road. See that lamp over there?'

Brady looked at the gas lamp, about two hundred yards away across the frost-stiffened grass. 'What about it?'

'I saw three men waiting just behind it. The Peelers are here already, Joe.'

'Bastards,' muttered Brady.

Just then they heard a footstep, and looking towards the lamp standard at the head of the steps, they saw a figure mount the top step onto the pavement. Unaware of their presence in the darkness of the trees, the heavy-set man moved briskly along the footpath towards them.

'Joe.' Kelly's voice was the merest whisper. 'Let's do it anyway – Peelers or no Peelers.'

'Right,' answered Brady without hesitation.

The man hurrying along the pavement had all the appearance of one rushing to keep an appointment, but Brady had to be sure he really was Flynn. He waited until the

51

approaching figure was almost level with him, then he suddenly stepped out onto the path.

The man started badly.

'Oh sorry,' said Brady, 'didn't mean to give you a fright. I'm looking for the Conyngham Road steps . . .'

'Just up there,' answered the man nervously. As he spoke Brady could see Kelly silently moving in behind him.

'It's . . . it's Matt, isn't it?' asked Brady in apparent recognition. 'Matt Flynn?'

'Yes . . .' answered the man automatically, the surprise on his face clear in the moonlight.

'I have something for you, Matt,' said Brady pleasantly, then swiftly he plunged the twelve-inch blade into the man's chest. 'That's for all the men you betrayed, you squealin' bastard!'

Pain and disbelief mingled on the man's face, and he stumbled sideways as Brady savagely wrenched the knife out. Managing somehow to stay on his feet, the man brought his right hand up to his mouth, and suddenly there was a high-pitched and piercing whistle.

'Jesus!' cried Brady, lunging towards him, but Kelly had already sprung from behind, burying his knife in the man's back, halfway through a second whistle blast. The whistle fell from the man's mouth, and Kelly, gripping him fiercely while pulling out the knife, realised that the whistle was attached to the man's wrist.

'The Peelers, Joe, the Peelers!' cried Kelly urgently.

Looking around, Brady saw three figures about one hundred and fifty yards away, running across the moonlit grass towards them. He quickly plunged his knife into the collapsing Flynn in a final deadly thrust, then threw him to the ground. 'Quick, Tim,' he cried, 'into the trees.'

Together they sprinted into the darkness of the evergreens. 'Down to the wall,' called Brady, and they ran, stumbling, down the incline. Reaching the wall at speed, Brady leapt onto its top and quickly dropped down onto the still-deserted Conyngham Road, followed a couple of seconds later by Kelly.

Suddenly there was a series of loud whistle blasts from behind them in the park.

'Let's go,' cried Kelly, turning towards Kilmainham.

'No! This way! Come on!' Brady sprinted across the road to the parked horse and carriage, and Kelly, responding to the note of command, ran to join him.

'Let off the break!' cried Brady.

As Kelly swiftly did so, Brady grabbed the gas lamp from the side of the carriage as another burst of police whistles rang out.

'Gee up!' shouted Brady, smacking the horse hard on the rump, and causing him to bolt. 'Let them chase that!' he cried as the animal ran wildly down the road.

'Over the wall, Tim, quick!' said Brady, scaling the wall at the side of the road. Kelly followed immediately and jumped down on the other side of the wall.

'Down to the railway line,' whispered Brady.

'What?'

'The tunnel leads under the park – while they're after the horse we'll be miles away. Come on!' With considerable agility for a man of his size, Brady swiftly descended the steep railway bank. Moving quickly in his wake, Kelly finally caught up just as they reached the gaping black of the tunnel entrance. The sound of police whistles in the distance carried down to them.

'Listen,' said Brady softly. 'They're movin' down the road. They mustn't have seen us gettin' down here. Right, let's go!'

He stepped forward into the dark tunnel, the carriage lamp casting distorted shadows onto the soot-blackened roof. Stretching ahead, outside of the lamp's glow, was an absolute blackness.

'God, Joe,' said Kelly, following closely behind, 'this place would give ye the creeps. It's well you took that lamp.'

'Yeah – I heard once that the tunnel's half a mile long.'

They moved forward hurriedly, stepping from one wooden sleeper to the next as they followed the curve of the tunnel. Suddenly Kelly stopped. 'Joe!' he called softly.

'What?'

'I heard something . . .'

'Where?' said Brady, also stopping.

'I'm not sure – listen.'

A rumbling sound started to fill the tunnel, the noise quickly growing louder.

'Jesus – it's a train!' cried Brady.

'Which way is it comin'?'

'I can't make out . . .'

The track started to vibrate as the rumbling sound became a roar. 'Quick, Tim! Off the track!'

'Where will we . . . ?

'Up against the wall – fast!' shouted Brady, as the lights of the approaching train started to swing around the bend before them. The two men flung themselves against the wall and the train suddenly rounded the bend, red sparks flying through the darkness as the driver braked for the curve.

Swathed in a mass of smoke, the train roared towards them, and the two men squeezed fearfully against the wall as, with terrifying closeness, the engine went past. The long line of goods wagons seemed to be rocking by only inches from their heads and then, suddenly, the train was gone, a distant rumble and the smoke-filled atmosphere the only signs of its passing. Relieved, they stepped back from the damp tunnel walls.

'Do you think the driver saw us, Joe?' asked Kelly, his voice slightly shaky.

'Probably – I had the lamp. But he wouldn't have seen our faces.'

'He could report it in Kingsbridge,' said Kelly.

'He mightn't be stoppin' in Kingsbridge, and even if he is, by the time he makes a report we'll be out of it. Now let's go!'

They strode swiftly ahead through the smoke, occasionally stumbling on a damp sleeper. After a few minutes the smoke seemed to thin out and suddenly they were at the tunnel mouth. The high, frost-covered embankment looked eerily beautiful after the dark, smoke-laden tunnel, and both men breathed in deeply.

'Come on,' said Brady, 'the second bridge up here is Blackhorse Avenue.'

'What's the first?' asked Kelly.

Brady suddenly smiled. 'A side entrance to Marlborough Barracks. So no more talking.'

Swiftly but quietly they followed the curve of the track, the

54

brightly lit windows of the barracks appearing above the embankment on their left. They carefully observed the bridge for signs of a sentry, but the side entrance was obviously not guarded at the bridge, and after watching for a few moments they passed uneventfully beneath its arch. Thirty seconds later they cautiously started to climb the steep embankment to Blackhorse Avenue bridge.

'OK, Tim,' said Brady, when they reached the top, 'we brush our clothes and look respectable, then climb down separately onto the road, right?'

'Right, Joe.'

'I'll take your knife first.'

'Here ye are,' said Kelly, handing it over.

'Right. Now the Peelers will be sealin' off around Conyngham Road, so I'll walk home down Aughram Street, and you get the tram from the North Circular Road.'

'OK, Joe.'

'And, Tim . . .' Brady paused. 'You did well. That bastard Flynn won't be singin' any more songs in Mallon's ear.'

'This is only the beginning, Joe,' answered Kelly eagerly.

'That's right,' Brady said softly, 'the Invincibles are only warmin' up . . .'

Nine

Monday had finally arrived, and Kate walked expectantly along Westland Row to her rendezvous with James Carey. There was something very pleasant about walking in the city centre, with the warm, yellow-lit windows of the elegant buildings in attractive contrast to the crisp evening air.

Passing an alleyway, her mood of adventure and well-being was suddenly dampened by the sight of a shivering, barefoot little girl, standing before the door of a hovel. There was a stench of urine from the alley, and in the gaslight the child's face looked wan and under-nourished, and Kate wondered again at how, in a city like Dublin, elegance and poverty could so readily exist side by side.

She turned into Denzille Street, still disturbed by the image of the shivering child. Perhaps, she thought, if tonight's meeting went well, she could take action against those who allowed such things to persist. Feeling a little less cavalier, but more determined, she came to number 19a. The house was a sturdy one, its door freshly painted and the brasses gleaming. Pausing briefly, she gathered herself, then knocked confidently. A moment elapsed, then suddenly the door swung open and a tall, heavily built man with a full but carefully trimmed beard stood before her.

'Mr Carey?' asked Kate.

'At your service Mam.' The man, whom Kate judged to be in his mid-forties, did a sort of mock bow that was obviously meant to be amusing.

Kate smiled briefly. 'I'm Kate Lannigan . . .'

'Come in, Kate Lannigan, come in,' he replied jovially.

Kate stepped into a long hallway, handsomely – if a little gaudily – furnished. Carey closed the door, then turned and faced her.

'I'm very pleased to meet you,' he said, shaking her hand, 'very pleased.'

Oh God, thought Kate, *not an ogler*. With her good looks and striking auburn hair she was used to men staring at her – something which had made her neither arrogant nor falsely modest – but she hated a certain type of smarmy physical assessment, usually followed by a would-be smooth charm. Watching Carey smile as he held her eyes, she sensed such might be the case here.

'Let me take you coat,' said Carey.

'Thank you.' Before he could assist her, she had swiftly taken off the coat and handed it to him.

'We'll slip into the parlour,' said Carey, hanging her coat on a stand, 'we won't be disturbed there . . .'

'Fine,' answered Kate.

With a flourish, he opened a door off the hallway and ushered Kate ahead of him into the parlour. It was a large, high-ceilinged room, over-adorned with pictures of Daniel O'Connell, the Manchester Martyrs and much other patriotic bric-a-brac. A cheerful log fire burned in the grate, and a large, professionally taken photograph of a resplendently dressed Carey hung over the fireplace. The centre of the room was taken up by a large mahogany table, and Carey pulled out a chair for Kate at the end near the fire.

'Thank you,' she said, taking the seat.

'Well, Miss Lannigan,' said Carey expansively, standing hands on hips, 'I'm not disappointed, and that's the truth.'

'Not disappointed in what?'

'I was told you were a fine-looking young woman, and begod it's not a word of a lie!'

Kate realised that this was her cue to be coyly pleased; instead she looked at Carey and asked evenly 'Who told you that?'

'Oh now,' answered Carey easily, 'I have to be careful not to reveal my sources . . .'

'I dare say,' said Kate, 'and I assumed you'd have to be careful in vetting me too. I hope this will help establish things.'

Opening her bag, she held out a sheet of paper to Carey. He took it, then sat opposite her and started to unfold it.

'My Baptismal Certificate,' said Kate.

'Very good,' answered Carey, having read it carefully. He put it down, then looked at Kate seriously and without any flirtation. 'Your request to me was an unusual one, Miss Lannigan. The sort of request to which I had to reply with caution . . . considerable caution.'

'Of course,' answered Kate.

'Before agreeing to this meeting I had to make enquiries; quite detailed enquiries. You see, I have to be certain you really are who you say you are.'

'Well, yes. That's why I brought my Baptismal Cert.'

'With all due respect, that's not enough. If . . . if for argument's sake, Dublin Castle wanted to forge a Baptismal Cert, I'm sure they could.'

'You don't really think I'm . . . some kind of a spy?' asked Kate.

'No I don't, but I must be certain. So I have some questions for you. Questions only the real Kate Lannigan could answer. I even took the train down to Wexford in compiling them.'

'That was very thorough of you,' said Kate.

'You don't mind if we start then?'

'No. Ask away.'

Carey took several sheets of paper from his jacket pocket. 'Your brother who was in prison – what was his full name?'

'Michael Patrick Lannigan.'

'And when was he released from prison?'

'January the twentieth.'

'He and his father were injured during the eviction. Can you tell me what injuries they received?'

'Yes,' replied Kate, 'Michael got a broken arm, my father a cut face . . .'

'And when is your father's birthday?'

'March the fourth,' answered Kate without hesitation.

'Very good.' Carey referred to a second sheet of paper. 'What was the nearest village to your farm?'

'Knockcarney.'

'And the name of the parish priest there?'

'Father Quigley. The other curates were Father Owens and Father Murray.'

Carey nodded in affirmation. 'Looking up the aisle towards

58

the altar of your parish church, in which wall is Father Quigley's confessional?'

Kate paused a second, then looked Carey directly in the eye. 'Neither, his confessional is off the side chapel.'

Unperturbed, Carey turned over the sheet. 'Finally, Lord Masefield, your ex-landlord lives in . . . ?'

'Birchpark House.'

'Where he lives with . . . ?'

'His sister, Miss Catherine Prescott.'

'Masefield attended your eviction, didn't he?'

'Yes.'

'What colour was his horse?'

'A grey,' answered Kate, impatiently. 'And he was sitting on it when he gave me this!' Leaning forward, she pulled back her thick auburn locks to reveal the scar on her temple.

'I'm sorry,' said Carey gently, laying the papers back on the table. 'I am sorry. The English have a lot of spies and informers. I had to be sure you were who you said.'

'And now you are?'

'Yes, now I am. I hope you'll forgive all the questions, but we do have to be careful.'

'Yes, I suppose you do . . . Well,' said Kate, suddenly smiling, 'now that we all know who we are – where do we go from here?'

'That's really up to you. You said in your letter that you were prepared to take risks?'

'That's right,' answered Kate.

'I've studied the details of your case and I can see why; your family have been treated terribly. The question is – how far are you prepared to go to avenge that?'

'As far as necessary. And . . . it's hard to explain this, but it's not just vengeance. I want to do something . . . something that will make the Lord Masefields of this world think twice. I want other families to be spared what we've suffered.'

'That's very commendable,' said Carey.

Kate looked at him suspiciously, but there appeared to be no irony in his comment.

'Very commendable indeed,' repeated Carey. He rose and moved absently towards the window. Turning, he looked directly at her for a moment, then spoke a little more softly. 'Well, Miss Lannigan, I think we may be able to help each other. First though, I'll need your word of honour that everything said in this room is secret. Absolutely secret. Even if you decide, on reflection, not to help us . . .'

'You have my word.'

'Forgive me for saying this, but if ever anything leaks out . . .'

'It's alright, Mr Carey,' said Kate, raising her hand to stop him, 'I'd never be an informer. Believe me, you don't have to worry about that.'

Carey approached, leaned on the table and looked at her piercingly for a moment. 'No,' he replied, 'no I don't think I do. Very well then . . .' he said, sitting in the chair opposite her. He leaned forward and spoke earnestly. 'As you might imagine, it's most unusual to give an assignment to someone who's not a tried and trusted nationalist; however, in your case it so happens that there's a particular job for which you might be ideal.'

'And what would that be?' asked Kate.

'I'll come to that. Supposing . . . supposing I were to tell you that there were people planning to strike against the English, against the rotten ones at the top who allow the Masefields to flourish. Would you be prepared to help such people?'

'Yes,' answered Kate immediately.

'The people I am talking about are very serious. They know the only way to get listened to by Gladstone and his lackeys is through action . . .' Carey paused dramatically, looked appraisingly at Kate, then continued, 'so they're going to wipe out the top British officials in Ireland . . .'

'Murder them . . . ?' asked Kate.

'*Execute* them, for the crimes committed in their names. It's the only way. You have to take action, it's no use arguing with them . . .' He waited a moment, then sensing that she needed more convincing, he looked Kate straight in the eye. 'Do you think your Lord Masefield would listen to reason?' he asked slowly. 'Do you really think that the man who gave you that scar would be swayed by argument?'

There was a long pause, then Kate answered. 'No, I don't

60

suppose he would. What do you want me to do?'

'You're sure about this?'

Kate looked pensive, then nodded. 'Yes,' she said softly, 'yes I'm sure.'

'Certain?'

'Certain.'

'OK,' said Carey, 'what we want you to do is to work in Thomas Burke's residence.'

'Burke – the Under Secretary?'

'That's right. Cowper the Viceroy, and Forster are the top two targets. But Burke has been Under Secretary for fourteen years. He's number three in seniority but he knows more than the other two put together.'

'But how on earth am I supposed to get into his employment?'

Carey smiled. 'Your father did some dairy-farming, didn't he?'

'Yes,' said Kate bemusedly.

'Well, Burke's estate is about to lose a dairy maid. She's marrying the nephew of a sympathiser of ours. We know that an advertisement will be placed in the papers on Monday week. Burke, Forster and the Viceroy all have residences within a stone's throw of each other in the Phoenix Park, so it's a golden opportunity to infiltrate them!'

'But there's no guarantee I'd get the job,' said Kate.

'There are three reasons why you'll get the job. Firstly, there's this.' Carey picked up a letter on good-quality headed paper. 'It's an excellent reference from your last employer.' He smiled. 'No, not Enniscorthy Hospital, but a Lady Beresly. She has a large dairy herd on her Waterford estate – you'll find she recommends you very highly. Secondly, we know in advance when the advertisement is being placed, therefore you can be sure to be the first applicant. You'll deliver your reference by hand first thing on the Monday morning.'

'But that doesn't guarantee anything,' replied Kate.

'Ah, but thirdly,' continued Carey with a smile, 'the house steward on Burke's estate is responsible for the hiring of staff. His name is Jeremiah Hackett, and the man is – how shall I put it – he's very fond of attractive young women.'

Continuing to smile, Carey looked at Kate knowingly. 'I'm sure I don't have to tell you what an attractive young lady you are . . . So, you deliver your reference to Hackett in person first thing on Monday week. I'm sure you'll . . . impress him – and I'll be most surprised if you don't get the job.

He's enjoying this, Kate realised.

'Well?' said Carey.

'Supposing I were to get the job, what would I be expected to do . . . to help your group?'

'You'd probably have to stay there for a few months. Would you be prepared to do that?'

'Well . . . yes, if necessary,' answered Kate. 'But what would I actually do?'

'Report to us on security in the grounds. Try to log the movements of Burke and Forster – when they meet socially and so on. You might be able to lay your hands on photographs that would help our men identify their targets.'

Kate looked slightly puzzled. 'How would a dairy maid have access to photographs?'

'I'm not saying you definitely would, but it's a live-in position. Your room would be on the upper floor – you'd have reason to move through the house.'

'I see.'

Carey leaned forward slightly. 'Look, I'll be frank, Miss Lannigan. There's risk attached to this. When we kill them, you'll have to disappear – and quickly; but you did say you were prepared to take risks.'

'I still am,' said Kate. 'Where would I have to disappear to?'

'America is probably the safest bet. If Burke is killed the police will be sure to question all staff.'

'And my forged reference wouldn't hold up?'

'Precisely,' answered Carey. 'The house steward in hiring an attractive dairy maid isn't going to take the trouble of writing to a former employer – especially when the girl has a perfectly genuine-looking reference on authentic headed paper. The police investigating a killing, however, would be likely to check the backgrounds of all the servants.'

'Yes,' said Kate thoughtfully, 'I can see the logic in that . . .'

'Don't let money be a worry,' said Carey reassuringly. 'We'll look after you, and generously, from funds. Indeed while you're working as a dairy maid we'll augment the wages – I'm sure Burke doesn't overpay his staff,' he added with a grin. 'Also, I'd like to give you a lump sum now – towards your expenses in contacting me, applying for the job, and so on.' He smiled expansively. 'I can't do fairer than that, now can I?'

Kate regarded him coolly. 'Mr Carey, I'm not doing this for money.'

'My dear young woman, of course you're not!' He patted her arm. 'I know your motives are the purest, of course they are. But I'm not going to have you out of pocket. No indeed. Our supporters in America have funded us well, they'd want a patriotic woman taking risks for Ireland to be treated properly. So I must insist that you take something for your expenses.'

'Very well,' said Kate. 'There is one condition though, before I go ahead.'

Carey looked at her appraisingly. 'And what would that be?'

'I'm living with my aunt, and she must be kept out of all of this.'

'Ah yes, the reason for the Post Office Box . . .'

'She's a good woman, the very best,' continued Kate, 'but she's no nationalist. In fact she's always been a staunch loyalist. So when this is over I don't want her in any trouble – nothing is to be traceable back to her.'

'Her relatives are evicted and imprisoned, and she's pro-British?' asked Carey, raising an eyebrow.

'A lot of Irish people are pro-British, Mr Carey – you hardly need me to tell you that. My aunt regards Lord Masefield as one bad apple . . .'

'That's nonsense!' replied Carey with irritation.

'I know it is, that's why I'm here,' cut in Kate. 'But she's not going to change at this stage of her life, and I don't want her at risk. I'll do all that's asked of me, but she mustn't be traceable.'

'Very well, very well,' answered Carey, his amiability in place again. 'There won't be any problem. Move into a modest hotel or lodging house, and use that address when you apply for the job; then any police enquiries later on won't make any connection between you and her. You won't have been a resident in her house when you applied for the job.'

'Yes,' answered Kate, 'yes that makes sense . . .'

'Right, it's all settled then. The advertisement will appear this day fortnight, and you present yourself at the Lodge that same morning. Give the steward the reference, flash those lovely blue eyes of yours a few times, and if you don't get the job, my name isn't Jim Carey!'

'Let's hope your name remains Jim Carey then,' said Kate drily.

'Very good,' agreed Carey heartily, 'very good.' He rose to his feet. 'Just hang on a minute till I visit the safe. Then you'll be well able to afford your lodgings – and a nice costume for your interview.' He winked conspiratorially. 'Excuse me for just a moment.'

Kate watched him leave the room, her feelings a mixture of elation at how well the meeting had gone, and reluctance at having a man like Carey as a comrade. In spite of his off-putting manner though, she had to admit that his enthusiasm was infectious, and she felt determined that however distasteful Burke's house steward might be, she was going to do her utmost to get the job.

Thinking about it all, a part of her found it hard to believe that she was to be involved in plotting to kill the chief British officials in Ireland. How would Aunt Julia – or even her parents – feel about that? How would she feel *herself*, when the time came? Before her eviction she had never really wished evil on anyone – much less thought of killing them – but now she felt differently, now everything was changed. There were too many injustices, too many evicted families, too many Lord Masefields, too many hungry children like the little girl she had glimpsed down the alley tonight. If a few pampered aristocrats had to die to change things for the better, then so be it.

Waiting for Carey's return, she felt strangely relieved that the dreaming and hoping were over. Now, at last, she was about to go into action.

Ten

Joe Brady was ending his report on the killing of the traitor Flynn, as the Invincibles committee listened attentively in the upstairs bar of Mullett's public house.

' . . . so we split up at Blackhorse Ave,' said Brady. 'Tim got the tram, and I walked home down Aughram Street. Then I cleaned and hid the knives, and that was the end of it . . .'

'Well done, Joe,' said James Carey. 'A job very well done indeed.'

Mullett, flanked by Ned McCaffrey and Dan Curley, sat at the head of the table. 'Tell me, Joe,' he said, 'young Kelly played a full part, you say?'

'Yes,' answered Brady.

'That's very reassuring,' said Mullett. 'Do you think, if necessary, he could kill a man himself – without your support?'

'Yeah,' answered Brady without hesitation, 'Tim Kelly's not short of guts.'

'Neither of you are, Joe,' said Dan Curley, 'and I'd like to propose a vote of thanks for a difficult job, very well done . . .'

'I'll happily second that,' said Carey.

'Hear, hear,' added McCaffrey.

'Yes,' said Mullett proudly, 'as chairman I'd like to say thank you on behalf of the Irish Invincibles. With men like yourselves, we can't fail.'

'We can easily fail,' said Brady sullenly. 'And if you're all finished tellin' us what a great job we did, I want to say something.'

'Fire ahead, Joe,' said Mullett, his surprise at Brady's attitude apparent on his face.

'Me and Tim did the job, and you all think it was a great success – but it could have been a disaster.' Brady turned to Carey. 'You told us Flynn would be early, that he was always early.'

'He normally was, Joe,' said Carey defensively, 'what happened on this occasion I don't pretend to know.'

'*I* know, Mr Carey,' said Brady. 'We were given the wrong information.'

'Well I'm sorry Joe, but every eventuality can't . . .'

'I'm not interested in eventualities!' interrupted Brady, 'I'm interested in facts. And the fact is, the Peelers were there before Flynn. And the other fact is that the bastard went around carrying a police whistle tied to his wrist.'

'We weren't to know that, Joe . . .' said Carey.

'There's a lot of things you didn't seem to know,' said Brady sharply. 'And the difference between gettin' away with it and gettin' caught could be knowin' these things . . .'

Relishing Carey's personal discomfort, Mullett allowed the awkward silence to last for a couple of seconds before he spoke. 'I can see your point, Joe, really I can. In fact, we're hoping in the near future to gain a useful source of inside information. Access to the kind of facts you're talking about. So don't worry, we'll get our targets alright – and without getting caught.'

'I'm sorry you were put at risk, Joe, genuinely I am,' said Carey, 'but this person we're lining up is going for a job right inside . . .'

'That'll do, Jim!' snapped Mullett. 'Only the committee need to know the details.'

'Well surely Joe . . .' started Carey.

'Only the committee – you know the rules,' said Mullett.

'No offence, Joe,' added Dan Curley placatingly.

'It's just that the less people who know the details the better,' continued McCaffrey, 'you never know when one of us might be hauled in by the Peelers.'

'Are you suggestin' I'd squeal?' asked Brady, looking McCaffrey aggressively in the eye.

'Of course not, Joe, of course not,' he replied nervously.

'There's no squealers in the Invincibles,' said Mullet to Brady, 'but just like you and Tim wouldn't have wanted everyone knowing you were doing the job on Flynn, this person we're lining up deserves the same secrecy. OK?'

'Yeah . . . OK,' replied Brady.

'Well, thanks very much, Joe, for giving us your report, and well done again,' said Mullett, rising to indicate to Brady that his presence at the meeting was no longer required.

'Right,' said Brady, rising and taking his coat from the back of his chair.

'Tell Seán downstairs to give you a pint on the house, Joe,' said Mullett, 'and we'll be in touch.'

'Thanks,' answered Brady, then nodded to the three seated committee members who bade him farewell. Mullett crossed and accompanied him to the landing, waved as he descended the stairs, then closed the door.

'He's bloody touchy,' said Carey, as Mullett returned to the table.

'Maybe, but he's the sort of man we need,' answered Mullett. 'And he's right about the inside information – it really is important. How soon is this girl of yours applying for the job in Burke's residence?'

'Next week,' replied Carey.

'Let's hope she gets it,' said McCaffrey.

'Even if she doesn't get it, we'll find another use for her,' answered Carey. 'But I think she will. In fact, I've a feeling she's going to be very useful to us. Very useful indeed.'

Eleven

'Now, Sir, room 27, you won't be disturbed here.' The porter opened the bedroom door and carried in Scott's luggage. 'There we are now,' said the man, laying the cases beside the large bed, 'and if there's anythin' ye want, you've only to give the bellcord here a pull.'

'Thanks very much,' said Scott, slipping the porter a tip.

'Thank you, Sir,' said the man. He opened the bedroom door, then turned and smiled at Scott. 'And you're very welcome to Ireland . . .'

'Thank you,' replied Scott in his best Philadelphia accent.

The man nodded pleasantly, then gently closed the door.

Scott hoped he hadn't tipped too heavily by the standards of the hotel. It was important on a mission like this to blend into the crowd. Never draw attention to yourself, he had always been taught, even in such minor matters as tipping too much or too little. The same reasoning had made him choose the middle-of-the-road Eblana Hotel – it was the kind of place in which a modestly well-off horse breeder like Bill Ryan would probably stay.

Scott climbed onto the bed and lay back contentedly. It had been a tiring day's travel, with a rough ferry crossing to Dublin. Although they had travelled separately, he had seen Penrose being ill over the side of the boat; for a reason he couldn't quite fathom he had derived a certain satisfaction from it. Perhaps it was the idea of the colonel – for once in his life – not controlling a situation, he thought wryly.

At any rate Penrose would no doubt at this moment be ensconcing himself in the congenial comfort of the Officers' Mess in Marlborough Barracks, while he, Scott, was alone in a second-class Irish hotel room. Wrong! he quickly reminded himself. He must stop thinking of himself as William Scott – he was Bill Ryan now. What was it Uncle Philip used to say?

'Good actors don't say lines – they become characters.' He must *become* Bill Ryan.

Without rising from the bed, Scott reached out and from the top of one of his bags withdrew an Ordnance Survey map of Dublin. From what he had seen of it while travelling from the docks, it looked a lively and attractive city. He might even get in some theatre-going during his stay – it shouldn't be out of character for Bill Ryan to seek a little diversion, he told himself.

The first thing though was to execute his plan for infiltrating the Invincibles. For that he would need to familiarise himself with the streets of Dublin. He spread out the now-familiar map and studied it again. Tomorrow he would be visiting the Estate Agents to rent a cottage. He wanted somewhere secluded that would be within striking distance of the Phoenix Park and Marlborough Barracks, yet not too far from town, and he had circled a few potential locations on the map.

He looked at the map on whose streets he would soon be operating, and in spite of his tiredness he felt a tremor of excitement. He was here at last. The training and preparation were over now, and tomorrow his mission proper would begin. It was a pleasing thought, and on impulse he reached for the bell-cord. A whiskey and soda to celebrate would be in order. It seemed, after all, just the kind of thing Bill Ryan might do.

Twelve

Determined to look her best and get the job, Kate studied herself in the mirror again. She was pleased with the way her new pale blue velvet suit set off the auburn of her hair and highlighted her fair-skinned complexion. Matching her suit, she wore a blue bonnet, and under it she had arranged her hair in such a way that the scar on her temple was carefully concealed. The velvet suit, she felt, was just right; respectable enough for an interview, yet fashionable enough to make an impression – or so she hoped – on Jeremiah Hackett, the house steward.

Still looking in the mirror, she tilted her head to one side, then smiled suddenly in recognition of her vanity. Enough self-admiration, she told herself, it was time to go. She picked up her letter of reference, crossed to the door, and closing it behind her, descended the stairs. None of the other lodgers were about the hallway, and eager not to bump into any of them, she quickly opened the hall door and stepped out into Parkgate Street.

It was half past eight in the morning, and the busy thoroughfare was bustling with activity. She looked across the Liffey to the nearby Guinness Brewery and saw cart after cart emerging, heavily laden with wooden barrels, the great dray horses pulling vigorously at this early stage of the morning.

Turning right, she strolled along Parkgate Street, crossed Infirmary Road, and then turned in through the gates of the Phoenix Park. As soon as she had gone a few yards there was a noticeable drop in noise, and the surrounding bushes and trees masked the presence of the adjacent city streets.

The nearby lodging house had been a good choice, she felt; close to the park, modest enough to seem credible as the residence of a dairy maid newly arrived in Dublin and seeking employment, and yet big enough to enable her to avoid any sort of intimacy with her fellow lodgers.

Breathing deeply, Kate savoured the early morning freshness of the park air. It was about two miles from the entrance gate to the Under Secretary's Lodge, and she had allowed herself plenty of time to enjoy the journey. In these, the last few days of February, there was a touch of spring in the air, and although it was still quite cold, the rising sun was reflecting off and melting the ground frost, so that Kate felt a lightness of spirit as she headed up the main road.

She passed the Wellington monument, scene of the recent mysterious murder, where, according to the papers, a man had been stabbed to death for no apparent reason. Moving a little more briskly, she strode on by the statue of the mounted Viscount Gough, and past the now-deserted bandstand in the Hollow, where music was played in the summer months.

Ten days previously she had vacated Aunt Julia's for the lodging house, and knowing Julia's loyalist affiliations, she had said that a senior British civil servant, with a delicate child, had offered her a post as the child's nurse. It was a live-in position, and though based in Rathmines in Dublin, the family travelled abroad a good deal.

She had found herself lying fluently but with considerable guilt, and the upshot of it all had been that Kate had left the shop in Drumcondra, promising to keep in touch whenever the variable hours and foreign travel allowed. Despite her sorrow at Kate's departure, Julia had assured her that it was a good position, and cautioned her not to lose it through being cheeky or too independent.

If only she knew, thought Kate, as she approached the boundary fence of the Vice-regal Lodge. If only she knew her niece was seeking a job in the Under Secretary's residence in order to act as a spy for a group of extreme nationalists. Poor Julia, she'd be horrified. But then Julia had never been evicted from her comfortable home, Kate reminded herself. She would have to put Julia and all other distracting thoughts from her mind. Her mission today was to get the job and nothing could be allowed to distract her – she simply *must* succeed.

Before, whenever she'd really wanted something, she had

always prayed. Would it be wrong to pray for success now, she wondered, knowing that ultimately it might result in people being killed? She wasn't sure. What she was doing was right, she felt, yet praying for it somehow seemed a bit dubious. Better put it out of her head for now, she thought, she'd need all of her wits about her shortly. Putting aside the moral question, she continued on, but some of the zest seemed to have gone from the the fresh spring morning.

Kate stood hesitantly at the base of the Phoenix monument. It was a large stone column topped by a rising Phoenix, situated in the middle of the main road. She paused to gather herself, under the pretext of admiring the monument to the mythical bird. Looking to her right, she could see the gate lodge of the Under Secretary's residence, now only fifty yards away.

I'm an excellent dairy maid, she said to herself; I've a first-class reference from Lady Beresly – I'm *going* to get the job.

With a sudden surge of conviction she walked briskly towards the lodge. There was a small bell recessed into the wall but Kate waited in case the gate-keeper had seen her approach. Having paused a moment, she was about to ring the bell when a small white-haired man, dressed in livery, came out the door of the cottage and approached the gate. 'Yes?' he said.

'Good morning,' replied Kate pleasantly. 'I've something for Mr Hackett.'

'What is it?' asked the man gruffly.

Opening her bag, she produced the letter. 'I have to give him this.'

'Post, is it?' said the man. 'I'll have it delivered.' He held out his hand for her to pass the letter through the gate.

Kate smiled ingratiatingly. 'I'm sorry, it's a very important document. I've strict instructions to deliver it to Mr Hackett myself.'

'Have you now? And who might you be?'

'Kate Lannigan.'

'Of?'

She hardly paused a moment. 'Lannigan and Company Limited.'

There was a subtle change in the man's attitude. 'Oh . . . I see . . .'

'Mr Hackett asked my father that I deliver this in person.'

The old man looked at her appraisingly, then nodded his head. 'Aye, I dare say he did . . .' Lifting the catch, he slowly swung the pedestrian gate open for her.

'Thank you,' she said, stepping through.

'Up the drive and swing left before the house. The steward's bell is the top one at the back door.'

'Thank you very much,' answered Kate. 'Good morning.'

'Good morning,' answered the man, carefully shutting the gate before shuffling back towards the warmth of his cottage.

Kate walked up the long curving drive, flanked on both sides by well-tended parkland. Reaching the top of the drive, the residence itself came into view. It was a large, rambling building and before its front entrance was a long sloping lawn. The driveway forked and Kate took the left branch which brought her round to the back of the house.

A young groom was leading a chestnut mare towards a long stable-yard which, surrounded by extensive outhouses, stretched to Kate's left.

'Good morning,' he called, stopping the horse and looking at Kate in friendly enquiry.

'Good morning,' she answered, 'I'm looking for Mr Hackett.'

'He's just gone in. If you give the bell there a ring you'll catch him.'

'Thanks, I'll do that.'

With a smile and a nod, the youth set off again with the mare, as Kate crossed to the back door and rang the bell. Standing at the door, she could feel her heart pounding as she awaited an answer.

The door swung languidly open, and a well-dressed man in his late forties appeared on the threshold. Despite the grey of his hair, his clean-shaven face had a chubby, almost baby-faced appearance. He held his head to one side, and his pale blue eyes flashed appraisingly at Kate. 'Well, well, who have we got here?' he asked.

'My name is Kate Lannigan. I've come to see Mr Hackett.'

'Have you indeed?' A half-smile played about his lips. 'Well

I'm glad to say you've found him, my Dear . . .'

'I've come about the dairy maid's job in this morning's paper, Mr Hackett.'

'My, my, aren't we the early bird?'

'I was eager to apply for it. I have my reference and letter of application with me.'

'Really? I don't normally interview without an appointment.' He waited just until Kate's face clouded slightly, then continued playfully, 'But since you've come all this way, well we'd better have a look at them, hadn't we? Do step in.'

'Thank you,' said Kate.

She crossed the threshold, and Hackett closed the heavy door behind her.

'We'll talk in my parlour – we shan't be disturbed there,' he said pleasantly. 'It's this way.'

Kate followed him along the wood-panelled passage way, then along another corridor to the left, which led to his private quarters. Being a house steward, and thus the most senior of the household's servants, she knew that he would have his own rooms away from the servants' quarters, but the manner of the man's speech and his well-cut tweed suit indicated a higher position on the social scale than she had anticipated.

'Here we are,' said Hackett, ushering her into the parlour. 'Do take a seat.'

It was a well-furnished, medium-sized room. A long bookcase lined one wall, and in the opposite wall a bay window provided an attractive view of a nearby belt of evergreen oaks. Kate sat on a comfortable leather armchair and Hackett lowered himself onto a matching one, several feet away.

He leaned back easily. 'So, Miss Langan, isn't it?'

'Lannigan,' corrected Kate, choosing a tone which she hoped wouldn't make it sound too much like a correction.

Hackett gave a little nod to indicate his error. 'Miss Lannigan – you're interested in the post of dairy maid?'

'Yes. Very much so,' Kate forced herself to add with a bright smile.

'And you've already read the papers, written your

application, and walked here to deliver it – all by . . .' he glanced at the clock, 'seven minutes past nine?'

'Yes, I'm an early riser.'

'A good characteristic in a dairy maid. You have previous experience, I presume?'

'Yes, Sir, I worked for three years for Lady Beresly.'

'Where was that?'

'Blackwater Estate in Waterford. This is the reference,' said Kate, passing it over. She could feel her pulse pounding as Hackett opened the letter and read it.

'Hmm . . .' He looked her in the eye. 'Very impressive, very good indeed . . .'

'Thank you.'

'So why did you leave?'

'My family have emigrated. They've all left for America but I wanted to stay in Ireland, so I came to Dublin.'

'And why Dublin, pray?'

'I thought it might be nice if I could work as a dairy maid, and at the same time live for a while in the capital.'

'Aha,' said Hackett with a little laugh. 'You want to sample the delights of city life?'

'Well . . . yes. A little perhaps . . .'

'Might I be so bold as to enquire whether – how shall I phrase it – whether a factor in the equation might be a young man?'

'No, it's not a young man.'

'You're not averse to men, I hope?'

Kate forced herself to smile. 'No . . .'

'But you're not here in Dublin because of a young man?' persisted Hackett.

'No, I'm not.'

'Very wise, Miss Lannigan, very wise. Young men can be foolish. In fact as . . . companions, for an attractive young lady, young men can be quite unsuitable. They haven't the experience to know how to treat a woman . . . wouldn't you agree?'

How do I avoid agreeing with that without offending him, thought Kate. 'Well . . .' she replied, 'well I suppose it varies from man to man.'

'How very diplomatic!' laughed Hackett. 'Perhaps it's not the dairy where you should be employed, but the Diplomatic Corps!'

Kate smiled weakly.

'However,' continued Hackett, 'as it's a dairy maid we seek, we'd better discuss that vacancy.' He leaned forward in a slightly more business-like posture. 'Well, the head of our dairy here is a Mr Michael McDaid. He looks after milking, butter and cheese production and storage, the welfare of the herd, and so on. The dairy maid's job is to assist him in these and any other duties he might delegate.'

'I see,' said Kate.

'The annual salary is seventeen pounds, ten shillings, plus of course, food and board.'

'Very good.'

'Unfortunately Mr McDaid isn't here just now – he's gone to the veterinary surgeon – so you can't meet him.'

This sounds promising, thought Kate, I must say something to try and clinch it. 'I'm sorry to have missed Mr McDaid,' she said, 'but as regards the butter and cheese manufacture, we did that at Blackwater – I have experience in those areas.'

'Excellent,' replied Hackett. He looked directly at her, his eyes twinkling. 'I'm a great believer in experience. I always feel that those who have it should . . . pass it on. Wouldn't you say?'

'Eh . . . yes,' she answered uncertainly.

'How old are you Kate – I may call you Kate?'

'Yes of course. I'm twenty, I'll be twenty-one in June.'

'Ah, twenty . . . What a good age. So much to learn, so much ahead of you – and yet – probably a little experience already acquired, especially in the case of a pretty girl like yourself.'

Kate looked him in the eye. 'Are you talking of dairying, Sir?'

Hackett threw back his head and laughed merrily. 'You're a spirited girl, Kate Lannigan, I like that in a woman, upon my word I do!' He wagged his finger playfully at her. 'And you're a little bit naughty too. I think you knew I was referring to – how shall I phrase it – matters amorous?' He leaned forward. 'I think that you and I would get on well together, don't you?'

She looked at his leering expression and felt her skin crawl, but knowing she couldn't afford the luxury of disgust, she found herself meeting his gaze and smiling. 'Yes, Mr Hackett, I'm sure we'd get along,' she answered brightly, hating herself.

'I'm very glad to hear that, Kate,' said Hackett meaningfully. He rose with a smile. 'Leave me your letter of application then, and we shall be in touch.'

She rose and handed him the letter.

'Thank you,' said Hackett, his fingers brushing against Kate's as he took it. 'And now I'm afraid I have some duties to attend to. Allow me to escort you to the door.'

'Thank you, Mr Hackett,' said Kate with a smile, 'and I hope you can look favourably at my application. I'd very much like to work here.'

Hackett swung open the door for her. 'I don't believe I could look at a young lady like yourself other than favourably!' he replied smoothly. 'After you.'

Followed by Hackett, and conscious of his eyes boring into her, Kate moved down the corridor. Reaching the back door, Hackett opened it for her. 'Well, Kate, we shall be . . .' he paused and smiled, '*in touch*, and shortly. Good morning.'

'Good morning, Mr Hackett, and thank you.'

He nodded in farewell, and Kate turned and started towards the drive, aware of Hackett watching her. Let him look, she thought, it didn't matter now. 'We'll be in touch,' he'd said. Indeed they would, but not in the way Hackett thought. Not that way, she vowed, not in a million years. Stepping out determinedly, she started off down the drive.

Thirteen

'The place is surrounded, Superintendent. Ready to move whenever you say.'

'How many men are in the back lane now, Sergeant?'

'Four, Sir.'

'Very good.' Superintendent John Mallon of G Division, Dublin Metropolitan Police, allowed himself a wry smile. 'We wouldn't want Mr Mullett slipping out the back.'

'No, Sir.'

The previous week's spring-like weather had vanished, and Mallon pulled up the collar of his coat against the biting March wind blowing down the quays. 'Alright, keep the men out of sight, Sergeant. They'll be opening the pub any minute now; the moment they do, we go in.'

'Very good, Sir.'

'When the doors open I'll signal from across the road.'

'Yes, Sir, we'll be ready.'

'Right.' Mallon turned the corner from Merchants Quay into lower Bridge Street, then crossed the road, gaining the footpath directly opposite Mullett's public house. Just as he reached the pavement, he heard the sound of the pub's wooden doors being opened.

Punctual buggers, thought Mallon, the mental logging of such a detail being typical of his thorough approach to police work. For over twenty years the tall, grey-bearded Ulsterman had been dealing with subversive nationalists, and he knew well the importance in successful detective work of noting apparently minor details.

He paused for a moment, reaching in his pocket as though for a coin. His right hand closed around the cold handle of the pistol, concealed in his overcoat pocket. The manoeuvre had enabled him to turn about, and seeing both doors of the pub now open, he raised his left hand in a signal.

Immediately the sergeant and two constables rounded the

corner. Mallon swiftly crossed the road, reaching the door of the pub at the same time as the uniformed policemen. Without breaking his stride he pushed open the inside door of the bar and entered, the gun held firmly just inside the right pocket of his overcoat.

A tall, red-haired barman looked up in surprise from a table he was cleaning. 'What the hell . . .' he started.

'Superintendent Mallon, DMP. I'm looking for Mr Mullett.'

'He's not in,' said the barman.

'Keep this man here, Sergeant,' snapped Mallon, making for the door leading to the stairs.

Just then the door opened, and a bemused James Mullett stood in the doorframe. 'What's going on?' he asked.

'I'm Superintendent Mallon, DMP. You are James Mullett?'

'Yes.'

'I must ask you to come with me, Mr Mullett.'

'What the hell for?' asked Mullett belligerently.

'We'd like you to answer some questions.'

'Questions? About what? I've done nothing.'

'Then you'll have nothing to fear, will you?' answered Mallon.

'I'm not going anywhere till I know what this is about.'

The tall detective walked right up to the publican, paused, then looking down on him, he spoke slowly. 'It's about murder, Mr Mullett. It's about murdering a police informer, to put it at its bluntest. Now, shall we go?'

'Joe! Joe Brady!'

Brady looked up the stone mason's yard, the freezing chisel and his clearly visible breath bearing testimony to the coldness of the March afternoon.

'Over here!' he called, then started slightly in surprise as his visitor rounded a huge granite boulder. 'Mr Carey, I didn't expect you.'

'Have you heard?' asked Carey.

'Heard what?'

'Mullett was arrested last Saturday morning!'

'What?'

'Mallon of G Division picked him up at ten o'clock,' said

Carey, unable to keep from his voice a hint of relish at being the bearer of such dramatic news.

'Jaysus! I . . . I've been on a pavin' job down the country these last few days.'

'I know, I've been trying to contact you.'

'Are they onto us?' asked Brady.

'No. He was taken in as a suspect in the murder of an informer called Bailey.'

'Bailey?' said Brady. 'I though Flynn was his name?'

'That's the irony, Joe. It's a different killing. We didn't do it, and the one we did they don't know about.'

'Not yet,' grunted Brady.

'No, no, I know Mullett better than that, Joe. We've had our differences, but he won't squeal. You can be sure of that. And we left no evidence linking us to Flynn's killing.'

'How did they pick up Mullett in the wrong then?'

'I'd say they're guessing. If they were onto the Invincibles they'd have picked us all up by now. No, I'm sure they're just guessing – they know Mullett's pub is a nationalist house – that's no secret – so they pulled him in to question him about Bailey.'

'So what do we do?' asked Brady.

'Nothing, for a couple of days. Just sit tight. It would suit them if we panicked, but we won't. We've been in touch with the Directory in London and they're sending someone over to see us.'

Brady looked concerned. 'They're not going to call off the campaign?'

'No fear, Joe, no fear.' He looked at Brady and nodded. 'And your concern does you credit. In fact I've been talking to the other committee members, and we're holding our meeting on Thursday night.'

'So?'

'We'd like you to attend, Joe. I probably shouldn't tell you this before the meeting, but I know you'll keep it to yourself.'

'Keep what to meself?'

'In Mullett's absence – and knowing the way the Peelers operate, that could go on for quite a while – in Mullett's absence you're being co-opted onto the committee.' He smiled at the younger man's surprise. 'How do you feel about that?'

'I'm . . . I'm honoured, Mr Carey.'

'Not at all, Joe, you deserve it. I could tell from the word go that you had the right stuff in you.'

'Thanks . . . thanks very much.'

'Not a word to the others mind, that I slipped you the news, Joe. This will just be our secret. You simply show up and be surprised when we promote you, OK?'

'Yeah, fine,' answered Brady.

'Right, Mulletts at half eight on Thursday night then, the upstairs bar.'

'Mulletts? After the raid?'

'Exactly, Joe. We brazen it out. If we suddenly stopped drinking there because Mullett was picked up it'd look suspicious, like we'd something to hide.'

'Yeah, yeah I suppose so,' said Brady.

'Seán, the head barman, is running the place while Mullett is in custody, and I've arranged the upstairs bar with him. We arrive, one at a time, between half seven and half eight. You come last, at half eight. OK?'

'Right.'

'Fine. If anything develops in the meantime I'll let you know. Otherwise I'll see you on Thursday.'

'OK, Mr Carey, and thanks.'

'Not at all, Joe. Good evening now.'

'Good evenin' . . .'

Carey nodded, then turned and walked away across the yard.

Brady picked up his chisel again, unconscious now of the numbing cold. It was hard luck on James Mullett, but he couldn't deny his own elation. From now on he wouldn't be an Invincible obeying orders; now he would be deciding what the orders were. And if he had his way, there would be less talk and more action. Excited at the prospects ahead, he placed his chisel against a block of granite and returned vigorously to work.

Fourteen

The cottage was perfect. Sitting in the kitchen at the rear, Scott could work undisturbed, the only sounds reaching his ears being the occasional cries of the local children at play. The estate agent had described it as an attractive, compact home, adjacent to the Phoenix Park, yet truly rural in character, which description Scott had mentally translated as a small cottage near the edge of the city.

It was only the second house he had looked at, but he had known immediately it was what he wanted. Situated off Blind Lane, a narrow, leafy thoroughfare linking Blackhorse Avenue to the Navan Road, the cottage was sturdy and well kept, with four good-sized rooms and attractive gardens at the front and back. Its location was sufficiently off the beaten track to avoid all but the most prying eyes, and to further guarantee privacy, Scott had discouraged anything other than superficial passing of the time of day with the few nearby neighbours.

Marlborough Barracks, from which Colonel Penrose was operating, was only ten minutes walk away; the Phoenix Park, where the Viceroy, Chief Secretary Forster and Under Secretary Burke lived was within a five minute stroll; and although the estate agent's rural description was actually accurate, the city centre was only about three miles distant.

Sitting in the back kitchen, Scott closed the history book he had been studying and relaxed in his chair. Enough was enough. He had been conscientiously continuing his education in Irish politics and history during the two weeks he had been in the cottage, and he reckoned that by now he had mastered all that he was going to master.

The weeks, he had found, had passed quickly and pleasantly; Dublin had turned out to be an elegant Georgian city, its citizens for the most part friendly and extrovertedly humorous. He had been to several excellent theatres in his Bill

Ryan persona, and had developed a thorough knowledge of the city's geography during his surveillance activities.

Leaning forward, he picked up his whiskey and soda and sipped it appreciatively. It was the only one he would be having today – he knew he would need all his wits about him tonight. For he had done his planning, weighed his options and finally made his decision. All the preparations were complete, and tonight he would make his move to infiltrate the Invincibles.

The thought brought a touch of butterflies to his stomach, and lifting the glass again, he drained it. No point in worrying at this stage, he thought. He had made his plans and done all he could to ensure success; there came a point where one could do no more, when matters simply lay in the lap of the Gods. And only tonight would tell if the Gods were kind or cruel. So be it, he told himself, slowly lowering the glass and noting, with wry satisfaction, the steadiness of his hand.

Joe Brady quickly climbed the stairway to Mullett's upstairs bar, knocked on the door, and, deciding it would be in keeping with his new status, entered without waiting for a reply.

Carey, it turned out, had been wrong about the promotion to the Invincibles committee being sprung on him at this meeting. Ned McCaffrey, as acting chairman in Mullett's absence, and lacking Carey's innate sense of intrigue, had been in touch and had said quite openly why Brady was being invited to the meeting.

Entering the room now for his first Invincibles committee meeting, he encountered McCaffrey moving towards the door.

'Ah good evenin', Joe,' he said. 'It's only yourself.'

'Hello, Ned,' said Brady, then exchanged greetings with Carey and Curley, seated on opposite sides of the table, before looking curiously at the short, round-shouldered figure sitting directly before the fire. The man's plump cheeks were made to look even plumper by virtue of a bushy beard, and his pince-nez and good quality clothes sparked an instant assessment in Brady's mind; an office man, a softee.

'Let me introduce you, Joe,' said McCaffrey. He turned to the rotund stranger.

'Mr Tynan, this is Joe Brady; Joe, Mr Patrick Tynan, representative of the London Directory.'

The man removed his pince-nez and stood smiling, his hand outstretched.

'Pleased to meet you,' said Brady, shaking his hand.

'My pleasure entirely, Sir. Your performance to date has been much vaunted.'

'Yeah?' said Brady non-committedly, distrustful of the man for using a word like vaunted, which he, Brady, did not understand.

'Yes, much vaunted indeed,' added Tynan.

'Take a seat, Joe, and we'll start,' said McCaffrey. 'Well . . . eh . . . as acting chairman of the Irish Invincibles I'd like to formally welcome Mr Tynan here. He's been sent over by the London Directory of the Land League and . . . well I'm sure . . . I'm sure he has a lot to say . . .'

Brady had been watching Carey as McCaffrey was speaking and he sensed Carey's irritation. Probably believes that he should be acting chairman, thought Brady, and maybe he's right – McCaffrey just wasn't cut out for leadership.

'Well, Mr Chairman,' responded Tynan, 'it's most civil of you to cede me the floor. Suffice to say that I am here at the London Directory's instigation, to help you facilitate the speedy execution of our plans.'

A speech-maker, thought Brady derisively, all fancy words but useless when it would come to the crunch. He knew the type alright, and there would be little fear of this one getting any blood on his hands.

'Firstly,' continued Tynan in his sing-song, speech-making voice, 'firstly it is my privilege, and indeed my pleasure' – he smiled warmly at Brady – 'my pleasure to confirm the appointment of Mr Joseph Brady to the executive committee.'

'Congratulations, Joe,' said Dan Curley.

'Hear, hear,' echoed the others.

'Thanks, Dan,' said Brady softly.

'A pleasure soured, however,' continued Tynan, 'by the loss of Jim Mullett. Perhaps we could hear the current status on his position?'

'Eh yes . . .' answered McCaffrey. 'Well, Mallon's holding

him prisoner in the Bridewell. He can't have any real evidence, but he's probably trying to trip Jim into giving something away.'

'I see,' said Tynan.

'You needn't worry,' said Curley, 'Jim won't talk.'

'How long could he be held?' asked Tynan.

Carey leaned forward. 'There's no saying. Mallon's powers are wide-ranging – he could be held for weeks, months . . .'

'Obviously we can't wait that long,' said Tynan. 'At what stage are our preparations?'

'Well as you know, we have the weapons,' answered McCaffrey.

'And the kind of men who'll use them,' cut in Dan Curley, with a glance in Brady's direction.

'Quite so,' answered Tynan, 'I'm fully *au fait* with the execution of the traitor Flynn, by Messrs Brady and Kelly.' He gave a little nod of approval to Brady. 'The question is, though, how soon can we use the men and weapons to strike against our real targets?'

'When we have more intelligence on them,' said Carey. 'We have our sources inside Dublin Castle, of course, but I felt that an agent in the household of the enemy would be very useful in setting our plans.'

'Have you taken steps to procure such an agent?' asked Tynan.

'I have indeed,' said Carey importantly. 'In fact I'm glad to be able to inform you all that I've heard from our agent, Kate Lannigan.' He paused, savouring the moment. 'Next Monday she starts work as a dairy maid in the employment of Thomas Burke, Under Secretary for Ireland!'

'Excellent. Excellent work, Sir,' said Tynan.

'Thank you,' answered Carey, his pleasure obvious.

'And while I think of it,' said Tynan, 'is there anything we should be doing apropos our erstwhile colleague?'

'What?' asked Brady irritably.

'Regarding Mr Mullett,' answered Tynan. 'Should we be doing anything to assist financially while he's in jail?'

'That's already taken care of,' said Dan Curley. 'Seán, the

head barman, has taken over. He'll run the pub until Jim is released.'

Brady could feel his impatience slowly rising. When would they stop talking and do something? He leaned forward. 'What I want to know is this – when exactly are we planning to strike?'

'Well it's hard to be definite . . .' started McCaffrey.

'Within a couple of weeks, Joe,' Carey interrupted. 'I'm expecting Miss Lannigan to provide information about security in the grounds of Burke's residence – times when Forster visits him, and so on. Don't worry, Joe, you'll see action, and shortly. Till then, we bide our time carefully.'

'Quite right,' said Tynan. 'Let's be as fully briefed as possible when we strike. Meanwhile, might I suggest our next meeting be this time next week?'

'Certainly,' said Carey.

'Well if that's all . . .' started McCaffrey.

'Bastards! British bastards!' came a roar from the street below. 'Come on ye red-faced, red-coated bastards!'

'What the hell's goin' on?' said Dan Curley, going to the window.

'Let's go down and find out,' said Brady, already moving quickly to the door.

An excited crowd was gathering at the head of the laneway alongside the pub as Brady and the other Invincibles reached the street. Stripping off his coat on the pavement before the laneway was a dark-haired, well-built man of about twenty-five, his face reddened with anger.

'Come on!' he cried, 'come on ye overfed English bastards. Let's see what you're made of!' The man took up a fighting stance opposite his opponents, two sergeants in the red uniforms of the British Army.

'Alright, Paddy. We'll show you what we're made of,' said the smaller of the two soldiers with quiet venom. His pock-marked face looked grimly composed in the gaslight as he undid the buttons of his jacket. His bigger companion had already removed the tunic of his uniform, revealing a heavy frame and muscular arms.

He smiled mirthlessly. 'Alright, son. You don't like the English, eh? You think we should step into the gutter to let you pass? Well, I'm afraid we're goin' to have to teach you some manners. Ain't that so, Sergeant Bates?'

'That's right. And some bleeders got to learn the hard way.'

The dark-haired man held up his fists. 'Oh yeah?' he called, 'how about you try and teach me then?'

'Our pleasure,' said the pock-faced Bates, folding his jacket. 'Our pleasure, chum.'

'Maybe I should even the odds?' whispered Brady to Carey as the crowd expectantly made room for the fighters.

'Let's see what happens first,' answered Carey.

'Come on! One at a time or both together!' roared the black-haired man.

Sergeant Bates bent down, carefully placing his jacket on the ground, then suddenly sprang forward unexpectedly. Despite the appearance of having drink taken, his opponent reacted with great speed, rolling backwards under Bates's weight but swinging around and burying his knee in the soldier's stomach as they collapsed to the ground. Bates's cry of agony was cut short by a powerful uppercut which sent him reeling backwards.

The crowd cheered as the dark-haired man sprang to his feet, but the bigger soldier, moving with a speed which belied his size, was upon him. The sergeant gripped the man from behind in a bear's hug, squeezing with all his strength and pinning his opponent's arms to his side. His face contorted by pain, the younger man suddenly brought his heel down forcefully on the soldier's foot, and with a scream of agony the sergeant released his grip.

Pressing his advantage, the younger man moved in close, then unleashed a vicious blow to the head. It never landed. With his instincts honed by a thousand brawls, the big soldier pulled to one side, the blow missing him by a fraction of an inch. Quickly jabbing with his left hand, he split the lip of his off-balance opponent, a flow of blood immediately trickling down the younger man's chin.

Reacting in the manner of a trained boxer, the dark-haired man skipped back out of reach, raising his guard at the same time. The two men looked at each other for a moment, then as the crowd shouted encouragement, the younger man, weaving on his feet, started to circle the sergeant. Suddenly, over the shouts of the crowd, the sound of police whistles shrilled through the night.

'Peelers! Peelers! Quick, scatter!'

The big sergeant, knowing from experience when to make an exit, immediately ran to his semi-conscious companion, dragged him to his feet and quickly grabbed their tunics from the ground before making off in the direction of the quays.

Seeing the blood-stained, dark-haired man looking around in confusion, Joe Brady swiftly pushed his way to him through the crowd. 'Quick, this way!' he cried.

'What?'

'Down here before the Peelers – quick!' Pulling the man with him, Brady ran down the laneway, then turned a corner and immediately pushed open a door. 'In here!' They entered a room full of wooden casks, and Brady bolted the door behind them. 'Up the stairs,' he cried, 'come on.'

Followed by the dazed and bleeding man, Brady ascended the stairs, opened a door onto a landing, then opened another door and led the man into the small upstairs bar the Invincibles had recently vacated.

'Here,' said Brady, tossing the man a towel from the counter. 'Press it tight to stop the bleeding.'

'Thanks,' said the man, sitting and cleaning his blood-stained chin.

Brady crossed to him, then sat in the opposite chair and smiled. 'That was nice goin'. You would have done him in the end.'

'Maybe, maybe not . . .' said the man, 'but you can't let those English bastards walk on you.'

'True for ye! By the way, I'm Joe Brady.'

'Good to meet you, Joe,' said the man, shaking hands. 'My name is Ryan, Bill Ryan.'

'American?'

'Half, I guess. I'm from Pennsylvania but my parents were Irish. I guess I'm Irish too, in my heart. Coming here's been like coming home.'

'Welcome home then,' said Brady.

'Thanks, it's good to be here,' said Scott, who, despite his cut lip, was smiling with genuine satisfaction.

'We must clear the house! Time, Gentlemen, please!' The big red-haired barman strode back and forth among the tables of the downstairs bar, his voice a weapon. 'Finish up please, Gents!' he roared.

'OK, lads,' said Carey, draining his pint and rising, 'we better go before Seán gets cross.'

'He's not cross now?' asked Scott, his American accent unslurred, despite the night's drinking.

Carey laughed. 'He's just getting into his stride.'

Taking their coats they moved out of the cordoned-off snug. In the aftermath of the fight they had retired there, to be joined by Brady and Scott when the fuss had died down. They crossed now through the bar proper where there were many cheerful exchanges and goodnights; then they stepped out into the street, the evening air sharp and clear after the warm fug of the pub.

'Well now, Bill,' said McCaffrey, 'are you sure you don't want us to get you a cab?'

'No thanks,' said Scott. 'I'd much prefer to walk. Do me good,' he laughed, 'clear the head after all that Guinness.'

'Sure ye were only sippin' it,' said Brady. 'We'll have to teach ye the way to lower pints.'

'I guess you will, Joe,' said Scott, with a smile. 'Meanwhile I'm real grateful for what you did tonight.'

'Ah it was nothin',' said Brady.

'And it's a pleasure to drink with a man who sent the red-coated minions scurrying away, tails between legs,' said Tynan.

'No speeches, Mr Tynan,' said Brady, emboldened by the drink. 'No speeches or Bill here will never get home, what?' He laughed loudly at his imagined witticism, Curley and McCaffrey smiling briefly in acknowledgement.

Carey crossed over to Scott and shook hands formally. 'It's been a pleasure, Bill, a pleasure. And eh . . . regarding those other matters we discussed, we'll be back to you. We have your address and we'll certainly be in touch.'

'I look forward to it,' said Scott, 'I sure do. Well, I'll say goodnight then and eh . . . *Erin go brách!*'

'*Erin go brách!* Safe home Bill,' called the others as he walked away towards the quays.

Carey waited till Scott was gone from earshot, then turned to Tynan. 'Well, what do you think?'

'A sound man and a great fighter,' interjected Brady, his speech slurred.

'Indeed, Joe, but I was asking Mr Tynan here,' said Carey.

'Oh right . . . sorry.'

'He could be a most valuable acquisition,' said Tynan, nodding sagely.

'If he's what he says he is . . .' added Carey.

'Of course,' Tynan answered. 'But assuming he is genuine – and we'll tread very carefully till we're happy about that – assuming he's genuine, he could be a most useful member.'

'Especially if he buys the stud farm,' said McCaffrey. 'It would be an ideal place for hiding weapons or a man on the run.'

'Yeah, and he's obviously not short of money,' added Dan Curley.

'I think, Gentlemen, you're missing his main source of potential value,' said Tynan.

'What's that?' asked Carey.

Tynan stroked his beard reflectively. 'Well . . . it struck me that a wealthy man with plans to buy a stud farm is greatly enhanced in value to us when you consider that he has no record whatsoever. Being uninvolved with nationalism in America means the police have no knowledge of his existence.'

'Let's just hope he's not too good to be true,' said Carey.

Tynan nodded. 'Yes. But there are lots of Irish organisations in Pennsylvania, we can make enquiries about his family.'

'Why don't I write to Danny O'Sullivan in Clan na nGael?' said Carey. 'He knows every man, woman and child in Pittsburg, and he could make enquiries elsewhere in Pennsylvania.'

'Good thinking, Jim,' answered Tynan, 'would you look after that?'

'I will,' said Carey.

'I hope he is legit,' said McCaffrey. 'He seems like a very nice fella.'

'History, my friend,' said Tynan, 'is full of nice fellows who betrayed their kith and kin. But let's not pre-judge. If he's what he appears, we may have an excellent recruit, and if he's not . . .'

'If he's not,' said Carey, 'then our friend Mr Ryan will be getting a twelve-inch blade buried in his guts.'

Fifteen

With an apparent lack of interest, Captain William Scott glanced up from his bench at the side of the Glen Pond as his superior approached. He had chosen the most remote section of the Phoenix Park for their rendezvous, assuming correctly that on a cold March morning there would be few other strollers in such an area.

To any casual observer, Colonel Penrose – smartly dressed in civilian clothes – would look like a middle-aged gentleman out for a brisk walk. Unlikely as it was that anyone could see them here, Scott nevertheless remained seated, ostensibly gazing out over the wind-ruffled waters of the pond, as the colonel approached.

'Good morning, Sir,' he said.

'Morning, Scott,' said the colonel, sitting on the other end of the bench and unfolding his newspaper. He leaned back and opened the paper before him. 'I got your letter when I returned from London. Being a bit over-cautious, don't you think?'

'Sir?'

'Park-bench meeting in the wilds rather than your cottage?'

'Well contact has been made, Sir. That means lots of imponderables outside my control. So anything I *can* control, I think I ought to.'

'You don't think they've got your cottage under observation already?'

'Probably not, Sir,' answered Scott, 'but there'll be enough risks without taking unnecessary ones, however slight. So I'm afraid I must ask you to regard the cottage as out of bounds.'

Penrose shrugged. 'As you wish, Captain, as you wish. So,' he said, his tone brightening, 'you've finally made contact?'

'Yes, Sir. May I ask first about Sergeants Bates and Ross?'

'Both safely back from leave in Ireland, and each twenty guineas richer for their performances.'

'And the troopers who impersonated the policemen?'

'Back with their regiment in Aldershot, paid for their whistle-blowing, and all four men guaranteed to remain absolutely tightlipped – plus they're all due for shipment with the regiment to Calcutta next week. No security worries there, I assure you.'

'No indeed, Sir, very well organised.'

'You did rather make Bates earn his twenty guineas,' said Penrose, a hint of amusement in his voice.

'It had to look convincing,' answered Scott. 'Besides,' he continued, gently touching his sore lip, 'Sergeant Ross evened the score somewhat – the man's fists are like hams. The important thing, however, is that it worked. Not alone did it gain me entry, but it was actually one of the group – Joe Brady – who "rescued" me from the police.'

'Good show,' said Penrose.

'Thank you, Sir.'

'I also got to meet several other gentlemen of whom we're aware.'

'Namely?'

'Besides Brady, there was the builder James Carey, Ned McCaffrey, Dan Curley, and a Patrick Tynan.'

'Tynan? That's a new one,' said Penrose interestedly.

'Yes. Unusual sort of character, and rather taken with the sound of his own voice. . .'

'Nothing unusual about that in Ireland,' interjected Penrose.

'Perhaps not, but in spite of his being somewhat uninspiring, the others seemed fairly deferential to him.'

'Hmm.' Penrose looked thoughtful. 'That could be significant.'

'Quite. The other impression I got was that the others knew each other better than they knew Tynan. It occurred to me he might only recently be with them.'

'And yet you say he was treated like a figure of authority?'

'Yes. Which might suggest a man imposed upon them from above,' said Scott.

'Perhaps. But the London Directory of the Land League don't have a Tynan on their executive, as far as I'm aware.' Penrose nodded thoughtfully. 'We'll make a few discreet enquiries about Mr Tynan. Talking of enquiries, how deeply did they question you about your background?'

'Quite a bit,' answered Scott. 'I gave them the horse breeder from Pennsylvania story.'

'Were they suspicious?'

'Hard to say, Sir. They asked a lot of questions about America and why I was in Ireland. Difficult to be sure if they were testing me out, or genuinely interested.'

'Did they ask about the fight?'

'Oh yes, that was rather a good idea, if I say so myself. The split lip bought quite a bit of credibility.'

'What did you say caused the fight?' asked Penrose.

'A refusal to step out of the way of two British bullies. A point of honour, they being part of an army of occupation here in Ireland,' answered Scott with a grin.

Penrose turned towards Scott for the first time. 'You do rather enjoy cocking a snook at authority, Captain, don't you?'

'It was the appropriate line to take with them, Sir. I wanted to portray the risk-taking man of action. I had to sell them the idea that I'd come to Ireland because I was seeking my roots, this was where things were happening, I was eager to see Ireland for the Irish, all that sort of thing . . .'

'And did they nibble at the bait?'

'I think so. Tentatively mind, and no doubt further to some checking out. But on parting they had my address and promised to get in touch.'

'What exactly did they say they'd be in touch about?' asked Penrose keenly.

'Well, I let it be known that I wouldn't be averse to meeting some "active" nationalists. I didn't want to push it too far on a first meeting, but they got the message. If I don't hear anything within a couple of weeks I can always drop in to Mullett's for a drink, perhaps speed things up.'

'I doubt that you'll need to,' said Penrose, 'their security is rather haphazard. Besides, the inherent weakness in any secret society or terror group is that to expand and achieve their goals, sooner or later they have to take a chance on perspective members. And I think they will with you.'

'Let's hope it's sooner, rather than later.'

Penrose nodded sympathetically. 'Are you finding Dublin very dull?'

'Quite the contrary, Sir,' answered Scott, 'I find it rather appealing. But I am anxious to make progress on the mission.'

'Yes of course.' Penrose suddenly lowered his newspaper. 'Look here, Scott, there's not a soul about, and it's deuced cold sitting still. Let's stroll up towards the road above the Glen. We can talk as we go.'

'Very good, Sir,' said Scott rising.

Leaving the Glen Pond behind, they started up the steep, tree-lined road.

'Did you manage to bring the conversation with Carey and company around to the Viceroy and Chief Secretary?' asked Penrose.

Scott smiled. 'That wasn't difficult. They're prime topics of conversation.'

'And?'

'There's no question – as Chief Secretary for Ireland, Mr Forster would be the number one target.'

'A damn good man, Forster,' said Penrose.

'Yes, Sir. The Invincibles, however, see him as an out-and-out tyrant. He's much more hated than the Viceroy.'

Penrose snorted derisively. 'What would you expect from people who regard Parnell as a bloody hero? No, Forster is an excellent Chief Secretary, and he knows one must enforce law and order before granting any concessions. That's why he's right to keep Parnell in jail until terrorism is stamped out.'

'Well, yes, unless . . .' started Scott hesitantly.

'Unless what?'

'Well unless Parnell is released by Mr Gladstone. He *is* talking of granting a measure of local government for Ireland – presumably he'd want to work with Parnell's Irish Party to implement that.'

'If you ask me,' said Penrose, 'it's damn bad form. Forster's battling away here to stamp out disorder, and Gladstone is pulling the rug from under his own Chief Secretary with his kid-glove treatment of Parnell and his cohorts.'

'I suppose it is rather awkward for the Prime Minister, Sir –

after all Parnell is a Member of Parliament and leader of a party in the House of Commons.'

'Parnell is a sanctimonious hypocrite, who wants to have his cake and eat it,' said Penrose. 'He wants to be the martyred, non-violent statesman, imprisoned for his beliefs, while he knows his political power is maintained by violence and Land League terror in Ireland.'

'Yes, well I dare say it'll all be sorted out in the end by the politicians, Sir. Meanwhile I shall do my utmost to thwart any assassination bids by the Invincibles.'

'And you're convinced Forster would be the chief target?'

'Yes, I think Forster would almost certainly be Number One, followed by the Viceroy, and after that, probably Under Secretary Burke.'

'No harm to step up Forster's security then,' said Penrose.

'No indeed, Sir.'

'It makes one wonder, Scott,' said Penrose musingly.

'Sir?'

'If this whole democracy concept hasn't gone too far. Have you heard the Matthew Harris statement?'

'I don't think so, Colonel.'

'Chap in the barracks cut it out of the paper. Extraordinary.' He reached into the pocket of his waistcoat and withdrew a clipping. 'Outrageous really to think the most important figure in Ireland must go about in fear of his life, and Mr Matthew Harris of the *Ballinasloe Tenants' Defence Association* can state he'd have . . .' Penrose paused for a second, then read disdainfully: 'He'd have no objection if the tenant farmers of Ireland shot down landlords as pheasants are shot in the month of September!'

Scott burst out laughing, then quickly sobered under Penrose's glare. 'I'm sorry, Sir, I'm sorry . . . but it is, well, rather pithily stated.'

Penrose didn't reply but continued walking towards the nearby junction with the Upper Glen Road. At the intersection he stopped and faced Scott. 'Captain, you're an excellent soldier in many respects but you'd be wise to curtail your liberal tendencies. Perhaps you've found the ordinary Irish people you've met to be friendly. Perhaps your theatrical background makes you susceptible to their colourful way with words. If that is so, Captain, I'd strongly suggest you harden your heart and be on your guard. You're here to prevent murder. One slip, one wrong move, and your witty Irish chums may murder *you*.'

'Yes, Sir,' said Scott contritely. 'Point clearly taken, Sir.'

'I hope so. Very well, we'd better part here,' said Penrose. 'You will of course keep me posted.'

'Yes, Sir.'

'Very good, Scott. Good day to you.'

'Good day, Sir.'

Turning in the opposite direction to that taken by the colonel, Scott walked on. One wrong move and he'd be dead. Whatever about Penrose's other opinions, there was no disputing that one. He'd just have to count on making the right moves then. That and his normal good luck. Unperturbed by the colonel's glum advice, he walked on briskly through the park.

Sixteen

Sitting in his accustomed place at the head of the table, Jeremiah Hackett raised his glass in a toast. 'The master and mistress!' he called.

'The master and mistress,' responded the assembled servants respectfully, before lowering their glasses and commencing to eat the evening meal.

Tonight's the night, thought Kate, feeling a tremor of excitement in her stomach. She was midway through her second week in the Burke household, and was familiar by now with the rituals of the Servants' Hall, and how the varying shades of social strata were maintained in everything from modes of address to seating arrangements.

Sitting in the middle section of the long table, in keeping with her lowly status, Kate was surrounded by scullery maids, house maids, grooms and footmen; while at the table head, on Hackett's left and right, sat the cook, Mrs Galligan, and Imelda Roche, the ladies' maid. At the other end of the table sat the butler, flanked by the master's valet, and Mr McDaid, the dairy manager and Kate's immediate superior.

Mr McDaid was a soft-spoken, middle-aged widower, and Kate had taken to him from the start. He had soon reciprocated her friendliness, having quickly realised that she was an efficient and cheerful worker. Living alone and childless in the cottage adjoining the dairy, Mr McDaid's attitude to Kate had become more like that towards a daughter than a new employee. Kate was glad of this, as, apart from liking him in his own right, she knew she might well need an ally against Jeremiah Hackett.

The smooth-faced house steward had lost no time in visiting Kate at the dairy, and while up to now she had been able to deflect his innuendo and verbal advances with a sort of cheerful, laughing dismissiveness, Kate knew enough of

98

human nature to sense that Hackett would not accept rejection indefinitely, however good-humoredly phrased.

Still, she would worry about that when the time came. Tonight she had other plans. She had promised Carey that the Invincibles would have an initial report on the Under Secretary's Lodge as soon as possible, and dinner time was the one occasion when all the staff were assembled here in the Servants' Hall. If she could excuse herself while they were eating, it would be her best chance to explore the house without fear of interruption.

'Wasn't it awful, Kate?'

'Sorry?' Startled out of her musings, Kate turned to the stout house maid beside her. 'Sorry, Madge, what was that?' she said.

'Monsieur Artois, the trapeze artist, wasn't it awful?' repeated Madge.

'Yes, terrible,' answered Kate.

Agnes Horan, the scullery maid, pushed aside her plate and leaned across the table conspiratorially.

'My cousin saw the whole thing,' she said. 'He loves the music hall, goes to Dan Lowrey's every week.'

'He saw the accident?' asked Kate.

'Yes, he told me only this afternoon,' continued Agnes importantly. 'Monsieur Artois did his Leap for Life – twenty-five feet through the air he flew – and just missed the second trapeze.' She paused dramatically. 'You could hear his head crack when he hit the stage!'

'I believe they took him to Mercer's Hospital,' said Madge.

'For all the good it done,' retorted Agnes, 'he was dead in half an hour.'

'They take terrible risks, them acrobats, I wouldn't do their job for any money – would you?' asked Madge.

'No,' answered Kate with a shake of her head, but her mind was centred more on the risk she was about to take herself. She felt slightly guilty for the deceit she was about to practise on Agnes and Madge, and also for only half-listening to their talk, but she simply couldn't keep her attention focused on their conversation.

After a few moments she saw Hackett pulling back his chair

as most of the assembled staff finished their main course. 'Shall we retire?' he asked rhetorically, and without awaiting a reply he stood up, to be followed to his own parlour, as was the custom of the house, by the 'upper' servants – Cook, Mr McDaid, Ahern the valet, Lacey the butler, and Imelda Roche the ladies' maid.

Every evening they retired for dessert and coffee, served by the still-room maid, and Kate had planned to make her move on their departure. She waited a moment after they'd left, then just as dessert was being served along the table, she turned to Madge, a pained expression on her face. 'I don't feel well,' said Kate.

'What's wrong, love?' asked Madge sympathetically.

'I've just gotten a splitting headache. I . . . I think I'll go up to my room.'

'Do you want me to come with you?' asked Agnes.

'No!' said Kate, then more softly, 'No thanks, Agnes . . . I'll just lie down for a few minutes. A quiet lie-down usually cures it.'

'OK,' said Agnes.

'I'll see you later,' said Kate, 'excuse me.' Rising from the table, she left the dining hall and went through the kitchen, the heat from the huge black stoves still warming the food-scented air, then she passed out the kitchen door to the back staircase.

Moving quickly now, she ascended the stairway, but instead of continuing up towards her attic quarters she stopped at the first floor. In apparently casual conversation with Agnes, the house maid, Kate had discovered that Burke had his study on the first floor, adjacent to his bedroom. She slowly opened the door joining the back stairs with the corridor. A cautious look confirmed that no one was about.

She realised that this was the point of no return – a dairy maid had no business being in this part of the house. Gathering her nerve, she paused a second, then closed the door softly behind her and started down the richly carpeted corridor. Her contingency plan, if discovered here, was to claim she had heard a squeal of distress from one of the household cats and had gone to investigate. It was an excuse she fervently hoped not to have to use.

100

She reached the end of the corridor and came to large double doors on her right. According to her calculations these must lead to Burke's corner bedroom, therefore the adjoining study should have its entrance to the corridor one door back.

Kate moved to this door and listened for a moment. No sound carried from within. She dropped to one knee and looked through the keyhole, but it was blocked by the presence of a key on the inside. Her pulses racing, she knocked softly on the door. If someone opened it she would say that she had come in answer to a bellcord – the house maid having been taken ill – and was this the room which had rung? She waited a moment, and when to her relief there was no reply, she turned the door handle and entered the room.

There was nobody there. Kate quietly closed the door behind her and was struck by the rich lingering aroma of high-quality pipe smoke. She looked about the study, which was obviously well used. A large mahogany desk, situated before the window, had an array of pipes on its top alongside rows of papers held down by ornate glass paper-weights. The opposite wall was covered with bookcases, many of them filled with neatly stacked files. A fire burned in the grate, and over the mantelpiece were numerous photographs.

Kate moved swiftly now, knowing her crying cat excuse would be useless if she were discovered here. Her first task was identification. Despite working for the past ten days in Burke's employment she had never met, or even seen, the man. This problem was quickly resolved – all of the photographs on the mantelpiece had captions written in a round flowing hand. There were pictures of Burke at his desk in Dublin Castle, awarding a prize at a polo competition, in cap and gown as a student, on the lawn with his sister, playing croquet in a group, and one which immediately caught Kate's attention. Its caption read 'Chief Secretary W E Forster and Under Secretary T H Burke, Saint Patrick's Hall, 1881'. It was a clear, professionally taken photograph and Kate didn't hesitate. Knowing it was just what the Invincibles wanted, she slipped it inside her shawl, then quickly rearranged the other pictures on the mantelpiece so that no gap was apparent.

She crossed to the desk and carefully looked through the

papers on its top. Most of them seemed to be related to legislation concerning the Land Act. Kate tried the first of the desk's drawers, and finding it unlocked, pulled it all the way out.

A slim leather-bound book lay in the drawer and Kate opened it. Each page had names and times entered in black ink, and Kate realised that it was Burke's desk diary. Her excitement soared. His planned movements would be exactly what the Invincibles wanted!

Flicking ahead through the diary, it opened on 10th April. 'Polo prize-giving 12.00' read a neatly penned entry, 'Collect Forster 11.30.' Kate could hardly believe her good fortune. Carey would be ecstatic if she could supply him with information like this.

She took a piece of notepaper from the desk and was about to jot down the details when she heard the sound. Her stomach contracted with sudden fear as she realised it came from next door. Someone was in Burke's bedroom. Fighting back a sense of panic, she looked about the room for a hiding-place. Just as she replaced the diary, she saw the handle of the dividing-door depress.

With a speed born of desperation Kate moved to the window and slipped in behind the floor-length curtains. Her heart was pounding so loudly in her chest that she felt sure it must be heard, but unaware of her presence, the entering man moved casually to the desk and picked up one of the pipes.

Through a slight chink in the curtains, Kate looked out. The man was dressed in a red velvet smoking-jacket, and on his turning around she saw that it was Burke. She also saw, with horror, that in her haste she hadn't properly closed the drawer in which the diary had been hurriedly replaced.

Burke pocketed the pipe, then noticed the partially opened drawer. Kate thought her pounding heart would explode as he looked quizzically at it, then with a shrug he closed the drawer and returned to his bedroom, pulling the dividing doors behind him.

Kate felt an immense wave of relief wash over her. But if Burke had caught her with the diary . . . No, she thought determinedly, don't dwell on that or you'll be paralysed with fear. She waited a moment, taking deep breaths to try and calm herself, then emerged from behind the curtains and quickly crossed to the door, taking care to make no sound.

This was the risky part. If Burke, or anyone else, were in the corridor when she emerged, she would be caught red-handed, but if she stayed in the study Burke might return at any moment. Suddenly she reached out, quickly turned the door handle, and stepped out of the room. The corridor was empty. Kate quietly closed the study door, then swiftly moved down the corridor. Encountering no one, she turned out through the doorway to the safety of the stairwell.

Clutching the precious picture under her shawl, she climbed the stairs two steps at a time, then, reaching the sanctuary of her attic quarters, she locked the bedroom door behind her and withdrew the photograph, a mixture of elation and relief almost overcoming her. She crossed to the wardrobe and hid the photograph under the clothing she had stored in its depths; then she lay down on the bed, suddenly drained, but also thrilled, by the audacity of what she had done.

Seventeen

James Carey was looking forward to this evening's meeting, partly in anticipation of Kate's report from within the enemy camp, and partly, he had to admit, in anticipation of seeing again such an attractive young woman. Hearing a knock on his front door, he carefully adjusted the lie of his well-fitting jacket, and moved expectantly down the hall.

He opened the door, an easy smile on his face. 'Miss Lannigan,' he said warmly, 'as punctual as you're pretty. Do come in.'

'Thank you,' answered Kate.

'There's a roaring fire in the parlour – let me take your coat.'

'Fine,' said Kate, handing him the coat and entering the front room.

Carey hung her coat in the hall, then followed her in, indicating the armchairs before the fire. 'Can I offer you a little something to drink?' he asked.

'No, thanks all the same,' answered Kate, sitting in one of the chairs.

'Well,' said Carey, seating himself opposite her and smiling, 'I'm all ears . . .'

Kate sat forward seriously. 'Before I give you my report Mr Carey, a rather worrying thought occurred to me.'

'Oh, and what might that be?'

'That perhaps it wasn't very wise to meet here.'

Carey looked puzzled. 'Not wise, why not?'

'Well,' answered Kate, 'my first contact with you came about because it's generally known you're a nationalist, so obviously it's known to the police too.'

'It's not against the law to believe in nationalism.'

'No, but it struck me that the police might watch you in case you did something that is against the law,' said Kate.

'So?'

'So if they were watching this house, and saw me enter, and traced me to the Under Secretary's Lodge . . .'

Carey smiled reassuringly. 'I think the police have more to do than stand in Denzille Street watching who enters and leaves my house. I really wouldn't worry about it.'

'I'm afraid I would,' answered Kate, pleasantly but firmly. 'So in future I'd prefer to meet where we can be sure we're unobserved.'

'I think you're being a bit . . .' started Carey.

'*And*,' Kate cut him short, 'I'd like to leave here tonight by the rear entrance. You may feel I'm being over-cautious, but it's my neck, and I think I've already taken enough risks this week.'

Carey sighed, then shrugged in acceptance. 'If that's what you want.'

'Thank you,' said Kate. Suddenly she smiled. 'And now for the good news.' Opening her handbag, she withdrew the photograph of her employer and Forster. 'Courtesy of Under Secretary Burke,' she said, handing him the picture.

Carey studied it a moment. 'Excellent,' he said, 'first class. Where did you get this?'

'From the mantelpiece of Burke's study,' answered Kate, unable to keep a note of pride from her voice.

'You just walked in and took it?'

'Yes. When all the staff were having dinner I slipped in to the study.'

'Sound girl yourself!' said Carey admiringly. 'That was smart thinking too – waiting till they were all eating.'

'Not quite smart enough,' replied Kate. 'Burke came in while I was there.'

'What?'

'I managed to hide behind the curtain when I heard him coming,' explained Kate. 'I was lucky.'

'You were indeed,' said Carey, a new note of respect for her in his voice. He indicated the photograph. 'How long can I hold onto this?'

'I think you'd better keep it.'

'Keep it?'

'Yes, I rearranged the other pictures on the mantelpiece. It's

105

very unlikely he'll notice the difference. I don't think it's worth the risk of getting caught trying to replace it.'

'Yes, you're probably right,' said Carey. 'Tell me, what's security like in general, around the residence?'

'Unpredictable. As you probably know, there's a sort of moat – well, more a ditch really – all around the perimeter. There are two principal entrances: the main drive where the gate-keeper's cottage is, and the tradesman's entrance at the rear, leading out by the stables and outhouses. I've also found two pedestrian gates in the perimeter fence.'

Carey leaned forward eagerly. 'If we gained access to the grounds, what then?'

'Gaining access is the easy part,' said Kate, 'the fence isn't high and the moat isn't deep. Inside though, there are soldiers to guard Burke. Mostly they stay in a barrack house near the back entrance, but they also move through the grounds at random.'

'I see,' said Carey.

'The other problem, even if you avoided them, would be finding Burke. It's a big house and I haven't been able to find out much about his routines, so far.'

'Hmm,' said Carey, 'probably be simpler to get him somewhere else.'

'On that subject, I've one final piece of information,' added Kate.

'Yes?'

'Before Burke disturbed me I got a quick look at his diary. On the tenth of April he's going to a polo match, and he's collecting Forster at half eleven.'

'Christ!' said Carey excitedly, 'that's just the information we need. They'll be leaving the Castle together – we could get the Chief Secretary and the Under Secretary in one fell swoop!' He looked seriously at Kate. 'You've done well – you've done very well.'

'Good,' she answered. 'If I pick up anything else I'll let you know.'

'Excellent,' said Carey. 'And now, I have something for you.' He reached into his breast pocket and withdrew an envelope, passing it over to her.

Kate accepted it and opened the flap to find the envelope contained a wad of five pound notes. 'What's this for?' she asked.

'The executive committee wanted you to have it.'

'Look, I told you before . . .' started Kate.

'I know,' said Carey, raising a hand to stop her. 'I know – you're not doing this for money.'

'So why are you offering it?'

'For several reasons. You've lost your home, your nursing career has been disrupted – we think you deserve some compensation for that.' Seeing Kate about to protest, Carey raised his hand again. 'No please, let me explain. There's a very practical reason also. This is a dangerous business we're embarked on, the whole thing could explode at any minute.'

'How do you mean?' asked Kate.

'If we kill the top targets – Burke especially – you may have to get out of the country fast. There may not be time to wait for banks to open, withdrawals to be made. This way you'll have money for boat and train tickets, money to live on if you have to leave suddenly for America – it speeds everything up.'

'I see.'

'Look, you've shown your commitment and bravery. We in turn want to show our concern for your well-being. Take it in the spirit in which it's being offered.'

'Very well,' said Kate, 'and thank you. I . . . I do appreciate it.'

'Not at all,' said Carey jovially, 'and to celebrate we'll have a little toast. What'll you drink?'

Kate hesitated, then not wishing to appear ungracious, said, 'A dry sherry please.'

Carey rose and moved to a cabinet on the far side of the room. 'One dry sherry coming up.' He opened the drinks cabinet, poured a whiskey for himself and the sherry for Kate, then returned to the armchair before the fire. 'Actually the committee felt there was one other service you could do for the Invincibles,' said Carey, seating himself again.

'Oh. What's that?'

'It's not a dangerous mission – in fact you might well enjoy it,' he added with a smile.

Why do I mistrust him already? wondered Kate.

'Here,' said Carey, passing over the sherry. 'Let's have our drinks, and I'll tell you all about it.'

Eighteen

Scott leaned back comfortably, book in hand, as the late March sunshine streamed through the kitchen windows, warming the alcove in which he sat. The local children were playing in Blind Lane as they often did, but their cries and chants had become familiar and didn't distract him from his book.

Over two weeks had now elapsed since his meeting with the Invincibles in Mullett's pub, but despite his impatience at their slowness in making contact, he had forced himself to bide his time. It would be much better, he reasoned, to let them come to him, rather than appear suspiciously over-eager. They would no doubt be making enquiries with their sources in America, which would take some time.

Knowing it was always easier to pace oneself with a deadline in view, he had decided to give them until the following Wednesday, then if contact hadn't been made he would casually drop into Mullett's for a drink and try to speed things up.

Aside from his desire to make faster progress on his mission, he had found Dublin life quite rewarding. He had been to music hall at the Harp, and the Star of Erin; theatre at the Grafton; and opera at the Gaiety. He had had slight qualms about the opera, recognising that *Aida* was more in line with the taste of Captain William Scott than with his Bill Ryan persona. But why be snobbish, he had rationalised. Why not a horse breeder who loved opera? And in fairness to himself, he had immersed himself in the breeder role, visiting stables and stud farms in the Castleknock and Clonsilla areas. In fact the more he pretended to be interested in premises and animals for breeding, the more it had struck him as a very satisfactory career for one who loved horses. Perhaps, he thought, it would be worth looking into when he eventually retired from the army.

Suddenly the peace of the sunlit kitchen was disturbed by a

loud knock on the cottage door. Scott glanced up quizzically, then closed the book and rose. He moved to the hall and opened the door, his heart skipping a beat on seeing the bulky frame of Joe Brady before him.

'Hello, Bill,' said Brady.

'Joe!' cried Scott, his American accent immediately falling into place. 'Good to see ye! Come on in.'

'I'm. not disturbin' ye?'

'Not at all,' said Scott. 'Step right in.'

'Thanks.'

'Come on out to the kitchen, that's where the sun is.'

'I was workin' in Inchicore this mornin',' said Brady. When I knocked off I decided to stroll across the park and see ye.'

'I'm sure glad you did. Take a seat.'

'Thanks.'

'Can I fix you a drink?'

'Well . . .'

' "Well" means yes in Ireland,' laughed Scott, 'I've learned that much. How about a whiskey?'

'Fine,' answered Brady, 'no water.'

'Two neat whiskeys,' said Scott, crossing to the dresser for the bottle and glasses.

'So,' said Scott, pouring the drinks, 'I was wondering when I'd hear from you fellas . . .'

'We've been busy.'

'Here you are,' he said, handing Brady the glass, and sitting in the armchair opposite him.

'*Sláinte*,' said Brady, raising the drink.

'*Sláinte*.'

Lowering his glass, Brady leaned back easily. 'So, what have you been doin'?'

'Oh, looking at horses, stud farms, accommodation . . .'

'This is a nice place you have here.'

'It's only rented. If I set up as a breeder I'll want something attached to the stables.'

'And will you – set up here permanently?' asked Brady evenly.

'Yes, I believe I probably will.'

'That's good. I'm glad to hear it. By the way, you said you were from Pennsylvania, right?'

'Yeah,' answered Scott.

'A fella I work with spent some time out there, in a place called Scranton.'

'Really?'

'Yeah. Do you know it?'

'Sure I do.'

'What did you think of it?' asked Brady.

Scott paused and shrugged. 'Alright if you like anthracite, it's a mining town.' Was he being tested again, he wondered, or was this just chit-chat? Brady's impassive face gave nothing away.

'Yeah,' said Brady, 'my friend didn't fancy it much. He worked as a miner there and in another town called Dodsville.'

'Dodsville?'

'Yeah, do you know it?'

'No, can't say I do,' answered Scott easily. He *was* being tested. Part of his preparation had been to study the mining regions of Pennsylvania, and there was no Dodsville that he'd ever heard of. 'Whereabouts is it?' asked Scott in apparently innocent puzzlement.

'Oh don't ask me,' said Brady, 'I could just about point out New York on the map.'

'You've never been to America then?'

'I've never been out of the country.'

'Really?'

'There were twenty-five born into our family, Bill, and we were always short.'

'You're kidding me!'

'What?'

Twenty-five born into your family?'

'Yes.'

'Jeez, that's some family.'

'Yeah, and it was a struggle to keep a roof over our heads, never mind travellin' abroad.' Brady's voice was bitter. 'Maybe it's different in America, but here if you're poor, they like you to stay poor.'

'Yeah?'

111

'Yeah, it's easier for the English to rule us and keep us down if the people aren't educated, if we're busy strugglin' just to stay alive.'

Scott nodded but thought to himself: *you can't blame the English if you impoverish yourself with a family of twenty-five.*

'Yes, I suppose so,' he said to Brady. 'You're OK now though, aren't you?'

'I was lucky. I left school at fourteen and my father got me into the paving. There's loads will never get that chance – they're born paupers and they'll die paupers.'

'Is that what stirred your interest in nationalism?' asked Scott.

'Only part of it, it's political too. Why should my future in Ireland be decided by some fat bastard, sitting on his arse in London?'

'Why indeed?' answered Scott, then seeing as the issue had been raised he decided to probe a little. He leaned over towards Brady. 'Maybe we can do something about that, Joe, together.'

'Maybe,' responded Brady. 'Mr Carey will contact you about that when the time is right.' He raised his glass, took a long drink of the whiskey and leaned back in the chair. 'Meanwhile,' he said, 'how about some diversion?'

'Diversion?' replied Scott.

Brady smiled. 'Have you a girlfriend in America?'

'No. No I can't say I have.'

'Have you found one since you came here?'

'Well no, I haven't gotten . . .'

'Right,' snapped Brady, 'you've been lookin' at too many horses and not enough girls. Meself and Tim Kelly are goin' to a dance on Friday night. Why don't you come with us?'

'Tim Kelly?' asked Scott.

'Yeah, he's a pal of mine, a nationalist too, you'll like him. Are ye on?'

'Well . . .'

' "Well" in Ireland means yes,' laughed Brady.

'Sure,' said Scott with a smile. 'Why not?'

'Sound man.'

'And thanks for thinking of me, Joe. It was good of you to come all the way from Inchicore.'

'Not at all,' answered Brady. 'We'll meet you in Hanrahan's of Parliament Street at eight o'clock, OK?'

'Fine.'

'And now I better go or I'll be late for me dinner.' Brady knocked back the remainder of his whiskey and rose. 'We'll see ye on Friday night then, Bill?'

'Wouldn't miss it, Joe,' said Scott, leading him from the kitchen to the front door.

'Right, see you then,' said Brady.

Scott waved a friendly farewell as the muscular paviour walked down the garden path. He waited till Brady turned off onto the road before closing the front door and allowing his excitement to show. He had obviously passed his first test with the Invincibles and they were drawing him closer for further inspection – which would enable him to do precisely the same to them. Things were finally starting to move, and Penrose would be very pleased when he notified him, and passed on the name of Tim Kelly for the files.

He returned to the kitchen and in celebratory mood topped up his glass of whiskey, then he sat back happily in the alcove, and wished that it were Friday already.

Nineteen

'Aw, Joe, it's raining,' said Tim Kelly plaintively, as he stepped out of Hanrahan's pub.

'What do ye want me to do – wave a magic wand?' retorted Brady.

'Is it far to the dance hall?' asked Scott.

'No,' said Kelly, 'it's just off Dame Street.' He smiled brightly at Scott. 'The thing is, Bill, this is me good coat – cost nearly ten bob – I don't want it gettin' all wet.'

'Oh that'd never do,' replied Brady sarcastically.

'It might ease off if we wait a minute,' said Kelly hopefully.

'Come on, it's only a bit of drizzle. We'll be there in a couple of minutes,' said Brady, stepping out from under the awning of the pub.

Avoiding the busy, Friday night traffic of splashing cabs and landaus, the three men briskly crossed the rain-washed Parliament Street.

Scott was pleased with the night's progress so far. In the hour they had spent in the pub he had answered the apparently friendly questions of Brady and Kelly, regarding life in America. It was difficult to know how much was genuine interest and how much he was being tested, but he thought he had acquitted himself well, and in return he had felt entitled to question them about their lives in Dublin.

Though somewhat cautious at first, it had transpired that both men were really fervent nationalists. Scott sensed a more radical conviction with these two than with their older colleagues like Carey and Tynan. And although never discussing the topic of assassination, Scott felt sure that if it arose, Brady's brusque, no-nonsense approach would make him a natural candidate for carrying out the actual deed.

Kelly, he thought, was a more curious case. Only twenty years old, he had a youthful innocence about him, which, allied to his friendly, outgoing manner, made him very likeable. It was only when his fervour for Irish independence emerged that his natural exuberance became channelled into a frightening fanaticism. He turned to Scott now, as they rounded the corner into Dame Street. 'Well, Bill, are ye ready to meet some Irish colleens?' he asked with a smile.

'Ready, willing and able,' answered Scott easily.

'Sound man,' retorted Kelly, punching him playfully on the shoulder.

Following right behind Brady, they quickly walked down Dame Street, approaching the laneway leading to Dan Lowrey's music hall. Directly opposite was the entrance to Dublin Castle, centre of British administration in Ireland, and seeing the immaculately dressed sentries standing rigidly to attention before the gate, Scott took the opportunity to reinforce his Bill Ryan characterisation.

'Arrogant looking bastards, aren't they?' he said.

Brady looked over at the sentries, erect and unmoving despite the falling rain. 'They do it deliberately – think it'll impress us,' he said with contempt.

'Yeah, well, we're the ones who'll impress them, with twelve inches of Sheffield steel!' said Kelly heatedly.

'OK, Tim!' cut in Brady harshly.

Scott immediately recognised that Brady's tone was forbidding any further discussion of an obviously sensitive topic.

'Come on, it's gettin' heavier,' said Brady, in what Scott felt was an attempt to distract attention from a blunder.

'Yeah, it *is* getting heavy, Joe,' answered Scott, as though unaware that anything significant had occurred. 'How much further is it?'

'Next turn on the left,' replied Brady, 'won't be long.'

Twelve inches of Sheffield steel, thought Scott. And what had Kelly said? *We're the ones who'll impress them*. Could it be that Kelly and Brady had already been chosen by the Invincibles as the potential assassins? And using knives rather than guns? Knives – that would mean an assassination bid where the victim could be approached at very close quarters. Such as when travelling in a slowly moving carriage. He had better tell Penrose about this first thing in the morning, precautions would need to be taken. Or was he reading too much into a single remark? Perhaps; but his instincts told him that Kelly had revealed something important. Well he would let Penrose decide whether or not to take action.

'Here we are,' said Brady, arriving at a gaslit doorway.

'Great,' said Scott cheerily, 'lay on McDuff.'

Brady glanced at him uncomprehendingly, then knocked on the door.

No more Shakespearian quotations, Scott reprimanded himself.

The door was opened from within, and the sound of music and laughter spilled out into the street. A tall, broad-set man who opened the door nodded in recognition to Brady, then stepped aside to allow them in. They went to the pay-desk where a middle-aged woman took their eight pence admissions.

'Come on, we'll leave our coats in the cloakroom,' said Kelly eagerly.

They headed down a warm, darkly lit hall to a desk, attended by an attractive fair-haired girl. Kelly handed in their coats, all the while engaging in banter with the smiling girl. Watching him, Scott found it hard to reconcile this outgoing young man with the fanatical nationalist and potential murderer whom he knew him to be.

'OK, Bill,' Kelly said laughingly, as he gave them the tickets for their coats, 'the maidens of Ireland await you!'

'I hope they're not disappointed,' said Scott with a smile.

'Come on, it's down here,' said Brady, leading them towards the source of the music.

Entering a large, noisy, and softly but colourfully lit room, Scott saw a four-piece dance band on a stage, before which was the dance area, already crowded with waltzing couples. Along one wall was a refreshment area with tables and chairs, where teas and minerals were being sold, and along another wall sat the young ladies awaiting invitations to dance.

Scott turned to Brady. 'Eh, Joe.'

'Yeah?'

'What exactly is the drill here?'

116

'How do you mean?'

'Well, for seeking a dance partner. I don't want to do the wrong thing,' said Scott.

'It's dead simple,' interjected Kelly, 'you look at the girls, see one you fancy, and go over and ask her if she'd like to dance.'

'And if she declines?'

'Ah just ask another one,' said Kelly easily. 'But she probably won't – people are here to have a good time.'

Looking about him Scott was inclined to agree. There was an air of boisterous gaiety about the dancing couples, and even as he looked, several young men approached prospective partners and cheerfully asked them to dance. How far removed it was from the balls he had known in London, where formal introductions and rigidly adhered to dance cards were the norm. He tried to imagine a conservative like Colonel Penrose coping with the free-flowing informal atmosphere of this dance, and had to suppress a smile.

The music ended to vigorous applause, then the band launched into another waltz, and immediately the floor was awash with movement again.

'Do you want to come with me, Bill?' asked Kelly. 'We could ask a couple of girls together, just to break the ice for you.'

'No thanks, Tim, I don't want to cramp your style,' answered Scott smilingly, 'I'll just take a few minutes to find my feet here.'

'OK, it's every man for himself so!' cried Kelly. 'I'll see yis later.'

Scott watched with interest as Kelly approached a girl with curly blonde hair and smilingly asked her to dance. The girl nodded, and they joined the throng sweeping around the hall.

'I'm goin' to the Gents, Bill. I'll be back in a few minutes,' said Brady.

'OK, Joe,' answered Scott.

Left alone, he moved about the hall, intrigued by the cultural values in evidence. The whole atmosphere was so different to the regimental dances and society balls he had attended in London. Much less glamorous of course, but also far more lively, the participants here seeming to derive more pleasure and entertainment from their dancing.

In keeping with his Bill Ryan role, he knew he would have to ask some girls to dance. How fascinating it would be to socialise with girls both Irish, and, it had to be said, from a lower social station. Moving across the back of the hall, he glanced at the seated girls. As he did he collided with a young woman carrying a cup of tea.

'Mind!' she called.

'Oh Lord!' cried Scott. 'Oh I *am* sorry!' he said, seeing he had spilt the tea over her dress. Recovering from his shock he realised that for a word or two he had lost the American accent, but with the loudness of the music, and in the absence of Kelly or Brady, no harm had been done.

The girl had placed her cup on a table and was distractedly rubbing at her skirt with a handkerchief.

'Excuse me, Mam,' said Scott, 'my fault entirely.'

The girl looked up then and he was immediately struck by her beauty. She had thick flowing hair, a classically structured face and bright blue eyes. She looked directly at him with a hint of a smile. 'You were watching the girls, weren't you?'

'Well I . . . yes I was,' admitted Scott a little sheepishly.

'Well at least you're honest.'

'I'm really sorry,' answered Scott.

'And well you might be. If you'd been watching where you were going, I'd be able to drink my tea instead of wiping it off my dress.'

'I truly apologise,' said Scott, but in spite of the girl's complaint he thought he sensed an element of playfulness in her tone. 'May I make recompense by getting you another cup of tea?' he asked, with slightly mock gravity.

She looked at him evenly. 'Is this something you do, to get to meet young women?'

Again Scott sensed a twinkle in her eye as the question was asked. He decided to risk cheekiness. 'Yes,' he answered seriously, 'whenever I see an attractive lady I throw a cup of tea over her. Never fails.'

The girl looked at him for a second, then laughed warmly. 'I see. Well, personally I only like one cup a night thrown at me.

If you buy me another one I'd prefer to be allowed drink it.'

Scott smiled back. 'In the circumstances I think we can probably allow that. If you'd like to keep a table I'll get the teas.'

'Teas – plural?'

'I was hoping you'd allow me to have a cup with you, keep you company while you have yours.'

The girl looked at him with a pretence of seriousness. 'Well, I suppose if I don't, you'll only throw it over some other unfortunate.'

'Pretty likely,' nodded Scott.

'OK then,' smiled the girl.

'With or without sugar?'

'One spoon and plenty of milk please.'

'Yes, Mam. Two teas coming up.'

Pleased with his boldness, he made his way through the throng towards the refreshment counter, paid for the teas, and was going back towards the table when Brady approached.

Seeing the two cups and the sitting girl, Brady raised an eyebrow. 'Quick work, Bill, we can let you out,' he said quietly. Scott winked, then Brady passed smilingly on.

'Here we are,' said Scott, seating himself and handing over the tea.

'Thank you.'

'It's not bad,' he mused, sipping his.

'I thought you Americans only drank coffee?'

'Ah, so my accent has given me away.'

'Well,' answered the girl with a grin, 'let's say no one would think you were from west Cork.'

'No, I guess not. I'm from Pennsylvania.'

Her face lit up. 'Really? I have an uncle there, in Philadelphia.'

'That's my home town.'

'Have you ever met Jack Geraghty? He's a fireman out there?'

Scott shook his head. 'Can't say I have. It's a big place, Philadelphia.'

'Yes, yes I suppose so.'

'Still, if I ever set the house ablaze I'll certainly watch out

119

for him,' added Scott with a smile. 'You can give me a letter of introduction. Talking of which . . .'

'Yes,' answered the girl. 'I suppose it would be more respectable to take tea with a man you've been introduced to.'

Scott rose and extended his hand. 'I'm Bill Ryan.'

Shaking his hand, the girl smiled pleasantly. 'Pleased to meet you, Bill. I'm Kate Lannigan.'

The band, having exhausted its repertoire, was repeating itself by now, as Scott and Kate waltzed around the floor to the strains of 'The Blue Danube'. He was aware of envious glances from other men, and in spite of himself couldn't but feel a certain pride at being her chosen partner for the evening.

She had proven a good dancer, and they glided along easily despite the buffeting of other couples on the crowded floor. In fact, Scott secretly welcomed the crowded conditions, which caused them to dance sufficiently closely for him to smell her perfume, and to dance with an intimacy which, while not exactly improper, was somewhat more advanced than would be usual between a lady and gentleman who had just met.

Part of the excitement, he realised, lay in the knowledge that Kate Lannigan, beautiful and intelligent as she was, would not, in fact, qualify as a lady. In his Bill Ryan persona, however, Scott was free to relax with her in a way that would not normally have been possible. The upshot of it all had been an immediate rapport, with Kate's flirtatious playfulness being matched by Scott's newfound style of humour.

Kate had been talkative and friendly, with an eagerness to know all about his life in America, and he in his turn had been fascinated to hear, at first hand, details of how life was lived by the ordinary Irish people.

Dancing before the foot of the stage, they swirled past Tim Kelly, still in the company of the curly-headed blond girl he had met earlier in the evening. Kelly caught Scott's eye, nodded briefly at Kate, then gave a conspiratorial wink. In spite of the schoolboy sense of bravado which Scott clearly recognised in himself, he couldn't help but feel rather pleased as he nodded back to Kelly.

Sensing the slight movement, Kate looked up, an enquiring

smile on her face. God, but she's beautiful, thought Scott.

'Someone step on your toes again?' asked Kate.

'No, I'm fine,' he answered with a smile of reassurance.

Just then the band finished the tune with a flourish. The dancers all applauded, Kate and Scott standing easily together as the band leader stepped forward.

'Thank you, Ladies and Gentlemen, thank you,' he called. 'The next set of dances will be the last of the evening, so take your partners please.' He raised his violin and the band struck up, but instead of dancing Kate turned to Scott.

'I'm afraid I'll have to be going now,' she said.

'What about the last dance?'

'There'll be a terrible rush for coats at the end. My cousin wanted to leave before that.'

'Your cousin?' asked Scott.

'I came here tonight with my cousin and her boyfriend. They're up from the country on a visit and they're leaving me home.'

There was a slight pause, then Scott decided to continue in the bold vein in which he'd started the evening. 'I was hoping I might have that honour.'

Kate laughed gently. 'Aren't you the forward one?'

'Well?'

'My cousin's expecting me . . .'

Sensing the lack of conviction, Scott felt a surge of confidence. 'I bet she wouldn't be heart-broken at travelling home alone with her boyfriend, especially if she knew you were safely escorted.'

'By Mr Bill Ryan?'

'Why not? We're almost neighbours, and I'd be getting a cab anyway. Look, I've really enjoyed your company – it would sure be a pleasure to escort you home.'

Kate smiled. 'Well when you put it like that . . .' She handed him a ticket. 'Why don't you get both our coats from the cloakroom before the queue gets too big, and I'll find my cousin and tell her.'

Scott took the ticket happily. 'You got yourself a deal, Mam.'

*   *   *

121

The rain had stopped now, but the horses hooves splashed in a gentle rhythm along the wet road. The gas lamps flanking the long straight course of the main road of the Phoenix Park seemed to stretch away into infinity, and the night air was sweet and clear after the rain.

Sitting in the back of the cab, Scott had been reflecting that his evening could hardly have gone any better.

'You've gone very quiet,' said Kate softly.

'Sorry,' he answered, turning to face her. 'I was just admiring it all,' He indicated the parkland gliding by the carriage window. 'It looks so lovely in the moonlight.'

'Oh dear, now I *am* going to have to be careful,' said Kate seriously.

'What do you mean?'

'I've found that when men start talking about the moonlight, it's time to be on your guard,' she answered with a grin.

'Madam,' said Scott in mock horror, 'you obviously haven't encountered the gentlemanly conduct for which Pennsylvania is renowned.'

'Is it?'

'Absolutely.'

'I must check it out with my uncle,' said Kate with a smile.

'Uncle Jack Geraghty, the Fearless Fireman?'

She looked at him in surprise. 'I only mentioned him in passing – you've a very good memory.'

'All part of the training – as a horse breeder you need to remember lineage.'

'Look,' said Kate pointing out the window. The carriage had started to swing around a tall column in the centre of the road, on top of which was a statue of a bird. 'The Phoenix monument – isn't he a queer looking creature?'

'Yes, but then wouldn't you be, if you had to spend your life rising from the ashes?'

'What a prospect.'

'Oh, I don't know, every job has its good points.'

Kate laughed. 'Tell me one thing that's good about being a Phoenix?'

'Well, you'd never be cold – think of all those flames.'

'98.6 is hot enough for me.'

'98.6? What's that?'

'Eh . . . the temperature of blood, body temperature.'

'How did you know that?' asked Scott.

'Oh, I was just talking to the vet last week. One of our cows had a fever, and we were talking about temperatures.'

'Ah.'

'We're just here,' said Kate brightly. 'You can drop me at the turn.'

'Oh, let me leave you right up.'

'No, please,' Kate replied softly. 'I don't want the staff knowing . . .'

'Oh . . . Oh yes, of course.' Scott stuck his head out the carriage window. 'Driver! Can you stop at the turn please?'

The cab slowed, then came to a halt.

Rising, Kate moved to the door. 'It's been a lovely evening, Bill. Thank you very much.'

'Hold on, Kate,' he said, as she turned the door handle. 'I . . . I'd really like to see you again. Could we . . . would you like to come out with me?'

'I don't have all that much time off.'

'You must have one night off?'

'Well, yes . . .'

'What about that then? We could go somewhere really nice.'

She paused a moment, then smiled. 'Why not? You can tell me more about gentlemanly Pennsylvania.'

'Great,' said Scott happily. 'What night then?'

'Perhaps next Saturday. I could be out by around eight.'

'Eight it is next Saturday. Will I meet you at the back entrance to the lodge?'

'No, not there. Down at the park wall would be better. You know the "Hole in the Wall"?'

'Yes.'

'Eight o'clock there. And now I must run. Goodnight, Bill.'

'Goodnight, Kate.' He opened the door, taking her arm as he helped her to alight.

'Straight home now,' she said with a laugh, then waved cheerily. 'Night . . .'

'Goodnight,' answered Scott. He waited at the carriage door, watching her retreat up the road.

123

'Where to, Sir?' asked the driver.

'Eh . . . Blind Lane, please.'

'Right ye be.'

Scott took one last look at the retreating figure, then entered the cab and leaned back contentedly as the carriage moved off through the moonlit park.

Twenty

'It was a shambles! A bloody shambles!' said Brady.

James Carey kept his patience. 'Let's be realistic, Joe,' he said. 'We never thought that killing Forster would be easy. We must expect some setbacks.'

'Setbacks?' Brady turned and spat venomously into the fire. The hissing noise produced was the only sound in the quiet of the upstairs lounge. He turned and faced the other committee members. 'Setbacks and wrong information seems to be all we're gettin'!'

'Now be reasonable, Joe,' said Carey. 'Our man in Dublin Castle got word Forster was leaving at three o'clock. He took a chance slipping out to notify me.'

'And *we* took a chance,' snapped Brady, 'hanging around with twelve-inch blades in our pockets for someone who never came!'

'I know . . .' started Carey, but Dan Curley held up his hand stopping him. Curley had recently been made chairman at Tynan's suggestion, replacing the acting chairman Ned McCaffrey, who, far from being offended, seemed relieved to cede the leadership to the popular Curley.

Curley now took control. 'Look, Joe,' he said sympathetically, 'all of us took a risk waiting for Forster. All of us were frustrated when he didn't show. And all of us would take the same risk again tomorrow if there was a real chance of getting Forster. But he's Chief Secretary, a busy man, he's going to chop and change his schedule. OK, we missed him yesterday; but we'll get him eventually – because we're committed to getting him. Right?'

Brady looked at him, then softened. 'Yeah, OK, Dan.'

'I'd like to say something,' interjected Tynan. Leaning forward, he removed his pince-nez, blinking eagerly at his listeners. 'Although yesterday's mission was ultimately abortive, I shall report – and report with pride, may I add –

that the Irish Invincibles responded with enthusiasm and alacrity when yesterday's opportunity to execute the tyrant Forster arose.'

Christ Almighty, thought Brady, how did we get saddled with this clown? A bloody dreamer, as much in love with his own voice as with the fight for independence.

'A truly admirable body of patriots,' added Tynan.

'Thank you, Mr Tynan, we appreciate that,' said Curley with diplomacy, 'and now we'd better move on to the next item of business – our would-be recruit, Bill Ryan. Jim has been making the enquiries so I'll let him tell it.'

Carey straightened up importantly, then withdrew an envelope from his pocket. 'As you know,' he said, 'I've been asking questions about Mr Ryan with our contacts in Pennsylvania. This is the reply, it arrived today.'

'Isn't that rather risky?' asked Tynan. 'As a known nationalist your mail could be intercepted.'

'Indeed, Mr Tynan,' said Carey with a smile. 'Which is why it was sent to a Box Number, under a false name.'

'Ah, you've been appropriately pre-emptive. I do beg your pardon, Sir.'

'Not at all.'

'Well, don't keep us in suspense, Jim,' said Ned McCaffrey. 'What do they say about Ryan?'

'Absolutely nothing,' replied Carey, 'they've never heard of him.'

'Is that in Pittsburgh or Pennsylvania generally?' asked Curley.

'I wrote to Danny O'Sullivan in Pittsburgh,' answered Carey, and he wasn't known at all there.'

'That's not surprising,' cut in Brady, 'he lived in Philadelphia.'

'True,' said Carey. 'Danny is checking there, but so far he hasn't been able to turn up anything.'

'So where does that leave us?' asked McCaffrey.

'It seems to me,' said Tynan, 'that it does little to hasten a resolution one way or another.'

'Odd though that no one in the Irish community has even heard of him,' mused Curley.

'Well I wonder is it?' said Carey. 'After all, Philadelphia is a big place, and he did say that he'd had no contact with any political groups.'

'We don't want to lose a good man just because he wasn't involved with the cause before,' said Brady.

'Good point, Joe,' said Carey, 'and we know from the fight that Ryan has guts. If we succeed in killing Forster it'll be that much harder to get the Viceroy and our other targets. We may be glad to have someone like Bill Ryan in our ranks.'

'Indeed we may,' agreed Tynan, 'and I do bear in mind the value attached to the potential uses of a stud farm. On the other hand, we mustn't risk exposing our plans too hastily to someone of unproven pedigree.'

'What about this girl we lined up?' asked McCaffrey.

'Ryan left her home from the dance we went to,' said Brady. Tynan nodded approvingly. 'Excellent. Good work, Joe.'

'She'll be reporting to me on Wednesday,' said Carey, eager to re-establish his role as Kate's controller. 'I'm expecting her to supply a good deal of background information on Mr Ryan; then we can check if it matches everything he told us in the pub, and see if he's telling the truth.'

'Or perhaps lying consistently,' suggested Tynan.

'If he's lying we'll catch him out,' said Carey. 'I'll get Kate to encourage his affections, get him to reveal more about himself.'

'Supposin' she can't?' asked McCaffrey.

Carey smiled. 'You've never seen her, Ned.'

'No.'

'Believe me,' said Carey, 'if she leads him on, he'll be happy to follow.'

'Between that and her position in the lodge, she sounds like an excellent acquisition,' said Tynan.

'Thank you,' said Carey. 'If I say so myself, I think we struck gold when Miss Lannigan looked me up.'

'When did she say Forster and Burke are goin' to the polo?' asked Brady.

'April the tenth, next Monday.' Carey looked meaningfully at Brady. 'That's assuming Burke keeps to his diary entry.'

'Let's get the bastards then, and no mistakes this time,' said Brady.

'We could do it in the road leading to the polo grounds,' suggested Curley.

'No,' said Brady. 'Let's get them comin' out of Dublin Castle, show them we can strike right on their own doorstep.'

Tynan nodded sagely. 'Hmm . . . I think Joe may have a point. An execution within sight of the seat of British control, it has a certain poetic quality.'

'The carriage will slow down just as they come to Lord Edward Street,' said Brady, 'that would be the place to strike.'

Curley nodded in agreement. 'That's fine by me, if you approve, Mr Tynan.'

'I'm happy to say I agree wholeheartedly,' answered Tynan.

'Right,' said Curley, 'Monday it is. I'll notify the men, and issue the weapons.'

Twenty-One

Warmed by the evening sun, droves of ragged children scampered in play, their screams and cries unheeded by Joe Brady as he walked through the city slums. Warm weather always heightened what he thought of as the smell of poverty – a sickly combination of the odour of unwashed bodies and that of urine and excrement from the tenement hallways.

With as many as seventy desperately poor people crammed into each house, and all sharing a single tap and outside toilet, it was hard to blame them for their poor hygiene, and yet, in spite of himself, Brady couldn't deny his sense of distaste. He knew he was more fortunate than many with his regular wage as a tradesman, and his resultant ability to buy decent clothes and have them laundered when necessary, yet the anger he felt at the social system which kept so many in misery was extended to the victims too. Despite his sympathy with their plight, part of him also held a degree of contempt for the poor, particularly their resigned acceptance of their wretched lot. He had come to think of shabby clothes and stale-smelling bodies as the mark of the oppressed, and as a free man he took a pride in his clean appearance. Although no one would have dared to say a word to his face, he knew that some of the neighbours smirked as he carried his change of clothes when going to take his Saturday bath.

Let them smirk, he thought, as he now left the alleyways and approached the redbrick bath-house, the same smirkers were the ones who would always be downtrodden losers. He entered the cavernous doorway of the baths, paid the twopence entry fee, then collected his towel and climbed the stairs to a vacant cubicle. He undressed as the bath filled up, then stepped in and soaped himself all over, the dust from the day's paving floating away as he washed in the sud-filled water. He lay back in the bath, enjoying its warmth. This was a time to savour, when he could relax and think things out, free from the endless noisy squabbling of his brothers and sisters at home.

He reflected on the Invincibles and their failure to kill Forster, his frustration eased by the thought that on Monday that would all be put right. Thanks to Kate Lannigan's information they would get the bastard then, right in front of Dublin Castle. It was a deeply satisfying thought that he, Joe Brady, was the one who would do the actual deed. For years to come he would be remembered as the man who killed the tyrant Forster. No more would he be a mere stone mason, but a hero like Robert Emmet or Wolfe Tone.

Of course killing Forster was just the start. Winning freedom from the British would be no easy task, but the Invincibles had the stomach for the fight, and when they showed what could be done by wiping out people like the Viceroy and Chief Secretary, more Irish men would swell their ranks.

The notion of new members made him think of Bill Ryan, and once again he felt impatient with Carey's approach. Weeks had passed and nothing useful had come of the enquiries to America. How long were they going to wait? For, despite a slight touch of jealousy regarding Bill's good fortune in being set up with Kate Lannigan, he liked the American's direct, action-seeking style, and wanted him in the group.

He did recognise that they had to exercise some caution, however, and now he tried to weigh up the situation and work out how he would handle it if he were in charge. He had been mulling it over for several minutes when suddenly the answer came to him. Pleased with his flash of insight, he stood up in the bath, the water cascading from his powerful body.

Yes, he thought, towelling himself vigorously, on Monday they would get Forster; and then they'd settle the Bill Ryan question. It was going to be a good week.

Twenty-Two

Filled with a sense of anticipation, Kate sat before the mirror carefully brushing her hair. Her eagerness was fuelled as much by the prospect of meeting Bill Ryan again tonight, as by her mission of checking him out for Carey. James Carey – what an irritating man he could be. When she had reported to him after meeting Bill at the dance, Carey had been pleased. Pleased, but evasive regarding Kate's questions about why Bill should be checked out. When pressed, the most he would say was that Bill Ryan could be an important supporter of the Invincibles, but that it was essential that they know more about him.

The one point about which Carey had been emphatic was that Kate should be careful not to give any hint that her role in the Under Secretary's Lodge was anything but authentic. She thought of her slip into nursing terminology when she had spoken to Bill of 98.6 being body temperature. No need for Carey to know that of course, but she would have to be careful tonight not to make any more such errors.

She laid down her brush and dabbed perfume on her wrists and behind her ears. Appraising herself carefully in the mirror, she noted with satisfaction how the green of her good velvet suit set off the auburn of her hair. Suddenly she smiled in recognition of her vanity, winked playfully at herself in the mirror, and rose.

She crossed the room, locked her door behind her and quickly descended the service staircase to the hall. Leaving the house by the back door, she walked towards the tradesman's entrance, aware of the soldiers' glances from their hut inside the boundary wall.

It was a lovely warm April evening, and as she headed to her rendezvous with Bill she felt a sense of elation. He was, undoubtedly, the most handsome man with whom she had yet walked out. There was something about his dark brown eyes, especially when he smiled, which suggested an attractive, but partially hidden, warmth of personality. She wondered what the night might reveal about him, and, looking forward to her assignation, continued happily through the sunlit park.

Scott stepped forward as Kate approached the Hole in the Wall. 'Miss Lannigan,' he called, bowing in mock gallant fashion.

Kate smiled. 'Hello, Bill.'

'I'm sure glad you could make it,' Scott said warmly.

'I nearly didn't.'

'Oh?'

'We're calving at the moment so I'm really needed, but my boss – Mr McDaid – let me off.'

'I'm glad,' said Scott.

'I am too,' answered Kate, 'but he's really nice and I don't want to take advantage of him. Would you mind very much if we didn't go into town? I want to be able to get back reasonably early.'

'OK.'

'Do you like walking?' she asked.

'Sure I do.'

'We could walk out to the Strawberry Beds if you liked?'

'The Strawberry Beds?'

'It's just on the other side of the park, by the banks of the Liffey. There're tea-rooms there and it's a lovely walk.'

'You've just sold me,' said Scott with a smile. 'Let's walk to the Strawberry Beds.'

He moved to the outside of the footpath, and they strolled along the tree-lined road.

'So you're delivering calves at the moment,' said Scott.

'Yes, it's a bit hectic.'

'And what's life in the Under Secretary's Lodge normally like?'

'Oh, good and bad I suppose . . .'

'I'm intrigued,' said Scott, 'what's good and what's bad about it?'

'Well, working with the animals, an open-air life, watching the sun rise over the pastures, having a nice boss like Mr McDaid – they're all really good.'

'And the bad?'

Kate grimaced. 'The worse thing is the house steward, Mr Hackett.'

Scott's eyebrows rose in interest. 'What's he done?'

'I'll tell you about him again. It's too nice an evening to be spoiled by him. Besides,' she added with a smile, 'I'd much rather hear all about Pennsylvania. By the time we reach the Strawberry Beds, I'll expect you to have me an expert!'

Sitting at a table in the Liffey Tea Rooms, Kate gazed out the window at the river's placid waters, darkening now in the blue light of dusk.

She had been relieved to discover that the easy rapport she had felt with Bill at the dance had been swiftly re-established this evening, and as she turned to look at him now, standing over at the counter ordering tea and scones, she felt a sudden dart of guilt. It seemed mean-spirited somehow to be asking questions with a view to reporting the answers back to Carey, yet it had to be done.

'Right, that's settled,' said Scott, returning to the table and sitting.

'You were telling me about the canal boats,' said Kate.

'Yeah, so I was, but the thought struck me – all the way here I've been going on about Pennsylvania.'

'That's OK, I'm really interested in America.'

'Do you know what day it is tomorrow then?'

Kate looked slightly puzzled. 'Tomorrow? Well, it's Easter Sunday . . .'

'And also April the eighth,' said Scott, 'the last day of the American Civil War. Lee surrendered to Grant on April the ninth in 1865.' He laughed. 'You did say you were interested in America . . .'

'Well perhaps not *quite* to that extent,' said Kate with a smile.

They were interrupted by the waitress arriving with the tea and scones. Placing them on the table, the woman nodded pleasantly before returning to the kitchen.

'To tell you the truth I wouldn't have remembered the date

myself,' continued Scott, 'but I was looking through a book of famous dates before I came out.'

'You seem to have books on everything.'

'Well I like to read up on stuff. This book was fascinating – there's hardly a day of the year when something interesting didn't happen.'

'Tell me another one so.'

'Well, let's see,' said Scott with a smile. 'You want a really vital piece of information?'

'Absolutely.'

'OK. On April the twelfth – next Tuesday – in 1858, Big Ben was cast.'

'That's pretty vital,' said Kate with a laugh. 'I must tell that to Mr McDaid. He'll be very impressed.'

'He's your boss – the one you like?'

'Yes, he's a lovely man.'

'So tell me about the other guy, the house steward you don't like.'

'Oh, don't remind me of him.'

'Now you've really whetted my curiosity. Come on,' said Scott, 'I've been telling you all about my background. Tell me about this guy.'

Kate sipped her tea, thinking how she would tell the story, then put her cup down. 'Well,' she said, 'as house steward he's in charge of the servants, and when I started about a month ago he used to come down to the dairy when Mr McDaid wasn't about . . .'

'And?'

Kate grimaced. 'He was always making double-meaning remarks, brushing up against me, saying we'd have to get to know each other better.'

'I think I know the type.'

'Anyway I tried to stay pleasant, but keep him at arm's length. It worked for a couple of weeks, then he got more insistent. One day when Mr McDaid was away he came to the dairy.' Kate shrugged. 'This time he wouldn't take no for an answer.'

Scott looked at her concernedly. 'What happened?'

'He grabbed my shoulders and kissed me. When I tried to

pull away he twisted my arm. It really hurt, so after a while I relaxed and let him kiss me; then when he eased off my arm I grabbed a pail of milk and emptied it all over him.'

'Good for you!'

'While he was coughing and spluttering I got a pitchfork, and I told him if he took a step towards me I'd use it. I was roaring angry and he looked at my face, looked at the pitchfork, and backed off a bit.'

Scott nodded approvingly. 'I'll bet he did.'

'He tried a different tack then,' continued Kate, 'said he'd have me sacked if that was my attitude. I'd been expecting something like this for a couple of weeks, so I had an answer ready for him.'

'Which was?'

'That if I was dismissed I'd write to Mr Burke himself, telling him what was happening in his house; that I'd also write to the newspapers; and that I'd ask my parish priest to intervene in the matter.'

Scott laughed in admiration. 'Ten marks out of ten, Kate.'

'Well, I decided that a fuss like that might be Hackett's big fear.'

'So he backed down?'

'He's never bothered me since, but I've made a real enemy there. If I make the slightest wrong move I know he'll be down on me like a ton of bricks.'

'Maybe, but I reckon you handled yourself pretty well. You're very independent.'

Kate looked at him questioningly. 'Do you mean for a servant?'

'No, not at all. There's many a high-born lady wouldn't have shown such fighting spirit. It was a genuine compliment, I admire your bravery.'

'Thanks, Bill,' said Kate softly, touched by his earnestness. After a moment she looked at him playfully. 'I suppose then that the girls in Philadelphia are all timid, obedient creatures?'

'I wouldn't go so far as to say that . . .'

'Oh? You've known a few who weren't?'

'Well, let's say I haven't met many with your particular style,' said Scott lightly.

'It must be my fiery Irish blood.'

'Really?' He raised his eyebrows. 'I'd like to see more of this fiery side of your nature . . .'

Kate laughed. 'Now you're starting to sound like Mr Hackett.'

'God forbid; I don't want a pitchfork in my chest!'

'Then I suggest you behave yourself,' she said with a laugh, 'and eat up your scone.'

The warm night air was scented with hawthorn as Kate and Scott walked back through the darkened Phoenix Park. They strolled arm in arm now, and were comfortable enough together to enjoy a companionable silence.

The evening had gone as well as Kate could possibly have hoped, the only problem having been her distaste for the deception required of her, and so, after her probing about Pennsylvania, she had decided to relax and simply enjoy Bill's company.

She had described some of the concerts she had attended with Aunt Julia, and it had turned out that Bill too was a music lover. He had enthralled her with descriptions of Gilbert and Sullivan productions he had seen in New York. It almost seemed to her too good to be true – a handsome, well-read, music-loving man who was both good fun and considerate, keeping company with an apparent dairy maid.

She knew of course that while such an arrangement would be most unlikely in European society, things were ordered differently in America. There, an ordinary man could presumably make his fortune, develop cultivated tastes, yet not be hidebound by social convention.

The importance attached to social status reminded her of Lord Masefield and her eviction, and as usual the thought fortified her conviction that what she was doing for the Invincibles was necessary. If only, she thought, her meeting with Bill had no connection with such matters.

'Penny for your thoughts,' he said.

'Oh, just . . . thinking of the calving.'

'The calving – that's pretty romantic,' said Scott jokingly.

Kate indicated the nearby Under Secretary's Lodge. 'It was

seeing the lights at the gate,' she explained. 'Back to reality . . .'

'I know what you mean. It's . . . it's been a lovely evening Kate.'

'It has; so let's end it here. I don't want any nosey parkers at the gate looking to see who I'm with.'

'OK,' said Scott, stopping and turning to face her. 'I'll see you again?' he said softly.

'Yes.'

'When?'

'I'm off all day next Saturday.'

'Let's spend it together then.'

'OK. We could have a picnic if you like.'

'I like very much,' he said with a smile.

'Don't expect anything too fancy. I haven't really got much access to the kitchen.'

'Well . . . look, why don't I do it?'

'You?'

'Yeah. I could make an American picnic.'

'What's that?'

'Ah, that would be telling. Suffice to say I'm a fairly dab hand at outdoor eating.'

Kate laughed. 'You're a bundle of surprises, aren't you?'

'Renowned for it.'

'Well, if you're sure.'

'Consider it done. One American picnic, next Saturday . . .'

'Weather providing.'

'Sure. The Hole in the Wall again?'

'Yes,' answered Kate, 'about ten.'

'Great.'

'Well, goodnight, Bill, and thanks for a lovely evening.'

'Kate?'

'Yes?'

'I have to . . .'

He leaned forward and softly placed his hand on her shoulder, then bent and kissed her. She had hoped he would and now she gently touched his cheek and kissed him in return. After a moment they parted.

'Goodnight, Bill.'

'Night, Kate.'

Twenty-Three

Brady stood at the corner of Parliament Street, his pulse starting to race now that the moment was nigh. All the years of smouldering resentment against the system, all the weeks of frustration and inactivity with the Invincibles, all would soon be swept away, for in two minutes time, at eleven thirty, Forster and Burke were due to leave Dublin Castle for the polo grounds.

William Edward Forster, the scourge of nationalists, the tyrant of the tenant farmers, would be getting his desserts when he, Joe Brady, killed the most powerful and hated man in Ireland. The thought sent his adrenaline pumping, and he fingered the concealed, twelve-inch surgical knife in anticipation.

Across the street he could see Tim Kelly, apparently enjoying a conversation in the weak April sunshine with Ned McCaffrey, and over at the corner in line with the Castle gate, Dan Curley sat on a street bench reading a newspaper.

Tynan had worked it all out. When the carriage emerged from the Castle, Dan Curley would identify the occupants, and, assuming that Burke and Forster were in the carriage, Curley would fold his newspaper. This would alert the assembled Invincibles, and at a signal from Tynan they would strike.

Tynan had decided on a moderately large group, partly due to a recent tightening in Forster's security, and partly due to the proximity of the soldiers on guard duty at the Castle gate.

From the shop window into which he pretended to be looking, Brady could see the rest of the group: Carey strolling down the far side of Lord Edward Street, Tynan approaching on the near side, and four volunteers, Delaney, Fagan, Hanlon and Kavanagh posing as workmen at a manhole.

Much as Brady despised Tynan as a talker, rather than a doer, he had to admit that the planning was good. When the carriage stopped at the junction with Lord Edward Street they would don face-masks and move in. He, Brady, had been given Forster as his target, and Burke was allocated to Tim Kelly. Surprise would be important, and they were counting on the fact that the last place in the world where the British would be expecting an attack would be outside Dublin Castle.

Once the carriage halted, the manhole volunteers would engage the coachman and footmen, and the armed detective who sat in the front. Dan Curley would tackle the policeman at the rear, and he and Kelly would deal with the two targets. With luck it should all be over in twenty seconds, after which they would disperse by pre-arranged routes.

Brady glanced across the street at Curley, but he still sat reading the paper. Come on, thought Brady, his watch now reading eleven thirty-one. *Come on*! This was the worst part, not knowing whether in thirty seconds time he would have committed the execution of the century or whether this might just be another false alarm. He hoped that Kate Lannigan's information was accurate, and that Forster would adhere to his appointment; after four months the Invincibles needed to stop talking and actually achieve something.

Moving to another section of the shop window, he reflected on how time passed with agonising slowness at a moment like this. He looked at bridles, bits and stirrups, and although he tried to appear interested in the shining brass and polished leather of the harnesses, he was already beginning to feel conspicuous. Suddenly he caught a movement from Curley's bench. Turning around carefully, Brady could see Curley looking towards the Castle, then after a moment the sound of horses' hooves came clattering from the cobblestones.

Brady felt his heart start to pound. He watched Curley intently as the sound of the hooves increased. Suddenly Curley lowered the newspaper and folded it. Christ!, thought Brady exultantly, it was them!

He nodded to Tim Kelly, then started up the pavement towards Tynan, his hand firmly clutching the knife. The carriage was beginning to slow as it came to the junction. The volunteers at the manhole started to climb out, and Brady was about to step into the street when Tynan whispered hoarsely: 'Hold on!'

'What?'

'Hold on, Joe!' Tynan called to Kelly also. 'Wait, Tim, wait!'

'What the hell . . .' started Brady as Tynan pulled him up onto the pavement beside Kelly and McCaffrey. Brady could see the carriage was now stationary, then he turned angrily to Tynan who was looking at the vehicle despairingly.

'It's off, we can't do it!' said Tynan.

'You're crazy,' snapped Brady, 'it's them! Come on!'

'We can't do it,' whispered Tynan desperately, 'there're women in the carriage.'

'So what?' snarled Brady, 'we won't kill them!'

The carriage was about to pull out into Lord Edward Street, and Brady could see the assembled Invincibles waiting on Tynan's signal. He gripped the older man by the arm. 'For Christ's sake give the signal before they're gone!'

Tynan turned on him, eyes blazing. 'No damn it, no! It's off – off!'

Just then the carriage swung round and moved briskly up Lord Edward Street past the bemused Carey and the Invincibles at the manhole. In fury Brady tightened his grip on Tynan's arm. 'You lily-livered bastard – we could have had them!'

'You'll take your orders like any soldier, Mr Brady; now be good enough to remove your hand from my arm,' answered Tynan angrily.

Brady looked defiantly at him without releasing his grip.

'What the hell happened?' asked Curley breathlessly as he approached them on the pavement.

Brady released his grip and looked at Tynan with contempt. 'He let them go.'

'There were women in the carriage – we're not at war with them,' snapped Tynan. 'Now split up, we're causing a spectacle here.'

'Split up, my arse,' snapped Brady, 'I want this discussed.'

'Take it easy, Joe,' said Curley. 'Look, why don't we meet in an hour in Carey's yard? We can talk safely there.'

'Right,' said Tynan, 'pass on the word, then split up. And quickly,' he added, looking at Brady. 'That's an order.' Turning on his heel, he walked away towards the quays.

'Bastard,' said Brady.

'What's going on?' asked Carey as he joined them.

'He called it off,' said Brady bitterly, indicating the retreating Tynan.

'Why?'

'The king of the fuckin' talkers couldn't offend the women in the carriage.'

'Damn it!' muttered Carey.

'We're all to split up now,' said Curley, 'and meet in your timber yard in an hour's time.'

'In my yard – what for?'

'To do the only thing the Invincibles ever do,' said Brady with venom. 'To talk . . .' Turning suddenly, he strode off, his anger and frustration unabated as he walked away down Dame Street.

Warmed by the mid-day sun, a pleasant smell of wood enveloped Carey's timber yard.

'Very well,' said Dan Curley, 'now that we're all here, Mr Tynan wants to say something about this morning.'

Tynan paused dramatically, looking from one man to the next before speaking. 'You've all – each and every one of you – worked hard, made sacrifices and taken risks. This morning's execution of the tyrants Forster and Burke should have been the culmination of all those efforts. There's no doubt that we could have succeeded today, and I know some of you may be angry that we didn't.'

'That's putting it mildly . . .' started Brady.

'No please, Joe, allow me to elucidate.'

'What?'

'If you'd be kind enough to allow me to explain my reasons for aborting our plan,' said Tynan.

'We're listenin',' answered Brady.

'The Irish Invincibles are at war with the British Crown,' continued Tynan. 'It's a war of independence, and our enemies are the British authorities in Ireland, and those who work for, and collaborate with them. But, Gentlemen, we are not, and never shall be at war with women and children, even the wife and child of a villain like Forster.'

'We didn't have to kill *them*,' said Curley.

'No, perhaps we could have stabbed their husband and father to death without injuring them,' answered Tynan. 'Perhaps in the mêlée with footmen and the police they'd only have been blood-splattered. But, Gentlemen, that is not how the Invincibles will operate. When we go down in history – as we most certainly will – the blows we've struck must not be tainted. Our supporters and sympathisers, here and in America, will rejoice when we fell the tyrants, but it will be clean blows, delivered man to man. No matter how long it takes, now matter how frustrating, we shall have the self-discipline of soldiers and we shall only attack the enemy when it is honourable to do so.' He paused and looked around the group. 'I take it that is clearly understood and accepted?'

There were nods of assent.

'Joe?'

Brady didn't answer immediately, then he too nodded. 'Yeah, alright.'

'Good. No hard feelings about this morning then – words spoken in passion and so on,' said Tynan conciliatorily.

'OK,' answered Brady.

'Fine, fine.'

'By the way,' interjected Carey, 'Kate Lannigan reported to me last night.'

'Well?' asked McCaffrey.

Carey smiled. 'It seems her date with Bill Ryan went well.'

'And what he told us?' asked Curley. 'Did it tie in with what he told Kate?'

Carey paused briefly, savouring their expectancy.

'Yes,' he answered, 'nothing he told Kate contradicted his story to us.'

'Which still proves nothing, mind,' said Tynan.

'Indeed,' answered Carey. 'However, I've instructed Kate to encourage the courtship. They're meeting next Saturday and she'll delve further into his background.'

'It's a very slow way of finding out about him,' said Curley.

Carey shrugged. 'Well, Danny O'Sullivan hasn't come back yet with further information from Philadelphia, I'm afraid it's the best we can do.'

'I don't think so,' said Brady.

'Sorry?'

'I said I don't think it's the best we can do, Mr Carey.'

'Have you a better idea?'

'Yeah, I was thinking about it.'

'Indeed?'

Brady ignored the sarcasm. 'There is a way that could show if Bill Ryan's genuine.'

'What's that, Joe?' asked McCaffrey.

'Well, me and Tim Kelly were going to do the ferry job . . .'

'So?'

'Supposing we offered Tim's place to Bill Ryan?' suggested Brady.

'That's putting you at risk if Ryan *isn't* genuine,' said Curley.

Brady shrugged. 'I'll chance that. It would give us a good idea of what Ryan is really made of.'

'I'll be seeing Kate at nine o'clock next Sunday morning,' said Carey, 'she's to report to me on her Saturday date with Ryan. We should at least wait and see if she comes up with anything.'

'We were thinkin' of doin' the job on Sunday,' said Brady. 'If she finds out nothing definite, I could call for Ryan and spring it on him. What do you think, Mr Tynan?'

Tynan removed his pince-nez and fingered it absent-mindedly. 'We'd be revealing ourselves to a certain extent and that's a risk; on the other hand, any new volunteer is a risk, and as you say, the assignment would show us what sort Ryan really is.' He looked thoughtfully into the distance.

'Well?' asked Brady impatiently.

'You really are eager for action, Joe, aren't you?'

'Yes.'

'As you wish then,' said Tynan. 'You may wait in the park on Sunday morning, and if Mr Carey's young lady hasn't uncovered anything, call straight away on Mr Ryan. All agreed?'

'Agreed,' they answered.

'Good luck then, Joe – and be careful,' said Tynan.

'Right. Eh, there is one thing,' added Brady. 'If he takes on the job, that suggests he's genuine – but what if he doesn't?'

'In that case,' replied Tynan carefully, 'we may well have to . . . *curtail* Mr Ryan's stay in Dublin . . .'

Twenty-Four

Scott lay contentedly on the rug, his closed eyes soothed by the heat of the sun. The warm breeze carried the scent of gorse and the only sound in the glade was the occasional trill of birdsong.

It was, he reflected, quite idyllic, as indeed had been the whole day so far. With the sun shining in a clear blue sky, Kate had suggested that they have their picnic on the peninsula of Howth, eight miles north-east of Dublin, and in high good humour they had taken the train, Kate pointing out views and places of interest along the way.

As their carriage skirted the sparkling sea on the approach to the fishing village of Howth, Scott had realised that Kate's descriptions of the peninsula's beauty were well founded. Across the channel from the harbour mouth lay the picturesque island of Ireland's Eye, its vivid green slopes in contrast with the blue of the sea, and forming a backdrop to the village itself were hills and peaks ablaze with heather and gorse.

They had taken a pony and trap up the steep incline out of the village and towards the summit, then proceeded on foot into the woods at the base of one of the peaks. Their leisurely wanderings had brought them to a small glade, its carpet of grass adorned by a profusion of bluebells.

Laying down the rug, Kate had proclaimed that this would be the site of their picnic. She had also said that as Bill had prepared the food, she would serve it up, and as she had undone the strap of the large picnic basket to lay out its contents, Scott had lain back, eyes closed and blissfully at one with the pastoral surroundings. He had relaxed almost to the point of dozing when a mocking cry sounded in his ear.

'Mr Van Winkle!'

Slowly he opened his eyes.

'Are you quite refreshed?'

'Yes, I think so,' he answered with a smile as he sat up.

'I'd hate to feel I was disturbing you,' said Kate.

'Quite right, a growing lad needs his rest!'

She smiled. 'It's a bit early for lunch, but I thought I'd set the places. You're supposed to admire my efforts.'

Scott took in the neatly laid out cups, plates, and utensils. Kate had also brought crisp linen napkins and a small vase which was now filled with wild bluebells. 'Highly civilised,' he said smilingly.

'Oh well, your American picnics are very grand, what with clams and crab and God knows what; I wouldn't like to let our side down,' answered Kate cheekily.

'I think, Madam,' said Scott with mock formality, 'that your preparations have been admirable.'

'Have yours?'

'*My* preparations?'

'Yes; have you checked your book to see what they were doing in China on this day three hundred and seven years ago?'

'Oh, my book of dates! Well as a matter of fact I did consult it . . .'

'And?'

'Well I'm sure you know this already, but next Tuesday, April the 17th, in 1839, the Republic of Guatemala was founded . . .'

'Yes I knew that,' answered Kate with a straight face.

'And April 16th, 1521?'

'Eh, that's tomorrow . . . let me see now . . . tomorrow three hundred and sixty-one years ago . . . No, no it was on the tip of my tongue but it's gone.'

'Martin Luther arrived at the Council of the Diet of Worms.'

'How could I have forgotten?' asked Kate, then burst out laughing.

She really is beautiful when she laughs, thought Scott.

'God,' she continued, unaware of his admiring stare, 'I know who I'd like to put on a diet of worms.'

'Who?'

'Mr Drooling Mouth Hackett – who else?'

'Is he still bothering you?'

146

Kate grimaced. 'Ah, nothing in particular. He just bothers me, being around. Always gaping, you know.'

'Why do you stick it? You're a very intelligent girl, Kate, I'm sure you could find other employment.'

'It's OK for the moment, and apart from Hackett I do enjoy the work.'

'I'm not suggesting there's anything wrong with being a dairy maid, it's just that . . . well, you could achieve more, a lot more.'

'You think so?'

'Definitely. Maybe . . . maybe I could help . . .'

She looked at him warmly for a moment, then laid a hand on his arm. 'Bill, you really are a nice man, it's good of you to be concerned . . .'

'Not at all . . .'

'Yes, it is, but listen,' said Kate seriously. 'Can you keep a secret?'

'Sure I can.'

'Well . . . the truth is, Bill, I'm not really a dairy maid.'

'You're not?'

'Well I mean, I am in so much as I'm working as one, but that's not really what I am . . .'

Scott looked at her enquiringly. 'What are you really?'

She paused briefly. 'I'm a nurse.'

'A nurse? Well, I reckon you'd be a pretty good one.' Suddenly he pointed at her in mock accusation. 'The other night – 98.6; that's how you knew about temperatures!'

Kate nodded sheepishly.

'But why give up nursing to work in a dairy, and why hide the fact?'

'I was working in the hospital in Enniscorthy, but then my family gave up our home in Wexford to go to America. I didn't want to leave Ireland yet, so I came up to see what Dublin was like. In July I'm hoping to be able to get a nursing job here. The reason I've kept it quiet is because I wouldn't have got the job in the dairy if they'd known I planned to leave.'

'No, I guess not. And don't you miss your family?'

'Yes, but it's not forever. I'll be qualified in one more year. I can join them then if I want.'

'I see,' said Scott, looking at her with curiosity. What other secrets, he wondered, did this intriguing girl have. His own need to deceive her was something he had regretted, and it had made him feel guilty, despite the fact that deceit was essential in his job of preventing murder. Now he told himself that perhaps secrets were held in all relationships. Certainly the more Kate revealed of herself, the more he wanted to know – like how, for instance, had she got the scar on her temple. Could she possibly have been beaten by her family? Could that be the real reason why she had stayed behind when they emigrated?

'You won't tell anyone, Bill?'

'What? No, no of course not.'

'I haven't told anyone else.'

'Don't worry,' he replied, returning to a lighter tone, 'I shall take your secret to the grave!'

Kate smiled, then looked him in the eye. 'Now it's your turn,' she said softly.

'My turn?'

'I told you a secret. Fair's fair, now you've to tell me one.'

'A secret?' he answered, playing for time. *I'm a British officer spying in Ireland.*

'Well?' asked Kate.

Scott shrugged. 'I'm not sure if I really have any.'

'Bill Ryan, you're a fibber!' laughed Kate. 'Everyone has secrets, and you owe me one.'

'Alright, let's see . . .' *Always keep your lies as near as possible to the truth*, that's what they had constantly stressed in training. 'Well,' he started, then paused. 'I've never told this to anyone else, Kate, but . . . well for years I resented my father's preference for my older brother over me . . .'

'I thought you'd no brothers or sisters.'

'I haven't now,' answered Scott, improvising, 'my brother was killed in the civil war – he died at Gettysburg.'

'Oh I'm sorry, Bill.'

'It's OK.'

'What was his name?'

Scott thought of his real brother, Graham. 'Eh, Connor,' he answered, 'Connor Patrick Ryan.'

'Were you close?'

'No, not really. He was seven years older than me. My father always . . .' He paused.

'Go on . . . please . . .'

'Everything my brother did seemed to be right in my father's eyes,' said Scott, realising even as he said it that he was telling his own childhood story. 'I always . . . I always seemed to have to prove myself. To be a better horseman – because Connor was at my age; to be a better student, a faster swimmer, a braver sportsman. I've never said any of this before, but looking back I seem to have spent half my life proving something about myself to my family.'

'Poor Bill,' said Kate softly. She laid her hand on his arm, then smiled gently at him. 'You'll never have to prove yourself to me.'

'No?'

'No.'

He looked at her smiling face, framed by the flowing auburn hair glowing in the sunlight. 'Kate . . .'

'Mmm?'

'You take my breath away . . .'

They looked at each other a moment, then kissed, tenderly at first, then more passionately. Scott ran his hand gently down her cheek. 'I think you must be the loveliest girl I've ever known.'

Kate locked her arms around his neck as they sank onto the rug. 'Don't tell me, Bill,' she whispered, 'show me . . .'

Twenty-Five

A startling series of knocks sounded on the front door as Scott finished a leisurely Sunday breakfast. He wondered who on earth could be calling at half past eight, then, laying down his teacup on the kitchen table, he moved cautiously to the parlour window, and standing to one side, glanced through the net curtains. Immediately he recognised the bulky figure of Joe Brady.

Scott felt a quickening in his pulse; Brady would hardly be making a social call at half past eight on a blustery Sunday morning. Something must be on, he thought excitedly, perhaps they were finally going to involve him in some action. Moving to the door, he resolved to be ready for anything. He mustn't hesitate, whatever might be sprung upon him.

'Joe,' he cried, opening the hall door. 'This is a surprise!'

'Hello, Bill,' answered Brady, 'can I talk to you a minute?'

'Sure, step on in. I was just finishing breakfast. Can I fix you something?'

'No thanks.'

'Are you sure? I'm having a cup of tea myself . . .'

'I thought you Yanks only drank coffee,' said Brady, stooping to enter the sunlit kitchen.

'I guess I've been civilised since I came here,' answered Scott with a laugh. 'Are you sure you won't join me?'

'Sure thanks, but you go ahead . . .'

'Right, take a seat then,' said Scott, regaining his own chair.

Brady sat, looking at Scott for a moment without speaking.

'That's a change from yesterday, chilly despite the sun . . .' said Scott, uneasy at the intensity of Brady's stare.

'Bill,' said Brady softly, 'the time has come . . .'

Lowering the teacup, Scott looked at him quizzically. 'How do you mean, Joe?'

'You said you wanted to be involved in the cause of nationalism, right?'

'Sure.'

'You still feel that way?'

'Of course.'

'I'm talking about *action*, not talking.'

'The way I see it, Joe, there's been too much talking. I want to join the men of action.'

'Have you ever killed a man?'

Scott paused a moment, then looked Brady in the eye. 'Not yet, Joe.'

'But you would?'

'Yes.'

'I'm on a mission today,' said Brady simply. 'Will you help me kill an enemy?'

Scott felt his heart begin to pound. 'Sure, Joe,' he answered, trying to keep the excitement out of his voice, 'who is he?'

'His name isn't important. He's an enemy of Ireland.'

'Fair enough . . .'

'You're in then?'

'All the way,' said Scott with conviction.

'Good man. I'll give you the details when we get there. No point havin' sweaty palms before the time,' said Brady with a wry grin.

'When are we doing it?'

'As soon as you're finished here.'

'I'm through with breakfast. Just give me five minutes to shave.'

'Unshaven's better – and dress in old clothes. Have you a cap and muffler?'

'Well, no, actually . . .'

'OK, you can borrow these,' said Brady, withdrawing a cloth cap and well-worn muffler from his overcoat pocket.

'Thanks. I'll change into older clothes then,' said Scott, heading for the bedroom.

'Right, and don't be long, Bill, we've a tram to catch.'

'OK.'

Closing the bedroom door behind him, Scott quickly dressed in his oldest clothes, then crossed to the wardrobe and took out a polished wooden box. Opening it, he withdrew his service revolver and carefully slipped the loaded weapon into the inside pocket of his jacket. The wooden box had an ammunition compartment and he quickly withdrew a handful of extra cartridges, placing them in his trousers pocket. They might well be needed, he thought, if, single-handedly, he had to stop an Invincible assassination bid.

He paused a moment to gather his thoughts. Was there any way he could alert Penrose? No, Brady would be with him all the time. Besides, he wasn't even sure if Forster were the target – it could well be the Viceroy or Burke.

'Are ye right, Bill?' called Brady.

'Coming, Joe!' Scott quickly slipped the gun-box back into the wardrobe. 'Coming . . .'

Alighting from the tram at O'Connell Bridge, Brady and Scott turned down Burgh Quay. A sharp east wind blew up the river, and despite the bright sunshine they each wore a heavy overcoat, cap and muffler.

Nothing in Brady's demeanour would suggest anything other than a man out for a casual stroll, and Scott tried to match his manner to that of his companion.

Brady had been talking easily, giving no clues however as to their destination. 'By the way, Bill,' he asked with a smile, 'how's your girlfriend?'

'My girlfriend?'

'You're not going to tell me ye didn't follow up on that girl at the dance?'

'Well . . .' Scott smiled vaguely, instinctively wanting to keep Kate firmly separated from his mission with the Invincibles.

'Have you seen her since?' persisted Brady.

'Yes . . . actually I have.'

'Well, don't keep us in the dark – what's she like?'

'She's very nice. Different . . . from girls I've known in America.'

'She's a fine-lookin' woman . . .'

'Yes,' answered Scott, then, anxious to conceal his distaste for discussing Kate with Brady, he broke stride as they reached Butt Bridge. 'Which way, Joe?'

'Straight down the quays.'

'Towards the docks?'

'That's right.'

What would Forster or any of the top targets be doing down there?, thought Scott, as they walked alongside the wind-ruffled Liffey. Could this be a circuitous route to somewhere else? No, that hardly made sense, it wasn't as though they were being followed. Why walk then towards the heart of dockland, deserted on a cold Sunday morning? Deserted. Suddenly alarm bells seemed to ring in his ears. Supposing somehow they had found out the truth about him? Supposing he, Scott, were the 'enemy of Ireland' and it were Brady's mission to dispose of him down one of the deserted dockland alleys?

He adjusted his muffler, surreptitiously loosening the top button of his overcoat to afford easier access to his revolver, then came to a halt. 'Joe?'

Brady stopped, looking at him enquiringly. 'Yeah?'

'I'd like to be put in the picture. What are we doing down here?'

Brady regarded him a moment, then shrugged. 'OK, Bill, I'll tell ye. We're goin' to take care of a squealer.'

'A squealer?'

'A British informer.'

Scott felt his blood run cold. 'Who would that be?' he asked softly.

Brady moved closer and put a hand on Scott's shoulder. He spoke reassuringly. 'You wouldn't know him, but he's the ferryman, down at the Grand Canal docks. Alright?'

'Yes. Yes, OK.'

'Come on then.'

Matching his companion's stride, Scott set off again, his initial relief at not being the target now turning to horror. What was he to do now, he thought desperately, he could hardly take part in the murder of someone assisting the British forces.

'You're lookin' worried,' said Brady. 'Are ye gettin' a bit nervous?'

'Well, yeah, I suppose I am . . .'

'That's why I didn't want to tell ye the details too soon. Don't worry, Bill, you'll be OK when the time comes.'

153

'I thought it would be Forster. Kinda easier to build yourself up to doing it to someone like him.'

'Don't worry, this bastard has well earned what he's goin' to get.'

'What exactly is he getting?'

'This,' replied Brady, reaching into his overcoat pocket and partially displaying a heavy wooden baton, topped with steel. 'I've one for each of us,' he continued. 'A couple of good wallops on the head, then into the Liffey with him. It'll be a warnin' to anyone else thinkin' of squealin' . . .'

Christ! though Scott, what a dilemma. Could he justify killing a British informer in cold blood, in the hope of saving the Chief Secretary later on?

'We're just there,' said Brady.

'Oh, right.'

'See the little boat over at the slip?'

Scott looked across the choppy expanse of the river to see the small ferry docked on the far shore.

'That's the one,' said Brady. 'We'll stroll up by the canal docks while he's crossin', let the passengers get off, then circle back and get him. OK?'

'Yeah . . . yeah sure,' answered Scott hoarsely. Pull yourself together for God's sake! he thought. You've got to think clearly. If the Chief Secretary is murdered there'll be anarchy, and penetrating the Invincibles is the best chance of preventing that. No, he simply couldn't show his hand so soon. The ferryman would have to be sacrificed, just like the life of any soldier might have to be sacrificed for Queen and Country.

They were approaching the large sea-locks where the Grand Canal enters the Liffey when Brady steered him round a corner to the right. 'They're movin' off now, so we'll hang on here,' he said. 'When the boat's nearly dockin' we'll cut down this lane. By the time we're back on the quays the passengers should be gone.'

Brady withdrew one of the batons and handed it to Scott. 'OK, Bill, give him one on the skull with this. I'll distract him by talking.'

'Right,' answered Scott, pocketing the weapon. He *was* being tested, no doubt about it. He decided that if his conscience would allow him kill the unfortunate ferryman, he might as well be convincing about it and gain credibility. 'This squealer, Joe,' he said hoarsely, 'he's betrayed a lot of men?'

'He's been singin' in Superintendent Mallon's ear for years.'

Scott suddenly smacked the heavy metal baton into his open palm. 'His next song will be to the fishes . . .'

'Now you're talkin'!' said Brady with a grin. 'Hold on and I'll check the boat.'

Scott watched Brady look around the corner, and despite the approval with which Brady had greeted his remark, he experienced a sense of guilt, an instinctive distaste for the crudeness in which he had had to engage.

'Right, they're nearly here,' said Brady returning, 'let's go!'

They moved briskly up the lane and came to a junction, then turned right to approach the quays again. 'There were only five passengers in the boat,' said Brady. 'Probably all going over the canal to Ringsend.'

'Supposing they're not?'

'We'll soon see,' answered Brady as they reached the corner. Carefully he peered around it.

'Well?' asked Scott.

'All clear. Come on.'

The passengers had all departed, presumably up by the sea-lock and towards Ringsend. Rounding the corner, Brady and Scott walked along the deserted cobbled quays towards the ferry, the early morning sunlight reflecting on the noisily lapping waters. Scott took in the whole scene, his senses appearing to sharpen as his heart began to pound.

Reaching the steps leading down from the quay, Brady glanced round to ensure that they were unobserved, then nodded to Scott. They descended the steps and went on board, the ferryman not bothering to look round from his newspaper as they embarked.

Scott tightened his grip on the baton, then moved towards the man, observing his broad shoulders and thick greasy hair under a soiled sailor's cap.

'Seán!' called Brady.

The man turned around, his eyes narrowing in surprise and fear on recognising Brady.

155

'I believe you've been doin' a lot of singin', Seán.'

The man moved towards Brady, arms out in appeal. 'No, Joe . . . I . . .'

'Yes, Seán!' cried Brady, grabbing him by the lapels. 'And I'm told Superintendent Mallon is your biggest fan!'

'No, Joe! No really . . .'

'Yes,' insisted Brady, pulling the man so close that their faces were almost touching, 'but you've sung your last aria, Pal . . .'

With surprising speed for one so heavy, the ferryman suddenly swung Brady to one side, simultaneously pulling a knife from his jacket pocket. He jabbed at the off-balance Brady, narrowly missing, then with a leap Scott threw himself forward, the baton swinging in an arc towards the ferryman's head. There was a thud as the weapon struck home, and with a cry of agony the man fell to the ground. Quickly regaining his feet, Brady pulled out his baton and delivered two more savage blows. 'Bastard!' he cried.

Scott looked in horror at the battered skull, then in one swift movement Brady lifted the body and tipped it into the Liffey. 'Let's go!' he snapped.

Unmoving, Scott stared in disgust at the body, floating bloodied-face up in the river.

'Let's go, Bill!'

'Right – right!' Swiftly he followed Brady up the steps and along the quay.

'Down Benson Street,' said Brady, indicating the first turn left.

Rounding the corner, they walked briskly down the street, Scott's stomach still in a knot, then turned right, following the line of warehouses along Grand Canal Dock. It was only when they were approaching the busy thoroughfare of South Great Brunswick Street that Brady reverted to a more leisurely pace.

'OK, Bill, we're just Sunday strollers again.'

'OK.'

'And, Bill,' he said, turning to face Scott, 'you did well, you did very well.' He held out his hand and Scott shook it. 'You're one of us now.'

'Thanks, Joe.'

'Come on, we'll get a tram into town and have a few pints.'

'Yeah, right.'

Brady's words seemed to ring in his head. *You're one of us now.* He was in. He had passed the test alright – and he felt awful.

Twenty-Six

The Phoenix Park was almost deserted, despite the return to warm spring weather, as Scott proceeded to his early morning rendezvous in the Furry Glen.

Walking round a curve in the hawthorn-flanked road, he saw the glen pond ahead, and, sitting on a park bench by its banks, the waiting Colonel Penrose. The older man partially lowered his paper as Scott sat on the far end of the bench.

'Morning, Scott.'

'Good morning, Sir.'

'I presume a nine o'clock rendezvous on a Monday morning is significant?'

'Yes, Sir,' answered Scott who, despite the absence of any other strollers, looked out over the pond rather than at his superior. 'They made contact yesterday, Sir. I was offered a mission.'

'Capital! What precisely is involved?'

'It's already occurred. Joe Brady called yesterday morning and asked if I'd assist him in a killing.'

'And?'

'I said I would, thinking it might be Mr Forster and I'd have a chance to intervene.'

'But it wasn't?'

'No, Sir, it was a test for me. I was asked to help kill an informer.'

'I see,' said Penrose. 'I take it you did?'

'Well, not quite so readily as that, Sir.'

'What?'

'I did do it; but with grave misgivings.'

'Grave misgivings? Nonsense man, you had no choice. You couldn't expose yourself. To have shied off could have wrecked the whole mission.'

'Quite. But to have to kill a man working for us . . .'

'You're too scrupulous, Scott, you really are. Besides,

you've fought in Afghanistan, Zululand – you've killed men before.'

'Not those on our own side, Sir,' answered Scott quietly.

Penrose lowered his paper impatiently. A quick glance round assured him that they were unobserved, then he turned to the younger man. 'Look here, Scott, an informer is not on our side. A lot of the Irish are against rebellion, thousands of people here are pro-British, but informers aren't among them. The informer is not on anyone's side, he's in it for the money. They're scum, the dregs of the earth. Even these Invincible chaps – fanatics and murderers though they be – at least they're motivated by some sense of duty, however misguided. But a paid informer? My dear man, lose no sleep over such a creature.'

'No, Sir.'

'Where did all of this happen?'

'Down the docks. We beat him over the head and threw the body into the Liffey.'

'Brady and you?'

'Yes, Sir.'

I take it your hesitancy was kept from Brady?'

'Yes. I think you could safely assume that in his eyes I'm now an accredited nationalist.'

'Excellent! Look here, Scott,' said Penrose, his tone softening, 'I dare say it was an unpleasant spot they put you on. Distasteful piece of business naturally, but you've got to understand what we're up against here. We're fighting anarchists, terrorists, people to whom human life means nothing. They don't fight by the rules, and if we're to defeat them we can't either. You do see that, don't you?'

'Yes, Sir.'

'Good fellow. You are still maintaining the role, I presume? Looking at horses, stables and such like?'

'Oh yes, that part's rather pleasant. Looking at thoroughbred horses is certainly no chore.'

'Quite so. As it happens your infiltration couldn't have come at a more opportune time.'

'How's that, Sir?'

'Well, you know about Parnell?'

'Just that he's been released on parole to attend a funeral in France.'

'Compassionate grounds,' Penrose snorted derisively. 'And of course since he's been out there's been a flurry of political activity. The upshot of all the skullduggery and wheeling and dealing is that the Viceroy is resigning, and Gladstone wants to find some way to release Parnell and the Land League people. Forster is our one rock of strength. As Chief Secretary for Ireland he's the only one who'll stand up to Gladstone and keep Parnell behind bars. That's why your mission is vital. Forster *must* be protected.'

'I'll certainly do all in my power, Sir.'

'Do, Captain, do.' Penrose lowered his voice. 'I'll tell you something, Scott, in the strictest confidence, mind . . .'

'Of course, Sir.'

'Later this week Forster will be going to London for a cabinet showdown. If he wins there'll be a new Coercion Act passed in Parliament, which will give him the powers he needs to stamp out lawlessness in Ireland. And Forster will only release Parnell and company *after* law and order is restored. We need that Act, Scott. Badly. It's no exaggeration to say that the future of Ireland may be determined in the coming weeks; that's why preventing an attack on Forster is absolutely crucial.'

'I do appreciate that, Sir.' He paused a moment. 'There is one thing, Colonel . . .'

'Yes?'

'Can Mr Forster's security not be improved – altered itineraries, higher levels of protection and so on?'

'Yes, that's already in hand; only so much can be done however without seeming to be running scared.'

'Yes, quite. Could all known Invincibles be arrested perhaps? We don't know them all, of course, but rounding up those we do know would certainly lessen their threat.'

'It's tempting alright, but if we're patient we may get the whole organisation – lock, stock and barrel. In particular we want to get the ones at the top. If we can find any link with the

Irish Party, we could discredit the allegedly non-violent Parnell.'

'I see,' answered Scott thoughtfully. 'Murky waters, Sir.'

'That's putting it mildly, Captain,' said Penrose with a wry smile. 'That's putting it mildly indeed.' He closed the newspaper. 'So, your best course now is to intervene only to prevent an actual assassination bid, otherwise gather intelligence on them but don't show your hand. You'll keep me posted, of course.'

'Yes, Sir.'

Penrose suddenly stood up, folding his paper as he looked out across the waters of the pond. 'You've done well, Scott, keep up the good work.'

'Thank you, Colonel.'

'Good day to you then.'

'Good day, Sir.'

Scott remained seated as Penrose strode away. Dissatisfied with the encounter, he sat staring at the water; then he rose and moved off slowly in the opposite direction.

Twenty-Seven

'Jesus Christ Almighty, when are we goin' to get this bastard?'

'Take it easy, Joe,' said Carey.

Brady looked at him malevolently. 'Take it easy? That's the whole fuckin' problem!'

'Now look, Joe . . .'

'No you look, Mr Carey. I took the mornin' off work trackin' that bastard Forster. We were supposed to cover his every move. We were supposed to be pullin' out all the stops to get him before he went to London. All volunteers mobilised . . .' he added scornfully.

'It was just one of those things, Joe,' said McCaffrey.

'It wasn't!' snapped Brady. 'It was sheer carelessness. Sheer fuckin' carelessness!'

Tynan donned his pince-nez, and leaning forward on the table, looked directly at Brady. 'Let me ask you a question, Joe,' he said softly. 'Are you blaming someone here present?'

The muted street noises were the only sounds penetrating the upstairs bar as Brady allowed an uncomfortable silence to develop. Eventually he looked away from Tynan. 'No, I suppose not. But the gobshite who lost sight of Forster . . .'

'Was a drayman, not a trained soldier,' interjected Tynan. 'One accepts whatever volunteers one can get.'

'He was still careless.'

'Indubitably,' answered Tynan, 'which is why his services will not be called upon again.'

'There's another consideration,' said Carey. 'I think Forster must be deliberately changing his itinerary. I mean, getting the early train rather than the connecting boat train sounds like evasive action to me.'

'It looks that way,' agreed Dan Curley, 'but then we could hardly expect him to oblige us; he'd be dead now if he *had* tried to board the boat train.'

162

'Assumin' our men at the station didn't botch that up too,' added Brady caustically.

'The fact of the matter is that our quarry has, for various reasons, eluded us,' said Tynan. 'As a delicate stage has now been reached, apropos political developments . . .'

'What?' interrupted Brady irritably.

'It would seem that Forster and Gladstone are at loggerheads,' explained Tynan, 'over a new Coercion Act, and the possibility of Parnell's release.'

'So?'

'So I think we may assume that our erstwhile quarry, Mr Forster, may be out of the picture for a time.'

'He wouldn't be if we went after him and finished him off in London,' said Brady.

'I think Joe's right,' said Dan Curley thoughtfully. 'Forster really has it coming to him, and they wouldn't be expecting an attack at the centre of their precious empire.'

'It would be a great boost for morale,' added Carey, 'the men need a lift.'

'Gentlemen,' said Tynan, raising a hand, 'your enthusiasm does you credit. But looked at objectively one must conclude that our quarrel is not with Forster *personally*.'

'Mine is,' said Brady. 'I won't be happy till that swine is six feet under.'

Curley nodded in agreement. 'Yeah, when you think of all the injustice that's gone on under Forster's reign.'

'Granted,' said Tynan, 'but our quarrel is with the institution of Chief Secretary, not the individual incumbent.'

'I'm not quite with you Mr Tynan,' said McCaffrey.

'What I'm saying, Gentlemen, is that the *idea* of a British Chief Secretary running Ireland is what is objectionable, not the specific man himself. We must be seen to be fighting for national freedom, not pursuing a vendetta against Forster.'

'Fair point,' said Carey.

'A minute ago you wanted to boost morale by killin' him,' said Brady.

'I've changed my mind,' snapped Carey. 'Mr Tynan's view makes sense.'

'I see your point, Mr Tynan,' said Dan Curley, weighing his

words carefully, 'but I still think Forster has been such a tyrant, that he deserves to be followed and executed.'

'Hear hear,' said Brady.

'Mr McCaffrey?' asked Tynan.

'Eh well, really I suppose . . . I think Mr Tynan is probably right, it wouldn't look good if we seemed to be settling a grudge . . .'

'Thank you, Ned,' said Tynan. 'Jim?'

Carey nodded sagely. 'I think, on balance, our main target should be the rulers here – if Forster's gone, then good riddance.'

'That's settled then,' said Tynan. He turned to Brady and Curley. 'Gentlemen, as representative of the London Directory I'm afraid I must instruct you not to consider following Forster to England. I'm not, however, putting off vigorous action – far from it. If Forster has his way with Gladstone, and returns to Ireland, he immediately becomes our principal target again. And I suspect that if he doesn't get his Coercion Act he'll have to resign, in which case we shall await his replacement. Meanwhile, in Forster's absence, Burke is Acting Chief Secretary for Ireland. I propose, therefore, that Thomas Burke becomes our target for execution.' He looked around the table. 'Agreed?'

Carey and McCaffrey nodded, then somewhat reluctantly Brady and Curley did also.

'Very well, Gentlemen,' said Tynan. 'Let us discuss, therefore, how we may best arrange for Mr Burke's demise . . .'

Twenty-Eight

The gas lamp outside the Hole in the Wall public house cast a flickering yellow circle of light, and standing in the dark shadow of the adjacent park wall, James Carey waited.

The letter from Danny O'Sullivan in America had finally arrived and, frustratingly, had explained in detail how difficult it was to track down one individual in a vast country receiving millions of immigrants. The letter neither proved nor disproved Bill Ryan's story, and the only interesting point in it was that O'Sullivan had been unable to locate a death certificate for Ryan's father, despite Ryan's claim that he had died in Philadelphia the previous year. Hardly a damning point, Carey had thought, there could, after all, be any number of bureaucratic reasons why the certificate might not be readily to hand.

Carey had mentioned the fact to Tynan and the other committee members, and the general consensus had been to adhere to their plan of using Ryan in the attempt on Burke's life. Deeds, after all, did speak louder than vague doubts, and according to Brady's account, Ryan's performance in the ferry killing had been swift and lethal.

Everything pointed to Bill Ryan being a patriot and a man of action, but at the same time why not continue to probe a little, thought Carey, especially since they had gained the man's confidence through Kate.

Kate Lannigan – what an attractive young woman she was. Carey had to admit that he always enjoyed meeting her, even if she was a little too self-confident for his liking. Still, he reflected, it had been a real feather in his cap recruiting and placing an agent in the enemy camp. He had said nothing to the others about meeting her tonight – the less they knew about her, the stronger his position as her controller, an important point if, as he suspected, Tynan were trying to edge him out a little. The thought of the power invested in the plump little speechmaker irritated him. He still couldn't understand why the London Directory had landed them with Tynan in the first place, when he, Carey, could have orchestrated everything, given the authority.

'Mr Carey!'

He turned, a little flustered by the sudden proximity of the whisper. 'What . . .'

'It's Kate.' She moved closer, carefully avoiding the pool of light as she gained the shadow of the boundary wall. 'You wanted to see me . . .'

'Yes, I'd like to have a chat,' said Carey pleasantly.

'I don't have much time. I'm after slipping out.'

'I know, that's why I made the rendezvous for ten at night – to facilitate slipping out.'

'OK,' she replied. 'Let's walk up this way through the trees – we won't be visible from the road.'

Moving towards the belt of trees running parallel to the wall, Carey turned smilingly to Kate. 'It's a long time since I scampered in the park with an attractive young lady,' he said playfully.

'*Scampered*? Your letter said you needed to brief me on something.'

'I jest, Kate, I merely jest,' said Carey easily, pausing as they reached the trees. 'To business then. You're seeing Bill Ryan next Saturday, correct?'

'Yes.'

'I'd like you to steer the conversation round to the death of his father. Try to find out exactly when and where he died. The cause of death for good measure, if you can.'

'May I ask why?'

'I'd rather not say, really.'

'I'd rather you did.'

'I think, Kate, that the less you know about these things the better.'

'But the more you know, the better?'

Carey smiled. 'In an army, Kate, a general needs all the facts, but he doesn't necessarily share them with the foot soldiers.'

'I think I'm a little more than a foot soldier, I mean I am going out with him.'

'That, I suspect, is not an unpleasant chore?'

'No.'

'I thought not,' replied Carey knowingly.

'Look, asking questions about America is one thing, but I'd like a good reason if you want me to pry into something like his father's death.'

Carey looked at her enquiringly. 'He's really gotten to you, hasn't he?'

'What's that supposed to mean?'

'That you don't want to offend the sensitive nature of handsome and dashing Mr Ryan, but you don't seem to mind offending me by quibbling about your mission.'

'It's not the same thing.'

'Evidently not,' said Carey sarcastically. 'A couple of dates and already you're protective towards him. He must have wooed you very convincingly . . .'

'Let's say his manner is more appealing than yours, Mr Carey,' said Kate, looking at him coldly.

'OK, OK . . .' Carey raised his hands appeasingly. 'Let's not fight among ourselves. Sure we're all on the one side.'

'Are we?'

'Of course we are, of course.'

'Does that include Bill Ryan?'

'Yes,' said Carey thoughtfully, 'I'm fairly sure it does. Look, I'll tell you the facts then. Bill has presented himself to us as an Irish American dedicated to the cause of Irish freedom. Now we're eager to include him in our plans, but in fairness to our other volunteers we have to be sure of his bona fides.'

'I see . . .' answered Kate reflectively. 'And has anything he's said to me contradicted what he said to you?'

'No it hasn't – except that a death certificate hasn't been found for his father, who apparently died last year. Now I'm ninety-nine percent sure it's just some clerical error or bureaucracy; but I'd like to be one hundred percent sure if possible.'

'Right . . .'

'So, just ask him gently, and in a roundabout way about his

167

father's death. I'm sure, Kate, you'll find a way of doing it sensitively. OK?'

'Yes . . . alright then.'

'Good girl. I knew I could count on you. And eh . . . I know he's a handsome devil,' said Carey with a conspiratorial smile, 'but don't let him turn your head.'

Kate didn't smile back. 'I'll ask him the questions for you, Mr Carey, and give you the answers.'

'Can't ask for more than that. Oh, by the way,' he added, 'our interest in your employer is increasing. Any more intelligence from the Burke household?'

'Yes, actually. I was going to mention that the reason I'm in a rush is because of food hampers . . .'

'Food hampers?'

'Yes, I'm up to my eyes packing cheese and butter. Mr McDaid says it's for a party of people Burke is entertaining at the regatta on Saturday.'

'What regatta is this?'

'It's held at one of the boat clubs on the Liffey. I was afraid to ask which one, in case too much interest might sound suspicious.'

'Quite right,' said Carey, a note of excitement in his voice. 'This could be very useful information, Kate – we'll find out which club ourselves. Good work,' he added sincerely, 'very good work.'

'Thanks. Now I really must go.'

'Yes, yes of course, and you'll keep me posted on the other matter with Bill?'

'Yes.'

'Goodnight then, Kate, and congratulations on a job well done.'

'Goodnight.'

He stood, immobile but excited, then after a moment he turned and strode off happily towards the Hole in the Wall, eager, suddenly, for the noise and good fellowship of the nearby pub.

168

Twenty-Nine

Paddy on the railway pickin' up stones,
Up comes an engine and breaks his bones,
'Ah,' says Paddy, 'that's not fair!'
'Ah,' says the engine, 'I don't care!'

The lilting children's skipping song carried through the open kitchen window as Scott sat reading the Saturday newspaper. Normally he liked to listen to the amusing words of the children's songs, but this morning he was engrossed in the newspaper's account of an eviction in Wicklow.

Suddenly his reading was disturbed by a loud knocking on the front door. Laying down the newspaper, he quietly went to the parlour window and carefully glanced out through the curtains. Standing on the doorstep were Tim Kelly and Joe Brady, both dressed in their working clothes. Switching mentally to his Bill Ryan role, Scott moved into the hall.

'Hi there!' he said jauntily, pulling open the front door.

'Mornin', Bill,' said Brady.

'Hope you weren't expecting a lady-friend,' said Kelly smilingly.

'No such luck,' laughed Scott. 'Come on in.' Leading his visitors back into the kitchen, he pulled out two chairs and motioned for them to sit. 'How about a cup of tea or coffee?'

'No, thanks all the same, Bill,' answered Kelly without sitting.

'Sure?'

'Yeah,' said Brady, 'Skin-the-Goat's waitin' outside.'

'Skin-the-Goat?'

Brady smiled. 'It's a nickname. He's a cab-driver who helps the cause.'

'And he's parked outside?'

'Yeah, he said he'd feed the horse while we collected you,' answered Kelly.

169

'Collected me – where are we going?'

'First things first,' said Brady. 'I've good news, Bill, you've been formally accepted into the Invincibles. If you raise your right arm, we'll do the oath now.'

'My right arm . . . eh, OK.'

Brady removed a lethal-looking surgical knife from a scabbard inside his overalls, and with a surge of panic Scott realised that his raised arm left his chest exposed. Unobtrusively he placed his other hand in front of his heart, but his anxiety proved ill-founded as Brady raised the weapon high in the air and administered the oath.

When it was finished Brady lowered his arm and sheathed the knife. 'Congratulations, Bill,' he said, extending his hand with a smile.

'Thanks.'

'Congratulations, Bill, welcome aboard,' said Kelly.

'Thanks, Tim. So,' he said enthusiastically, 'now that I'm a fully fledged Invincible, where are we going?'

'Trinity Boat Club,' answered Kelly, 'the Under Secretary's attending the regatta.'

'Except that we're goin' to attend to him first,' added Brady.

Kelly smiled eagerly. 'We're turning out in force today, Bill.'

'Great,' said Scott. 'I thought though that Forster was the number one target?'

'He still is,' answered Brady, 'but he's in England. Burke is his right hand man. He's got it comin' too.'

'Sure,' said Scott. 'And where is this regatta held?'

'Islandbridge,' replied Brady. 'Give him the parcel, Tim.'

'What's this?' asked Scott, as Kelly handed him a rumpled brown paper parcel.

'Overalls,' answered Brady. 'We're goin' to pose as workmen while we're waitin' on Burke.'

'Good thinking,' said Scott, his mind racing. To have any chance of stopping them he would have to get his revolver. 'Listen, I'll just change into these in the bedroom,' he said, moving to the door. 'Make yourselves comfortable . . .'

Once inside the bedroom he quickly withdrew the gun and extra cartridges from the wardrobe. Swiftly changing out of his clothes, he donned the overalls, concealing the pistol and cartridges within their voluminous folds.

He stood with eyes closed at the window, breathing deeply to steady himself and compose his thoughts. The sound of the children singing 'Paddy on the railway' carried in through the open bedroom window, distracting him, then suddenly he opened his eyes with a start.

Snapping into action, he crossed to his bedside table, took up a pencil and paper, and wrote swiftly. Sealing the paper in an envelope, he wrote COLONEL PENROSE – MOST URGENT on the outside, underlining the URGENT, then slipped the envelope into his overalls pocket and made for the door.

'Sorry to keep you,' he said easily, 'I'm not used to these duds . . .'

'Ah, you're too much of a gentleman, Bill,' said Kelly with a laugh, 'but we'll make a workin' man of ye!'

'Are we right then?' asked Brady.

'Sure, Joe,' answered Scott, 'just gotta do one thing before we go.'

'What's that?'

Scott smiled. 'I guess even Invincibles use the lavatory?'

'Yeah OK. Don't be long, right?'

'Sure,' replied Scott, heading out the back door and round the corner towards the outside lavatory. Once out of sight of the kitchen he ran down the side of the house towards the front hedge and the sound of the chanting children.

He peered very carefully through a gap in the hedge and looked towards the cab. The driver, holding a bucket from which the horse was drinking, was looking in the opposite direction. Scott paused, realising that the man could turn at any moment. He couldn't wait, he decided, he'd just have to chance it.

Shifting his attention to the skipping children, he swiftly appraised them, then decided on a lithely built red-haired girl of about eleven, who stood near the footpath awaiting her turn at the rope. He checked that the cabman was still turned away, then called softly to the child. She turned around in surprise, but didn't approach when Scott called her forward. 'It's OK,' he whispered, 'I just want you to do a message.'

Standing her ground, the child looked at him dubiously.

'Look,' said Scott encouragingly, 'here's a half-crown if you'll deliver a letter.'

Looking at the proffered silver coin, the child's eyes widened.

'OK?' asked Scott urgently.

The girl nodded her head, then approached gingerly. Scott glanced up again at the cabman. Fortunately the other children were still skipping away, and he hadn't looked around.

'You know Marlborough Barracks?'

'Yes,' answered the girl.

'Run as fast as your legs will carry you and give this to the soldier on the gate, OK?'

'OK,' said the child.

'Straight away and as quick as you can. It's very important.'

'Alright,' said the child, taking the letter and coin, 'I'll fly . . .'

'Good girl,' Scott answered, then looked with concern as the other children stopped skipping to observe her speedy departure. Without waiting to see if the cabman had turned, he quickly withdrew from the hedge and sprinted back up the garden, slowing down to a brisk pace as he approached the kitchen.

'OK, fellas,' he said jauntily, opening the back door and rejoining Kelly and Brady, 'let's keep our date with Mr Burke.'

The sweat trickled down his brow, and mopping it away, Scott leaned heavily on his shovel. The warm spring sunshine had made the unaccustomed physical labour more tiring than he had expected, but the roadside trench he had been digging with Brady, Kelly and four other volunteers was convincing and workmanlike – the occupants of the carriages passing in to the regatta had barely given them a second glance.

Looking up towards John's Road, he could see another group of Invincibles manning a fruit stall, while on the far side of the road Tynan and Curley sat on a bench apparently reading their newspapers.

He took his watch from his overalls and glanced down surreptitiously. A quarter to twelve. If Burke were coming it

172

would be any moment now. The opening of the regatta was scheduled for twelve noon, and the Invincibles were expecting him to perform the opening ceremony. Looking nervously down the road, Scott prayed that the message had been delivered to Penrose in time to halt the Under Secretary.

'Leaning on your shovel, Bill?' said Kelly cheerily. 'You'll never make a living as a navvy!'

'I suppose not,' answered Scott, marvelling at how Kelly could be so boyishly good-humoured, minutes before the planned stabbing to death of a man. It would be a pity to have to kill Kelly, he reflected, but he and Brady would have to be stopped if an attempt were made on Burke's life. Penrose had said that the killing of Forster could mean anarchy, and Scott reckoned that the murder of his linchpin, the Under Secretary, would be almost as bad.

The plan which Brady had outlined seemed simple and effective. If Burke were accompanied in the carriage by his sister they would allow it to pass, infiltrate the boatclub on foot, and slay the Under Secretary when the opportunity arose. If, as they hoped, Burke were in the carriage alone, then the fruit stall would be thrown across the road and the volunteers from the trench would surround it. Brady, Kelly and Scott had been chosen to strike the actual blows and they each carried a razor-sharp twelve-inch surgical knife.

Scott knew that the sheer numbers of Invincibles would rule out any question of drawing his pistol and making arrests. He would have to hope he could immobilise Kelly and Brady and as many of the other volunteers as possible, if Burke were to escape; a plan which depended, he recognised, on rather a lot of imponderables . . .

He picked up his shovel and returned to the front of the trench.

'Any minute now, Bill,' said Brady.

'Is he coming?' asked Scott hoarsely.

'No sign yet, but he's due. Just be ready.'

'Sure, Joe,' he answered.

As he dug fitfully, Scott's mind wandered back again to the delivery of the letter. Supposing the child had simply run round the corner and pocketed the money? Or brought the letter home? Or sprinted to Marlborough Barracks, but been too late to catch Penrose? Stop fretting, he told himself, it was the best that could have been done on the spur of the moment. In fact, the only thing that could have been done. And numerous lives would be saved – his own included, perhaps – if the child reached Penrose, and if Penrose halted the Under Secretary's trip. Anxiously looking down John's Road, he wished there weren't quite so many ifs.

The one o'clock hooter from the Guinness plant carried on the breeze, as Brady, his face tight with anger, walked back from the fruit stall to the trench.

'What's the story, Joe?' asked Kelly.

'Another balls-up! Another bleedin' balls-up! Ye can pack your gear,' he added bitterly.

'It's off?' asked Kelly disappointedly.

'Yeah,' snapped Brady.

'It's only one o'clock, Joe, he might arrive late,' suggested Kelly.

'The bastard's not comin' at this stage, Tim. Ye heard the startin' gun – they've been racin' for the past three quarters of an hour.'

'What did Mr Tynan say?'

'He said the longer we all hang around here, the more suspicious it gets, and for once he's right.'

'I thought Mr Carey was certain that Burke was attending?' persisted Kelly.

'He got it wrong then, didn't he? And not for the first time either.'

Scott shook his head sympathetically. 'It sure is disappointing, Joe,' he said softly, hoping the relief wouldn't show in his voice.

'Yeah, I'm sorry, Bill, but don't worry, we'll get the swine sooner or later. Right lads, pack your tools in the back of the cart and let's get out of here.'

'Maybe Burke switched his plans for security reasons,' said Scott, his heart-felt relief making him unable to resist the disguised jibe.

'Why would he do that?'

174

Scott shrugged. 'Make his movements unpredictable, keep would-be assassins guessing.'

'Maybe,' answered Brady, spitting on the ground with venom, 'he'd a lucky escape today anyway.'

'Yeah, a lucky escape.' And that makes two of us, thought Scott, as he eagerly loaded the tools back into the cart.

Thirty

It was marvellous to be alive, Kate thought, as she walked through the sweet-smelling meadow, the weak moonlight faintly casting shadows on the landscape. It was wonderful to be alive on a warm spring night, especially on a night spent in the company of someone as exciting as Bill Ryan. He had left her to the small pedestrian gate in the boundary wall of the Under Secretary's Lodge, and she still felt a glow from their lingering goodnight kisses as she took the short-cut over the fields towards the house.

The evening had gone perfectly, with Bill insisting that having dined on a picnic, and in the Liffey Tea Rooms, they were surely due a proper sit-down meal. Kate had happily agreed, and dressed in their finery they had gone to a luxurious – and to Kate's mind, horrendously expensive – hotel restaurant.

Despite its size, the restaurant had actually turned out to have an intimate atmosphere, with each party allocated its own alcove, and the candlelight and piano music had heightened the already romantic mood of the evening. They had eaten well; drunk a bottle of white wine; danced closely together when the pianist played a selection of slow waltzes; laughed like children when Kate had insisted that the stuffy head waiter worked part-time in the Liffey Tea Rooms.

It had been a magical evening, and in the circumstances Kate couldn't bring herself to quiz Bill about his father's death. It seemed too devious, too disloyal. She wanted to be able to look back on the meal without the memory being marred by deception, and so she had put Carey out of her head and had given herself up to the pleasure of Bill's lively company and what had turned out to be a wonderful evening.

Travelling home in the carriage, however, she had reluctantly accepted that, devious or not, she would have to confront the problem sooner or later. Since her talk with Carey

176

she had thought a lot about what Bill's position might be regarding the Invincibles. Certainly he had given no hint of fervent nationalism during their dates, but then it made sense that he would be discreet about his political motivation, just as she herself tended to avoid such subjects when they were together. While they had been chatting earlier about music, she had spoken of the concerts attended with Aunt Julia, and so, on the journey home, without appearing too contrived, she had managed to bring the conversation around to Julia's late husband Peter, and how much of a shock his death had been.

How, she had asked, hating herself, had he, Bill, reacted to his father's death? Was the illness a protracted one? Yes, Bill had said, he'd been very upset, the fever had taken a long time before finally claiming his father last October. Did he die in hospital? No, Bill had answered, they had a nurse in at home. Kate had thought to herself that Carey wouldn't be pleased. A hospital death could be traced, given time, but to try to locate a home nurse, last employed six months ago and four thousand miles away . . . 'I know a lot of nurses who went to America,' she had said. 'Your Dad's nurse wasn't Irish, was she?'

'No, American.'

I *can't* ask her name, Kate had thought, it would be pushing too far. To hell with Carey, she'd decided suddenly, she had done enough snooping for one night.

'Let's not talk of the dead on a night like this,' Bill had said.

'No, no it's a night for the living,' Kate had softly answered, as they moved closer together in the darkened cab.

Walking across the meadow now, she could see the yellow glow of gas lamps from windows in the lodge. A light burned in Burke's bedroom, and she thought of her employer, the man whose death she was helping to plot. Despite working in his service for the last six weeks she had only seen him on three or four occasions.

He probably doesn't even know I exist, Kate thought. And yet, despite the rigidly observed class consciousness and the knowledge that he was a major controller of a political system she abhorred, she found it impossible to take any pleasure in the thought of his imminent death. She had realised that the attempt on his life at the regatta must have failed when she had seen the party return, yet her disappointment had been oddly mixed with something akin to relief.

Everything Carey had said about rulers like Burke tolerating the evils of the landlords may have been true, and looked at objectively Kate could see the logic of the Invincibles' strategy, yet she had increasingly found herself wishing that violence wasn't necessary. There was something about cold-blooded assassination, which, while not actually undermining her mission, nonetheless dulled her enthusiasm. Could it be that her passions were being diverted from the land war to Bill Ryan, she wondered, as she reached the back door of the house and stepped into the hall.

'Miss Lannigan!'

Kate looked around in surprise to see the house steward standing in the dimly lit passageway leading to his quarters.

'Good evening,' she said.

'Good evening,' mimicked Hackett, slurring his words slightly. 'Out for a night with our fancy man, were we?'

'I was out for my night off, Mr Hackett.'

'Oh, I see.'

Kate could smell the whiskey on his breath as he approached, bringing his smooth-cheeked face close to hers. 'No debauchery for the . . . the virginal Miss Lannigan . . .'

'If you'll excuse me, Mr Hackett,' said Kate stepping back.

'No I won't excuse you!' he answered, grabbing her arm. 'Not till I'm finished with you!'

'Let go my arm please,' said Kate, struggling to keep her voice reasonable.

'Let go my arm,' mimicked Hackett. 'Don't touch my milk white flesh!' He pulled her close. 'You know what you want? You know what you *need*, Miss High and Mighty Lannigan? Well I'll tell you, and I'll give it to you!'

'Get your drunken paws off me – now!'

Startled at the venom in her voice, Hackett hesitated a moment, and Kate pulled her arm away.

'Who the hell do you think you are?' he asked, lurching towards her again.

Standing her ground, Kate kept her voice unwavering. 'I'm

an employee of Mr Burke's, and if you lay a finger on me I'll shout the house down.'

Hackett paused, and swaying slightly looked at her scornfully. 'Little milk and water virgin. I know what you want. I've met your type before – and I've given them what they needed!'

'Really? How awful for them, how awful to be slobbered over by a drunken bully!' Turning on her heel, Kate walked away.

'Stuck up bitch! I'll show you! I'll fix you!'

Don't rush, Kate told herself as she moved to the stairs. Don't let him think you're afraid. Reaching the bannister, she started to climb steadily, aware of Hackett having followed her to watch from the base of the stairs.

'This isn't over yet!' he hissed. 'This isn't over by a long shot!'

The words echoed in Kate's head as she climbed without looking back. *This isn't over yet.* Instinctively, and with a sense of dismay, she somehow knew it to be true.

Thirty-One

'Come in, Sir,' said Scott in a startled voice.

'You look like you've seen a ghost, Captain,' observed Penrose, stepping from the twilight of the garden into the warmly lit cottage.

Scott quickly closed the door behind him, then turned to face the older man. 'I thought we had an understanding, Sir, that you would never call here.'

'And I thought you had been seeking me urgently for the last five days.'

'Yes, Sir, but coming straight to the house . . .'

'Please, Captain,' said Penrose, raising a hand. 'I've been travelling non-stop since leaving London this morning. I'd rather like to sit down.'

'Of course, Sir, the kitchen is in here,' said Scott, opening a door off the hallway.

'Thank you.'

'I don't wish to appear rude, Sir, it's just that . . .'

'Security is of the utmost,' interjected Penrose. 'I know, Captain, I know. You may rest assured I was not observed calling here.'

'Very good, Sir,' answered Scott, pulling out a chair from the kitchen table.

Penrose lowered himself gratefully into a reclining position. 'At ease, Scott,' he said, indicating for the younger man to sit also.

'May I offer you a drink, Colonel?'

'I won't, thank you all the same. We'd better get down to business.'

'As you wish, Sir,' said Scott, seating himself. 'I've been trying to contact you since the assassination bid last Saturday . . .'

'Yes, I had to go to England immediately afterwards,'

interrupted Penrose. 'Left in rather a hurry and only got back an hour ago.'

'I see. I needed to talk to you, Colonel, about what happened on Saturday.'

'Yes?'

'Brady and Kelly called here for me. I was sworn in as an Invincible.'

'How very colourful,' said Penrose sardonically.

'It wasn't very entertaining, Sir. Not when they told me we were going to kill Under Secretary Burke on his way in to the regatta.'

'Quite. How did you manage to get the message to the barracks?'

'On the pretext of going to the lavatory, I slipped a note to children playing out on the road.'

'Good thinking, Scott.'

'Thank you, Sir. Of course I'd no idea whether or not you'd ever get it. If you hadn't, or if you'd gotten it too late . . .'

'You would have been in a tight spot. Yes, I can quite see that. Luckily you caught me in the barracks, and I was able to raise the alarm. Superintendent Mallon spoke to the Under Secretary and persuaded him to cancel the visit.'

Scott looked at his superior searchingly. 'Does that mean Superintendent Mallon knows of my operation, Sir?'

Penrose smiled. 'Ever mindful of your personal security, Scott . . .'

'It tends to keep one alive in the field, Sir.'

'I dare say. To answer your question, no, he doesn't know of your operation.'

'Surely he wished to see the warning note?'

'Oh I gave him the note. The anonymous one I wrote myself, in block letters, warning of an attempt on Burke's life. It served the purpose of raising the alarm without giving away our role.'

'Didn't Mallon ask why it was addressed to you, Sir?'

'Yes, I told him I didn't know why, although I pointed out to him that my identity is not unknown in military circles.'

'He accepted that?'

Penrose smiled wryly. 'Outwardly at any rate. Mallon is both influential and a damned good policeman, so I dare say he knows I'm in Military Intelligence. He must also know that I'm not likely to reveal my activities to the Dublin Metropolitan Police.'

'Actually, Sir, I believe the time has come for police involvement. That's what I wanted to put to you as a matter of urgency.'

'Police involvement?' Penrose's voice rose in puzzlement. 'A moment ago you were anxious about concealing your mission.'

'I'd still be anxious not to reveal any more of our operation than was necessary, particularly until we actually strike. The fact of the matter however is that I think it's time the Invincibles were arrested.'

'And why is that, pray?'

'Because it was sheer good luck that my note reached you in time last Saturday. The assassination bid was a large-scale operation. I'd have had a serious problem trying to prevent it single-handedly. The Invincibles are lackadaisical in many ways, Sir, but there are a lot of them, and they're sufficiently organised to turn out in force at short notice; and with the likes of Brady on the committee there's no questioning their determination. We can't rely on being lucky again, Sir. That's why I believe they must be rounded up.'

'Do you indeed?'

'Yes, Sir, I do.'

'It wouldn't be the appropriate action right now.'

'I really think it would, Sir.'

'I hope you're not questioning my authority, Scott?'

'I'm sorry, Sir, I mean no disrespect, but as the man on the spot, I can see the dangers. Two or three assassins I can arrest, but there were twelve men in last Saturday's bid. They must be rounded up now if we're to forestall them.'

'I think you're forgetting your rank, Captain Scott. Colonels in the British Army are not told by captains what they must do.'

Scott's face reddened in anger. 'Sir, I'm trying to save the lives . . .'

'I know what your task is, Scott!' Penrose cut in sharply. 'I did, after all, choose you for it. The fact of the matter is that arrest at the present moment would be inappropriate.'

Scott breathed in deeply. 'May I ask why, Sir?'

'There are political considerations. The cabinet is still deliberating over Forster's demand for a tougher line. If we can establish a link between the Invincibles and Parnell and his cohorts, then Forster's position is greatly strengthened.'

'Assuming, Sir, that Mr Forster or his Under Secretary are not murdered first by the Invincibles.'

'Superintendent Mallon is increasing their protection,' answered Penrose coldly.

'But, Colonel, we can't link them to Parnell. I've already reported that Tynan is the senior Invincible in Dublin. You said yourself that investigations showed him to be a . . . a glorified bookseller from Peckam Rye! Hardly a traceable colleague of Charles Stewart Parnell, Sir.'

'Tynan is relatively small meat, I concede you, but if, as you say, he's enamoured by the sound of his own voice, then on closer acquaintance you may be able to persuade him to reveal the source of his orders.'

'I may, Sir, but I wouldn't like to be relying on it.'

'I'm not asking you to like anything, Captain. I'm telling you what your orders are.' He leaned forward a little, softening his tone. 'Look, Scott, this is a damnably tricky operation and you've shown pluck and ingenuity. Just hang on for a while more, and we may be able to hit these chaps for six.'

'Yes, Sir,' answered Scott flatly.

'Good fellow,' said Penrose, suddenly rising. 'Stay as you are, I'll let myself out.' He smiled fleetingly. 'Don't worry, I'll take a different route back to the barracks. And remember, Scott, any evidence linking Parnell to the Invincibles would be of great value, very great value indeed. Good evening to you.'

'Good evening, Sir.'

Hearing the front door close, Scott gazed absent-mindedly out the kitchen window. *Very great value indeed*, Penrose had said, and probably cheap at the price, in the colonel's scale of values – even if it cost the life of Captain William Scott . . .

Thirty-Two

Kate angrily washed her hands under the dairy's cold water tap, then picked up the towel, her annoyance evident in the brisk manner of her drying. She had known that her recent confrontation with the house steward wouldn't be forgotten, but she hadn't anticipated that Hackett would wait until the morning of her night off, then insist that she be seconded to the allegedly short-staffed kitchen to help out.

Kate was certain that the illness preventing two of the kitchen maids from working was one fabricated by Hackett, and designed to allow him to spite her for the boldness with which she had stood up to him the previous Saturday. The galling part was that Hackett had succeeded admirably in his intention of irritating her, by insisting that she cancel her night out, for the good of the household. She had been really looking forward to her Saturday night date with Bill, but if Hackett wanted the additional gratification of her appealing to him, he could sing for it. She was damned if she would suffer the humiliation of asking the house steward for permission to walk over to Bill's cottage to cancel the date, and so she prepared now to slip out unobserved.

Looking around the corner of the milking parlour, she saw the fields behind the dairy to be deserted, and pausing only to pick up her basket, she quickly set off. The late April sunshine was warm upon her shoulders, and despite the disappointing task of cancelling with Bill, she relaxed a little as she crossed the back meadows. It was funny, she reflected, how the badness of someone like Hackett often brought out the best in others. Only half an hour ago Mrs Galligan, the cook, had called her in to the kitchen, and suspecting Kate's disappointment at her cancelled night off, had presented her with a mouth-watering strawberry flan. In spite of herself, Kate smiled at the memory of the cheerful Mrs Galligan suggesting that the flan would 'take the edge off your young man's disappointment.' Without confirming or denying the existence of a young man, Kate had thanked her sincerely, touched by the older woman's concern to offset Hackett's vindictiveness.

With the cake lying securely in her basket, she now rounded the sun-warmed wall of the orchard and suddenly came upon a patrol of armed soldiers.

'Morning, Miss . . .'

'Good morning,' she answered, hoping her voice didn't betray any uncertainty. She told herself there was no earthly reason why they should suspect her of being on anything but dairy business, and so with a smile and a nod she continued on her way.

'All right then,' cried the sergeant, 'you've seen a lady before. Get on with it.'

Conscious of the admiring glances of the soldiers, Kate walked on towards the pedestrian gate. Was it her imagination, she wondered, or had they stepped up the number of patrols? Perhaps she should mention it to Carey at their next meeting; meanwhile she had better get down to Bill's and back, before Hackett discovered her absence. Quickening her pace, she made for the nearby exit gate.

Kate turned left onto Blind Lane, hoping Bill would be in. She had never before visited him at the cottage and she was curious to know what his home would be like. Would it be neat and tidy in keeping with Bill's own appearance? Yes, she thought, it probably would be, but then again, with men you never knew. Perhaps the atmosphere would be casual, disorganised, needing a woman's home-making touch. She half hoped it would be, then, recognising the drift of her thoughts, she smiled ruefully.

Crossing the road, she saw the high hedge and at its end a sign saying 'Rose Cottage'. She opened the gate, walked to the door and knocked.

What a lovely garden, she thought, glancing around from the doorstep as she waited. She envied Bill living here; it was certainly more attractive than her own accommodation in the servants' quarters.

Receiving no answer to her knock, she felt her heart sink a

little. She really wanted to explain to Bill in person, and, she had to admit, she longed to see the inside of the cottage and how he lived.

Once again she knocked, and getting no answer, withdrew an envelope and paper from her basket, then set it down on the doorstep. She took a pencil from her pocket, leaned against the door, and wrote.

Dear Bill,

I am sorry to have missed you. Bad news I'm afraid, but horrible old Hackett has cancelled my night off. I'll tell you the full story when I see you, and I'm sorry again, especially at such short notice. I'm sure to get a night off during the week instead and we can paint the town then to make up for tonight. I enclose in the basket a strawberry flan from Mrs Galligan, the cook. She says it may 'take the edge off my young man's disappointment', but I must warn you that I'll be highly insulted if it does. You have my full permission to be so upset at not seeing me that you can only pick at the cake!

Anyway I'd better run as I just slipped out to tell you the bad news and I mustn't get caught. I'll pop out to the Hole in the Wall at one o'clock on Tuesday and let you know what night I'm off, and assuming you're still my young man, and that you were unable to enjoy the cake *too* much, we'll have a night on the town!

Take care,
Love,
Kate

She quickly sealed the letter, then slipped it into the basket which she moved to the side of the doorstep. She knew she ought to return quickly but on impulse crossed instead to the window and looked in. The net curtains made it difficult to see clearly, but she could make out a neatly made bed. The wardrobe and tallboy were properly closed and no discarded clothes could be seen.

Well, thought Kate, if ever they were to marry, it would be

for love, not because Bill sought a housekeeper. Turning from the window, she smiled wryly at the fanciful course of her thoughts, then started back, walking briskly towards the Under Secretary's Lodge.

Thirty-Three

It had been an amazing week. Scott could still hardly believe that in the space of a few days Gladstone had released Parnell and the Land Leaguers from jail; Parnell in turn had pledged to end the No Rent campaign and discourage unrest in expectation of a new Arrears Bill; the Coercion Act was to be ended; and in protest at all of these revolutionary steps Forster had resigned as Chief Secretary for Ireland.

The citizens of Dublin were jubilant at the sudden breakthrough, apparently worked out, via intermediaries, between Parnell and Gladstone, and throughout the country Parnell's release and the new eviction-preventing Arrears Bill were seen as great victories. It seemed that Forster and the hard line approach had had their day, to be replaced by a more consultative regime, and there was a tangible air of hope on all sides regarding this new policy.

At the music hall which Scott and Kate had attended that evening there had been an atmosphere of festivity which was almost intoxicating. It seemed to be a mixture of relief at the prospect of an end to strife and violence, joyful triumphalism at Parnell's release and Forster's defeat, and genuine hope for the future.

Looking out the carriage window as they travelled along the quays, Scott saw a group of men carrying a pro-Parnell banner and singing merrily.

'Now I know what you mean by an intoxicating atmosphere,' said Kate with a smile.

'In every sense of the word,' replied Scott, indicating the crate of stout bottles beside the men on the pavement.

'God bless Parnell!' shouted one of them to the carriage.

'Amen!' answered Kate cheerfully.

Scott looked at her appraisingly. So far he had subtly minimised discussion of politics with her. It was one thing having to misrepresent his views to the Invincibles, but he hadn't wished to lie to Kate any more than was necessary. Now, however, seemed an opportunity to probe a little.

'Do you mean that?' asked Scott, keeping the enquiry casual.

'Of course. Who else could have beaten Forster and had the small farmers' arrears written off?'

'No one, I guess. They say though he wouldn't have succeeded in his negotiations without the violence of the Land League activists.'

'Maybe not, but now he has succeeded, isn't it great? And the Land League has really raised the farmers off their knees. Now there'll be justice for the tenants, and that's all they wanted.'

'You reckon?'

'Of course, there's no more need for violence now.'

'I sure hope you're right.'

'Well it's common sense now, isn't it? Bloodshed can be a thing of the past.'

'Sure . . . sure it can . . .' *Common sense*, but would fanatics like the Invincibles listen to common sense? Scott thought anxiously. And if, with all the radical changes taking place, they somehow did, how would his mission end? And if his mission in Dublin were to end, what about himself and Kate?

'Hey,' she said, poking him playfully, 'no staring into space – you're supposed to be entertaining a lady.'

'I beg your pardon, Madam, most remiss I'm sure. Perhaps I can make it up to you by offering a nightcap?'

'Back in your cottage?'

'Yes.'

Kate looked at him, then smiled. 'Grand.'

Scott smiled back. 'I'll tell the cabman.'

'This sure is one abstemious nightcap,' said Scott, leaning over the kitchen table to pour tea for both of them.

'Well my Daddy always warned me about men who ply you with drink,' answered Kate with a grin.

'Your Daddy seemed to do a lot of warning,' he said, sitting beside her.

189

'For all the good it did, and you gallivanting in the back of the cab.'

'There's no law against kissing in the privacy of a carriage.'

'Just as well or we'd be master criminals!'

'And what would Daddy say then?'

'That you led me astray, all men being brutes!'

'Not with you, Kate . . .' he answered softly.

'I was only kidding.'

'I know, I know. Here, have some apple tart.'

'Is it your own?'

'My own?'

'Did you make it yourself?'

'I *bought* it myself. I'm afraid my talents don't extend to baking cakes.'

'I wouldn't be a bit surprised if they did. You have the house like a new pin.'

'Must be my . . . my years of self-sufficient bachelorhood!'

'Is that a life that appeals to you?'

The question was asked with a smile, but Scott sensed the seriousness behind it. 'So far it has, yes,' he answered. Despite the easy tone which they were both adopting, he felt a moment of truth was approaching. With the complications of the Bill Ryan/William Scott role he had tried to take a one-day-at-a-time approach in his relationship with Kate, yet all the while he knew that sooner or later matters must come to a head. But how was he to reconcile the duties and loyalties of a British Officer with loving an Irish nurse, for he may as well face it, he was enraptured by this woman.

'But you're not one of these confirmed old bachelors?' she asked.

'Hardly old at twenty-six,' he replied, playing for time.

Kate looked at him. 'You know what I mean,' she said softly, the bantering tone gone from her voice.

'No, I'm not a confirmed bachelor, far from it.' Looking at her face in the soft glow of the gas lamp he realised with a sudden rush of conviction that his future lay with this woman. Whatever the cost, whatever the problems, he mustn't let Kate slip through his fingers. He reached out and took her hand. 'Kate . . . I . . . I . . .'

'Yes?'

'I love you.'

She raised one hand and touched his cheek. Scott could feel his heart pounding as she gazed into his eyes.

'Oh, Bill, I love you too.'

Rising, he drew her into his arms and they kissed tenderly. After a moment he opened his eyes. Kate looked at him fondly, a small smile about her lips. 'I'm so glad, Bill . . .'

'I am too, Kate, I am too.' Absently he stroked her hair, then he looked at her seriously. 'You said once that you missed your family in America.'

'Yes?'

'When were you planning to join them?'

'As soon as I'd finished my last year of nursing here.'

'Could your training be finished in an American hospital?'

'I suppose it could – why?'

'I was thinking. I don't have a lot of money but I've often felt that ranching would be a good life.'

'I thought you wanted a stud farm in Ireland?'

He smiled. 'That was before I met you. America's a young country. I think it would be a good place for people making a new life . . .'

Kate looked at him, her eyes aglow. 'Yes?'

Scott held her gently in his arms, but just as he was about to speak a loud knock sounded on the hall door.

'Damn!'

'Who could that be?' asked Kate.

'I don't know, but I'd better answer it,' he said, struggling to contain his annoyance at the extremely bad timing of the caller. Gently he squeezed Kate's shoulder. 'I won't be a minute.'

'OK.'

He closed the kitchen door behind him, quickly crossed the hall and opened the front door. Tynan, Brady and a swarthy, heavily built man stood on the doorstep.

'Good evening, Bill,' said Tynan pleasantly, 'sorry to call at such a late hour, but we wanted a word . . .'

Scott's irritation was worsened by the smell of drink on

191

Tynan's breath. 'I'm afraid your timing is poor, Mr Tynan; I'm entertaining a guest.'

'My sincerest apologies for discommoding you, Bill, but a confab is rather called for.'

'Can't it wait until tomorrow?'

'Can't your love life wait till tomorrow?' asked Brady.

'My private life is no business of yours, Joe.'

'It is when it comes before the Invincibles!'

'Gentlemen, gentlemen, let us not squabble,' said Tynan amiably, 'we're all colleagues in nationalism. However, I must remind you of your oath of allegiance, Bill, and if you're wooing a young lady, I'm afraid I must ask you to put that in abeyance until another time.'

Scott paused a moment, then, realising that his credibility as Bill Ryan called for precedence over his private life, he stood aside. 'You'd better step in then.'

'You haven't met Major Thomas Quinn,' said Tynan as they entered the narrow hallway.

'How do you do,' said Scott, shaking hands.

'Pleased to meet you,' replied the swarthy man in a strong American accent. He looked about forty, but the grin on his face gave him a boyish air as he shook hands enthusiastically. 'I've heard good things about you, Bill,' he said.

'Glad to hear it.'

Scott had intended to bring them into the front parlour, but while Quinn had been speaking Joe Brady had quickly walked towards the kitchen and opened the door.

'Good evening,' he said, stepping into the warm room.

'Good evening,' answered Kate, without any trace of recognition in her voice.

Realising that there was no avoiding Kate meeting them now, Scott showed Tynan and Quinn into the kitchen.

'May I present Miss Lannigan?' he said. 'Kate, this is Mr Murphy, Mr Roche and Mr O'Brien. These gentlemen are horse breeders, and being in the vicinity they were adamant we engage in some late-night shop-talk.'

'I do most profusely apologise if we've interrupted your supper,' said Tynan.

'That's alright,' answered Kate, her irritation not quite concealed.

'I'm sure yourself and Bill can have many another,' said Brady pointedly.

'Yes, I'm sure we can,' said Kate. Reluctantly she rose. 'Well, if you'll excuse me, I'll leave you gentlemen to your business. Goodnight.'

'Goodnight, Miss.'

Scott followed her to the hall, closing the door behind him. 'Kate . . . Kate, I'm really sorry . . . They were absolutely insistent, they'd been drinking . . .'

She smiled and laid a hand on his arm. 'It's OK, Bill, it's not your fault.'

'We can talk as I walk you home. I'll tell them to wait.'

'No, no I'll slip up myself; it's only ten minutes.'

'But we've so much to talk of . . .'

'I know, and it's lovely and too important to be rushed. Why don't I come over tomorrow night for an hour?'

'Can you get out?'

She squeezed his arm and smiled gently. 'For you I can do anything, Bill.' Reaching up, she kissed him lingeringly. 'It's been a wonderful night . . .'

'All nights are with you.'

'I better go before you turn my head entirely! Eight o'clock tomorrow then?'

'Eight o'clock.'

'Goodnight so.'

'Goodnight.'

He watched as she moved jauntily down the garden path, and returned her wave as she shut the gate; then reluctantly he closed the hall door.

In spite of all that had happened during the evening, he knew he would have to try to remove Kate from his thoughts if he were to concentrate on his Bill Ryan persona before the waiting men. The presence of the American was unnerving. He'd need to be more alert now regarding his concocted life history, and somehow he felt that Tynan's reference to an important confab didn't suggest that the Invincibles might be

193

appeased by the new political climate. Returning to the kitchen, he found the three men seated around the table.

'Can I fix you drinks?' he asked.

'Thank you, but no,' answered Tynan, 'I think we've imbibed sufficiently as it is.'

'Whatever you wish,' said Scott, seating himself at the table.

'Well, Bill,' said Tynan, 'I dare say you're *au fait* with the latest political developments.'

'Sure, it's been quite a week.'

'You say that as though the news was good.'

'Well, Forster defeated, Parnell released, a Bill to wipe out rent arrears and prevent eviction, I'd call that progress.'

'It's window dressin'!,' said Brady bitterly.

'Ending the No Rent campaign was a betrayal of gigantic proportions.' Tynan's cheeks reddened as he spoke. 'A betrayal of all who risked life and limb in the cause of Ireland. The Irish Party and the Land League have been chucked a bone by their English masters, and they're almost choking on it in their pathetic gratitude.'

'We're supposed to jump for fuckin' joy because in future we won't be evicted off our own land,' added Brady.

Scott clenched his teeth in frustration. Couldn't they see? Couldn't they grasp that a milestone victory had been won in the matter of tenants' rights? That having defeated Forster, Parnell and the Irish Party could now make real progress – peacefully, and in Parliament – without the backdrop of evictions, burned crops and crossroads assassinations? Couldn't these fanatics see that the vast majority of Irish people were delighted at the gains made and the prospect of a new administration?

'People are so easily misled, Bill,' said Tynan. 'They think it's a concession having the Land League prisoners freed from jail. They think replacing a tyrant like Forster with this . . . this Lord Frederick bloody Cavendish is a mark of progress.' He snorted in contempt. 'Cavendish the moderate for Chief Secretary and the future is assured . . . They forget that Ireland is *our* country and no Englishman should be ruling it – not this Cavendish, not Forster, not any of them.'

Brady and Quinn nodded in agreement, and Scott knew

there could be no reasoned argument with these men about the parliamentary route to Home Rule for Ireland. If he wanted to maintain credibility with them he would have to pretend agreement with their philosophy. 'You're right, of course,' he said, as though now seeing things in perspective. 'When you look at it that way we mustn't let ourselves be fobbed off.'

'We won't be,' said Brady.

'Indeed we shall not,' added Tynan. 'Before the ink is dry on this so-called Kilmainham Treaty we're going to strike. Major Quinn here will lend his highly valuable military expertise to help ensure success.'

Quinn smiled engagingly. 'I fear you flatter me, Mr Tynan.'

'Not at all, not at all. Major Quinn has fought in your civil war, Bill, rose through the ranks and won a chest full of medals.'

'Really? Which side Major – Union or Confederate?'

Quinn's smile faded. 'Union of course. They fought for freedom and against slavery, just like the Invincibles are doing here in Ireland.'

'Of course,' answered Scott apologetically. 'Forgive me, I should have known . . .'

'Well I guess you were too young for the civil war,' answered Quinn, his amiability restored.

'Yeah, I was only nine when it ended.'

'The Major here was only seven when his family emigrated to America,' said Tynan, 'but like yourself, Bill, he's Irish and a nationalist in his heart and soul.'

'You know the Fenian raid of '67 into Canada?' said Brady, 'well Tom was on that.'

'And lots of other missions against the British, all over the world,' added Tynan.

'I'm impressed,' said Scott, wondering if Penrose had a file on this man.

Quinn laughed dismissively. 'They're making me sound like a hero when I'm just a soldier doing my duty. Were you in Clan na nGael back in the States, Bill?' he asked easily.

Scott felt a tightening in his stomach but kept his reply casual. 'No, I only became interested in Irish politics last year, around the time of my father's death. It was only then he

195

explained about being evicted and having to leave Ireland.'

'You were born in the States?'

'Yes, the wilds of Kentucky.'

'Our family settled in Ohio, moved there in '49 after the potato famine. You ever been to Ohio, Bill?'

'Yes, actually,' said Scott, thankful now for all the hours he had spent on American geography. 'As a child, my father once brought me to Cleveland.'

'Hey, I'll bet that was something to remember?' said Quinn with an easy smile.

Scott wondered was he being tested. Looking at Quinn's friendly face it was hard to know, but he was pleased at the choice of a childhood visit – he could sound credible while still being hazy about details. 'Well I was pretty young,' he answered, 'the main thing I recall was how big Lake Eyrie was, I thought it was the ocean . . .'

'Sure,' laughed Quinn, 'that would figure; Ohio's pretty impressive even if I say so myself. Still, I guess Kentucky's a good place to live if you're breeding horses.'

'Oh I didn't live in Kentucky, I just happened to be born there.'

'Oh, so where did you live?' asked Quinn interestedly.

'Philadelphia.'

'Philadelphia? I've an uncle there. What part did you live in?'

'Oh various parts,' answered Scott easily, 'we moved premises a fair bit.'

'No I meant where was your house?'

'Caroline Street.'

Quinn's eyes lit up. 'You're kidding me?'

'No.'

Quinn looked to Brady and Tynan in pleased astonishment. 'That's amazing. My uncle Peter has his bakery in Caroline Street. Which end did you live at?'

'Towards the church end,' answered Scott.

'You must know it then! You know Quinn's the bakery on the corner before the church?'

'Eh . . . I think so . . .'

'That's my Uncle Peter's! Hell, you can't miss it. How many

bakers sell loaves shaped like the map of Ireland?' laughed Quinn.

'Not too many,' Scott forced a grin.

'Did you know Peter well?'

'No . . . no I don't know if I knew him at all. I travelled a lot . . .'

'No you'd definitely know him to see, Bill. You must remember the red-haired man who rang the baker's bell up and down Caroline Street every day, with the picture of a loaf on his placard, right?' laughed Quinn.

'Right,' said Scott with a smile.

'Well that was my Uncle Peter,' said Quinn, delighted with this common ground. 'Hell, he probably poisoned you with his map of Ireland loaves!'

Scott smiled non-committedly, and suddenly Quinn looked at him with suspicion. 'You're not . . . you're not going to tell me, Bill, that you bought your bread in the little Jewish bakery, that you didn't support a fellow Irishman?'

'No, of course not.'

'You got your stuff in Quinn's then?'

Scott paused briefly, then realised he'd have to commit himself. 'Yes,' he answered suddenly, 'naturally we bought in Quinn's. Us Irish Americans have to stick together.'

Quinn punched him playfully on the shoulder. 'That's the spirit, Bill, that's the spirit!' Settling back comfortably, the American addressed Tynan and Brady. 'Well, Gentlemen, I guess we've achieved our objective.'

'So it would appear,' answered Tynan coldly.

'I'm not quite with you . . .' said Scott.

Brady leaned forward aggressively. 'No you're not with us, that's it in a fuckin' nutshell!'

Quinn turned to Scott, an easy smile still on his face. 'Fact is, Bill, you're a liar.'

Scott felt his stomach lurch. 'What?'

'A liar, Bill – you know, someone who tries to fool everybody.'

'I'm sorry, I'll have to ask you to explain,' said Scott, struggling to keep his voice steady.

'Oh I'll explain alright,' answered Quinn, the smile

197

suddenly leaving his face. 'There's no map of Ireland loaves, no red-haired bell-ringer, because there's no such place as Quinn's bakery. I don't have an Uncle Peter, in Philadelphia or anywhere else. Is that clear enough for you?' Reaching into his coat, Quinn withdrew a heavy revolver which he pointed at Scott.

'You've been playing a dangerous game, Bill,' said Brady menacingly.

'No, no . . .'

'Yes! A very deadly game. You remember the boatman and what happens to informers?'

'No! No you misunderstand . . .'

'Do we indeed?' Tynan's voice was ironic. 'I rather think not, Mr Ryan, or whatever your real name is.'

'My real name is Ryan.'

'Then why all the lies?' asked Quinn.

'I . . . I had to . . .'

'Why?'

Scott sighed. 'I really didn't want to have to tell you this but . . .'

'Don't worry, pal,' said Brady venomously, 'you'll be telling a lot of things you don't want to by the time I'm finished with you.'

'Just a moment, Joe,' said Tynan, raising a hand. 'Very well, Ryan, if you've something to say, now is the moment.'

Scott leaned forward, praying that the back-up story he had devised for a situation like this would buy him time. His cover gone, his best hope now was the gun hidden in the bedroom.

When he spoke he kept his voice low-key and dejected. 'All that stuff about Philadelphia . . . it's . . . it's lies, all the stories about my father and I breeding horses – they're not true, and I made them up because . . . well . . . I was ashamed to tell you the truth . . .'

'Go on,' said Tynan.

Scott lowered his eyes. 'Well the truth is, my father *did* die last year, and on his deathbed he did tell me, for the first time, all about being evicted and having to leave Ireland. But . . . well . . .'

'Go on, man,' said Quinn.

'It wasn't in a hospital, it was in prison.'

'Your father was in prison?'

'Both of us were.'

Tynan regarded him curiously. 'For what?'

'For . . . for horse-thieving,' muttered Scott. He looked up at them earnestly. 'I was afraid that you'd turn me down for the Invincibles if I told you the truth.'

'How do we know this isn't another pack of lies?' asked Brady.

'I can prove it's not.'

'How?'

'I have my discharge papers from prison. I can get them from the bedroom,' said Scott, starting to pull back his chair.

'Don't move!' Brady's voice was cold and harsh.

'No need for you to go,' said Tynan. 'Joe will get them.'

'No, they're hidden. I'll have to dig them out.' They stared at him in suspicion. 'Look, they're not the kind of thing I was going to leave hanging about, are they? I had to hide them,' he added, trying to keep his hands from shaking. His mouth felt dry and his heart pounded, but he knew he must keep thinking coolly.

'Very well,' said Tynan suddenly rising. 'We shall all procure the documents together.'

'Thank you,' said Scott, pulling back his chair. 'They're in the bedroom.'

'You go first, Joe,' said Tynan, 'the Major and I shall escort Mr Ryan.'

Brady rose and opened the door leading from the kitchen to the bedroom, to be followed by Scott, Tynan and Quinn, the latter with the revolver carefully trained on Scott.

'I've got them in the wardrobe over here . . .'

'Stay where you are!' called Tynan. 'Don't move from that bed. Now just indicate to Joe where the papers are hidden.'

Scott felt beads of sweat forming on his brow. He *had* to get to the wardrobe. 'I'll need to show him, Mr Tynan,' he said, trying to keep the fear from his voice.

'And why is that, pray?'

'It's . . . there's a false bottom . . .' answered Scott, improvising desperately.

'A false bottom in what?'

'In a wooden box holding the papers.'

'Then tell Joe where the box is.'

'It's tucked away. If I could just show . . .'

'Tell him where the god-damn box is!' snapped Quinn impatiently.

'It's . . . it's under the blankets in at the back, top shelf,' answered Scott, figuring that a break for the wardrobe would be suicidal.

Brady took a chair, and standing on it, reached forward into the deep recesses of the wardrobe.

'I can't see anything in here,' he called back.

'No, further in and to your right,' answered Scott.

Brady leaned further in, then with lightning speed Scott swung around and buried his knee in Tynan's crotch. The older man screamed in agony, and Scott forced him back onto Quinn. Knocked off balance, and with Tynan in the way, the American was unable to fire his pistol before Scott was upon him, leaping over the collapsing Tynan.

Recovering quickly, Quinn swung round his gun hand, but Scott caught him by the wrist and punched him in the stomach at the same time. Quinn reeled from the blow but held doggedly onto the gun, its barrel pointing towards the ceiling as they struggled.

From the corner of his eye Scott saw Brady jumping down from the chair, and exerting all the strength in both his arms, he swung Quinn's gun hand around. Forcing the hand downwards, he levelled the gun at the rapidly advancing Brady. Scott managed to work his finger through the trigger guard, then screamed in pain as Quinn smashed him in the ribs with his free hand. Swiftly jabbing backwards with his left elbow, Scott caught the American in the face, and as Quinn staggered backwards Scott pulled the pistol from his hand.

He grasped the weapon and twirled round suddenly, only to take a full force punch on the chin from Brady. The gun fell from his hands as he reeled across the room, then the burly stone mason was upon him. Brady had whipped his wooden baton from his pocket, and gripping Scott by the hair, he swung fiercely with the heavy weapon. Taking the blow directly on his skull, Scott instantly collapsed to the floor. Brady raised the baton again over the head of his unmoving opponent, then, seeing Scott's condition at close range, he slowly, and reluctantly, lowered the weapon.

Thirty-Four

Lord Frederick Cavendish, second son of the Duke of Devonshire, couldn't dispel his anxiety. His marriage to Gladstone's niece, Lucy Lyttleton, had been an eminently happy one, but now his sense of duty both to his beloved Lucy and to the Prime Minister had been put to the test, for two days previously Gladstone had asked him to accept what many considered to be a poisoned chalice – the post of Chief Secretary for Ireland, in replacement of William Forster.

Despite a deep reluctance to take the post and his doubts regarding his own suitability, the middle-aged aristocrat felt duty bound to accept his being chosen by the Prime Minister – a choice much derided in the newspapers, where it had been widely accepted that the job would go to the dynamic Mayor of Birmingham, Joseph Chamberlain.

Sitting now by the window of his drawingroom, Cavendish looked up as the butler entered carrying the newspapers on a silver tray.

'I'll take the papers, Bradberry,' said Lucy from her place on the *chaise longue.*

'Very good, Milady.'

If the man thought it unusual for Lady Lucy Cavendish to intercept her husband's newspapers he gave no indication of the fact, but instead bowed politely, then left, closing the drawingroom door quietly.

'No need to spare me, my Dear,' said Cavendish. 'What have they to say about me?'

Lucy scanned the columns, shaking her head in anger. 'It really is too bad of them. How can they be so hurtful?'

'What does it say?'

She read with disdain. 'Lord Cavendish is a gentleman whose distinction it is to possess no conceivable qualification for the office . . .'

'Perhaps they have a point, my Dear.'

'Nonsense, Freddy.'

'I've never been an accomplished public speaker.'

'That's not important. What is important is your experience at the Treasury. How can the newspapers overlook the knowledge of Irish affairs you gained there? Who else has your grasp of the Land Purchase question?'

He gave a small smile. 'Dear Lucy, you'd be a fine advocate. What does the other one say?'

Lucy studied the paper for a moment, then breathed out in exasperation.

'Well?'

'Never was so small a politician appointed to so great a post at a crisis so important.'

'That's . . . that's rather rum . . .'

'It's quite disgraceful, and really, Freddie, you mustn't heed it. They're simply ill-tempered and disagreeable because they predicted Chamberlain was certain to get the post, and now they've been proven wrong. You'll be a first-class Chief Secretary.'

'One can't be sure in such matters. Even Father spoke against my accepting – what was the phrase – "so odious and thankless a task".'

'Your father was looking at it selfishly. One can't do that when a public figure. There's a duty involved.'

'I know, Dear.'

She crossed to him and took his hands. 'You mustn't underrate yourself, Freddie. You could really do some good in Ireland. With Spencer as replacement Viceroy, and you as Chief Secretary, a fresh start is being signalled. And reaction in Ireland has been very positive.'

'To Parnell's release and Forster's departure, not to me personally.'

'Nevertheless the public mood has shifted. The people want peace, they want justice. With you at the helm, that could be brought about.'

'It's the one thought that keeps me going.'

Before he could say any more there was a knock on the door and Bradberry entered carrying an envelope. 'I'm sorry to disturb you, Sir, but it's an urgent message from Lord Spencer.'

203

'That's alright,' said Cavendish, rising. 'Thank you, Bradberry.'

'Thank you, Sir.'

Cavendish opened the sealed envelope as the butler left the room.

'Well?' asked Lucy.

'Spencer is leaving for Dublin on the early train tonight. He wants me to join him.'

'But you're still clearing your desk.'

'He says Treasury affairs will be taken care of, and could I make the eight-twenty train to Holyhead.'

'What will you do?'

'I suppose I'd better join him. I shall have to be packed in rather a hurry.'

'We can dine early. I'll arrange it with Cook.'

'Dear Lucy, what should I do without you?'

'What you will do in your new post.'

'And what is that, pray?'

'Manage very well.' She squeezed his arm. 'They're all wrong, Freddie. They don't know you as I do. You'll be a wonderful Chief Secretary.'

Cavendish leaned down and kissed her tenderly. 'You'll join me in Dublin as soon as possible?'

'Of course, the moment I've settled our affairs here. And now I'd better speak to Cook.'

'Very good.' He watched with affection as she left to make the arrangements, her words of encouragement buoying his spirits somewhat, then he crossed and pulled the bellcord to have his valet summoned.

Now that his departure was imminent, he told himself that for better or worse he had been chosen, and so he must serve the people of Ireland to the best of his ability. It was time to suppress his doubts and worries and concentrate on doing his duty, for this time tomorrow, after due pomp and ceremony, he, Frederick Cavendish, would take office as the new Chief Secretary for Ireland.

Thirty-Five

Her heart beating excitedly, Kate walked along Blackhorse Avenue, unconscious of the sights and sounds of the early summer dusk. Ever since her conversation with Bill the previous evening her head had been in a spin. It had been the first time they had professed their love for each other, and Bill's suggestion of a future in America was almost fairytale-like in its appeal.

The burning sense of injustice which had initially fuelled her actions with the Invincibles was now largely quelled by the reforms of the forthcoming Arrears Bill, and with a replacement Viceroy and Chief Secretary arriving tomorrow to head the new administration, there seemed no point in further violence or intrigue. It was time for a fresh start, both for the country and for herself and Bill. She reasoned that the visit of Brady and the other two men the previous night must have been to cancel whatever scheme they had been involving Bill in, and with the disbandment of the Invincibles normal life could now resume.

Turning left into Blind Lane, Kate felt her heart lift in anticipation of seeing her handsome American. Soon she would be with him, sharing in his laughter, savouring the tender expression that came into his eyes when he spoke to her seriously, waiting for the formal proposal of marriage which she knew, with exquisite certainty, was at hand.

She reached the garden gate, swung it open, and started up the path, the smell of nightstock heavy in the air. Kate gave a loud playful series of knocks on the front door, then waited eagerly for Bill's response.

A moment passed, and, receiving no answer, she frowned, then knocked a second time. The loud knock echoed down the hall, and getting no answer again, she felt a sinking feeling overcome her. After a third knock and a long wait she knew he wasn't there, and with the knowledge came the disturbing

205

thought that something must really be wrong. Bill would never have missed such an important rendezvous of his own choice.

Kate pressed against the door, and, finding it locked, moved around the side of the house. Despite the deepening dusk, none of the windows had a light burning. She reached the back door and turned the handle, and to her surprise it swung open.

Standing on the back step, she had a strong urge to run away, fearful of what might lie within the darkened cottage. Her mouth had suddenly gone dry, and with pulses pounding she told herself she must investigate. She gathered her nerve, then took a deep breath and stepped in, taking care to leave the door ajar in case she might want to leave quickly.

Threading carefully, she crossed the kitchen and opened the door to the hall. She felt her way in the gloom, and moved to the small table just inside the door, on which she had seen an oil lamp the previous night. She ran her hand along the table and found the lamp, still in place, and beside it a box of matches.

Kate lit the lamp, her fingers trembling, and seeing nothing untoward in the hall, she opened the door to the parlour and stepped in. The oil lamp cast shadows along the wall of the neatly kept room, but again all seemed in order.

She nervously opened the door leading from the parlour to the scullery and entered the room, only to find it too deserted. Her heart still pounding, she quickly crossed to the kitchen. By the lamp's glow she could now see that the cups from their supper still lay in place on the table, and the sight sent a shiver up her spine. It meant that Bill had taken no meals here in nearly twenty-four hours. Which suggested that he must have left with Brady and the other men. Unless . . .

Kate tried not to dwell on the alternatives, but in spite of herself her thoughts were on what might lie behind the bedroom door. She looked at it with a sense of dread, all her instincts telling her to put down the lamp and run from the darkened cottage, but she knew that would be letting Bill down. She stood staring at the door as though paralysed, then suddenly she moved forward, swung the door open and stepped into the bedroom.

To her relief the room was empty. Looking around, she saw

a chair over against the wardrobe, the top press of which hung open. Immediately it struck a jarring note. Everything else in the room was neat and orderly, so why would Bill leave the chair and open press if he were getting something from the wardrobe?

Crossing to the chair, she stood up on it, and holding the lantern, looked into the open press. There was nothing in it but blankets, the top one badly crumpled. She stepped down in puzzlement and tried to marshal the facts. The only explanation seemed to be that Bill had left in a considerable hurry. But why? And knowing the importance of their meeting tonight, why had he not returned?

The answer had to be that whatever business the Invincibles had with Bill wasn't yet concluded. And then an even worse thought struck her. Supposing *Bill* had been their business. Could he conceivably be some kind of traitor to their cause? Surely not, she told herself, she was letting her imagination run away with her. There was probably a perfectly plausible and much less dramatic reason for his absence. And yet, she couldn't shake off her unease.

She moved back to the kitchen, and setting the lamp on the table, sat down to think. She knew she couldn't stay here waiting on Bill, her absence would only draw Hackett's attention, and attention was the last thing wanted by either the Invincibles or herself and Bill. For the same reason she couldn't risk going to Carey's house. Even if by chance he were at home, and prepared to tell her the truth, it would all take too long.

Even slipping out for an hour tonight had been a risk, and Kate knew that Hackett was only waiting for such a misdemeanour to create a scene. That left the police. If she were certain that the Invincibles had abducted Bill she could always notify the Dublin Metropolitan Police. But in that case, what could Bill's objective have been with the Invincibles, and could she betray Carey and the others to the police in order to save him? Would it be right to put her love for one man before every other consideration? She didn't know; and, she decided, for now it didn't arise – any such action would be jumping the gun by a mile.

No, she would call back tomorrow. Bill might well be back by then. In fact he would probably get word to her, knowing she would be worried. Seeing a pen and paper on the bookcase by the window, she rose and crossed to it. She had dipped the quill in the ink when something that Carey had said about evidence arose from her memory. 'The legal system stands or falls on evidence,' he had cautioned her. 'Leave as little as possible linking you to the Under Secretary's residence; and none at all linking you to Bill Ryan or anyone to do with the Invincibles.'

There was no doubt that a letter to Bill would fall within Carey's description. She paused, but only for a moment, her concern for Bill easily outweighing the importance of Carey's rules of conduct. She leaned on the bookcase and wrote.

Dearest Bill,

I found the back door open and let myself in. I know something important must have happened to prevent you from meeting me like we said. I pray you're safe and well, Bill, I really do. Tomorrow at lunch time I'll get out and come over, by which time I hope you're back.

Till then,
All my love,
Kate

She crossed the room and placed the note prominently on the table, wedged by the two cups, then moved to the still-open back door. Blowing out the lantern, she placed it on the window ledge, then she closed the door behind her, stepped out into the garden and made towards the gate.

The scent of nightstock struck her again but this time she hardly noticed. She tried to convince herself that all would be well but she knew in her heart that only Bill's presence would allay her growing sense of unease. Closing the gate in the deepening dusk, she headed back, unhappily, towards the Under Secretary's Lodge.

Thirty-Six

'Shall we make a start, Gentlemen?' said Tynan impatiently, as Carey, Brady and Curley accepted drinks on a tray carried by McCaffrey. Although the upstairs bar was a secure and convenient venue, Tynan sometimes wondered at the wisdom of holding committee meetings there, with the attendant distraction of available liquor.

'Ready and willing, Mr T, ready and willing,' answered Carey cheerfully, his glass of whiskey at hand on the table.

'Very well then. We've a number of points to consider, Gentlemen. Let us commence with our erstwhile colleague, Mr Ryan.'

Lowering his pint of stout, Ned McCaffrey shook his head in wonder. 'Bill Ryan a traitor. God it's hard to credit, what?'

'He certainly had me convinced,' agreed Curley. 'All of us really, I suppose.'

'Well I don't know, I always had a . . . a sort of reservation,' said Carey. 'That's why I kept up the questioning via Kate Lannigan.'

'For all the good that did.' Brady's tone was dismissive.

'I beg your pardon, Joe,' answered Carey, 'but it yielded very useful data for Major Quinn. That's what provided the background information for him to set his trap.'

Brady shrugged. 'We were lucky there, that's all. Gettin' a tip-off when Quinn arrived from America was just good luck.'

'The thing I can't get over is the ferryman business,' said Curley. 'Bill seemed such a nice fella, it's hard to believe he'd kill one of his own just to impress us.'

'It's not that hard to believe, Dan, not if one looks at history,' said Tynan. 'Mr Ryan should serve to remind us of the need for vigilance. We're up against a ruthless foe, we must be prepared for all manner of back-stabbing and duplicity.'

'I'll tell ye one thing,' said Brady, his voice venomous, 'I don't know how I stopped meself from finishing off the bastard last night. I felt like buryin' the baton in his treacherous bleedin' brains!'

'As an enemy agent he's much more valuable to us alive,' said Carey, 'we could learn a lot about British intelligence from him.'

'And he's in Shanley's place now?' asked McCaffrey.

'Since last night. We brought him out to Glasnevin in Skin-the-Goat's cab,' answered Brady.

'He's a dangerous man,' said Curley. 'I think we should finish him off as quickly as possible.'

Tynan smiled reassuringly. 'Don't worry, Dan, I've seen the place they're holding him in; there'll be no escaping from those premises. Besides, it's only for a few days, and our men are armed and alert. I don't imagine Mr Ryan will be going anywhere.'

'Yes, but it's what he may have already told the authorities that I'm worried about. He knows a hell of a lot about us.'

'A worry shared by all of us, Dan. But the fact is, no effort has been made to detain us. And as I've said before, one mustn't forget that for all their numbers and might, our opponents are constrained by the intricacies of the law. They'd need firm evidence to convict us of anything, and with Ryan disposed of when we're finished questioning him, they won't have that evidence.'

'I take your point, Mr Tynan,' said Carey, 'but the sooner we question him and finish him off, the better. Am I right, boys?'

The others nodded assent.

'You're perfectly right, Jim, and we shall hold him for no more than a couple of days,' answered Tynan, a speech-making lilt coming into his voice. 'Time, I grant you, is of the essence. Rapidity of action, one might say . . .'

'Look, what's our next move?' cut in Brady bluntly.

Tynan regarded him for a moment. 'Our next move, my precipitous friend, is to respond to the probability of the authorities knowing about the Invincibles. There's a risk, naturally, of some of us being detained for questioning. Therefore I propose that while we're at full strength, we redouble our efforts to get Burke.'

'He'll be certain to meet the new Chief Secretary's boat tomorrow. Maybe we could get him on the way?' suggested Curley.

'Maybe we could get them both,' put in Brady. 'That sort of welcome for Lord Frederick bleedin' Cavendish would show the English what we think of their soft-soapin' and bribery!'

'Hear hear!' said Curley enthusiastically.

Tynan ran his hand absently through his beard. 'It would indeed be a spectacular gesture . . .'

'Especially if we were to pull it off on Cavendish's very first day,' said Carey.

'Hang on! Listen . . .' cried McCaffrey suddenly. The sound of footsteps could be heard quickly ascending the stairs.

'Who the hell . . .' started Curley. He was cut off by a loud knock from the landing.

Brady rose quickly and crossed to the locked door. 'Who is it?' he called belligerently.

'Kinsella!' came the answer, 'I must see Patrick Tynan!'

Recognising the voice of Tynan's friend, the Blackrock station-master, Brady turned the key and opened the door, locking it again immediately Kinsella bustled into the room. The excited man crossed to the table. 'Have you heard, Patrick? Have you heard the news from Ballina?'

'No, what is it?'

Breathless from the stairs, Kinsella leaned against the table. When he spoke his voice was laden with horror. 'A group of children was celebrating Parnell's release. They were making a lot of noise and the police . . . the police used buckshot. They shot the children! The bastards shot the children!'

'Oh Jesus,' said Carey softly. 'Oh no . . .'

'They shot them . . . they shot the children,' repeated Kinsella.

Tynan's face was pinched in shock and anger as he slowly rose to his feet. 'By Christ!' he shouted. 'By Christ the bloodshed of our children won't go unanswered! This massacre will be paid for, and dearly, by the blood-thirsty invader!' He looked around the room. 'We've got to see that this hideous deed is answered by the destruction of the tyrant

211

responsible. The tyrant whose official hands are already stained with our children's gore! Gentlemen, we must mobilise our men immediately. Whatever the cost, whatever the risk, the enemy must be punished. Tomorrow we execute Messrs Burke and Cavendish, come hell or high water! Agreed?'

'Agreed!' they answered vigorously.

Thirty-Seven

Lying on the gloomy barn floor, Scott felt his head throb with pain. The make-shift bandage he had fashioned from a strip of his shirt was tightly wrapped around the blood-caked wound which Brady had inflicted on him the previous night. Scott reckoned that the improvised dressing might just about keep out the dirt and prevent infection, but the pain was something he knew he would simply have to endure.

He took out his watch. Despite its face being cracked during the fight in the cottage, it was still working, and he placed it in the shaft of light coming in under the door. 9.30 pm. He had been a captive here almost twenty-four hours, assuming they had brought him here immediately after the fight.

Not that he knew his whereabouts. It was, he presumed, a location isolated enough to make cries for help pointless, a theory supported by the birdsong all about. On the other hand he had frequently heard trains in the distance, and the Invincibles would hardly have wanted the trouble of moving him somewhere deep in the countryside. His guess was an isolated house on the edge of the city.

A painstaking exploration of his immediate surroundings had suggested that the room in which he lay had once been used as a barn of some kind. There were no windows, but a big, unyielding pair of double doors, no doubt padlocked on the outside. The place was now largely filled with empty wooden packing cases. Opposite the double doors was a heavy metal door under which a shaft of yellow light appeared. This door, he had discovered, led to a kind of passageway linking the barn with the kitchen of the adjacent house.

Coming to at around eleven that morning, he had found himself lying on the floor beside the metal door, a heavy blanket thrown roughly over him. He had heard the voices of his captors as they drank tea in the nearby kitchen, then he had feigned unconsciousness while trying to get his bearings.

213

The episode with Brady, Tynan and Quinn had come back with a rush, and he realised from the throbbing ache in his head how his desperate struggle in the cottage must have ended.

Lying on the cold floor of the barn, he listened to the men's voices. He reckoned there were three of them, an older and a younger man with Dublin accents, and another who sounded as though he were from Cork. Unaware of his having woken, they were talking freely. The topic of conversation was the expected arrival the following day of Cavendish and Spencer, the new Chief Secretary and Viceroy, and in common with the other Invincibles the men were deploring the enthusiasm with which the people were greeting the recent political developments.

'This Kilmainham Treaty business is a bloody cod!' said the Corkman. 'Release Parnell and replace Forster, and half the country goes mad.'

The older Dubliner snorted. 'Yeah, if we're good boys and lick their boots for another fifty years maybe they'll consider Home Rule for Ireland then!'

'Kilmainham Treaty me arse!' said the other Dublin man, 'the only treaty worth havin' is a treaty grantin' us full independence.'

'True for ye boy!' said the Corkman. 'And I'll tell ye something else. Lord Frederick Cavendish and his lap-dog Burke are making a big mistake if they think the Irish National Invincibles can be bought off.'

'We'll teach them a lesson alright,' said the older man. 'Ireland still has some true men left.'

'And true women. Don't forget Carey's girl played her part; that helped put a halt to the gallop of our friend here.'

'Oh yeah, fair play to her,' said the Corkman. 'Joe was saying she's a fine bit of stuff too, lovely auburn hair . . .'

'Get outta that!' said the young Dubliner, 'it's sayin' your prayers ye should be at your age!'

'Ah there's life in the auld dog yet,' laughed the Corkman.

There was the sound of a chair being pulled back. 'I'm glad to hear how lively you're feelin' – there's a mound of dishes to be washed here. So come on, let's be havin' you!'

Laughingly they rose from the table as Scott lay numbed on the floor. *Don't forget Carey's girl played her part; that helped put a stop to the gallop of our friend here.* Oh, God, no, he thought. No! Not Kate. Not Kate working for the Invincibles . . . *Lovely auburn hair . . .*

Closing his eyes in anguish, he knew it had to be true. With a sickening lurch of recognition, he saw now the reasoning behind a series of events previously unsettling in a vague, subconscious way: the fluke of his chance meeting with Kate when Brady suggested a night's dancing; their instant rapport; her allowing a stranger to escort her home that night; all the questions she had asked him about America and his supposed father's death.

How could he have been so naïve? And then he thought, could they perhaps have been blackmailing her in some way? And the more he thought about it, the clearer it was that he had to escape and see her.

That had been this morning, but as the day had passed he had realised how slight the possibility of escape was. His jailers had wordlessly brought him food at lunchtime and again at six o'clock, but each time as one had carried in the food, the younger man with the Dublin accent had covered Scott with a pistol.

Lying uncomfortably on the ground, he cursed Penrose bitterly. Why couldn't the damned man have acted when he had asked him to? If the colonel hadn't been so pig-headed, he could have rounded up the Invincibles, in which case Cavendish and the new Viceroy wouldn't be arriving tomorrow to potential assassination, and he, Scott, wouldn't be lying here with an aching skull and wondering if these were his last nights on earth.

Looked at dispassionately, it seemed they might well be. The only reason he could think of why they weren't interrogating him now – prior to putting a bullet in his head – was because they had bigger fish to fry. Time was running out, and with no prospect of rescue it was up to him to save his own life, and very possibly the lives of the country's rulers.

And see Kate. That, he reflected guiltily, in some ways seemed the most important thing of all. But first he had to escape. And looking at the thick stone walls and locked doors, he had no idea how he could.

Thirty-Eight

Kate tried hard to keep the worry from her face as she carried two heavy pails of milk towards the dairy, its granite walls reflecting the late afternoon sunshine. Entering the door, she saw Mr McDaid sitting at the table in the corner, his shortsightedness causing him to hold a newspaper up close to his face.

'Time for a cup of tea, Kate,' he called. 'I've poured one out for you.'

'Thanks,' she answered, forcing herself to sound pleasant and normal. She emptied the pails into a churn, then sat at the table, thankful for Mr McDaid's preoccupation with the paper. The headline read 'Messenger of Hope', referring to the eagerly awaited arrival that morning of Lord Frederick Cavendish, as new Chief Secretary for Ireland.

'Begod that was a great reception for Cavendish and the new Viceroy,' said Mr McDaid.

'Really?'

'Oh aye, military bands, a special train, crowds cheering, according to this. Good luck to them too. No more than they deserve.' He smiled. 'Did you hear about the students at Trinity College?'

'No . . . no I didn't.'

McDaid lowered the newspaper laughingly. 'God, but they're right scamps. You know the Lord Mayor is a baker? Well, didn't they shower him with crusts of bread when the cavalcade was passing the college! Aren't they desperate?'

'Yes,' said Kate, sipping absently at her tea.

'It says here that Spencer is a fine figure of a man, wore his collar and star of Saint Patrick, and was mounted on a beautiful horse.'

Kate realised she had better show some interest or McDaid would be asking her if there was something wrong. She lowered the teacup. 'And what about Lord Cavendish – how

217

did he travel?' she asked, wondering if her voice really sounded as strained and unnatural as it seemed to her.

'Oh a carriage for his lordship. I suppose he'll need his energy to run the country,' answered McDaid, unaware of Kate's anxiety as he casually returned to the paper.

Kate knew that to many people this was a great day, the dawn of a new era in Anglo-Irish relations, but she couldn't work up any enthusiasm for the political breakthrough that was taking place. Her thoughts kept returning to Bill's empty cottage and the reasons why he should still be missing. Not having received any message from him, she had slipped out again at lunchtime, but the cottage had been just as she had left it the previous night, her note still propped undisturbed on the kitchen table.

She didn't want to panic, but her instincts told her something was seriously amiss. A meeting with Carey, she had decided, was the only answer. As soon as she finished work this evening she would go to his house. By now she didn't care if it got her into trouble with Hackett. She would even risk the possibility that Carey's house might be under police surveillance. She had to know if Bill was alright, and if need be she would wait at Denzille Street all night to see Carey, and either have her fears allayed or confirmed.

McDaid sipped his tea noisily. 'Well, Kate, this could be a day to tell your grandchildren about, if all that the papers say is true. A "future bright with hope" they're calling it.'

'Let's hope it is,' said Kate, trying for a smile, but feeling instead a growing sense of foreboding.

If only they knew, thought James Carey as he observed the patrons crowded into Wrenn's public house. The bar's regular Saturday afternoon drinkers had been joined by the crowds in the city for the lunchtime procession, which had preceded the swearing-in of the new Chief Secretary and Viceroy, and a large group of Invincibles had taken over an entire corner of the pub, their initial irritation with the flag-waving crowds gradually abating as they lowered creamy pints of stout.

Carey looked at the other drinkers and smiled to himself. Yes, if only they knew. If only these docile idiots who cheered their new masters knew how short would be their reign. If only they knew that in Skin-the-Goat's cab, parked just outside, lay the concealed weapons which would soon be unsheathed to devastating effect.

He looked around the assembled Invincibles, some of them anxious-looking, some maintaining an air of easy bravado, and all, he knew, excited at the mission they were about to undertake. Tynan had sent a message to Dan Curley, regarding intelligence he had received about Burke and Cavendish's schedule for the day, and the plans had been laid accordingly. All they had to wait was another few hours, and then they'd make history.

From the corner of his eye Carey saw Joe Smith enter the pub. Smith was one of their sources in the British administration in Dublin Castle, and watching him approach, Carey thought he detected a nervousness in the man.

'The bould Joe, take the weight off your feet.' Carey made his tone cheerful, hoping to calm Smith with a relaxed and confident manner.

'Hello, Mr Carey.'

'Dan, can you put in a shout for Joe here?' said Carey expansively. 'Pint of Guinness, isn't it, Joe?'

'Yes, thanks – porter please.'

'Pint of porter when you're ready, Michael,' called Curley to the barman.

'Well, Joe,' said Carey, 'I'm glad you could make it. You won't be in any hurry home on a nice sunny day like today, sure you won't?'

'Eh no . . . not really.'

'Good man, because we need your assistance. Isn't that so, Dan?'

'We do indeed,' answered Curley.

'In what way?'

'Well, Joe,' said Carey, lowering his voice conspiratorially, 'I know pretty well what Burke looks like, but you see these hob-nobs all the time in the Castle. So we'd like you to come with us and make sure there's no mistake about identity.'

'What do you want Burke for?' asked Smith, a touch of alarm in his voice.

Curley smiled. 'We have some unfinished business with the gentleman.'

'It's alright, Joe,' added Carey reassuringly. 'We don't want you to do anything, just point him out to us, OK?'

Smith hesitated, then nodded. 'OK, Mr Carey, OK.'

'Sound man.'

'Ah, here's your pint,' said Curley, paying the barman the two pence, then passing the tankard to Smith.

'And a few more pints if you want them,' suggested Carey, 'we won't be leaving here until about five.'

'Where do we go then?' asked Smith.

'The Phoenix Park.' Carey smiled broadly. 'Sure where else would we go on fine summer evening?'

At a quarter to six Superintendent Mallon of the Dublin Metropolitan Police strode up Parkgate Street and in through the main entrance to the Phoenix Park. The fine weather and the festive air generated by the earlier cavalcade through the city seemed to have combined in lifting the spirits of the citizens, many of whom were strolling and relaxing in the park.

Apart from the pinching of his new boots, which was becoming painful, the superintendent was in a good mood. The day's events had gone perfectly, from the arrival of Cavendish and Spencer in Kingstown, through their triumphal procession across the city, and culminating in the solemn swearing-in of the new Chief Secretary and Viceroy.

The crowds in town had been enthusiastic in their welcome for the new administrators, and apart from a boy at the station starting some cheers for Parnell, there hadn't been the slightest sign of trouble. It was a great relief, he reflected, how the mood of the people had radically changed since Forster's resignation and the release of Parnell. The departure of Forster had seemed like a millstone lifted from Mallon's neck, the former Chief Secretary having been a constant target for extremists, and the police workload had certainly lightened in the new climate of hope.

There was still plenty of routine police work however, such as the rendezvous to which he was now making his footsore way. A message had arrived in the office that John Kenny, one of his underworld informants, wanted to see him at a quiet spot behind the Vice-regal Lodge. Mallon had no idea what it might be about, but he had left the office early, deciding to meet Kenny and then walk from the park to his home in the nearby North Circular Road.

Moving briskly along, Mallon caught the strains of a military band playing for the entertainment of the crowds. As he reached the turn to the Zoological Gardens he saw a man gesturing to him. Recognising one of the plain-clothes police officers who had been mingling with the crowds, Mallon approached.

'Good evening, Superintendent.'

'Good evening, Gilroy. Something up?'

'Possibly, Sir. I've seen a couple of ne'er-do-wells a while back.'

'Namely?'

'Joe Brady, James Carey and Patrick Delaney. May I ask, Sir, if you're meeting one of our underworld friends?'

'Yes, actually, I am . . .' Mallon saw the worried look on the policeman's face. 'You think they may be setting a trap for me?'

'Well they know who you are, Sir, and they have it in for you.'

'Yes, yes I dare say.' Mallon looked thoughtful for a moment. The message to meet Kenny had been rather out of the blue.

'Were you to meet him in an isolated spot, Sir?'

'Fairly. Back of the Vice-regal Lodge.'

'I don't like the sound of it, Superintendent.'

'No, Gilroy, nor do I.' Even if it were all just a coincidence, he thought, the idea of a walk all the way up to the lodge and back, in the increasingly chaffing boots, wasn't very appealing. And with the early start in Kingstown it had been a long day. 'I think perhaps Mr Kenny's information can wait,' said Mallon.

'Yes, Sir, better to be on the safe side. May I ask if you're armed?'

'No, no I was coming off duty.'

'This may all be nothing, Superintendent, but I'd feel happier if you borrowed my second revolver.'

'Hmm . . . very well, Gilroy; surreptitiously, if you would.'

Casually moving closer, the policeman passed the weapon to his superior.

'I appreciate your concern, Gilroy. Sharp of you to spot Carey and company. Keep up the good work.'

'Thank you, Sir.'

'Good evening, Gilroy.'

'Good evening, Superintendent.'

Turning down by the Zoological Gardens, Mallon set out for home, comforted by the feel of the pistol in his pocket, but wondering if it wasn't perhaps a bit fanciful to think that Carey and his cohorts were lying in deadly wait for him.

Dan Curley strode purposefully towards Carey, who leaned casually on the rail bordering the polo ground.

'What's up, Dan?' asked Carey, as the worried-looking Invincibles' chairman reached him.

Curley laid a hand on his arm and drew Carey out of earshot of the nearby spectators. 'What the hell are you doing over here?'

'Just enjoying the polo.'

'You're supposed to be our lookout!'

'Take it easy, Dan, I can see the road from here. Besides, they're not due yet.'

'They might come early.'

'We'll be ready if they do. I was watching the road, and Joe Smith is on the bench over there.'

Curley glanced at Smith, sitting uneasily on the roadside bench. 'I'm worried about him, he's very nervy.'

'Ah he'll be alright. I just had to get away from his fidgeting for a while – that's why I wandered over to the polo.'

'I want you to stay with him, Jim. We don't want any foul-ups.'

'OK, OK. Come on, we'll stroll over now.'

They turned away from the polo match and walked back towards the nearby main road. 'All the lads in place?' asked Carey.

'Yeah. Brady's already issued the weapons, they're in position, and Skin-the-Goat has the cab ready.'

'Begod, Dan, I can feel it in me bones. This time I think we're really going to do it.'

'We have to,' said Curley grimly, then reaching Smith on the park bench he changed his tone to a friendly, bantering one. 'Well, Joe, I've found our wandering friend.'

'Found, and confined to quarters,' said Carey playfully, sitting beside the anxious-looking Smith. 'You can leave meself and Joe here to it, Dan, we'll be as right as rain.'

'OK. I'll send Kavanagh back down with the second cab. Make sure he parks it facing up towards us, and the minute you see them coming, into the cab and up to warn us. Alright?'

'Rest easy, Dan. We'll play our part. There won't be any problem, sure there won't, Joe?'

'No . . . no problem, Mr Carey.'

'Good luck then,' said Curley, shaking hands with each of them, then striding off briskly.

Carey reached into his pocket and withdrew a cigar, a perfectly rolled Havana he had been saving for a suitable occasion. Well this, he thought, is certainly an occasion. Tonight we change the course of Irish history. Lighting the cigar, he leant back on the bench and waited.

Scott picked at his food, unable to concentrate on what he was doing. It was twenty past six in the evening of his second day in captivity, and if he didn't get to make his move soon it might be too late. For all he knew, it might already be too late; the Invincibles might have launched their attack on Burke and the newly arrived Chief Secretary and Viceroy during the day. He could only hope that they wouldn't have chosen to strike during the procession or ceremonies, but instead would leave it until the evening when the men would eventually have to return to their residences in the Phoenix Park.

Scott pushed the food aside and waited, knowing he couldn't start his escape plan until Mick, the younger of his captors, had left. In the two days in which he had been held prisoner, he had mentally logged all his captors' movements. He had carefully noted what times meals were eaten, when washing water was supplied, and the times of all movements to and from the house.

It seemed that the older men slept on the premises, to be joined in the mornings by Mick, who, having eaten dinner, had left the previous evening at a quarter to seven. The vital question was whether he would leave after dinner again this evening. He *had* to, for Scott's escape plan to have any chance. It all hinged on the absence of the pistol-wielding Mick and his insistence that Scott stand at the far end of the wall whenever the door was unlocked.

Lying in the darkness of the barn, he had had plenty of time to work out his scheme and what he should do if it succeeded. The first priority was to make the journey to the Phoenix Park as quickly as possible. Once there, he could alert the households of Burke, Cavendish and Spencer, whose lodges were all within several hundred yards of each other. With time being of the essence, he had decided this would be a better option than making for the nearest constabulary barracks, with the inevitable loss of time while he tried to convince them of his identity and the risk to the country's rulers.

Making for the park also meant that he could seek out Kate. But what if she hadn't been blackmailed into helping the Invincibles? Could he override his love and turn her in to the authorities?

Finding his thoughts going round in circles, he had decided there could be no answers to any of his questions until he had spoken to Kate; instead he had simply hoped against hope that his instincts had been correct and that despite everything, her declaration of love had somehow been genuine. But first he had to escape.

He rose carefully now and stepped over his plate, then moved quietly to the door and listened as the three Invincibles ate their dinner. From the conversation it was evident that they were nearly finished. He could feel his heart starting to pound. Soon he would know if Mick was going or staying. And if the young Invincible left, then he would make his own move.

The well-dressed man walked along the city quays savouring

224

the mellow summer evening. Few of the passers-by recognised him as Lord Frederick Cavendish, newly sworn-in Chief Secretary for Ireland, and those who did recognise him nodded pleasantly and with respect.

He was pleased at his decision not to travel with the Viceroy's private secretary, but rather to walk home with Under Secretary Burke on this fine evening. Burke had been delayed at the last moment, and he had headed on alone, eager to see from a stroller's perspective the city over which he would, in effect, be ruler.

His reservations about taking the job had been considerably allayed by the reception afforded him today by the people. It was quite remarkable how the populace had turned from confrontation and violence, now that political reform was being offered them. One really had to admire Gladstone for his vision and daring. The Prime Minister had had to overcome considerable opposition in releasing Parnell, but the gamble of the so-called Kilmainham Treaty was clearly paying off, paving the way for a new era of political progress in Ireland.

Pausing at the Liffey wall, Cavendish turned and looked back towards the centre of Dublin, second city of the Empire, and bathed now in the golden evening sunshine. It looked a fine city, and he fervently hoped he would be a fitting ruler of its citizens and all the other people of Ireland.

He thought now that perhaps he had been somewhat premature in his pessimism. Life here might not be so unpleasant after all, particularly when Lucy would join him. Looking at the city, he felt a sense of hope and a new warmth towards its people. Not withstanding their tendency for rebelliousness, the Irish, he believed, had been treated unfairly and with harshness in the past. It was time now for a period of just rule and genuine reform. His task was an honour, and, to go by his initial briefing by Burke, would no doubt be a challenge; but the future was undeniably exciting.

Turning away from the view, he resumed his course along the quays, walking a little more briskly now, towards where the sun was starting to set over the Phoenix Park.

*   *   *

Thomas Burke, Under Secretary for Ireland, walked quickly along the city streets, eager to catch up with his new colleague, Lord Frederick Cavendish. Burke was in good spirits after the warm welcome they had received from the crowds, especially having had personal experience of the animosity of the people prior to the Kilmainham Treaty.

Could it really only be three weeks, he thought, since the previous Viceroy had departed to jeers and catcalls? Since the hated Forster had travelled in fear of his life? Even Burke himself, with his fourteen years' experience as Under Secretary, had been surprised at the swell of goodwill created by Parnell's release and the proposed new Arrears Bill.

The recent atmosphere of peace and goodwill was so tangible that he had had no misgivings about suggesting to Cavendish that the two of them walk home. The day of the crossroads ambush had clearly been swept away by Gladstone's radical approach to the Irish Question.

He had been impressed by Cavendish and his desire for political movement when they had had their first briefing that afternoon. It was obvious that the new regime was going to be an exciting one, and he found himself eager to catch up with the new Chief Secretary to continue their discussions as they walked home.

Moving at a faster pace, he crossed the Liffey at Kingsbridge and turned into Parkgate Street. He looked ahead but could see no sign of Cavendish in the busy thoroughfare. A cab was called for, he decided, that way he'd be sure to catch him. Burke briskly crossed the road, then made for the line of cabs waiting at the gate of the Phoenix Park.

Carey sat on the roadside bench, trying hard not to let Smith's restlessness disturb him. The Havana cigar had been a mistake, his pleasure in it marred by Smith nervously cracking his knuckles. The awful thing was that the man's unease was infectious, and Carey had found his excitement being replaced by a sense of anxiety.

He had consciously stopped himself from continually looking down the main road. It was a long straight thoroughfare, he thought, there was no possibility that he would fail to see them approach. Besides, he was supposed to look like a gentleman taking his ease.

Looking across the road, Carey could see Kavanagh standing by the carriage and feeding the horse from a nose-bag. Relax, he told himself, everything is in position and you're ready to move at a moment's notice. All that needed to be done now was to stay cool, and await the arrival of Burke and Cavendish.

'Goodnight, Mick.'

'Goodnight, lads. See you in the morning.'

'God bless.'

Scott listened, ears strained as the younger of his captors departed. He heard the front door of the house slam, then took out his watch. Eight minutes to seven. He felt a surge of excitement now that he could finally start his escape bid.

Lifting the enamel mug from the floor, he held it in readiness. He had originally intended simply to punch himself in the nose to gain the blood-splattered look his plan required, but during the long hours of captivity he had had time to refine the plan. He would have to wait five minutes to allow Mick to be well clear of the house, and so he had decided to collect the required blood in the mug and then use the waiting time to stop the nosebleed; that way if his ruse worked he wouldn't be slowed down by a bleeding nose when he ran from the house. But first of all he had to get the blood.

He steeled himself, raised his fist, took a breath, and then suddenly punched his nose. A shaft of pain ran through his head, but on careful examination he found, to his chagrin, that no blood had come forth. Come on, he told himself, this could save your life.

Screwing up his eyes, he punched again, harder this time, and was rewarded almost immediately by a flow of blood. He lifted the rim of the mug to his nose and allowed the blood to dribble down into it for a minute, then, gently lowering the mug to the ground, he knelt on the floor with his head tilted forward, pinching his nose to speed the clotting.

He waited a couple of minutes, then carefully released his fingers. To his relief the bleeding had stopped. Quickly checking his watch, he realised that four minutes had passed since Mick's departure. He lifted the mug from the ground and thoroughly daubed his face and hands in blood, then swapped the mug for his enamel plate, crouched on the floor inside the door, and screamed. 'Help! . . . Help! Quick . . . for God's sake . . .'

There was a flurry from the adjacent kitchen. 'What's up? What's wrong?' demanded the man with the Cork accent.

'My face . . .' cried Scott. 'Oh Christ! Quickly, please . . .'

'You take the gun, Seán,' said the older Dublinman, then there was the sound of the key turning in the lock.

Scott's groans of pain increased, then suddenly the door swung open, flooding the barn with light from the kitchen. Seeing the blood-covered face and hands of their captive, the two men were clearly taken aback, just as Scott had hoped.

'What . . . what happened?' asked the older man, moving forward.

'Oh God,' groaned Scott, crouching in apparent agony. The approaching guard reached out to touch him, then Scott sprang upright, punching the man viciously in the stomach. The winded Invincible sank to his knees in pain, and seeing the Corkman swing the gun around, Scott flicked the metal plate, which he had concealed under his arm. The rim of the plate caught the Corkman full in the face, causing him to stagger backwards with a cry of agony. In an instant Scott was upon him. He wrenched the gun from the shocked man, then pushed him into the centre of the room where his partner, still clutching his stomach, was starting to rise.

Scott levelled the gun. 'Lie on the floor, both of you! Quickly!'

Still dazed by the sudden turn of events, the two men did as they were bid.

'Face down, arms and legs out!' As soon as they complied, Scott held the gun in one hand, then searched them for weapons or spare keys. Satisfied that they had neither, he immediately made for the steel door, slammed it after him, and locked it.

He withdrew the key and quickly took in his surroundings. He was in the kitchen of what looked like a sturdy country cottage, with fields visible from a big bay window through which the setting sun cast a red glow. Seeing a basin of water beside the sink, he crossed over and swiftly washed the blood from his hands and face, then towelled himself dry. He threw down the towel and moved, gun in hand, to the back door and carefully stepped out into a farmyard. There was no one about.

A grass track led away from the house, and crossing the yard he felt a sense of exhilaration at his freedom, then picking up his pace he sprinted down the May-blossomed lane, unconscious of its fragrant charms in his desire to get to the park.

Thomas Burke sat comfortably in the carriage, scanning the evening saunterers on both sides of the road as he travelled through the park. He spotted Cavendish ahead, just as the carriage drove past the statue of Lord Gough. 'Driver! Pull in to the kerb twenty yards ahead, please!'

'Very good, Mr Burke.'

As the cabman slowed the horse, Burke gesticulated to his strolling colleague. 'Lord Frederick!'

'Ah, you took the easy way,' said Cavendish with a smile, then halted as Burke dismounted from the carriage.

'We shan't be needing you,' said Burke, handing the cabman a coin. 'Thank you very much.'

'Thank you, Mr Burke,' answered the driver, respectfully tipping his hat before pocketing the coin and clipping the horse into action.

'I'm sorry I got delayed,' said Burke, as Cavendish came forward to join him.

'That's alright, to stroll in anonymity was quite pleasant actually.'

'Yes, I dare say. I'm afraid unaccompanied walks were a luxury in which your predecessor could not indulge.'

'Yes,' said Cavendish thoughtfully, 'Forster was an honest man, no questioning his integrity, but my word he did seem to make enemies in Ireland.'

'One could say that . . .' answered Burke wryly.

'I'd like more details regarding his policies. Shall we walk on, and you can apprise me as we go?'

'Certainly,' said Burke, falling into step beside the Chief Secretary as they made their way up the main road of the park.

*   *   *

Scott slipped the gun into his pocket as he reached the end of the flower-scented lane and stopped to get his bearings. He had arrived at a surfaced road, and to his right could be seen a row of cottages and beyond them open countryside; but to the left he could see a large building like a school or hospital, and in the distance rose rooftops and steeples. He was, as he had hoped, on the edge of the city.

He turned left, the road soon broadening into a wide thoroughfare with terraced houses on either side. Ignoring the stares of passers-by, Scott continued running as the road crossed what looked like a well-used railway line, then passed a large flour mill on the banks of a canal. He suddenly recognised the thoroughfare as Phibsborough Road, the end point of a walk he had once taken along the towpath of the Royal Canal. If he continued on for several hundred yards, then turned right along the North Circular Road, it would bring him to the Phoenix Park.

Just then a baker's cart came out of the flour mill, and without breaking stride Scott ran towards the driver, waving frantically for him to stop. The driver, a heavy-set man with flour-dusted red hair, looked at him quizzically. 'What's your problem, friend?' he asked.

'I need you cart. It's a matter of life and death,' said Scott breathlessly.

'Bejasus it'd be a matter of death alright if I came home without me cart!' he answered with a derisive laugh. 'Are ye mad or what?'

Scott quickly drew the gun and pointed it at the man's head. 'Off the cart! Now!'

'OK . . . OK . . . take it easy.'

The fear in the baker's eyes was obvious as he got down from the cart, his hands held high in the air.

'I'm really sorry about this, but lives are at stake,' said Scott.

'Yeah . . . right . . .' The man's voice was hoarse.

'I'll leave it safe for you. Consider it a hiring,' said Scott, slipping a pound note into the startled man's pocket before leaping onto the cart. He grabbed the reins and flicked the horse into action, pulled out to the right, and swiftly left the bewildered baker behind as the cart sped towards the North Circular Road.

'Mr Carey!' Joe Smith sat upright on the park bench. 'Mr Carey, it's him!'

'OK, take it easy, Joe,' answered Carey, a tremor of excitement in his own voice. He looked keenly down the road. 'Yes . . . yes I'd recognise Burke myself . . .'

'The other one is Cavendish.'

'You're sure?'

'Certain.'

'Right, let's go.' Rising from the bench, they crossed the road to where Kavanagh waited by the cab. He looked at them expectantly, and Carey nodded. 'It's them alright, let's move.'

'Right, I'll just take off the horse's feed,' said Kavanagh.

'Quickly man, quickly!'

Kavanagh hurriedly removed the nosebag, mounted the cab and whipped the horse into motion. Moving off, they travelled up the carriageway, finally slowing down as they approached Skin-the-Goat's parked cab.

The gnarled cab-driver stood leaning against the back wheel of his vehicle, casually reading a newspaper. Seeing Carey wave a white handkerchief as they approached, he immediately folded the paper, placed it on the back seat, and mounted his cab in readiness.

Kavanagh drove some yards past, halting when he reached the assembled Invincibles. Carey jumped down from the cab, his face bright with excitement.

'They're coming?' asked Dan Curley.

'They're coming!' Carey's voice was triumphant. 'Burke and Cavendish, alone and on foot. By God, lads, but this time we have them!'

Leaning eagerly forward in the cab of the baker's cart, Scott flicked the reins again, anxious to coax extra speed from the horse. He had been unheeding of the stares of strollers and other drivers as they had careered through Phibsborough and

231

along the North Circular Road, and now he could see the gates of the park looming ahead.

There seemed to be some congestion just opposite the entrance gates, and as he drew nearer he realised that a coal cart had shed its load. The coal was scattered all over the junction of Infirmary Road and the North Circular Road, and carts were backed up on both sides of the thoroughfare.

Damn, thought Scott. He turned the horse towards the pavement, then cracked the whip over the animal's head. 'Go on, boy! Go on!' Driving forward, the horse mounted the footpath. The baker's cart hit the kerb with a shuddering jolt, then it too was on the pavement.

'Jesus, Mary and Joseph, where do ye think ye're goin?' screamed a startled woman.

'Emergency! Clear a path!' shouted Scott. 'Emergency!'

The people around the coalman's cart scattered as Scott drove along the footpath, flanking the stationary vehicles before descending with a bang over the kerb and onto the road again.

'Bloody madman!' shouted one of the cart drivers, but Scott went on unheedingly. He quickly checked that the pistol hadn't been jolted from his pocket, then guided the horse through the wrought iron gates and into the park.

Waiting to kill Burke and Cavendish, symbols of all he hated, Joe Brady had never felt more alive. This part of the operation was his responsibility, and his nerve ends were tingling with anticipation.

'They're comin', I can see them in the distance,' said Tim Kelly eagerly. 'God, Joe, we're goin' to do it! We have them this time!'

'Don't get cocky, Tim,' said Brady, turning to his younger companion. 'We won't have done it till they're dead at our feet.'

'Yeah but . . .'

'No buts! Just follow the plan, Tim.'

'OK, Joe, you're the boss,' said Kelly equably.

Carey came forward, placing a guiding hand on Brady's

arm. 'A quick word in your ear, Joe,' he said, steering him out of earshot of the others.

'Yeah, what is it?'

'Smith has been nervous all afternoon and now he's getting worse. Does he have to stay?'

Brady looked down the carriageway. 'These two comin', that's definitely them?'

'Absolutely,' responded Carey.

'Then he can go, ye both can. We'll handle this end of it.'

'You're sure you don't need me?'

'Yeah. You head off now with Smith. We better get him out of the way.'

'Alright, Joe, and good luck,' said Carey, shaking hands.

'Thanks.' Brady nodded brusquely, then watched while Carey quickly wished the others well, before heading off towards the Islandbridge Gate with the much-relieved Smith.

'OK, lads,' said Brady briskly, 'time to move. Remember we stroll towards them casually, they think they're safe.' He looked derisively at the approaching men. 'They think they've bought off all the Irish. Now we'll show them just how wrong they are.'

Burke and Cavendish walked along slowly, engrossed in conversation regarding the forthcoming Arrears Bill. Burke was impressed by the range of the new Chief Secretary's knowledge of the land purchase issue. It was evident that Cavendish's previous post in the Treasury, where he had worked closely with the Prime Minister, had made him knowledgeable about Irish problems in general, and the crucial land-ownership question in particular. Despite his gentle manner, Cavendish was going to make a considerable impact. Already Burke found himself liking the man and his earnest desire to serve the nation.

Teasing out the details of the Arrears Bill, they walked on, too caught up in their discussion to be aware of the group of men heading in their direction.

Curley, Fagan and Hanlon walked easily down the carriageway. A short distance behind them sauntered Brady and Kelly, with Thomas Caffrey and Patrick Delaney taking up the rear.

Brady was well pleased with his plan. They would let Burke and Cavendish pass through the first group. This group would then turn, and, with the victims thus surrounded, Brady and Kelly would carry out the execution. Using the two waiting vehicles they would then make a quick escape by separate routes before it was realised who the dead tyrants were.

His hands thrust into his pockets as he walked along, Brady tightened his grip on the handle of the surgical knife. Glancing to his left, he could see from the determination on Kelly's face that he too was anxious to use his weapon, now that the moment was finally approaching.

Burke and Cavendish drew closer to the first group of Invincibles. The two men were immersed in their conversation, but Brady's satisfaction at their unsuspecting advance was marred by the brisk approach of a cart up the main road. At the rate it was travelling he reckoned it would reach the Invincibles at the same time as their intended victims. Having obviously realised this, Curley turned around, his expression a wordless query as to what they should do. Brady nodded sharply, indicating to continue.

Burke and Cavendish were now only five yards away as Curley fell into step again with his companions.

'Joe! Joe, the cart!' said Kelly.

'I see it,' hissed Brady.

'What'll we . . . ?'

'Shut up, just follow my lead.'

Burke and Cavendish had finally looked up from their conversation as they reached the leading Invincibles. Curley nodded to them as he and Hanlon stepped aside to let them pass. Cavendish nodded back graciously, then the two men moved on.

Damn, thought Brady, seeing the horse and cart almost draw level with Curley, Hanlon and Fagan. Burke and Cavendish were coming towards him now, their well-bred faces animated in discussion. Blast it all to hell, thought Brady, gauging the cart's progress, we can't stab them just as it's level with us. 'Let them pass, Tim,' he muttered.

'What?'

'Let them pass!' he hissed venomously.

Suddenly they were face to face with their quarry. The two aristocrats stood on the narrow footpath waiting for the group of men to step off onto the grass. Every instinct Brady possessed urged him not to clear a path, but rather to use the hidden knife. Gripping the handle even more tightly, he glanced at Burke, took in the cart which was almost abreast of them, and reluctantly stepped aside. The two men walked blithely on as Brady laid a restraining hand on Kelly's arm. 'Just for a second, Tim . . .' he said.

The cart was passing now, a red-faced farmer and his sturdy wife returning in it from their day's outing to the city. Further down the road Curley's group had halted and turned, but Brady continued on as the farmer drove past. After a few seconds Brady stopped suddenly and turned. The man and woman in the cart had passed on, travelling briskly up the carriageway towards the Castleknock Gate. 'Now, Tim! Now!'

Kelly needed no urging, the razor-sharp blade appearing in his hand as he sprang forward. Unsheathing his own knife, Brady ran towards the unsuspecting Burke.

The evening sun glinted on the steel blade as Brady raised it high in the air, then he drove it down powerfully, burying it in the back of the Under Secretary. Burke screamed in agony, and as he collapsed Brady struck twice more, stabbing him in the chest and neck.

As Brady stooped over his blood-splattered victim, Kelly had already delivered a stunning blow, catching Cavendish in the shoulder. With blood pumping from the wound, the Chief Secretary had stumbled, horror-sticken, into the roadway. Falling to his knees, he raised his hand in self-defence, only to have it almost severed by Kelly's next blow. Cavendish screamed in pain, then fell back onto the ground, his cries cut short by a swift blow from Brady's knife, followed almost immediately by another from Kelly.

'He's had it, Tim,' said Brady, 'make for the cab!'

'Right!'

'And for good measure . . .' said Brady, moving back to the body of Burke. He raised the prostrate Under Secretary's blood-stained head, placed the knife at his neck, and in one swift movement slit his throat.

Rising quickly, Brady ran towards Kavanagh's cab and leapt aboard. Seeing the other Invincibles already piling into Skin-the-Goat's carriage, he raised his fist in a victory salute, then shouted to them. 'Go! Go!'

Skin-the-Goat waved farewell, then immediately lashed his horse into action, heading south towards the city.

Kavanagh had been nervously flicking his mare with the whip to keep her alert, and as Brady seated himself with Kelly, Caffrey and Delaney, he turned around anxiously. 'Right, Joe?'

'Yeah. Let's get the hell out of here!'

'Gee up!' shouted Kavanagh, whipping the horse into motion. Galloping along the Fifteen Acres Road, they made for the Chapelizod Gate. Brady looked back across the broad expanse of parkland, but there was no sign of any pursuit. He turned around to his companions, unable to keep the excitement from his voice. 'We did it, lads,' he cried triumphantly, 'this time we bloody-well did it!'

Even as he leapt down from the baker's cart, Scott knew he was too late. A shocked crowd had gathered around the blood-stained bodies, and it came as no surprise when he heard the horrified onlookers say it was Lord Cavendish and Mr Burke.

Damn, he thought, Damn! Damn! Damn! If he had been here minutes earlier, if he hadn't been slowed down by the traffic outside the Zoo, if he had escaped from the barn a few minutes sooner – all ifs, and all, he realised, quite useless now.

He heard a policeman say that Spencer was safely guarded within the Vice-regal Lodge, but as Scott looked at Burke's hastily covered body and the face of the dying Cavendish, he felt an overwhelming sense of sadness. His own mission had failed, but even more importantly the whole future of the country would be in jeopardy because of this dreadful and futile act. The promise of change which the unfortunate Cavendish had signified for Ireland might not come to pass now, and never had Scott seen a country more in need of peace and reform.

A sudden buzz from the crowd brought him from his

reverie. 'The surgeon said it!' he overheard a man cry.

'What's that?' asked Scott.

'The surgeon, Dr Myles from Steevens' Hospital.'

'What about him?'

'He's after just sayin' that Lord Cavendish is dead.'

What an appalling waste, thought Scott, and the more he reflected upon it, the more angry he felt towards Colonel Penrose and his games of political brinkmanship. Damn him! Damn him and his smug conviction that it would be better not to round up the Invincibles. They should all have been arrested, but instead Penrose had risked Burke and Cavendish in his obsession with linking Parnell and the Irish Party with the extremists. Blast the man, thought Scott, blast him and his cold-blooded gambling with the lives of others. If he had only listened to reason, the murders need never have happened.

But it had happened now, and Scott knew it wasn't all over yet. Far from it. For there was still the matter of Kate. Could she really have been involved in something like this? And if so, what was he to do about it?

Turning from the crowd, he made his way to the baker's cart, mounted the cab, and set off worriedly towards the Under Secretary's Lodge.

Thirty-Nine

'It's OK, Joe, nobody will ever know you were involved.' Carey spoke soothingly as he led Smith out the Islandbridge gate of the park.

'God I . . . I hope not, Mr Carey.'

'It's over and done with. The lads all escaped and we were two hundred yards away when it happened. We've nothing to worry about.'

'I suppose not,' said Smith without conviction.

'I can understand your unease, Joe, for a long time it's been talking and planning. But sooner or later plans have to be put into action. They had to be executed.'

Smith nodded nervously. 'There'll be hell to pay though. Lord Cavendish was the son-in-law of Gladstone's wife.'

'Let me tell you something, Joe,' said Carey calmly. 'The day is gone – and good riddance to it – when Irishmen quivered in case they'd offended their lords and masters in England. That's what this whole business is about – self-determination. Do you follow me?'

'Yes . . .'

'Then don't be getting yourself into a state worrying. Just keep your head down until it blows over. You know, in years to come you'll look back on this and be proud you were involved. We all will. And I'll tell you something else, Joe. I've been called names in the past. People have said I'm a loudmouth, a spoofer, claimed I was all auld guff and talk. Well those people were wrong, dead wrong. Because today, Joe, we went into action. History was made here this evening, and James Carey and Joe Smith were part of it. That's something to treasure, Joe, that's something to treasure forever.'

The summer dusk had cooled suddenly with the setting of the sun, but Kate was unconscious of the temperature as she hung her apron on the wall hook in the dairy.

All afternoon she had been fretting over what might have happened to Bill, and with each passing hour her foreboding had increased. She wanted to believe that the Invincibles had called off their campaign – it seemed such an obvious course in the new political climate – and yet she found it increasingly difficult to hope that Brady and his companions had called to the cottage to cancel whatever scheme they had involved Bill in. For if they had, where had he been since Thursday night? And if they hadn't cancelled, was he now on some dangerous mission, or – and she tried not to dwell on this possibility – had their enquiries unearthed something about Bill? Something that might cause them to abduct him? All the options seemed disheartening, but she would soon know one way or the other, she consoled herself, for she wasn't going to leave Carey's house tonight until she got some straight answers.

The evening milking was finished now, and with Mr McDaid departed for his Saturday night game of cards in Clonsilla, Kate planned to slip unnoticed from the grounds of the lodge and make her way to town.

Moving to the door of the dairy, she suddenly stopped, hearing the loud snapping of a twig in the gloom outside the entrance.

'Who's there?' she called. No one answered. Kate peered out into the fading light, then she drew back in shock as Bill quietly emerged from the shadows.

'We need to talk, Kate,' he said softly, as he stepped into the dairy and swung the door behind him.

'OK, Mick, lt's safe to stop now,' cried Brady.

The Invincibles had slowed down their pace, having reached open countryside, and Kavanagh halted the sweating horse at the grassy verge.

'Where are we, Joe?' asked Kelly, his boyish face still flushed with excitement as he looked about him in the growing darkness.

'We're out on the Blessington Road.'

'God, I've really lost me bearings.'

'That's the idea, Tim, just in case anyone tried to follow us.'

'No one did, I watched for ages.'

'I know, that's why it's safe to stop now. We'll head towards Tallaght, then turn off down to Terenure.'

'What's in Terenure?'

'The southern approach to town. This way we'll be comin' into the city from the opposite direction to any hue and cry from the park.'

'Fair play to ye, Joe, ye have it all worked out,' said Kelly admiringly.

'Yeah. Come on, jump down from the cab and we'll clean our knives. We won't be a minute, Mick.'

'OK, lads,' answered Kavanagh.

Jumping down, Brady stepped into the long roadside grass after Kelly. 'Make sure to wipe your hands as well, Tim,' he said, 'and check your clothes for blood-stains.'

'Right,' answered Kelly, crouching down in the gorse-scented roadside.

They pulled handfuls of grass and carefully wiped the blood from their knives and hands. 'Clean as a whistle,' said Kelly cheerfully as he sheathed his knife, 'and no sign of any stains on me clothes either.'

Sheathing his own knife, Brady looked at his younger companion in the gloom. 'You're a cool customer, Tim, even if you do look like a kid.' Brady punched him playfully on the shoulder. 'I was proud of ye tonight; ye did well.'

'Yeah, yeah we really showed them, didn't we, Joe?'

Brady nodded grimly. 'We gave the bastards something to think about alright. Come on,' he added, slipping the knife into his pocket, 'the lads will want to celebrate with a few pints.'

'Eh, I think I'll skip that, Joe, if ye don't mind. They can drop me at the tram terminus in Terenure.'

'For what?'

'Well I promised me mother I'd call up . . .'

Brady shook his head in wonder. 'Jasus, Tim, you're a funny kid. One minute executin' enemies, the next runnin' to your mother.'

'Well it's just that I promised her . . .'

'It's OK,' said Brady, raising a hand. 'You earned the right to

240

do what ye like tonight. Come on.' Returning to the cab, he called up to Kavanagh. 'We're droppin Tim in Terenure.'

'Terenure?'

'Yeah, he has some personal business. And after that the next stop for the rest of us is Davy's Tavern!'

The others cheered boisterously, then Brady and Kelly climbed aboard. 'We've waited a long time for this night,' said Brady, 'so let's get back to town and do some real celebratin'.'

'Hear hear!'

'Gee up!' shouted Kavanagh, flicking the whip.

Startled by the cracking sound, the horse pulled away down the darkening roadway, while in the back of the cart Joe Brady sat back contentedly, well pleased with the evening's outcome.

Forty

Kate stood in the dimly lit dairy, her shock at Scott's sudden appearance being replaced by a flood of relief.

'Bill . . . oh Bill, I've been so worried about you,' she cried, coming forward.

'Have you?' asked Scott, standing just inside the door but not moving to her.

'When you weren't there on Thursday night I was afraid something might be wrong,' she said, her words coming in a rush. 'I went back again yesterday and today. What happened?'

'Don't you know?' he asked flatly.

'How would I know?' She looked at him askance. 'What's wrong, Bill, you're so . . .'

'So what?'

'I don't know. Distant . . . sort of strained . . .'

'A lot has happened, Kate, I need to know what's . . .'

'Bill!' she interrupted, 'your head.' She moved quickly to his side and gently reached up her hand. 'What happened to you?' she asked concernedly.

'I was abducted by your friends,' replied Scott, moving a little so her hand didn't rest near the wound.

'My friends?'

'Don't play games, Kate. I know you're involved with Carey and the others. I came here tonight to hear the truth from you.'

She felt a sinking sensation in her stomach. 'Oh, Bill . . . I . . . I wanted to explain to you myself when the time was right. It's . . . they shouldn't have told you . . .' she said in confusion.

'They didn't tell me. I overheard them when they thought I was still unconscious.'

Kate indicated his cut head. 'They did that to you?'

Scott nodded. 'Brady did.'

Kate laid her hand on his arm. 'Why, Bill, what's been going on?'

242

'I'll tell you in a minute. I'd like to hear your side of it first.'

Kate sighed. 'OK, I'll tell you my part. You obviously know that our first meeting wasn't accidental,' she said softly. 'Carey asked me to . . . to get to know you. He said you were a nationalist and they wanted to know more about you.'

'And you were to . . . encourage me?'

'Please, don't make it sound awful. How was I to know that I'd . . . how things would develop between us? I'm sorry I had to deceive you, Bill. I didn't know the person I was to check out would be as . . . as special as you . . .'

Scott looked down in confusion, running his hand distractedly across his brow.

'Bill, you're not what you pretended either, sure you're not?'

'No.'

'What are you?'

He looked up. 'I'm a British Officer. My real name is William Scott.'

'Oh my God!' Kate's hand went involuntarily to her mouth.

'I may as well revert to my normal accent,' he added. 'You see I was sent here to protect Forster and Burke from the Invincibles. That's why Brady and the others abducted me, but I managed to escape before being killed.'

Kate looked at him earnestly, her eyes widened in shock. 'So . . . so you were fooling me too . . .'

'I'd no choice, Kate.'

'All along you were leading a double life.'

'All along I was carrying out a mission to prevent murder, a mission that's failed, I may add.'

'How do you mean?'

'Lord Cavendish and Mr Burke were murdered this evening. Stabbed to death here in the park.'

'Oh God, no!' cried Kate. 'Oh sweet Jesus, they weren't?' She looked at Scott in horror.

'It *is* what the Invincibles were set up for.'

'But not now,' she cried despairingly. 'There was no need, everything had changed.'

'Tell that to Brady and his friends.'

'But it's so pointless now, so . . . futile . . .'

243

'I know, Kate, I know.' He looked at her searchingly. 'There's something I have to ask you,' he said softly.

'What?'

'Had they a hold over you, or were you acting of your own free will?'

'They'd no hold over me,' she answered distractedly.

'Then how did you get involved in this madness?'

'You'd never understand.'

'Try me.'

Kate hesitated.

'Please,' said Scott, ' I really want to understand.'

'Alright then. It all started before Parnell was released. At the time there seemed no hope of progress. The country was in chaos, something drastic had to be done . . .'

'So you joined the Invincibles?'

'I offered to help.' She looked directly at him, emotion making her voice harsh. 'My family had been evicted. You can't imagine what that was like, to be left bloodied and homeless at the side of the road. We were thrown off a farm we'd worked all our lives! It was awful, really terrible.' She paused, then spoke more softly. 'There was no law to protect people like us, so I decided to take the law into my own hands. Carey lined me up for this job here; helping the Invincibles seemed like a chance to fight oppression.' She shook her head despairingly. 'I didn't realise then that they were such fanatics.'

'Oh, Kate . . .'

'I really thought it would all be stopped after the Kilmainham Treaty. I wanted to get out, to . . .'

'To what?'

She slowly lifted her head, looking him directly in the eye. 'To go to America with you.'

Scott breathed out deeply. 'I see.'

'Do you?'

'Yes, I think so. You see all the time I was held captive, more than anything else I wanted to believe that . . . that your feelings for me were true. That in spite of my deceit, and your deceit, and the Invincibles, and everything, that what we said, what we felt, was true.'

Kate took his arm. 'I don't know what's going to happen now, Bill.' She smiled ruefully. 'I can't think of you as William, even when you speak in your English accent.' Kate looked at him seriously, the smile quickly vanishing. 'Whatever happens though, I meant it when I said I loved you, more than I've ever meant anything else in my life.'

'I did too, Kate,' answered Scott softly, 'I did too.'

'Are you going to have to arrest me?'

Scott looked at the floor, then briefly shook his head. 'I can't.'

'What *is* going to happen then?'

'There'll be a manhunt. The country will be turned upside down to catch the murderers; it's only a matter of time, they'll get them all.' He looked at her. 'That's why you've got to get out of Ireland quickly.'

'You'd turn a blind eye, let me go?'

He shrugged. 'Nothing will bring back the lives of Burke and Cavendish, will it? And besides, you're no murderer, Kate. You got caught up in something evil, but I don't think you could ever be evil yourself.'

'I . . . I don't know what to say . . .'

'You don't have to say anything. What you have to do is get to your family in America as quickly as possible.'

'And you, Bill?' asked Kate hoarsely. 'What about you?'

'I don't know . . . I . . . I just don't know . . .'

'Might I suggest a court martial for assisting the enemy?'

Scott and Kate swung round in shock as Hackett stepped into the dairy. The house steward smiled at their startled expressions. 'Yes, I think perhaps a firing squad for an officer committing treason, and the gallows for a murderous little Fenian bitch. How does that sound?' he asked, carefully training his shotgun upon them.

Forty-One

The sudden knocking on the door startled Superintendent Mallon. He sat in the armchair, his aching feet raised on a footstool, and as he had puffed contentedly at his pipe he had been looking forward to the warm soothing bath which was being run upstairs.

Sensing the urgency of the caller from the vigour of the knocking, he reluctantly rose, then made his way briskly to the hall door. Looking out through the leaded glass, he recognised Gilroy, the policeman who had earlier lent him the revolver.

As soon as he opened the door, Mallon realised from the other man's face that something was seriously wrong.

'I'm sorry to disturb you at home, Superintendent, but . . .'

'Never mind that. What's happened?'

'Mr Burke and another man have been murdered in the park, Sir.'

'Oh Christ! You're sure it's Burke?' he asked anxiously.

'Positive, Sir, and we think the second man may be Lord Cavendish.'

'God damn it,' said Mallon venomously, 'God damn it to hell!' Regaining control, he breathed out deeply. 'Right, we'd better get up there straight away.'

'I have a cab waiting outside, Sir.'

'Just give me a minute,' said Mallon. Returning to the sittingroom, he hastily pulled on his boots, slipped the loaded pistol into his pocket, then went to the foot of the stairs and called up to the maid to stop the bath as he had to go out.

He slammed the hall door and ran down the steps with Gilroy, then mounted the waiting cab which took off at full speed for the nearby Phoenix Park.

'It's Cavendish alright, God rest his soul.' Mallon had no doubts about the body, on which the gas lamp at the edge of

246

the park's main road cast a small pool of yellow light in the darkening summer night.

'What do we do now, Sir?' asked Gilroy.

Mallon indicated to the uniformed constable to cover the body again, then turned to Gilroy. 'I want you to make for Dublin Castle immediately,' he said. 'Tell them I want all seaports telegraphed and every police station in the Dublin area notified of what's happened. I want a watch put on every train leaving Dublin, and tell them to make arrangements to have the telegraph stations manned all day tomorrow, Sunday or no Sunday. Have you got all that?'

'Yes, Sir.'

'When that's done we'll have all the hotels and lodging houses checked, and I want every cab driver in the city questioned.'

'Very good, Sir.'

'Has the news of this been broken yet to Burke's sister?'

'I believe that's in hand, Superintendent,' answered Gilroy. 'The Viceroy has been informed, and his people will tell Miss Burke, and presumably Lord Cavendish's wife in London too.'

'Right,' said Mallon, 'that frees me for the troops.'

'The troops, Sir?'

'There's a unit of soldiers at Burke's lodge. I want armed groups of them to seal off all the park gates. It's probably too late, but if any of the killers lingered I want them hemmed in. Right, Gilroy, you head off for the Castle and I'll join you there later.'

'Yes, Sir,' said the policeman, running to the waiting cab.

It was going to be one hell of a night, thought Mallon as, the boots pinching his aching feet, he mounted one of the police cabs.

'Where to, Superintendent?' asked the driver.

'Under Secretary Burke's Lodge, and quickly please.'

Forty-Two

Keeping the shotgun trained on Kate and Scott, Hackett closed the dairy door with his foot. Kate watched, her heart pounding from the shock of his sudden appearance, as the house steward smiled sardonically.

'Well, well, well. The rebel girl and her foolish lover, gallantly compromising himself to save her neck. I have to say I find it very romantic. Drawn together by love in spite of the chasm of political differences. It's really quite touching.' He looked at Kate enquiringly. 'Or perhaps "touching" is an indelicate word for a woman of Miss Lannigan's pristine purity?'

Kate stared straight ahead, unwilling to gratify him with a reaction.

'Struck dumb with shock, are we? Or perhaps . . . perhaps it's just a good old sulk, eh? Well, we'll soon change that. No sudden movements please!' called Hackett, levelling the gun as Scott shifted position slightly. 'We wouldn't want to pre-empt the firing-squad, would we?'

'What firing squad is that?' asked Scott evenly.

'Oh come come,' answered Hackett, 'I heard the entire conversation. You see I followed you from the far side of the dairy, Captain – or should I call you Bill? I feel as if I really know you at this stage. At any rate I'd like you to turn around carefully.'

'For what?'

'Just do as I say,' snapped Hackett, his tone suddenly hardening.

Scott slowly turned towards the wall.

'My, my, that's a nasty cut on the side of your head. I'll tell you what, we'll be sporting about this. We'll choose the other side,' said Hackett, suddenly swinging the stock of the shotgun and clubbing Scott.

'No!' screamed Kate, but already the house steward had

248

turned the gun on her as Scott slumped unconsciously to the ground.

'Don't move. Stay just where you are.'

'You coward! You . . . you pig!'

Hackett waved a finger admonishingly. 'That's not very lady-like, Kate. I'm going to have to teach you manners. But first . . .' Quickly crossing to the sprawled figure of Scott, he searched him, taking the revolver from his right-hand jacket pocket. 'We'll just remove this from harm's way, shall we?' Standing back from Kate, but with the shotgun in the crook of his arm, he emptied the bullets from the chamber of the pistol, then slipped them into his pocket before putting the revolver aside.

Kate stared distractedly at where Scott lay slumped on the ground, a cold fury rising within her.

'Do I have your full attention?' asked Hackett.

Kate glowered at him.

He raised the gun threateningly. 'I said do I have your attention?'

'Yes.'

'That's better, because I've waited a long time for this. I'd like your full participation.'

'What are you talking about?'

'I'm talking about your lovely, milk-white body. The body you think is too good to share with a man. You're going to strip for me.'

Kate looked him directly in the eye. 'I'd die first.'

'Oh you'll die alright – on the gallows, for conspiracy to commit murder. But I'm going to have you first.'

'Rape is a crime too.'

'Rape? My dear girl, who on earth is going to believe such a claim? Obviously a fanatical nationalist is going to try to besmirch the man who captured her and her traitorous lover.' He shook his head. 'No one in authority will ever believe such ravings. And certainly no one will be concerned if you get a little . . . roughed up, in resisting capture. Wouldn't you think?'

'If you lay a hand on me I'll . . .'

'You'll what, scream the place down? Too bad we're so far from the lodge here, isn't it?'

'If you so much as touch me, I'll tear your eyes out.'

Hackett smiled. 'Bravely spoken, Kate. To tell you the truth I like a spirited woman. A little resistance makes the conquest decidedly more exciting.' Opening the shotgun, he removed the cartridges and put them in his pocket, then placed the weapon in the corner. 'Shall we begin?' he said, stepping forward smilingly.

Looking at his flushed, baby-faced features, Kate felt a wave of revulsion sweep through her. Come on, she told herself, don't stand there hating him, start thinking.

She stepped backwards, scanning the oaken shelves for the heavy butter paddles or any other potential weapon, but all the dairy implements had been tidied away.

Suddenly Hackett lunged forward, catching her wrist. Before she could pull away he grabbed the top of her blouse and yanked, ripping the material and exposing her shoulder. Kate lashed out with her fist and caught him in the ribs, but the force of the blow wasn't sufficient to make him free his grip, and swinging around, he slapped her hard in the face.

Kate reeled back, her cheek stinging, but Hackett quickly closed in, grabbing her shoulders and pulling her face close to his. Seeing him open his lips to kiss her, Kate angrily twisted her mouth away. Hackett jerked her shoulders, drawing her towards him again.

Fighting down the panic induced by his superior strength, Kate tried to think clearly, and as Hackett roughly tilted her chin towards himself, she jabbed upwards with her thumb, catching him in the eye.

Hackett cried out in pain and fury, and Kate managed to break his grip. She ran towards the ante-room at the end of the dairy, praying that Mr McDaid's shotgun would be on its customary rack there. With her hands trembling, she undid the bolt and swung the door open, then screamed in agony as Hackett pulled her backwards by the hair.

A series of shelves supporting churns of milk ran along one wall of the dairy, and Hackett pushed her towards the wooden supports, jamming her forcefully against the oaken beams.

'Alright!' he cried harshly. 'You've put up a fight to save your stupid honour, but unless you want to get hurt you'd better start co-operating. Understood?'

Her head aching from the pulled hair, Kate didn't reply, then Hackett slipped his hand inside the torn blouse. Feeling his fingers close about her breast, Kate twisted furiously, and forcing her head down, bit into Hackett's wrist.

The house steward pulled away his hand with a roar, his face contorted in pain, then lashed out with his fist, catching the side of her face. Kate felt a stab of pain in her cheek, but her cry was strangled by his other hand grabbing her throat, and to her horror she saw him produce a long penknife from his pocket.

For the brief moment that it took to open the blade with both his hands, Kate was free, but before she could take advantage of it Hackett had the knife at her throat.

'Now listen, you little Fenian bitch, and listen well. One wrong move and I'll bury this in you.'

Seeing the venom in his face, Kate realised that he meant it and she began to sob softly, the resistance ebbing from her body.

Hackett paused, savouring his triumph, then moved the blade to the shoulder strap of her slip. 'I'll bet a healthy young woman like you is soft and firm,' he whispered. 'Let's find out, shall we?'

Kate's sobs increased as he cut the strap and the material fell away from her shoulder. Hackett slowly ran his hand across the exposed flesh, then he lifted the fabric to reveal her breast.

She waited until just that moment, then suddenly kneed her distracted assailant in the groin. Hackett screamed, and Kate swung around violently, overturning a large milk churn which fell to the floor with a crash, covering the inert form of Scott with a flow of creamy white milk.

The knife fell from Hackett's hands, and Kate kicked it under the shelving as he grabbed madly for her. From the corner of her eye she saw Scott begin to stir as the cold milk flowed about his face; then a punch from Hackett caught her in the stomach. Temporarily winded, she stumbled backwards as the enraged house steward fell upon her.

She threshed fiercely, but Hackett closed first one hand, and then the other, about her throat. His flushed face was a contorted mask of fury and hatred as he squeezed, and Kate's vision began to blur just as she saw the milk-soaked figure of Scott heading towards them.

Suddenly the pressure on her throat disappeared as Hackett was yanked off her. With a cry of anger Scott buried his fist in the other man's stomach, then followed with a furious upper-cut which sent Hackett reeling backwards. Scott lunged after him, and the house steward, losing his footing on the milk-covered floor, was driven back by Scott's momentum.

There was a loud crack as Hackett's head smashed against the oaken shelves, then he slumped unconsciously to the floor. Scott quickly knelt by the house steward, seeking signs of life, but after a moment he looked up slowly at Kate, his face grim. 'He's gone . . .'

'Oh, Bill . . .' she cried, nervously fingering her torn clothing.

'Are you OK?' he asked, rising and moving towards her.

'Yes,' she whispered. 'Are you?'

'Yes.'

'Oh, Bill, is . . . is he really dead?'

Scott nodded. 'He's dead alright.'

'May God forgive me,' said Kate, with a catch in her voice, 'but I'm glad, Bill, I'm glad!'

Scott looked at her ripped blouse and marked cheek, then gently reached out and took her in his arms. 'It's alright, Kate,' he murmured, 'it's alright now.'

She laid her head on his chest, unperturbed by the milk-stained clothes in her desire to hold and be held. 'He was such . . . such a horrible man.'

Bill's arms enfolded her as he spoke softly. 'Not any more, Kate, not any more. It's over now, it's over.'

She held him closely as she spoke. 'Oh, Bill. I've . . . I've worried about you so much these last few days. You were on my mind the whole time.'

Scott gently raised her head, his hand cradling her cheeks as he looked into her eyes. 'You were on my mind too . . .' He paused, then slowly lowered his lips to Kate's. They kissed, softly at first, then with an urgent passion, as though desperate to offset all their tensions and anxieties. Eventually they parted.

'It's hard to . . . to take it all in,' said Kate. She looked up at him. 'Where do we go from here, Bill?'

He breathed out deeply, then met her gaze. 'To America. Together.'

She looked him firmly in the eye before speaking. 'You're sure?'

He nodded. 'Hackett settles it.' He indicated the body. 'I could never explain away all this. No! No that's not really it, Kate,' he quickly corrected. He paused, then continued earnestly. 'I know in my heart and soul that even if he'd never appeared, I couldn't have let you go alone.'

'In case I'd be caught, or . . .'

'Because I love you,' he interjected, 'and I want to spend the rest of my life with you. Because all that's happened is over now and can't be changed. Because I never want to lose you again, Kate.'

She gazed at him, her heart pounding joyfully, then gently she touched his face. 'You'll never lose me. I won't let you, I love you too much.'

They kissed again, then Scott pulled gradually away. 'I know it's very unromantic, but we really do have to move quickly now.'

'Yes . . . you're right. What . . . what should we do?'

'Get the body well hidden.'

'And then what?'

'Then we get out of here. If the lodge isn't already swarming with police, it will be very soon. We've no time to lose, we really need to get going.'

'Alright,' said Kate briskly, 'let's go then . . .'

Forty-Three

Superintendent Mallon quickly alighted from the cab as it pulled up to the rear gate of the Under Secretary's Lodge.

'Can I help you, Sir?' The corporal of the guard stepped forward, his tone polite but questioning.

'Superintendent Mallon, 'G' Division. I need to see your commanding officer immediately.'

Mallon's authoritative tone and his briefly proffered identification brought the soldier to attention. 'Very good, Sir. If you'd care to step in, Sir.' The corporal nodded to the armed sentries who swung the gate open.

Mallon quickly entered, beckoning to his police driver to follow with the cab.

'I'm afraid Lieutenant Simpson isn't here at the moment, Sir,' said the corporal. 'If you'd care to wait inside the orderly room, I can try and fetch him.'

'There isn't time,' said Mallon. 'Are there other officers?'

'Only NCOs, Sir.'

'Who's the most senior one?'

'Sergeant Davies, Sir.'

'Would you get him straight away please?'

'Very good, Sir,' cried the corporal, turning on his heel and briskly entering the barrack hut.

A moment elapsed, then he returned with a small, ruddy-faced soldier. 'Sergeant Davies, Sir!' the man called, snapping to attention.

'Superintendent Mallon, 'G' Division. There's been a double murder, Sergeant. Lord Cavendish and Mr Burke have been stabbed here in the park.'

'My eyes!' cried the sergeant, his cockney accent heightened in his surprise.

'Quite so,' answered Mallon. 'The point is, the killers could still be in the park. I want you to despatch two armed troopers

254

to all exit gates. Everyone leaving to be questioned, and anyone behaving suspiciously to be detained.'

'Begging your pardon, Sir,' said the sergeant, 'but Lieutenant Simpson would need to issue such orders.'

'Where exactly is he?'

'I couldn't say for certain, Sir, he was called away in a hurry. We knew there was a flap on, but my word, we didn't know the 'alf of it!'

'Look, we haven't time to chat, Sergeant, and we haven't time to clear this with Lieutenant Simpson. I want you to fall your men in immediately and despatch them in pairs to man the park gates. The rest of you will start a thorough sweep of the grounds. Understood?'

The soldier's indecision was evident in his face, years of conditioning prompting him to obey the voice of authority, yet his experience of the army – an army in which flogging had only recently been discontinued – inhibiting him from taking any initiative which might later rebound on him because of its unorthodoxy.

Sensing his dilemma, Mallon spoke reassuringly. 'It's alright Sergeant, I'll take full responsibility for this. I'll square it all later with Lieutenant Simpson.'

'Very good, Sir,' Davies answered, his relief obvious.

'Right, send them to man the gates, there's not a minute to lose. When you've done that, bring the rest of your force to the rear yard of the lodge and wait for me there.'

'Yes, Sir.'

'And Sergeant?'

'Sir?'

'Warn your men to be on their toes. The people we're seeking are armed and dangerous.'

'Yes, Sir.'

'Right,' said Mallon, turning away. He nodded to the police driver to accompany him, and, drawing his pistol, set off briskly towards the lights of the lodge.

Kate hid Hackett's shotgun under the straw on the top shelf of the dairy, as Scott retrieved his pistol and cartridges, then she climbed down, carefully jumping the last couple of feet onto the floor.

'I think that will have to do,' said Scott, indicating the row of milk churns in the darkest corner of the room, behind which he had concealed Hackett's body.

'You can't see anything from here,' said Kate.

'No. A thorough search will find him, but a casual look won't; if he mostly frequented the house, it should take a while before they get round to the dairy.'

'Bill, I was thinking . . .'

'Yes?'

'What you were saying about a manhunt and the ports being watched and all . . .'

'Well?'

'Your head injury will draw attention.'

'I can wear a hat.'

'No, no what I was thinking is that we should *use* it.'

'Use it?'

'Yes. You're injured and I'm a nurse, and that's the way to escape. Me in my uniform, and you as my patient in a wheelchair. It's the last thing they'd be looking for.'

'Maybe . . . but where would you get a wheelchair?'

'There's one right here. Mr McDaid's wife was confined to it before she died. It's still in the ante-room, we use it sometimes for moving heavy cheeses.'

Scott looked thoughtful. 'And your uniform?'

'I have one amongst my clothes in the lodge.'

'The lodge? That's sure to be a hive of activity, Kate, going back there would be a risk.'

'Not all that big a one for me. I work there and I'm not suspected of anything. Besides, I'll try to get in and out fast, without anyone seeing me.'

Scott sighed. 'I suppose it makes sense, but I don't like you going back in there.'

'I want to. I've over sixty pounds hidden in my room. That would give us a proper start in America.' She looked at him determinedly. 'I'm not going without it, Bill.'

'Alright.'

'Besides, I'll need some clothes.'

'No. No, leave your cases and clothes. When it's discovered that you're missing, the first thing they'll do is search your room. If all your clothes are there it won't seem like you've gone for good. It'll buy us more time.'

'OK, but I'll need something to wear.'

'Just take the bare minimum. I'll do the same at the cottage. We can buy new clothes once we've gotten away.'

'Is that where we're making for – the cottage?'

'No, not on foot. I took a baker's cart to get here, and I've hidden it over in the lane by the park school. We can make for there first. Then we'll drive down and go past the cottage, and if it looks safe we can go in. You can put on your nurse's outfit while I wash and change.'

Kate looked at him with concern. 'Brady and the others might come back. We can't stay there, Bill.'

'We won't. I'll collect my money and a few essentials, then we'll check into a hotel. Tomorrow we can book passage on the first boat to America.'

'America,' she said eagerly. 'I can hardly wait.'

'We're not out of the woods yet, Kate. There's the roving patrol in the grounds, and you've got to get in and out of the lodge. There'll be time for talking and planning later, but right now the longer we wait the more dangerous it gets.'

'OK, let's be away then.'

'The wheelchair?'

'Down here in the ante-room. We can carry it between us to the bushes near the yard, then I'll pop into the lodge.'

Scott paused suddenly and looked at her. 'You really are an amazing woman, Kate.'

'Of course I am. Sure why else would I be going to America with a man soaked in milk, and half the police in the country looking for us?' She smiled briefly at Scott, squeezed his arm, then turned and made for the ante-room.

Kate looked around the small attic bedroom that had been her home for the last two months. She knew she would never see it again, but apart from having to leave most of her clothes, her departure prompted few regrets. She had retrieved the money which Carey had insisted she take for just such a contingency

257

as this, changed out of her torn blouse, and packed her nurse's uniform and a small quantity of clothes in a light bag.

She had managed to force Hackett's assault and his subsequent death to the back of her mind, knowing there would be time later to ponder on what had happened, but for now all her energy had to be concentrated on escaping with Bill to America.

A final glance reassured her that the room looked lived-in, with no hint of its occupant's departure, then, satisfied, she stepped out onto the landing and closed the door quietly after her.

She quickly descended the narrow, staff stairway, hoping no one would emerge from any of the rooms, and, her luck holding, she reached the ground floor unseen.

At the base of the stairs the corridor passed the kitchen, and hearing someone approach from there, Kate dodged into the alcove under the stairs. With pounding heart, she watched as Nora O'Reilly, the youngest of the scullery maids, went quickly past. Kate waited a moment, then hearing no further footsteps she cautiously emerged and walked swiftly past the kitchen, around the corner and into the long hall leading to the back door.

She reached the door, gingerly opened it a fraction, and looked out. To her horror the yard was full of armed soldiers. She felt her stomach tighten in fear, her first thought being that Hackett's body had been discovered. Pulling back from the door, she breathed deeply, trying to calm herself. They couldn't have found the house steward already, she reasoned, it must be something to do with the killing of Burke and Cavendish. But what was she to do now, with the yard full of troops and her presence in the hallway in danger of being discovered at any moment?

Before she could think any further, she heard the sound of raised voices from the yard, and returning to the door, she peered cautiously out through the crack.

'I regret any breach of protocol,' said a tall man in civilian clothes, 'but there are murderers on the loose, and if there's any prospect of apprehending them I'll take it. That, Sir, is my responsibility!'

Kate could see that the man addressed was a young, blond-haired officer of arrogant bearing.

'If you'll excuse me a moment, Superintendent,' the young officer said, 'I don't wish to discuss this before the men. Sergeant!' he called, moving from Kate's line of vision, 'move the men to the top of the drive and wait for me there.'

'Very good, Sir!'

Returning, the blonde-haired man spoke icily. 'You talk about responsibility, Superintendent Mahon . . .'

'Mallon,' the policeman corrected.

'Superintendent Mallon. You talk about responsibility, but it is *my* responsibility to command these troops. You had no authority to despatch them to the park gates.'

'It was an obvious first move . . .'

'If you were issuing instructions to policemen, perhaps it would be. These men were not police, however, they were troops, *my* troops.'

'Lieutenant Simpson, I do appreciate that it was unorthodox,' said Mallon, his tone somewhat conciliatory, 'but your whereabouts wasn't known, and time was of the essence. I wanted an armed force to seal off all exits from the park, and until sufficient policemen could be mobilised to do so, your men were the nearest available force.'

Hearing of the exit gates being manned by troops, Kate felt her mouth go dry.

'Be that as it may, Sir,' answered Simpson, 'it is customary for British troops to take their orders from their officers, not from policemen.'

Mallon sighed, as though determined not to be goaded by the contempt in the younger man's voice. 'I've a long, and no doubt gruelling, night ahead, Lieutenant, and I don't want to waste energy arguing with you. Your men will be relieved as soon as possible; in the meantime I suggest you take the rest of your force and start a search of the grounds immediately.'

'Thank you for your perceptive advice,' said Simpson with disdainful sarcasm, 'it's unfortunate your policemanly perception didn't prevent the killings in the first place, isn't it? Goodnight, Superintendent,' he said, turning away.

'Lieutenant Simpson!' called Mallon.

Kate saw the young officer turn to the policeman.

'Yes?'

'We may not have prevented the murders, but you can rest assured, Sir, that we will apprehend the culprits.'

'Will you indeed?'

'Oh yes, Lieutenant, you may be certain of that,' said Mallon softly, then, turning, he walked briskly towards the rear gate.

Kate waited in the hallway as the young officer strode away towards his troops at the top of the drive, then, after a moment, she opened the door and carefully surveyed the dimly lit yard.

Although she could hear the soldiers moving down the drive, there was no one actually in sight, so she swiftly crossed the yard, skirted the dark outlines of the stables and then took to the shelter of the surrounding bushes.

Moving quietly, she soon reached the spot where Scott had hidden with the wheelchair.

'OK?' he asked.

'Yes and no,' replied Kate. 'I got in and out unseen, but the soldiers have started a search of the grounds.'

'We'd better get moving then.'

'That's not all, Bill. I overheard them talking, and they've sent armed guards to every exit gate.' She looked at him anxiously. 'It sounds like the whole park is being sealed off.'

Rifles at the ready, the two soldiers stood at the Cabra Gate, their checkpoint illuminated by the gate's twin gas lamps. The taller of the two stepped forward, his hand raised to stop the approaching baker's cart.

The cart came to a halt just where the gaslight merged with the shadows, and the first soldier levelled his rifle at the driver, a man stained with flour from his ill-fitting cap to his boots.

'Name please?'

'Matt Fitzpatrick,' answered Scott, in a convincing Dublin accent.

'Where are you coming from?'

'Chapelizod,' he replied without hesitation.

'What's in Chapelizod?'

'The Cottage Bakery,' said Scott. Then, feeling that an innocent man would show some indignation at being questioned at gunpoint, he called down to the soldier, 'What's goin' on here?'

'There's been a disturbance,' answered the man laconically, the gun still pointed at Scott as the other soldier walked along the side of the cart. 'Where are you bound for now?'

'Cabra Flour Mills,' answered Scott, beads of sweat forming on his deliberately flour-dusted forehead, as the unseen second soldier walked round the back of the cart.

Let them not be conscientious searchers, prayed Scott, painfully aware of the fact that by shifting three or four sacks of flour they could discover where Kate lay hidden with the folded wheelchair in the middle of the cart.

'Workin' a bit late, aren't you?' asked the second soldier, in what Scott recognised as a Liverpool accent.

He turned in his seat towards the man, now moving along the right side of the cart, and smiled. 'Not too late for a few scoops after I deliver this lot,' he answered jovially.

The Liverpudlian was feeling the flour sacks as the other man kept his rifle trained on Scott.

'What time did you enter the park?' asked the first soldier.

'About twenty minutes ago.'

'Were there troops on the Chapelizod Gate?'

Scott paused, his mind racing. He didn't know at what time the soldiers had been sent to seal off the park, nor how long it would have taken them to reach the distant Chapelizod Gate. He'd just have to take a chance.

'Yeah,' he said, 'they seemed to be just settin' up a checkpoint.'

'Eager buggers,' laughed the Liverpudlian from the far side of the cart, 'they must have quick-marched . . .'

'What's in all these sacks?' asked the first soldier.

'What's in any baker's sacks?' retorted Scott. 'Back-breakin' bleedin' flour!'

The soldier looked at him impassively, then turned as the Liverpudlian called: 'Oi, Fred.'

Scott turned also and saw a woman and a young man walking into the pool of light. The woman was dressed provocatively, her plunging neckline, clinging skirt and exaggerated strut suggesting a prostitute, a likelihood underlined by the sheepish demeanour of her companion.

'What ye think, Fred?' asked the Liverpudlian.

'Yeah,' said the first soldier, his face breaking into a leer. 'Yeah . . .' He turned back briefly to Scott. 'OK, on yer way.'

'Right,' said Scott, trying hard not to let the relief show in his voice. Clipping the horse into action, he drove briskly through the gate and out of the park.

Forty-Four

Spewing clouds of thick black smoke from its stack, the early morning express sped southwards towards the port of Queenstown. Despite the rocking of the train, Scott could read the banner headlines of his fellow passengers' Sunday newspapers. He noted that without exception they dealt with the park murders of the previous evening in terms of horror and outrage, a reaction which, if the conversation of his talkative fellow travellers was anything to go by, clearly mirrored the revulsion of the population at large.

With his bandaged head and distant expression he had stared ahead unspeakingly, as Kate, dressed in her nurse's uniform, had organised the storage of the wheelchair in the nearby guard's van, having first deposited him in the seat on which he was now propped.

After a few sympathetic and whispered words with Kate, the other passengers had obviously decided that here was a man unhinged by injury, and thus best left in tranquillity. It had been Kate's idea, and watching her doze on the seat opposite, Scott smiled in recognition of her perception.

Leaning back, he watched the Cork countryside rushing past. There was something almost unreal, he felt, about the normality of travelling on a train full of ordinary people after all that had happened. Could it really be less than twenty-four hours, he wondered, since he had been a captive of the Invincibles, since the discovery of the murder of Burke and Cavendish, his confrontation with Kate, the fight with Hackett, and the nerve-wracking escape from the park?

Little wonder if he felt a sense of disorientation as they sped towards the transatlantic steamer that awaited them in Queenstown. But would their luck continue to hold? They had been fortunate the previous night to find his cottage empty and unobserved, and having quickly washed, changed, and taken his money and a small case of clothes, he had left again with Kate in the baker's cart.

They had abandoned the cart around the corner from a cab rank, and with Kate pushing him in the wheelchair, they had approached the first driver in line and taken his carriage to the Railway Hotel in Parkgate Street. There they had taken two rooms as Nurse O'Sullivan and her patient Mr McPherson, and their good fortune had continued the next morning when – despite it being Sunday – the telegraph offices had been open, enabling Kate to book two cabins on that day's Queenstown-New York steamer.

Boarding the Dublin-Queenstown express had gone smoothly, despite a considerable police presence at Kingsbridge station, but Scott knew that the real test would be at the dockside in Queenstown. It was the obvious destination for anyone fleeing the country to the safety of America, and therefore liable to intense police surveillance. There was also the additional risk that by the time they travelled the one hundred and seventy-seven miles to the southern port, Hackett's body might be discovered, and Kate's disappearance probably would be. A telegram to the police in Cork, with a description of Kate, could mean ruination, but it was a risk which they had to take.

Scott's hopes lay in the consideration that with the police immersed in the Burke and Cavendish investigation, the disappearance of a servant girl – albeit one from the Under Secretary's Lodge – wouldn't be an immediate priority. But if the body of Hackett were found . . .

Stop, he told himself, no use worrying over factors beyond his control. He had enough to do to keep his McPherson characterisation convincing. He had slightly greyed his temples, and with Kate's expert bandaging the total image of the concussed highlander was far removed from the remembered Captain William Scott.

His Uncle Philip would have been proud of this performance, he thought wryly, and then, reminded of his family, he realised again the enormity of what he was doing. For once the idea was accepted of an agent being missing, presumed dead, there could be no going back; his army career was finished. And although the Scotts were not a close family, it was nevertheless a difficult step to sever all links, to know he would never again see his relatives, never again set foot on the family estate.

Just then the train started to slow down, and with the change in tempo he was jolted forward slightly, as was the dozing Kate. She opened her eyes and smiled at him, and in an instant his half-formed worries were swept away, and he knew instinctively that his future lay with this woman.

He resisted the impulse to smile back and instead looked vacantly out the window of the slowing train, to see that they were approaching Queenstown. His pulses starting to race, he leaned back and began breathing deeply, hoping to calm himself for the running of the final gauntlet.

Forty-Five

Kate felt her heart pounding madly as she guided the wheelchair along the station concourse towards the waiting ship. Her nurse and patient scheme, which had previously seemed so plausible, suddenly seemed hollow and unconvincing.

She followed the porter carrying the cases which she had hastily bought before leaving Dublin, and keeping close behind him she tried not to catch the eyes of any of the policemen along the station concourse and the adjacent dockside.

Apart from the uniformed constables, Bill had said there would also be a large force of plainclothes detectives to vet the crowds leaving the country on the steamer, but guiding the wheelchair along, Kate resisted the temptation to pick out the waiting policemen.

It was Sunday lunchtime, which meant that her absence from work would clearly be evident by now. For all she knew, they might already have telegraphed the ports with her description.

Think positively, she told herself; to be convincing you must first convince yourself. And after all, if they were searching for her they wouldn't be looking for a nurse with a patient, but rather for a single woman, and her two features most likely to appear on a description – her thick auburn hair and the scar on her temple – were both largely concealed by the long white nurse's bonnet.

Glancing carefully about, Kate could see many of the passengers being stopped for questioning by customs officers and the police, but she kept up a steady pace, the guiding of the wheelchair providing a plausible reason for keeping her head down.

'Just a second, Miss!' cried a voice in a sing-song Cork accent.

Kate looked up to see a tall, well-dressed man blocking the way.

'Detective Sergeant Harris. A few questions, if you wouldn't mind, Miss.'

'Of course,' answered Kate.

The porter, seeing that his customer was about to be questioned, lowered the cases impatiently.

'Your name please?' asked the detective.

'Nurse O'Sullivan – Mary O'Sullivan.'

'Where are you travelling from?'

'Dublin.'

'Whereabouts in Dublin?'

'Saint Laurence's Hospital.' She saw the policeman looking curiously at Bill, who stared ahead dreamily.

'What's the matter with your patient?' he asked, a note of confidentiality in his voice.

'Severe concussion. I'm taking him to a convalescent home in New Jersey.'

'And his name is?'

'McPherson. Mr Gordon McPherson.'

'Scottish, is he?'

'Yes, he was an engineer. He came over to Ireland on railway construction. There was an accident and . . . well . . .' She pointed at Bill sympathetically.

'Why doesn't he go home to Scotland?'

'His family emigrated. They've built a lot of the Trenton railway; he'll be well looked after there. No shortage of cash . . .'

The porter coughed loudly, his glance at the policeman seeming to suggest that the questioning had veered from the official to the conversational.

'Right, Nurse,' said the detective briskly, 'that'll be all.'

'Thank you,' said Kate, with a smile.

'Have a pleasant crossing,' added the policeman, as Kate prepared to follow the porter again.

'Thanks,' she answered, then moved on, her spirits soaring despite the pounding in her chest. She had done it, she had got

267

past the police, which presumably meant that the hunt wasn't on for Kate Lannigan, missing dairy maid.

She went on excitedly, forcing herself not to appear hurried, despite the fact that the nearest gangplank – and beyond it the ship to carry them to freedom – lay only twenty yards away.

She pushed the wheelchair on, the distance decreasing with agonising slowness, then reached into her pocket to have a coin ready for the porter.

They arrived at the base of the gangplank, and after lowering the cases the porter returned to the wheelchair to help Kate guide it up the plank and onto the ship.

'One moment, Miss,' called a heavily built, uniformed constable.

Kate felt her stomach suddenly constrict in fear as the policeman approached her, a slight smile playing about his lips.

He waved a finger at her admonishingly. 'Now, now, now,' he said softly, 'can't have this, can we?'

Kate looked at him evenly. 'Sorry?'

'Can't have this,' repeated the policeman, indicating the wheelchair which she had been about to guide up onto the ship.

'What's wrong?' asked Kate, with a calmness wildly at odds with her racing pulse.

'You're much too pretty to be pushing wheelchairs up ramps,' said the policeman, trying for a tone of easy gallantry. 'Allow me.' He indicated to the porter to return to the cases, then took the wheelchair and single-handedly guided it up the gangplank.

Hardly daring to believe her luck, Kate quickly followed, handed the boarding passes to the waiting ship's officer, and gave a coin to the porter, who laid down the bags, nodded his thanks, and left.

'Now,' said the policeman, applying the wheelbrake with bravado, and turning to look flirtatiously at Kate. 'Are you dropping him off here by any chance?'

'No, we're both sailing to New York.'

He smiled ruefully. 'Too bad.'

'Well . . .'

He shook his head in mock sorrow. 'Ah well, Cork's loss is New York's gain.'

Kate smiled. 'Thanks for your help.'

'You're welcome, and good luck over beyond.'

'Thanks.'

He tipped his helmet, then turned and descended the gangplank.

Kate watched him go, then, turning, she saw that Bill had shifted around, and realising that no one was observing them, he briefly dropped the faraway look, caught her eye, and winked broadly.

The warm afternoon breeze brought with it the tang of salt, as, standing at the ship's rail, Kate watched the shoreline glide past as they made for the mouth of Cork Harbour.

A steward had taken their luggage to the cabins below, but for this important occasion – her first time to leave the country – she wished to remain on deck, as did many of her fellow travellers.

She had steered Bill's wheelchair right up to the rail, the other passengers graciously making room on the crowded deck so he could enjoy a clear view of the sunlit water and green shoreline. All about them people were speaking animatedly, and while many of them were picking out landmarks along the side of the bay, it was evident to Kate that the engrossing topic of the day was the spectacular murder of Burke and Cavendish, on the new Chief Secretary's first day in Ireland.

'Desperate altogether, wasn't it?' said a black-shawled woman with a Dublin accent, to her two companions, 'and the poor unfortunate man only comin' here to bring peace.'

'They say his wife is heartbroken. It's a disgrace, that's what I think,' retorted her friend. 'Murdered in cold blood. They should be ashamed to call themselves Irishmen.'

'I heard that killing Lord Cavendish was a mistake,' said the third woman. 'They were supposed to kill Burke, but Cavendish tried to save his friend.'

'That would make sense, I mean Burke collaborated for years with Forster, but poor Lord Cavendish was only comin' here to make a fresh start.'

Kate tried not to listen, not wanting to dwell on her association with those who had carried out so senseless an act of violence, but the women continued their discussion, vying with each other for dramatic revelations.

The first woman declared in awe that the Carl Rosa Opera Company had sped up the last act in Dublin's Gaiety Theatre last night, so dismayed and shocked was everybody at the news; another claimed that the papers said London society was so horrified that shows there had been cancelled completely; and wasn't there a rumour that the killers weren't Irish at all, but Americans, the weapons used being Bowie knives? No, said another, the weapons were supposed to be butchers' knives, and the police were questioning all butchers known to be nationalists.

Kate breathed a sigh of relief when after several more moments of this the women retired to the bar below deck; yet the conversation had fixed her thoughts on the murders. She suspected that despite the sincerity of her motives in seeking out the Invincibles, she would always regret, and feel tarnished by, her association with them. But what could she do now? They had struck, and nothing would bring back the dead.

Lost in her thoughts, she had been staring down at the water, but feeling a change in the ship's motion she looked up suddenly to see that they were moving out through the mouth of the harbour. Looking back inland, Kate saw the fields and headlands of the bay diminishing, and seeing the fresh green landscape bathed in the May sunshine, she experienced a surge of regret. She was leaving Ireland and might never see it again.

As if reading her thoughts, Bill turned in the wheelchair, and seeing all the other passengers engrossed in backward glances, he reached out and squeezed her hand.

Kate looked down at him and, meeting his eye, her regrets seemed to fade away. She was touched by his sensitivity in reading her thoughts about leaving the country, and as he smiled affectionately she knew that whatever the future in America might bring, she could face it – and happily – once they were together.

She smiled back, then squeezed his hand tightly as the ship moved out into the open sea.

Forty-Six

In a quiet room high above the busy streets of Mayfair, Colonel Penrose addressed the meeting. Seated about the table were four middle-aged men, their fine clothing and assured bearing suggesting a background of power and privilege.

'Gentlemen, I shan't need to detain you long, at this, our final gathering,' said Penrose.

His listeners nodded in satisfied agreement.

'No doubt we shall all meet tomorrow at the funeral of Lord Cavendish, but this will be the final meeting of our . . .' He paused and smiled briefly, 'shall we say our *ad hoc group*? I'm told that tomorrow night Sir William Harcourt will introduce before Parliament a new Coercion Act for Ireland. Trevor, I believe you have some knowledge of its contents?'

'Yes indeed,' said the portly man whom Penrose had addressed. 'The Prevention of Crimes Bill, to give it its official title, will provide for abolition of juries in certain cases, power to arrest for questioning, special tribunals for crimes of violence, magistrates' powers to be extended, and special enquiries into criminal activities to be made easier.' He raised an eyebrow in amusement. 'I think, in general, a set of measures our liberal friends would regard as "Draconian".'

'Quite so,' said Penrose, 'though in the present climate of outrage I doubt if even they would be so foolish as to say so. If I may quote from the *Times*,' he said, consulting papers before him on the table, ' "Irish disloyalty is not to be caressed into quietude by any system of conciliation whatever", or as the *Observer* says, "There is only one remedy possible, and that is the declaration of martial law".'

Penrose looked around the group. 'I think, Gentlemen, that in the circumstances, the Home Secretary will have little difficulty in putting the Act through Parliament.'

'Pity about poor Freddy Cavendish, on a personal level,' said one of the assembled men.

'Yes,' answered Penrose, 'a decent chap by all accounts. But let us face it, Gentlemen, his death was a small price to pay for destroying Home Rule in Ireland.'

'Assuming of course that it does . . .'

Penrose looked up sharply. 'It's a little late in the day for reservations, Trevor. And it *will* stop the rot in Ireland. After the killings Gladstone can't possibly appear to be mollycoddling the Irish, the public wouldn't stand for it. No, Gentlemen, we had no choice; not when they overruled and replaced Forster. And the more disloyal the Irish became, the more they would have been appeased. There was really no option but to let these Invincible wretches do their worst. Cavendish simply had to be sacrificed. The backlash was essential.'

There were general nods of agreement.

'What about this agent chap of yours, Penrose? Might he have suspected what was being allowed to happen?'

'I doubt it. Not really in keeping with his boyish notions of fair play. Besides, we're quite safe, he won't be saying anything to anybody.'

'How's that?'

'Well I imagine that by now he's been taken care of,' said the colonel. 'The Invincibles were given an anonymous tip-off last week, and he hasn't been seen or heard of since.'

'I say, Penrose, that's rather rum.'

'The whole business is rather rum if it comes to that. Protecting the interests of Queen and Country often is. The fact of the matter is that we couldn't risk any talk or awkward questions afterwards, couldn't leave any loose ends.' He shrugged. 'Captain Scott was a soldier who went on a dangerous mission and gave his life for his country.'

'What about his people?'

'Decent family, they've got a place down in Devon. Have to be told he's missing, presumed dead. Their feelings will, of course, be respected. Memorial service with full military honours, posthumous decoration, died a patriot, that sort of thing. No, Gentlemen, you'll find there won't be any ghosts to haunt us after we part today.'

'Well done, Penrose. Tricky business. Very well handled.'

'Yes,' said the man called Trevor, 'I think all of us owe a debt to the colonel here. If we've helped secure a stable administration in Ireland, it's largely thanks to the efforts of Colonel Penrose, both as an intelligence officer in the field, and,' he permitted himself a dry smile, 'in the equally hazardous behind-the-scenes manoeuvring in Westminster!'

'Hear! Hear!'

'Thank you, Gentlemen,' said Penrose, his pleasure evident, 'it's been an honour and a privilege to work with you. And now, if we're finished here, may I suggest we vacate the premises? Discreetly, of course, and one at a time.'

'Ever on guard, eh, Penrose?'

'Yes,' answered the colonel with a smile, as he rose from the table, 'in military intelligence it tends to keep one alive.' He crossed to the door and unlocked it. 'Well, good day, Gentlemen, and thank you again for your support and encouragement.' He nodded, then turned smartly and walked out of the room.

Forty-Seven

Kate walked along Main Street savouring the winter sun which shone down brightly, its rays reflecting off the snow-capped mountains. The noon-day air had an invigorating crispness, and there was a lightness in her step as she crossed the narrow thoroughfare and entered the general stores.

The proprietor looked up eagerly, a wiry, grey-haired man whose watery eyes lit up as he leaned forward on the laden counter.

'Good morning, Mam!'

'Good morning, Mr Carter. I'm looking for some writing paper and envelopes, please.'

'Sure thing, got some nice vellum here. How many sheets?'

'Say about twenty, and a dozen envelopes.'

'You got it,' he said, withdrawing them. 'Anything else?'

'No thanks, that'll be all.'

'Newspapers arrived,' he said invitingly, 'came from Charleston just this morning . . .'

'Oh, well I'll take the *Tribune* so.'

'You got it,' said the shopkeeper, placing the newspaper with the other goods. 'Nothing else we can get ye?'

'No thanks,' said Kate with a smile.

'Right, that'll be three, plus four, and the paper – ten cents total please.'

She paid him and took the goods. 'Thank you, Mr Carter. Good morning.'

'Thank *you,* Mrs Jones, and good day to ye.'

Stepping into the street again, Kate smiled at old Carter's backwoods salesmanship, and reflected, yet again, on how strange it felt to be called Mrs Jones.

It was over five months now since her marriage to Bill, and

with their desire for anonymity and a fresh start they had chosen the name Jones, as being one unlikely to draw attention.

They had picked the name the previous summer, when, on arrival in New York, they had ditched the wheelchair and dropped the nurse and patient disguise. Kate could still remember the sheer joy of travelling together on the train to meet her family in Ohio, but journeying this time as a young woman and her fiancé, and no longer restrained by the nurse and patient pretence.

On arrival in Stanley they had discovered that the Lannigans had moved, and were now renting a holding on the Ohio/Kentucky border near New Boston, and it was here that Kate had been tearfully re-united with her family.

To her great relief, everyone had taken to Bill, except her brother Michael, who nursed a bitterness towards all things English since the eviction and his imprisonment in Kilmainham. But even Michael had been won round by Bill's good humour and obvious basic decency, so that by the time the wedding had taken place at the end of August, all lingering reservations had melted away, to make for an emotional ceremony, followed by a happy family celebration.

After discussing it with Bill, Kate had decided never to tell her family the truth about her involvement with the Invincibles. As it was, they accepted that Bill was a small-time horse-breeder from Devon, who had met Kate socially in Dublin. The horse-breeding part might soon be true, she reflected, for this very morning Bill was meeting with a representative of the West Virginian Bloodstock Bureau, and Kate had bought the writing paper in anticipation of contacting her family, to tell them the outcome of the meeting.

Looking towards the end of the street, where the Blue Ridge Mountains formed a spectacular backdrop, Kate hoped fervently that they would get the breeding contract, in pursuit of which they had come here. They had seen a lot of good places in America, but none that appealed to them more than this fertile valley.

Reaching an intersection, she turned off Main Street, then

climbed the steps of a modest wooden house and entered. The warmth and a smell of cooking made a pleasant contrast with the sharp outside air. She took off her coat in the hall, crossed to the livingroom where she laid her purchases on the table, then suddenly stood absolutely still. It had happened again. Several times in the last few days she had felt a flutter, but this time was the strongest yet. Her baby was moving inside her. The sensation filled her with joy and excitement, and no matter how much she thought about it, the wonder of herself and Bill creating a new life always seemed fascinating and magical.

Filled with a glow of happiness, she went to the kitchen and collected a prepared tray of crockery, brought it into the livingroom, and placed it upon the table. Her eye was suddenly caught by an article on the front page of the paper, and picking it up, she stood rooted to the spot, unconscious of Scott's arrival in the hall.

'I'm home, Kate,' he called, then entered the livingroom.

'Look, Bill,' she said softly, indicating the paper. 'Look at this.'

He came closer. 'Invincibles arrested . . .' he read aloud.

'They've caught them,' said Kate, 'Carey, Brady, Kelly, they've all been rounded up.'

Scott lowered the paper. 'It was always only a matter of time, Kate,' he said gently.

'I know.'

He looked at her troubled face, then touched her shoulder reassuringly. 'Don't worry, it's unlikely they'll mention your part, and even if they do, we're safe here.'

'I know, Bill, it's just . . . it sort of casts a shadow . . .'

'How do you mean?'

'Just now I really felt the baby move. It's such a thrill, the idea of a new life. I'd love to forget all about killing and death and . . . and everything to do with the Invincibles.'

'You will, darling, you will. We've got all our lives ahead of us.'

'I know, it's just . . . well I can't help feeling . . . feeling bad that those two men were murdered.'

'Kate, you had no act or part in that. You thought the Invincibles would be disbanded.'

'I know . . . I know . . .'

'Then look to the future, not the past. What happened then, happened in another time, another place. Nothing can bring those lives back, so we must leave it, and look to the future.'

'You're right,' said Kate. She smiled gently. 'But then you usually are . . .'

'And talking of the future, you never asked me . . .'

'Oh, Bill,' she said excitedly, 'you got it?'

He grinned, then nodded. 'A temporary contract, subject to our paying a hefty deposit, and to be terminated after six months if the Bloodstock Bureau so choose; but it is a start.'

'Oh, Bill, that's wonderful. And we can stay in Elk Springs? They'll rent us the stud farm?'

'Provided we pay through the nose. It's going to take every penny we've got.'

Kate threw her arms about him. 'Oh I'm so happy, Bill. And I don't care if we don't have a farthing to spare. We'll make it work, I just know it.'

Scott looked at her, then gently took her face in his hands. 'Kate Lannigan,' he said, 'I really love you.'

'Bill *Jones*,' she laughed, 'we love you too.'

'We?'

'My baby and I.'

'Yes, I'm inclined to forget that there'll be three of us.'

'Don't you dare! You're talking about the future heir to what'll be the finest stud farm in West Virginia.'

'That calls for a toast,' said Scott, crossing to the sideboard and taking out the sherry decanter and two glasses. He poured, then held one to Kate. 'To us, and our new farm,' he toasted, 'and the future heir!'

'Or heirs. I'm not finished with you yet, Mr Jones – not by a long shot!' And smiling happily, Kate raised her glass and toasted.

Epilogue

Superintendent Mallon, in keeping with his assurance to Lieutenant Simpson, was the man who apprehended the Invincibles. With the exception of Tynan, who found sanctuary in the United States, they were brought to trial in the spring of 1883. Mallon scored an even greater triumph in persuading James Carey to turn Queen's Evidence, a sensational development that helped secure convictions against all of the accused.

Joe Brady, Tim Kelly, Michael Fagan, Dan Curley, and Thomas Caffrey were sentenced to death, and duly hanged in Kilmainham Jail. The cab driver known as Skin-the-Goat received penal servitude for life, as did Laurence Hanlon and Patrick Delaney, while long prison sentences were handed down to Mullett, McCaffrey, Doyle, O'Brien and Moroney.

For turning informer, James Carey got a full pardon, and under police protection he and his family were quietly shipped to South Africa. Despite shaving off his beard and travelling under an assumed name, he couldn't resist chatting and playing cards with fellow passengers, and while sailing to Durban on the *Melrose Castle*, he was shot to death, having been recognised by an enraged Fenian fellow traveller.

Captain William Scott was posthumously decorated for gallantry, and although the body was never recovered, his memorial service took place with full military honours.

Kate lost her baby. Their remote region of West Virginia was poorly serviced for medical care, and the primitive treatment of complications during her delivery meant that she could bear no further children. Fuelled by her grief, she returned to her nursing career, specialising in obstetrics. Over the years she built up a scheme for the proper training and placement of community midwives, and with her commitment overcoming all obstacles, the success of the scheme resulted in its widespread acceptance throughout West Virginia and neighbouring states.

The prospect of Home Rule for Ireland, so feared by Colonel Penrose and his colleagues, took another forty years to arrive; it wasn't until 1923 that twenty-six of the thirty-two counties of Ireland achieved independence as the Irish Free State.

Four years later, in the winter of 1927, William Scott – or Bill Jones, as he was then known – died in his sleep at the age of seventy-one, leaving behind one of the largest and most progressive stud farms in West Virginia.

The already close relationship between himself and Kate had been deepened further by their inability to produce children, and their many friends worried about how she would cope in the absence of her partner of forty-five years. Devastated at first, she mourned his loss profoundly, then gradually returned to an active life, sustained by the thought that whatever she did, could – if he were in her thoughts – still be shared in some way with Bill.

It was because of this conviction that she decided to visit Ireland in the summer of 1928. Without fully understanding her motives, she felt a need to close an unfinished chapter, bidding the land of her youth a last farewell. And so, despite the reservations of her many nieces and nephews, she travelled alone, a sprightly woman of sixty-six, to visit a country not so greatly changed from the one she had left in haste all those years ago.

The fledgling Free State now had motor cars and electric lighting, and the pillar boxes were green instead of red, but the people, she was pleased to note, still had the same bantering sense of humour. She was delighted to discover that the dance-hall where she had first met Bill was still in business, still attracting couples such as she and Bill once were.

The only discomforting note was struck when she visited Glasnevin Cemetery, to place a wreath on the grave of Thomas Burke, her one-time employer, and a man for whom, along with Lord Cavendish, she had secretly prayed every day since their murder.

She left visiting the peninsula of Howth until last, afraid it might have been built on in her absence, but on the final day of her stay she visited it, still wild and beautiful, and climbed to the wood where she had first picnicked with Bill on that scorching April day so long ago.

Standing in the sunny glade, with a warm breeze blowing, she thought how it had all really been set in motion right here, when she and Bill had kissed for the first time. Lost in her thoughts, she stood immobile, until eventually the sudden bursting into song of a thrush took her from her reverie. She looked about, realising that she had been standing there a long time. Her final farewell having been made, it was, she decided, time to go home. She smiled at her sentimentality, and then, still pleasantly engrossed in memories, turned and started slowly down the hill.